'For my money, grenades are even more fiendish than bombs. They play more cruelly on the nerves. The noise they make is infernal, and they tend to fall where least expected ... The blockhouse had received its second direct hit. This time the roof collapsed and earth and sand rained about our ears, slabs of concrete crashed about us ... Major Hinka was thrown out headfirst and landed on a pile of debris. There was blood on his face, his uniform was in shreds, the stump of his right arm poked grotesquely through a rip in his sleeve—it was two years ago he had lost that arm and the stump had still not healed ...'

They were the same men who had fought and survived before—Major Hinka ... Little John ... the Legionnaire ... Barcelona ... the same men grown savage and brutal in a war that had led them from Russia to Monte Cassino—and now to the western front—to the battlefields of France and Hitler's last attempt to save the Third Reich ...

Also by Sven Hassel

WHEELS OF TERROR
THE LEGION OF THE DAMNED
COMRADES OF WAR
MONTE CASSINO

and published by Corgi Books

Sven Hassel

Liquidate Paris

Translated from the French by
JEAN URE

CORGI BOOKS
A DIVISION OF TRANSWORLD PUBLISHERS LTD
A NATIONAL GENERAL COMPANY

LIQUIDATE PARIS

A CORGI BOOK   552 08603 7

First Publication in Great Britain

PRINTING HISTORY

Corgi Edition published 1971
Corgi Edition reprinted 1971
Corgi Edition reprinted 1971
Corgi Edition reprinted 1972

Copyright © Sven Hassel 1971
Translation copyright © Transworld Publishers Ltd., 1971

This book is set in
Baskerville 10/10½ pt.

Corgi Books are published by Transworld Publishers, Ltd.,
Cavendish House, 57–59 Uxbridge Road, Ealing,
London, W.5.

Made and printed in Great Britain by
Richard Clay (The Chaucer Press), Ltd., Bungay, Suffolk.

EDITOR'S NOTE

The character who in this book is
called 'Little John' has appeared in
other novels by Sven Hassel under
the name 'Tiny'.

CHAPTER ONE

'I wonder,' said Little John, shading his eyes with his hand as he stared out to the horizon, 'if you could reach England by swimming there?'

'Probably,' said the Legionnaire, sounding bored.

'If you were a fish,' added the Old Man.

'And had a supply of food to keep you going——'

'Mind you, it would take some hell of a time.'

'Hm.'

Little John stared out across the sea again, frowning and scratching the top of his head.

'It has been done?' he said at last.

'Sure, but not from here. They don't set out from here.'

'Where would you arrive if you set out from here?' insisted Little John, who was nothing if not downright dogged when once he had embarked upon a subject.

The Legionnaire hunched a shoulder.

'Buggered if I know . . . Dover, perhaps.'

'Crap,' said Heide. 'This is in a straight line with Brighton. Nowhere near Dover.'

'How far do you reckon it is, then?'

Little John again.

'Mm . . . thirty kilometres. Eighty kilometres. A hell of a way, at all events.'

'Why don't we try it?'

The Old Man smiled.

'Because you'd drown before you were even half-way there.'

'You want to take a bet?'

'Why not? It's practically a certainty!'

'Of course,' murmured Barcelona, 'there is always

another point. If you missed your way, which you very likely would, because one bit of sea looks exactly the same as any other bit of sea, there's no knowing where you might end up. You could be lucky enough to bump into the coast of Ireland, but if you floated past that you'd have to carry on all the way to Greenland.'

'I'd take a chance,' said Little John. 'I'd sooner swim about the perishing ocean for the rest of my life than carry on fighting in this bleeding war.'

Absurdly enough, we actually began training for it. Each day we swam a bit further than the previous day, always pushing ourselves to the limits of our endurance, the rule being that the weakest must keep up with the strongest. I personally gave up the idea of swimming to Greenland on the day I nearly drowned with cramp. If it hadn't been for Gregor, the war would have been over as far as I was concerned. But one or two of the others pressed on with the training programme. They came back at midnight after their last excursion, all of them completely knackered but exultantly declaring that they had seen the coast of England on the horizon.

'Another couple of weeks,' declared Little John, 'and I reckon we'll be able to make it.'

They never had the chance. For some reason unknown to us the look-outs were doubled all along the coast, and before Little John and his team of aspiring Channel swimmers had found the means to evade them, history had put a stop to their ambitions in the shape of the Normandy landings. War had once again intervened.

NO QUARTER GIVEN IN SECTION NINETY-ONE

They were hurling grenades into our midst. The block-house had already received a direct hit and was leaning drunkenly at an angle, one side dug deep into the sand, the other rearing skywards. The roof sagged in the middle.

For my money, grenades are even more fiendish than bombs. They play more cruelly on the nerves. The noise they make is infernal, and they tend to fall where least expected. At least with a bomb you stand a chance of calculating its probable landing point.

Another explosion. The blockhouse had received its second direct hit. This time the roof finally collapsed. A shower of earth and sand rained about our ears, slabs of concrete crashed about us, all the lights were abruptly extinguished. Those of us that could, got out. Major Hinka was thrown out, bodily, head-first, and landed with a thump on a pile of debris. Cautiously he picked himself up. There was blood on his face, his uniform was in shreds, the stump of his right arm poked grotesquely through a rip in his sleeve. It was two years ago he had lost that arm. The stump had never yet healed properly.

A squealing horde of rats came bounding out from the ruins of the shattered blockhouse. One, in a panic, made a dart at the Major. It clung to his chest, rolling back its ugly mouth and revealing a row of sharp yellow teeth. With the back of his hand Little John sent the brute flying, and the minute it hit the earth it was seized upon by its companions and torn to ribbons.

From afar, the Marines artillery were firing non-stop upon us, slowly demolishing the stout concrete walls upon which we had relied for our protection. The newly-embarked infantry troops were advancing upon us, and we repulsed them as best we could with volleys of hand-grenades. Little John carelessly dangled a grenade as he helped pull a survivor from the wreckage of the blockhouse. I watched him in a state of suspended horror: the pin was half pulled out and he gave no signs of having noticed. But Little John knew what he was doing where hand-grenades were concerned. He and I were, so to speak, the champions of the section. Little John threw them from a distance of 118 metres; I from 110. So far, no one had been able to better our performances.

Meanwhile, the fun continued. It had already lasted for several hours and we were growing quite bored by it. It was rather like sitting inside an enormous drum beaten by a million maniacs. After a time your senses became blunted and you accepted it as mere background noise

Porta suggested a game of pontoon, but who could concentrate on cards? Our nerves were stretched taut, our ears cocked for the least change in the quality of sound of the inferno that raged all about us. It was child's play at the moment, compared with what was surely to come. Sooner or later, they would launch a full-scale attack; move in for the kill. God grant they wouldn't use flame-throwers! We should be lost if they did, and we knew they neither gave nor expected any quarter. They themselves had taken care to inform us that surrender was our only possible course, as they otherwise intended to fight until our last man had been wiped out. Propaganda, of course. We put out the same sort of rubbish ourselves. When it came to the point, flame-throwers or no, we should fight until we dropped, with our backs to the wall, with no thoughts of surrender in our well-drilled mind.

The Old Man was standing alone and forlorn in a corner, gently swaying from side to side and staring with glazed expression at his tin helmet, which he was holding before him in both hands. He didn't know that I was watching him, and I saw that his cheeks had two clear rivulets of tears running through the layer of smoke and dirt. There, I guessed, was a man who could not much longer endure the disgusting sights and sounds and smells of war.

The bombardment continued. Quite suddenly, and with no warning, the roof of our new shelter caved in upon us. For a moment there was panic and confusion. The thought ran through my head like a ticker-tape gone mad: so this is how it feels, to be buried alive. So this is how it feels, to be buried alive. So this is—— And then, suddenly, I was standing upright next to Little John, both of us straining to support the weight of a heavy beam and prevent yet another landslide. Little John said nothing; just stood and sweated and clenched his teeth. It seemed to me that every bone in my body was breaking beneath the strain. I half wished that Little John would give up the unequal struggle, and then I, too, with no loss of face, could let fall my share of the burden and sink down peaceably to die beneath the resulting debris. But

Little John stood stolidly on, and before I could disgrace myself Gregor appeared with a heavy hammer and some props. We weren't yet buried alive, but it had been a near thing.

One end of the shelter was clearly still unsafe, and we crowded silently together and passed round cigarettes and a bottle of calvados without a word. The only sound, other than the howling of the battle outside, were the pitiful moans of those who had been injured. A young kid of seventeen or eighteen was screaming his head off in agony, lying in a corner with both his legs crushed almost to pulp under the weight of a heavy cannon. They hauled him out and pumped him full of morphine, but I gave little for his chances. And certain it was he would never walk again.

Porta crawled about between people's legs, in search of his pack of cards, which had been scattered by the blast. The Legionnaire calmly unrolled a little green mat and began playing dice, left hand against right. The rest of us stood, or sat, or huddled together in an atmosphere as taut as a bow-string. We had reached that extreme of fear and tension that carried madness in its wake, when any chance remark or trivial incident could drive men over the borderline and turn them into wild beasts scratching and clawing at each other. It was a relief when a second horde of rats appeared: it gave us a legitimate excuse for violent action, and probably averted a small-scale disaster.

The hours passed; slowly, wearily, one after another in orderly procession, dragging onwards towards a new day, or a new night, we were no longer sure what time it was or how long we had been there. We just sat and waited. There was nothing else we could do. Some of us smoked, some of us talked, some of us slept. Most of us just sat and stared. The Legionnaire had long ago rolled up his little green mat, but Little John brought out his harmonica and gave us the same half dozen tunes over and over. A few of us swore at him, but the majority suffered in silence. The Army teaches you patience if nothing else.

Outside, there was no indication whether it was day or

night. A dense cloud of smoke hung like a pall between heaven and earth. It seemed unlikely that anyone—or, indeed, anything—could have survived the onslaught.

At one point, Porta pulled out the forty-nine playing cards he had managed to salvage from his pack and began dealing them out to his nearest neighbours, but even his enthusiasm waned in the face of our total lethargy. For one thing, it was almost impossible to see the cards without constantly lighting matches, and for another, who the hell cared anyway whether he won or lost?

'Not even bloody worth cheating any more,' grumbled Porta, sweeping up the pack and angrily shuffling the cards.

No one bothered to deny it. We just went on with our wearisome task of waiting.

'Might as well bleeding eat as sit on your bleeding arses and do nothing!'

Porta glared round at us in the gloom. No one so much as twitched a muscle. With an indifferent shrug of the shoulders he pulled out his iron rations and set about consuming them. We stared with vacant eyes. Not even Major Hinka passed any comment, though the opening of iron rations, never mind the actual eating of them, was expressly forbidden until or unless the order was given by a commanding officer. Porta munched stolidly on, using the point of his bayonet as a fork. When he'd finished his rations he drank the water used for cooling the machine-guns. No one protested. No one cared. Who wanted to cool machine-guns when any moment he was in danger of being blown to pieces by the enemy? Porta, apparently unmoved, concluded his meal by scrubbing his one remaining tooth with the piece of oily rag used for cleaning rifles. He then settled back with his hands behind his head and a beam of contentment on his lips, as one who has come to the end of a three-course meal and a bottle of wine.

At last the bombardment showed signs of abating. Cautiously we roused ourselves, picked up our rifles, pushed the armour plating away from the wall slits, set the machine-gun in position. That anyone should still be living in the hell of the outside world would be nothing short of a miracle. The scene had changed beyond all recognition since last we had looked upon it. Wreckage lay scattered for miles about. The barbed-wire installations so lovingly supervised by Rommel had completely disappeared. Major Hinka made several despairing attempts to contact base by the field telephone, but with no success. There was no telephone: was no base. All the positions we had held had presumably been crushed out of existence by the bombardment.

And now the enemy were pouring off the landing-craft and swarming up the beaches in their thousands. Wave upon wave of khaki-clad figures with never a thought in their heads that they might still have to encounter opposition. Who, after all, could possibly have survived the onslaught and be alive to offer any resistance?

And then, suddenly, the mortars were sending an uninterrupted cascade of grenades into the midst of the khaki hordes. For a moment the infantry hesitated, dropped back, evidently shocked by this unexpected reception. Their officers gave them no respite. They shouted orders back and forth and urged the men on with impatient arm movements and jerks of the head. The machine-guns sliced through their approaching ranks, mowing them down dozens at a time. Porta's flame-thrower sent its evil tongues leaping in among them, catching a man here, a man there. We rose up from our hell-hole and watched them die. It was our turn, now, to deal out wholesale destruction. The khaki figures fell over each other, trampled on their fallen comrades, stumbled and staggered but still came on. I saw one soldier trip on a pile of debris and become impaled on some hidden barbed wire. His screams were horrid even to my exultant ears. It was a relief when he was caught in the machine-gun fire and sliced almost in half. At least it put an end to the screams.

Major Hinka suddenly rose to his feet and dashed out into the open, yelling at us to follow him. We surged along in his wake, Little John and the Legionnaire at the head of us. I was dragging the gun with me, hanging round my neck by the strap. With my free hand I yanked grenades from my belt and hurled them into the mass of the enemy. All around us men were screaming, shouting, shooting, entangled in barbed wire, dying silently in the oil-sodden sand. Directly before me, a soldier in khaki. He had lost his helmet. I crashed my knee into his stomach, knocked him cold with the butt of the gun, left him lying there and ran on. I suddenly became aware that Barcelona was at my side. We ploughed on together, our heavy boots squelching in a sea of blood and bodies.

And now the enemy were retreating. Slowly at first, then speeding up by degrees until at length it was a mad dash to the sea, jettisoning arms, gas masks, helmets as they ran. Our turn had come, and we had triumphed. But how and why, for whom and for what reason? For the Fatherland? For the Führer? For honour, for glory, for medals and promotion? Not at all. Not a bit of it. We fought through instinct. To preserve our precious lives at all costs. And every minute a nightmare. One moment fighting side by side with a friend; the next moment, chancing to turn your head to see that what was once a human being is now no more than a bloodied mass of pulped flesh and crushed bone. And for a few minutes it breaks you up, you feel the tears choking you, you bang your head with the butt of your rifle, you feel that you're going mad, you can't stand it any longer. And then, seconds later, you're back in the thick of the battle, fighting again in deadly earnest, hating everyone and everything; fighting to kill and killing for pleasure.

As soon as the lull came, Porta's thoughts turned once more to food. I never knew anyone eat as much and as often as that man. And while he was sitting stuffing himself, Little John set about his usual macabre task of inspecting the mouths of corpses for gold teeth, which he carefully extracted and dropped into a little bag which never left his side. The Old Man used to create hell and mutter about hauling him up before a court-martial, but no threat yet devised had ever had the least effect on Little John.

Most of us stretched out on the ground behind the concrete shelter and watched Porta opening the booty of tins which he had purloined from somewhere or other. The first tin turned out to be full of gun grease. So did the second. And the third, and the fourth. The idiot had evidently pillaged an arms depot. He was the only one who seemed not to find it amusing, and, indeed, began threatening to knock people's heads off until the Legionnaire caught his interest by suggesting we should attach the tins to a hand-grenade, tie the whole lot to a stick of phosphorus and hurl it into the enemy ranks. Had it not been for the Old Man putting his foot down, Porta would doubtless have tried out the new weapon there and then.

The attack started up again. The machine-guns grew white-hot. Barcelona operated the large mortar, his steel gloves hanging in shreds. There was no respite, no breathing space, no pause for thought. It was kill or be killed, and both we and the enemy were splashing about ankle-deep in blood. The stretch of sand that separated us, once so smooth and silvery, was now churned up into a sticky, rusty-brown mess.

In the distance, the sea had grown a veritable forest of masts. Between the sea and the beach, a multitude of landing-craft were disgorging more khaki-clad figures. Many of them fell before they could reach dry land. Many more staggered only a few yards up the beach before collapsing. But still the assault continued. An entire army was being thrown into the attack on the Normandy coast. If the attempt failed, it must surely be a question of years before they could gather their forces to try again.

We were all of us, by now, half crazed with thirst, and were not so particular as we had previously been in following Porta's example and gorging ourselves on the water used for cooling the machine-guns. It was warm and oily and it stank to high heaven, but champagne itself could not have been more welcome. And we ourselves smelt none too sweet, if it came to that.

Indifferently, a group of us stood watching as an unknown soldier burnt to a cinder in a sheet of flame that was clear blue. It was a new type of grenade being used by the enemy. It contained phosphorus and it burnt fiercely on contact with the air.

Imperative blasts on a whistle sent us once more into action. We surged forward, impatiently brushing aside the dying and the wounded, many of whom clutched at our feet, came crawling towards us over the sodden sand. This was the counter-offensive; there was neither time nor room for pity. We rushed on, with grenades whizzing past our ears, exploding to right and to left. We ran unthinkingly, blindly like robots. A man who paused for reflection was a man who was lost.

More ships, more boats, more landing-craft. There seemed no end to the khaki figures that emerged from the water and launched themselves up the beach. But most of them were no more than kids. All that they knew had been learnt at home, on the barrack square, on manoeuvres, in the lecture room. This was their baptism of fire and they ran like crazed innocents into the mouths of our guns.

Slowly, we fell back. The English pursued us. We led them on, until at last they were there, where we wanted them, directly beneath us and in range of our flame-throwers. They threw themselves flat to the ground, seeking cover behind the chalky slopes that rose from the beaches. For our part, we took shelter amidst the concrete ruins of the blockhouse, wriggling our bodies into craters and shell holes. We were filthy, we were exhausted, and we stank. No doubt about it. I found myself irrelevantly wishing that we might be compared, in our present state, with the brave warriors of Nuremberg, loyal Party men all, who marched and counter-marched like clockwork toys on their everlasting parades, with all their glittering pomp and their oppressively scrubbed faces, banging on their drums and blowing on their trumpets and waving their pretty little flags in the air. We lay grimed and bleeding and louse-ridden in our dug-outs, but somehow I felt we could manage to make those puppets of Nuremberg look pretty stupid.

I glanced casually at my companion on the left. He bared his teeth at me in what passed for a smile, and it struck me that he was no longer a human being, he was a wild beast. We were all wild beasts, all of us who were

16

fighting in this lousy war. A sob of rage and fear rose up and choked me, set my whole body shaking and my teeth rattling. I bit hard on to the butt of my rifle, I yelled and I screamed, I shouted out for my mother as men always do when their nerve suddenly deserts them. It was a common affliction of the front line. Sooner or later it happened to us all. And when it did, there was but one thought uppermost in your mind: get the hell out of it! Get up and run! The devil with their courts-martial, the devil with their prisons, their Torgaus, the devil with the whole shit-ridden lot of 'em . . .

I was jerked to a bone-jarring halt by a knee thrust into the small of my back. A large hand caught hold of my hair. A second large hand jammed my helmet back on my head. I looked up and saw Little John.

'Just take a good deep breath and pull yourself together,' he said, quite sensibly for him. 'It'll pass, me old fruit, it'll pass . . . No need to panic, so long as your head's still on your shoulders.'

He grinned encouragingly at me, but it was no use: my nerve had gone, and all self-control with it. I had seen it happen to others in the past; I should see it happen to many more in the future. Porta, perhaps; Little John himself. The Old Man had been near to it, the Legionnaire had been through it several times, and he was a veteran of fourteen years' experience. But for the moment it was my turn to suffer, and I stood shivering in Little John's bearlike grasp. He wiped the sweat off my face with a piece of dirty rag, pushed me further back into the remains of the blockhouse, stuck a cigarette between my lips. Vaguely, I was aware of the Old Man crawling towards us.

'What's up? Not feeling too good? Take a deep breath and try to relax. Just hole up here for a while until it passes. No need for panic, things aren't going to start up again for a bit.'

Calmly, he pulled out a roll of sticking plaster, hacked off a length and covered up a long gash in my forehead. How or when I'd received it, I couldn't recall. My sobs continued, but the cigarette had a soothing effect. And, over and above all else, I was no longer alone. I was in the company of friends; friends who cared, friends who understood. I knew for a certainty that they would risk their lives for me and would share their last crust of bread with me. It is, perhaps, the one solace of war, this extraordinary and selfless friendship that exists among men who are forced to live and fight together day after day, week after week, for an indefinite period of time.

Gradually, I became calmer. The crisis passed, and I knew that for the moment, at least, I could carry on. There would be other attacks, that was almost certain. And they would came upon me suddenly, with no warning. But it was useless to dwell upon it, for that way lay madness.

The Old Man suggested a game of cards and we settled back in our concrete fissure and they let me win, and I knew that they let me, and they knew that I knew, but what the hell, we were friends. And quite suddenly, for no reason, we began to laugh, and while life was not exactly rosy it was not quite such hell as it had been.

D-Day plus 1. The day after ... Contact with the enemy had been broken. Losses on both sides were hideous. Hardly one surrounding village that had remained intact. Most were razed to the ground. Porta just went on eating. I do believe he could have consumed a whole cow and suffered no visible after-effects. Long, thin and bony, with hollow cheeks and sunken eyes, he ate, belched, farted, ate again, belched again, always seemed to be in a state of near starvation. And yet remained the picture of rude health. The war machine had evidently played havoc with his metabolism.

On this occasion, he had a bean-feast. No more tins of gun grease, he had uncovered a cache of real Argentinian corned beef. We made it into a hash and heated it up in our helmets over spirit stoves. Porta stirred it gently with the point of a bayonet, Little John added a tot of rum that he had picked up from somewhere. Even Major Hinka consented to join in the meal. It was the best we had had for many a day.

I was on guard near the machine-gun. An unpleasant

task, because a thick fog seemed to rise from every crater and smothered the earth like a shroud. Occasionally a rocket or a stream of tracer pierced a way through the mist. My companions were asleep, lying curled up on the ground, nose to tail like dogs. A light rain was falling, the wind was whipping itself up somewhere above the fog. I was alone, and it was bloody freezing. I huddled deeper into my great coat, pulled down my helmet over my ears, and still the rain found a way in and trickled in cold rivers down my back.

Check the machine-gun. Check the firing mechanism, check the shell-ejector, check the belt-feed. It was tedious, but our lives could depend upon it.

From somewhere beyond the point I judged the enemy to be there came a slight clicking noise. Ominous and steely. What were they preparing now? Listen hard for several minutes, but nothing happens.

Away to my right is a dandelion, bright yellow and all alone in the wilderness. The only flower that grows for miles around. What was this country like before the war came and destroyed it? Trees and fields and cows. Buttercups and daisies. Juicy green grass, rich earth, neat hedges and winding lanes. What is it now? Disfigured and bloody. I wonder where the people have gone, whether they still live, whether they will ever return.

Away to the north, the rumble of heavy artillery. The sky suddenly glows deep crimson. That must be Omaha, where the Americans are landing. I turn to the south and follow the pattern of the flaming rockets that are cutting through the night, extinguishing all forms of life wherever they come to earth.

Porta talks to himself in his sleep. You listen at first, in case he says something interesting, but after a while you get sick of it. His nocturnal soliloquies are always, predictably, on the same subject: food. Quietly, the Legionnaire curls out of his sleeping position and wanders away to a dark corner. Makes a noise like a waterfall. Hard to understand how anyone could sleep through such a racket, but surprisingly they do. The Legionnaire stumbles back and collapses with a grunt between Little John and Gregor. Little John kicks out in his sleep. Gregor gets on to his back and starts snoring.

The night drags on. After a bit I find I'm dreaming, and the dream is so vivid it seems it's actually happening. I'm fifteen years old again. Back in Copenhagen. I can see the streets, wet and slippy with the rain. It was a night like that when they nabbed Alex. We were just hanging about aimlessly, like all the out-of-work kids did in Copenhagen, when they jumped us; four of them against two of us. But we put up a bit of a fight and we got away, didn't stop running till we reached the Havnegade. I'd kicked one of them in the belly. I was pretty pleased about that. We hated the cops, Alex and I. It was a point of pride to give as good as you got.

But then, next evening, I waited in vain outside the Wivel Restaurant, near the station, and Alex never turned up. We'd agreed to meet there so we could hang about near the kitchens. Sometimes a toffee-nosed chef would open the back door and sling out the leavings from the plates of the rich into the eager hands of the down-and-outs and unemployed. But Alex never came. I never saw him again. I found out later they'd picked him up during the course of one of their periodical 'clean sweeps', along with a young Swede (what the hell was he doing in Copenhagen? Should have had more sense) and sent them both off to a remand home in Jutland. Alex escaped several times but was always picked up again. One day I saw his picture in the papers. He'd stowed away on board a steamer, the Odin, and had been drowned when she'd gone to the bottom. I'm not altogether sure, it was a long ime ago, but I rather think I cried when I read that. Alex had been my friend. My only friend. After he was dead I never quite got over the feeling of being totally alone in the world.

I ran my hand menacingly, caressingly, along the barrel of the machine-gun. I had only to push back the safety catch and she would be ready for her task of destruction ... God, how I loathed their so-called democracies with their sanctimonious tirades and their ceaseless lies! So easy to sit back and give advice when you're safe indoors with a full belly and warm feet. What about the 275,000 unemployed in Copenhagen? In Copenhagen alone? Why not shoot the lot and be done with it? That would solve a few of their democratic problems for them.

That last Christmas in Copenhagen ... how I remembered that last Christmas! I remembered slouching through the streets with my gloveless hands in my split pockets, scuffing up the snow with my threadbare shoes, looking up at the glittering lights on the tree in the middle of the Radhuspladsen. I hated that tree. It was a symbol of smugness and security. Their security, not ours. I walked over and pissed up it, right up as far as it would go, and then I walked away again leaving a steaming yellow stain in the crisp snow.

I wandered alone down the Vesterbrogade. Behind each window was a little tree or little lights or pretty paper baubles. Happy Christmas! Happy Christmas everyone! The catchphrase on people's lips. Happy Christmas, merry Christmas. Just a catchphrase, nothing more. It didn't mean a thing. You try knocking on a door and begging for a mouthful of Christmas goose and you'd find yourself on your arse in the gutter before you knew where you were. And yet for all that, it was the season of goodwill and they were satisfied with themselves and at peace with the world.

On the day after Christmas, late in the afternoon, I met up with a boy I knew called Paul. Most people were hurrying on their way to the cinema, for this was the day on which the programmes were changed and new films were shown. I remember there were many films about war, and one about the death of Al Capone. All very bloodthirsty and suitable for the season of the year. Paul and I seated ourselves in a café and shared one cup of coffee and a croissant. There was a police station down the road, so neither of us was quite able to be at ease.

'How'd you like a job?' said Paul, after a while.

Very casually, as if offers of work were an everyday affair.

I just looked at him and raised a sceptical eyebrow.

'A real job with a real pay packet every Friday,' he said,

as casual as ever.

'Get lost!' I said.

'I'm serious.'

There was a pause. I looked at him challengingly, not believing a word of it, daring him to go on and commit himself. After a bit, he hunched a shoulder.

'I thought you might be interested ... It's an address in Germany I was given. They're actually short of labour over there, if you can imagine that ... They're willing to teach you the work and pay you at the same time. It's a factory of some kind ... I'm told that by the end of a year you can save quite a tidy sum.'

I sat for a moment in stunned silence. A job ... a pay packet ... food in your belly and clothes on your back and a real bed to sleep in ... Even now I hardly dared believe in the truth of it. Before I could ask any more detailed questions the owner of the café was at our side, gesticulating angrily towards the door: there was a limit to the amount of sitting and talking they allowed for one cup of coffee and one croissant.

Fifteen days later Paul and I arrived in Berlin, having made the journey as stowaways in a goods train. Very shortly after that, Paul was killed in an accident at the factory, and I joined the Army as a result.

For the first time in more years than I could remember I ate three meals a day and slept in a bed at night. The work was hard, but the factory had been harder. I slowly put on weight, my hollow cheeks were filled out, my muscles developed. My rotten and broken teeth were cared for by the Army dentist as a matter of course, and all for free. I was issued with a smart uniform and knew the luxury of clean linen once a week. Suddenly, I was a human being. Suddenly, I realized what happiness was.

And then came the war, and with it the breaking up of my new-found joy in life. The companions I had lived with since I joined the army were killed or maimed or transferred to other units. As soldiers we were no longer treated as human beings but as a necessary commodity of war. We were essential, if the game were to go on, but so were tanks and guns and land-mines. The days of clean linen and free dental treatment were gone. We became ragged and filthy, unwashed and bug-ridden. The smart grey-green uniforms of which we had once been so proud faded until they were the colour and consistency of old dish-rags. The regiment lost its identity, merged with the rest of the war machine. And always we seemed to be on the march. We marched in the rain, we marched in the sun; we marched in extremes of heat and extremes of cold; in fog and snow and ice and mud. We quenched our thirst from scum-covered pools or rank ditch water. We bound our feet with rags when our boots wore through. And what did we have to look forward to, to keep alive any ray of hope? There were only three possible futures for any of us: either you could be so badly wounded that you were dismissed as useless; or you could be taken prisoner and sit out the war in a p.o.w. camp; or—most likely—you could end up under a solitary slab by the side of some unknown road.

My dreaming was brought to an end by the blinding light of a flare burning in the night sky. Instinctively I threw myself down and crawled to cover. No need to wake up the others: their reactions had been as immediate as my own. What was happening, out there in no-man's-land? I released the safety catch on the machine-gun. The Old Man fired the Very pistol and the ground ahead was illuminated by the crude light of the flare. We held our breath and listened. From somewhere in the distance we heard the throbbing of heavy motors, the occasional harsh chatter of a machine-gun.

'Tanks,' whispered Gregor, rather nervously.

'They're coming this way,' agreed Porta.

The Old Man fired another flare. Silence. Out in the blackness beyond the flare nothing moved, and yet we knew that something was there. We stood stiffly, with strained ears and staring eyes. Major Hinka's empty coat-sleeve flapped to and fro in the wind. The flare died away and as it did so we heard the grinding and clanking of chains coming out of the darkness. The tanks were arriving. Instantly, we moved into action, preparing the anti-tank guns.

There was a whole army of tanks. The ground shook and rumbled beneath them. We could see the first of them now, advancing along the top of the cliffs, part of a long, grey column of prehistoric monsters.

Under the cross-fire of heavy machine-guns we crawled out into no-man's-land to install the Pak anti-tank gun. It was not long before we had her in working order, and not longer before her missiles found their mark. There was a sound as of thunder, then a vivid streak of red lightning flashed across the sky. The leading Churchill had stopped a grenade just under the turret, and what, seconds ago, had been a menacing steel fortress advancing greedily upon its prey, was now abruptly transformed into a gigantic firework.

Fifty metres away on our right a Cromwell was lumbering towards us. Little John turned, calmly shouldered his bazooka, took aim, with one eye tight closed, pressed his finger on the trigger. A long tongue of flame shot out. Cromwell met the same fate as Churchill.

The scene was repeated, with variations, many times over. Many tanks went up in flames, many men were burnt alive, but always there were more moving up to take their place. Men and tanks came upon us in a relentless stream. The Pak had been wiped out, the enemy artillery were enjoying themselves at our expense. The air was full of flying debris, some of it human in origin. Acrid smoke filled our lungs, burnt our throats and our eyes. Our ears resounded painfully with the after-effects of constant explosions. I lay pressed into the ground, my fists clenched, my head half buried in the sand. I saw now why men called her Mother Earth and worshipped her. Dirty and blood-stained as she might be at the moment, she was still a great comfort.

A few metres away from me I saw an English private, flat on the ground as I was myself. He saw me at the same moment. And at the same moment, I dare say, we prepared to kill each other. I didn't want to kill, I had no personal animosity towards him, but then, on the other hand, I didn't want to be the one to die. And very likely it was the same with him. The laws of battle said that one of us had to die, and there was no time just then to sit and ponder whether the laws were wise and good. It was a question of killing someone else that you might live.

I had a grenade in my hand. So, no doubt, did the English private. I tore out the pin with my teeth. Lay there and counted. Twenty-one, twenty-two, twenty-three, twenty-four ... The grenade whistled through the air towards the English soldier. On its way, it passed his grenade whistling through the air towards me. He had thrown at exactly the same moment. But no damage done. We obviously share the same reactions and had both rolled out of range in time to save our skins. I leaped for the machine-gun and feverishly fired several rounds. A second grenade exploded. Almost had me, that time. There was a vivid flash in front of me; my head, safely encased in its steel helmet, nevertheless felt as if it were bursting open at the seams. For a second I felt fear, and then, almost immediately, a mad fury overtook me. Until that moment I had not personally hated my enemy. Killing him had been a necessity. Now it had become a perverse pleasure. I certainly had no intention of dying in the muddy fields of France.

We hurled ourselves bodily at each other. It was a fierce struggle for survival, no holds barred. We battered each other with rifle butts, kicked at each other with heavy boots, slashed and fought with bayonets. The Englishman caught me in the calf and I felt a sharp stab of pain. I dived at him with renewed fury. It was unfortunate for him that his helmet came off. He received a gash across his forehead, deep enough almost to accommodate a man's fist.

I myself was too exhausted to continue the fight. For the moment it was not necessary, the man was lying at my feet. I watched him, warily, wishing he would die and put an end to it. I could have put an end to it myself, but as suddenly as it had come my blood lust disappeared. The man was staring up at me, his eyes expressionless, his breath coming in quick, painful gasps. Blood was pouring down his face, trickling from the corner of his mouth. I felt weak and vulnerable. My leg was paining me, and if any of his companions found me there I could expect no mercy. I turned to go, but the rattling breath of the man I had tried to kill held me back. Impatiently I knelt at his side, bound up his forehead as best I could, held out my water canteen.

'Drink,' I said, curtly.

He continued staring at me, but made no move to take the water. What was the fool waiting for? For me to put it to his lips and risk a knife in the ribs? I left the water within his reach and ran hell for leather back to the shelter of my own side, regardless of the danger of flying shrapnel and stray grenades. I found the Legionnaire crouched beneath the burning wreckage of a Churchill, firing quick bursts from his L.M.G. Not far away I saw Little John, his face illuminated by the flames and looking almost satanic. I dragged a handkerchief from my pocket and tied it tightly round my leg.

The enemy had been beaten off—for the moment. We had a period of respite, but it might well be brief and we made the most of it. Porta noisily consumed his fifth tin of corned beef, Barcelona passed round a bottle of gin, the Old Man played idly with a pack of cards. Behind us, Formigny was on fire. The heavy Wellington bombers were in the air over Caen and the flames rose high into the sky. The ground beneath us trembled and shook, as if in anticipation of some catastrophe.

In an abandoned jeep Porta had found an old gramophone and some discs. We played them one after another, drunk with the sudden sound of music after the hideous and familiar sounds of battle, and when we had come to the last one we started over again at the beginning. We were on our third time round when a group of soldiers came up to us out of the dim light. They seemed unarmed. They carried a flag decorated with a large red cross, and their helmets bore the same emblem. Little John snatched up his rifle, but before he could fire the Old Man had knocked it angrily from his grasp.

'What the hell do you think you're playing at?'

Little John turned on him indignantly.

'Why are they only taking care of their own wounded?

What's wrong with ours?'

'Anyone fires on the Red Cross,' said the Old Man, grimly, 'and he gets a bullet from me straight through the eyes. Is that clear?'

There was a moment's uneasy silence, then Porta laughed.

'You're in the wrong war, Old Man! You ought to join the Sally Army, you'd be a general in no time!'

He turned and spat, but the Old Man wisely held his peace. No one showed any inclination to pick up a rifle.

The last of the wounded had been collected, the last of the stretcher-bearers was on his way back to enemy lines. All was peaceful. And then, suddenly, further up in the trenches, a young lieutenant gave a sharp cry and fell down in the mud. A bullet from a maquisard had found its mark. Another came sizzling across to us, and within seconds the whole bloody fight had started up again. Three machine-guns rattled out their reply and some of the stretcher-bearing party fell. The Legionnaire was on his feet before the rest of us and was running ahead, yelling to us to follow, as he had done so often before, on the frozen Russian steppes, on the slopes of Monte Cassino.

In the fierce skirmish that ensued, almost the entire stretcher party and the wounded they had collected were wiped out. The ground was once more strewn with the bodies of men from both sides. A new stretcher party was needed to pick up the new wounded. Attack, counter-attack. Death was the order of the day.

There was no quarter given in Section 91.

CHAPTER TWO

Porta was playing about with the radio set, twiddling the knobs this way and that, attempting to isolate the sonorous voice of the B.B.C. from all the other wild gabblings and cracklings that were going on.

'You're crazy,' said Heide, in disgust. 'You get caught at that game and you'll be for the chopping block and no questions asked ... What the hell's the point, anyway? You can't believe a word they tell you even when you've got them.'

Porta held up a hand.

'Put a sock in it, for Christ's sake! This is it coming through now.'

Sounds as of someone striking a heavy gong; very deliberate and menacing. And then the cold, correct voice of the B.B.C.:

'Ici Londres, ici Londres. B.B.C. pour la France ...'

Of course, what we didn't then realize was that practically the whole of the French resistance movement was also listening in to the broadcast.

'Ici Londres, ici Londres ... May we have your attention, please. Here are some personal messages: "Les sanglots longs des violons de l'automne." I will repeat that: "Les sanglots longs des violons de l'automne" (The long sobs of the autumnal violins.'

It was the first line of a poem, "La Chanson d'automne", by Verlaine. The message for which everyone had been waiting for many weeks. Oberleutnant Meyer, at the XV Army HQ, whose task it was to monitor all B.B.C. broadcasts, excitedly and in some haste informed the Military Governor of France, and also the commanders-in-chief in Holland Belgium. He was treated with the contempt that it was felt he deserved. Important messages, indeed! Just a load of drivel about autumn. The man was obviously a cretin. Oberleutnant Meyer hunched his shoulders and went on listening.

'Ici Londres, ici Londres. We are continuing to broadcast personal messages: "Les fleurs sont d'un rouge sombre. Les fleurs sont d'un rouge sombre" (The flowers are dark red.)'

That was the signal for the Resistance network in Normandy.

'"Hélène épouse Joe. Hélène épouse Joe" (Helen is marrying Joe).'

The signal for the entire region of Caen. It set off a whole series of sabotage attempts, many of which were successful: bridges collapsed, railway lines blew up, telephone connexions were severed. At the XV Army HQ it was now generally accepted that something, somewhere, was very seriously wrong.

'Can you make nothing of it, Meyer?' demanded General von Salmuth, anxiously.

Meyer just hunched a shoulder and went on listening.

For three days there was silence, and then the messages started up again with renewed vigour and inventiveness.

'Ici Londres, ici Londres ... "Les dés sont jetés" (The dice are cast). 'I repeat: "Les dés sont jetés." '

And as a result, many unsuspecting German sentries lost their lives, knifed in the back and their bodies flung into rivers or into the marshes.

'"Jean pense à Rita"' (John is thinking of Rita). '"Jean pense à Rita." '

The speaker enunciated his words very slowly and carefully, with a pause between each.

Porta laughed in delight.

'What a load of bullshit! John's thinking of perishing Rita ... I don't suppose the chap's doing anything of the sort. Who the hell are they, anyway? Who are this John and Rita? Sounds like a kid's story to me.'

'It's a code,' explained Heide, who always claimed to know everything. 'I was a radio operator once. They use messages like that all the time.'

' "Le dimanche les enfants s'impatientent" ' (On Sundays the children grow impatient). ' "Le dimanche les enfants s'impatientent." '

That was directed to Resistance members who were awaiting the arrival of parachutists in Normandy.

'Ici Londres. We shall be sending further messages in one hour.'

THE LAST HOUR

We wrapped the dead in canvas shrouds before burying them, and by the side of each corpse we left an empty beer tin containing the man's personal papers. Sooner or later, perhaps when the war was over, we reckoned that someone would have to see about proper cemeteries with real graves and row upon row of little white crosses, and when that time came, and they were ploughing up the decomposing dead from the ditches and the cornfields, it seemed best they should know the identity of each corpse as they unearthed it. Hence the beer tins and the papers.

It seemed to us a positive necessity for both sides to have decent graveyards filled with dead heroes. Otherwise, what could they show in the future to impress new young recruits?

'Now, you lads, these are the graves of our glorious dead who fell for their country in the last war ... Beneath this cross here lies Paul Schultze, a humble private soldier who had both his legs blown off by a grenade but who nevertheless remained at his post and held off the enemy. This humble private soldier saved an entire regiment. He died in the arms of his commanding officer, a patriotic song on his lips.'

There were so many bodies waiting to be buried that we didn't have enough beer cans for all of them. After a morning's hard work as grave-diggers we were allowed half an hour for food and were then packed off on a mine-detecting expedition.

That was worse than grave-digging by far. The life of

anyone working on mine clearance was generally accepted as being pretty bloody short and by no means sweet. The mines were magnetic, set to go off at the approach of the smallest and most insignificant piece of metal. We therefore abandoned every metallic object that we had about us, even stripping off our buttons and replacing them with odd bits of wood. We were not supplied with rubber-soled boots and for the most part had to make do with rags wrapped round our feet, but Porta, our tame scavenger, had had the good fortune to lay hands on a pair of genuine American boots of yellow rubber.

It was impossible to rely upon the mine-detecting device: it reacted not only for mines but also for the minutest particle of metal, so that in the end, according to individual dispositions, we either grew mad with perpetual fear or apathetic through over-familiarity. Either way, it was asking for trouble. To stand even a small chance of survival when working with mines a man needs to be continually alert, to have nerves of steel, and to act always with the greatest caution and the steadiest of hands. There where it looks safest might lurk the greatest danger.

Of course, it was Rommel who pioneered the innocent-seeming death-trap and brought it to such a high degree of perfection. The door that opens and blows up in your face; the wheelbarrow that bars your way, so that step to one side and the earth opens up beneath you; the cupboard door that remains ajar, and produces such a fury when closed that a whole row of houses goes sky high. Then there's the almost invisible wire, cunningly hidden beneath a carpet of leaves: the leading men tread on it and there's half a company wiped out in a split second.

We had learned a great deal about mines, and the more we learnt the less we liked. We'd met the P.2s, wired in relay, which set off a whole chain reaction of explosions. And that mines that had to be destroyed by detonating. And those—perhaps worst of all—that must be taken carefully to pieces, bit by bit until you come to the detonator, made of the thinnest possible glass ... If you had a death wish and that sort of mind that could happily spend a whole hour looking for a single piece in a jigsaw puzzle, then you were O.K., you could enjoy your work. But if you were anything like me, sweating with fright and hamfisted into the bargain, then without doubt you were a very square peg in a very round hole.

We advanced slowly in line, testing out the ground step after step, never too happy even when you were at the tail end and could expect to be reasonably safe. Every ten minutes we changed the leader (and the rubber boots). In this way, only one man's life was risked at a time and each man knew that his period of endurance at least had set limits. We kept a safe distance between each one, and each one trod carefully in the steps of the man before him. For a few seconds all would be well, your heart would begin to slow down its mad canter, your sweat glands would start taking things a bit easier—and then, with a blood-chilling shriek, the man at the head of the column would wave his hands in a frenzy and halt us in our tracks. The mine detector was reacting again . . .

We all come to a stop. The man unfortunate enough to be in temporary possession of the boots holds out the detector to the front, to the side, to the rear. He pinpoints the spot which is causing all the trouble, reluctantly crouches down beside it, begins timidly to scrape away the topsoil. Five minutes pass. Five minutes of sweat and terror. And all he unearths is a piece of shrapnel, a shell fragment or part of a grenade. Always the same story. Or nearly always.

We relieve our various tensions in bursts of ill temper and foul language directed towards the prisoner who declared the area to be heavily mined, towards the Information Service who passed on the news and were therefore responsible for our being here. Quite obviously the prisoner was lying, the Information Service were a bunch of gullible fools.

We press on at a slightly faster pace, angry and muttering. A sudden explosion cuts us all short. The miserable man who happens to be leading us is blown sky-high and comes back to earth in a thousand unrecognizable pieces.

So, the prisoner was not lying, the Information Service is not staffed by gullible fools but by highly intelligent people doing a grand job of work ... and getting us blown up in the process. Perhaps it's a T mine, fashioned specially with tanks in mind. If that's the case, you've certainly had it: hardly anyone survives a T mine. If it's an S mine, on the other hand, the outlook isn't quite so grim: you might well survive with only the loss of your legs. Well, that's not such a very great tragedy in these days of warfare. They'll fit you up with a pretty good pair of artificial limbs, and if you're not actually a certifiable cretin you'll probably be accepted for an N.C.O.'s training course. There are quite a few legless men in training nowadays. It could be worse. You can sign on for thirty-six years, expect to be a Feldwebel after perhaps fifteen to eighteen years, retire at sixty-five with a fat pension.

On the whole, therefore, when we weren't actually engaged on the job, we regarded mines as mixed blessings. On the one hand, you stood to lose your life; on the other hand, you stood only to lose your legs—with the enormous advantage of being invalided out of the front line once and for all. But let there be no mistake about it: it was no use losing one leg, or one arm. It had to be both or nothing. There were many one-legged men at the front, while those with one arm were so thick on the ground that you regarded them as entirely normal, well-equipped human beings. Major Hinka, for example, had waved his right arm goodbye a couple of years ago, and he had been in the thick of the action ever since.

And now, for the moment, it was me leading the column, me wearing the boots, me risking life and limb. With my nerves alert for the first sign of danger, I cautiously bent down and flattened a clump of thick grass. Something there ... something metallic? Directly behind me, Porta and the Legionnaire came to a halt. A strong temptation to turn and run. Unfortunately impossible. Slowly I bent down and laid my ear to the ground. Did I hear a faint ticking, or was that merely my coward's imagination? Was it a magnetic mine or a delayed-action mine? Already I was soaked with sweat, my teeth clacking

33

nervously together, my knee-caps dancing a jig. It was a mine, all right. Silent, for the moment, but none the less dangerous on that account. A cobra was less to be feared. The tips of my fingers felt the shape of the invisible antennae, the rounded dome, the shatteringly thin panel of glass. It was a classic T mine.

This is the moment. Control yourself, overcome fear if you want to go on living. Remember everything they taught you ... Two fingers under the dome, two turns to the left ... but slowly, slowly ... Break the glass and that's the end of you, Sven, my lad! Pray to God there's no hidden wire, that it's not linked up to other mines. They use their cunning, the sods that lay these death traps ... Two turns. That's that bit done. Now—two millimetres higher up, three turns to the right ... It's not moving! The bastard's not moving! What in blazes is that supposed to signify? A new sort of mine? One they haven't told us about? Christ Almighty, let me get out of here! To hell with their courts martial and their charges of cowardice! I want to go on living. With any luck the war will be over before they have time to sentence me.

My mind tells me to turn and run. Coldly and deliberately, my body stays exactly where it is. All right, I'm still here. So what do I do next? Take the damned thing out before I've defused it? Why not, it's only tantamount to suicide?

All the time I'm sitting doing nothing, the damn mine is lying there smug in the earth. Staring up at me. Mocking me. And then a new and horrific idea occurs: could it be a delayed-action bugger? Still gripping the dome with my right hand, I slide my left underneath the body of the mine. With my teeth, I begin tearing away the tufts of grass on either side. Why don't they train bloody monkeys to do the work? They could use their feet as well as their hands. And probably make a better job of it, too, not having to battle with fear all the time. Why hasn't anyone thought of it before? They already make use of pigeons and dogs, and horses and pigs, so why not monkeys? (We used pigs in Poland. Used to drive them across minefields in order to clear the way. Trouble was, pigs got to be

34

worth their weight in gold and it was eventually decided that men were more expendable.)

With agonizing slowness, I drew the mine out towards me. It was heavier than I had anticipated, but at last it was out in the open, exposed in all its horror. Great ugly thing. I longed to give it a mighty kick and send it flying, but that pleasure would have to be deferred until such time as I'd succeeded in defusing it.

I called to the others to come up to me. Porta and the Legionnaire crawled across. Porta, with no formal learning on the subject, was nevertheless a mechanical genius, and after one glance at the mine he threw me a look of contempt.

'Bloody idiot! You've been turning the perishing thing the wrong perishing way! It's not a normal French thread, I should've thought even you could've seen that.' He turned and waved at Little John. 'Bring us a Swedish key!'

The key duly made its arrival. Porta studied the mine for a while.

'O.K., screw it up again.'

Meekly, I did so. The Legionnaire wiped sweating hands down the seat of his pants. Porta picked up the key.

'O.K., you lot! Keep your heads down and your fingers up your bums!'

He bent over the mine, humming a casual snatch of song to himself as he did so:

> *'What will become of us, my sweet?*
> *Shall we be happy or sad?*
> *How shall we end up, my love?*
> *Shall we be sorry or glad?'*

Stiff as boards, the Legionnaire and I sat watching him. Unconcerned, Porta held up the mine in both hands.

'There you are!' He grinned at us. 'Harmless as an unhatched chicken.'

He turned and swaggered back to the others, the mine tucked under his arm like a rugger ball. Quite suddenly,

35

he flipped it towards Gregor.

'Here! You have a go! I can't manage the thing!'

Gregor gave a shrill cry of terror and dived earthwards. Porta stood over him, raising his eyebrows.

'What's up, little man? Something frighten you?'

'You stupid sod!' Gregor kicked out at Porta's legs. 'You stupid bleeding bastard!'

'Pack it up,' said the Old Man, wearily. 'I'm in no mood for fun and games. Try to remember we've lost six men so far on this job.'

'My heart bleeds,' said Porta. 'Come on, Sven, hand us the gums. My turn to be a hero.'

He took the boots and moved to his place at the head of the column, but he had gone only a few metres when he stopped, bent down, made his examination and gestured towards the Legionnaire and me, who were the two next in line behind him. We looked at each other. We knew what had happened: Porta had come across a mine wired in relay and he needed a second person to help him. Which of us should it be? For a second I wavered, and then the Legionnaire hunched a shoulder and went forward. It would be my turn next, and I immediately wished that I'd gone this time and got it over with.

Porta and the Legionnaire crawled over the ground, following the wire. There was a time when they could have cut the damned thing and be done with it, but the enemy had grown wiser since then. They now covered the wire with a thin coating of copper. Touch it with anything metallic and the current would pass through it and detonate the mine. It had taken us a while to discover this new trick. The enemy were careful to leave no operating instructions lying about, and we'd lost several men before stumbling on the secret.

This particular little present had been slung up in a tree and was connected to three 10·5 grenades. Porta shouted irritably over his shoulder.

'Come on, for Christ's sake! This isn't a church outing!'

I realized, with a sick-making lurch of the heart, that it was my job to go across with the necessary tools and remove the bloody detonator. No easy task, that. Many a good man has come to a bad end while removing detonators, and there was always the added risk that the enemy might have prepared some new little surprise to trip us up.

Porta, half-way up the tree, was holding the four wires that led away from the mine. I edged myself forward, clutching the tools. It was a T mine. The detonator was no larger than a packet of cigarettes, but that was quite large enough for me. On one of the grenades, some joker had written the message, 'Go to hell, damned Krauts'. It was signed with the simple name of Isaac. Really, you could see the unknown Isaac's point of view. No one with a name like that had any particular reason to love us.

By some miracle, the luck held. We disposed of the T mine and its booby traps and snatched a few moments' rest on the edge of the grave. We sat in a tight semicircle on the ground and smoked cigarettes, a pastime that was, in the circumstances, strictly forbidden.

'I'll tell you what,' said Porta, suddenly. 'I bet if old Adolf had to come and work in a minefield for half an hour he wouldn't be so bleeding cocky ... He wouldn't be so keen on fighting the bleeding war, neither!'

This simple reflection put us all in a good humour. We sat there laughing immoderately until the rest of the group came up to join us, led by Lt. Brandt, who was in charge of the operation. Brandt had been with us since the beginning. He had from time to time disappeared on training courses, but he had always returned to us and we tended to look upon him as one of ourselves rather than as an officer, even to the extent of addressing him by his Christian name and treating him with our own particular brand of generally obscene familiarity. He was a true officer of the front line and one of the few men to command our grudgingly given respect.

'Bloody mines,' he grumbled. 'Much more of this sort of thing and we'll all end up together playing oranges and lemons in the nut house.'

'We'll dream of bloody mines,' said Porta, 'when we're back home digging up the vegetable patch. We'll be try-

37

ing to detonate the bleeding spuds before we know where we are.'

Porta always spoke of 'when'; never of 'if'. On the whole I suppose we all thought in terms of 'when', though most of us were too cautious to say it out loud. But somehow you never could bring yourself to consider that one day it might be your turn to end up in a ditch with a beer can holding your personal papers. You often thought about death and broke into a cold sweat, but in your heart of hearts you couldn't seriously believe it would ever happen to you. Quite frequently, before a full-scale attack, we'd helped prepare the communal grave, lined it with hay, stacked up the little wooden crosses. And never once did you picture your own body flung into it along with all the others, though God knows death was a common enough experience. How many times a day did you hear the sharp whistling sound of a grenade, the heavy thump as it landed, then the explosion, then the shrieks of pain, then the realization that the man standing next to you a second ago was no longer there ... How many times had it happened that half the section had been blown up, that all round you men lay dead or dying, and you alone left standing there unharmed? You knew the luck couldn't last for ever, and yet instinctively you felt that your own personal luck was surely inextinguishable.

Porta was eating again. This time it was a case of tinned pineapple he had found in an abandoned American jeep.

'Funny how I never really appreciated pineapple before,' he mused. 'First thing I'm going to do when the war's over is go into a restaurant and stuff myself sick till it runs out of my ears.'

This, of course, was the cue for one of our favourite pastimes: playing the game of 'when the war is over ...' We discussed it each time with renewed vigour, and somehow it never lost its appeal, although of us all Heide was the only one who knew definitely what he wanted to do with his life. He was already an N.C.O., and he had long since decided to put in for officer training. To this end he consecrated a part of each day, no matter where we

38

were or what we were doing, to learning ten pages from the Manual of Military Campaigns. We teased him unmercifully, yet we were, perhaps, just a little jealous of his dogged determination to succeed. We all knew, though none of us would admit it, that we had been soldiers for too long to return to ordinary civilian life. The Old Man declared that only farmers could happily resume their prewar activities, and probably he was right. To me, farmers were a race apart in any case. Only show them a field of potatoes or a row of apple trees and the chances were they would go completely berserk. Many a farmer had turned deserter on account of an apple tree in full blossom. They were nearly all picked up two or three days later and were hauled off to the court-martial muttering feverishly about pigs or plum trees. Unfortunately, no court-martial that I ever knew could understand the sudden compulsion that came over these men upon being brought face to face with a chunk of your actual raw nature, and the outcome was, inevitably, the firing squad.

It was ten hours, now, since we had set out to clear a way through the minefield. Ten hours of tension; ten hours of walking, quite literally, in the path of death; ten hours with virtually no respite, because what's a twenty-minute break here and there when you know the job's not yet even half completed?

But at last it was nearing its end. We had just placed the final white marker indicating a safe passage for tanks, and we should soon be able to relax. I was on the point of driving in the last stake when from the corner of my eye I caught sight of something. I paused and looked up. The others were standing still as statues, their mouths dropping open, their eyes wide and staring. They were all looking in the direction of Lt. Brandt. He was standing rather apart from the main body of men, his legs straddled, his arms held slightly out from his body . . . I felt the goose pimples of fear break out over my limbs. I knew only too well what that awkward stance indicated: Claus was standing directly over a mine. The slightest move, and it would go off. I could see the wires running from it. Claus must know as surely as the rest of us that his hour had come.

Those nearest to him began slowly to retrace their steps, backing away one foot behind another. They, too, were in grave danger. It was evident from the presence of wires that the mine was linked to others. Only one person showed any desire to rush forward, in a heroic but undoubtedly suicidal attempt to come to the Lieutenant's aid, and that was Little John. We restrained him by brute force, and it took three of us to do it. No sooner had we succeeded in calming Little John than Barcelona was overcome by a fit of madness and began slowly to crawl towards Claus, still straddled over his death-trap.

'Catch the silly bastard!' yelled Porta.

The Lieutenant's face was a horrible leaden colour. He was one of the bravest men I knew, but even brave men are allowed a certain licence when standing on a live mine. Already we were preparing a syringe full of morphine, laying out the bandages and dressings. If by some miracle he survived, he would need all the dressings available. The Legionnaire had pulled out his revolver. His intention was clear: whatever happened, Claus should not suffer longer than was necessary. Call it murder if you will, but he had been with us for six years, fighting side by side with the men under him in some of the worst encounters of the war. When you know and love and respect someone as we did Claus, you don't bother too much about how the rest of the world is going to feel, you just go ahead and do what has to be done.

To be caught out like that, by a comparatively simple mine, lying there for all to see, was one of the incredible ironies of war that are so hard to bear. And yet, I suppose, it was almost inevitable that something of the kind should happen. After ten hours of concentrated work in the middle of a minefield it's not very surprising if a man's attention should lapse for a second or two. Unhappily, a lapse of even a fraction of a second is only too often fatal in such circumstances.

Porta suddenly cried out to Claus.

'Jump! It's your only chance!'

Claus hesitated—and who should blame him? It was

one thing to say it was your only chance; it was quite another thing nerving yourself to take that chance.

Meanwhile, we waited. And death waited none the less patiently, for a prey that was very sure.

After a time—ten minutes? Half an hour? Days, weeks, months? It seemed like eternity—Claus raised his hand to us in a silent, farewell salute, bent his knees, prepared to take his only chance...

I pressed my hands over my ears. Claus remained in position, like a runner waiting for the starting pistol. I suppose we must all have shared the agony of his final thoughts. So long as he remained where he was, he was still a live man; the second he moved, he would probably be a very dead man.

He pressed the tips of his fingers into the earth, preparing for the moment when he must take his chance. And then suddenly he straightened up again.

'Chuck me over your battledresses!'

Ten jackets were instantly thrown across to him. Only three reached him. Little John started up again, but Porta instantly fetched him a blow with a spade. He collapsed with a grunt.

'Tell him thank you from me,' said Claus, gravely.

He wound the three jackets round his body, protecting his stomach and chest as best he could. Then, once again, he raised his hand in salute.

'Jump! For God's sake, jump!'

I heard myself urgently whispering the command, but the sound was drowned in the sudden united pealing of bells all over the country. Bells that were ringing out for the liberation of France. The wind brought us the sound of the jubilant carillons, crying out that France was free. People forgot the horrors of war, the hell of the Normandy landings, the ruined buildings, the devastated countryside. They knew only that once more they were a free people. In the streets, American soldiers danced with French girls. Viva la France! Mort aux Allemands!

Lieutenant Brandt flexed his muscles. And jumped. And an explosion that shattered the eardrums drowned the pealing bells. A leaping tongue of flame ... We sprang forward. Both his legs had been blown off. One was lying neatly by his side; the other was God knows where. His entire body was covered in burns, and he was still conscious.

The Old Man at once set to work with the morphine. Porta and I bound torniquets round the two bleeding stumps of his legs. His uniform was hanging in shreds, there was a smell of roasting flesh. Claus gritted his teeth as long as he could, but then the suffering began in earnest and his screams of pain rang out and mingled with gay carillons.

'More morphine!' roared Little John, who had recovered consciousness after Porta's blow with the spade.

'There isn't any more,' said the Old Man, quietly.

Little John rounded on him.

'What the hell do you mean, there isn't any more?'

A pause.

'What I say,' said the Old Man, throwing away the syringe in a gesture of disgust. 'There is no more morphine.'

What else could we do? Nothing very much. Only sit by the Lieutenant's side and suffer his agonies with him. Someone placed a cigarette between lips that were already turning blue.

'You'll be all right——'

'A nice spell in hospital——'

'You're not going to die, it's the end of the war——'

'You'll be O.K. when we get you back to base——'

'Can you hear the bells? It's the end of the war!'

The end of the war, and very soon the end of life itself for our Lieutenant. He died within seconds, and we retraced our steps through the minefield, between the white markers that he had helped set up, carrying him shoulder high; a funeral procession with the triumphant bells as our accompaniment. Little John walked at the head. Porta brought up the rear, playing a melancholy tune on his flute. 'The journey of the wild swans', it was; one of the melodies that Claus had loved best.

CHAPTER THREE

The Russian, Lieutenant Koranin of the 439th East Battalion, together with his company of Tartars, had made an astonishing discovery: in an American landing-craft, lying by the side of three dead officers, was a document case crammed full of papers. Koranin instantly took possession of the document case and hurried off with it to his company commander, who with equal promptitude decided that it was a matter for General Marcks, commander of the 84th Army, to deal with. Accordingly the two men went off together with the precious document case.

The General at once appreciated the value of Koranin's discovery, and he lost no time in passing on the news to the Eighth Army. The Eighth Army, to his surprise and indignation, laughed in his face and gratuitously informed him that he was talking nonsense. For a while General Marcks was too stunned with anger to do more than sit and fume, while his aide-de-camp stood tactfully to one side and himself read through the contents of the wretched document case. Both men were firmly of the opinion that the papers were genuine.

'Do you think, perhaps, sir, the Secret Service . . .?'

The General did. The Secret Service should be informed immediately. No doubt about it, the papers were of the utmost importance. The next step was to contact Generalfeldmarschall von Rundstedt and tell him that he, General Marcks, had in his possession the Allies' top secret plans relating to the Normandy invasion. The plans clearly demonstrated the truth of what until now had been purely a matter for conjecture: that the recent landings were only a prelude to the full-scale invasion which everyone had been anticipating for the past four years.

'Rubbish!' screamed von Rundstedt, and slammed down the telephone.

He remained adamant. The plans were fakes. A deliberate trap. Had been planted there to catch just such gullible fools as General Marcks. Come to that, the landings themselves were intended to mislead. Von Rundstedt had his own ideas on the subject. Certainly the Allies were planning an invasion, any idiot knew that, but the Normandy landings were not the prelude to it. They had been laid on as an elaborate red herring.

'Relieve General Marcks of his command!' ordered von Rundstedt, irritably. 'The man's an idiot and a dreamer and has no right to be in charge of an army. Get rid of him.'

THE HILL OF GOLGOTHA

It was night. We were making our way back along the main road, three columns of us, to position 112. A damp North Sea mist hung in the air and worked its way under our clothes and our skin, down our throats and into our very bones. We were marching towards the rear of one of the columns. The vanguard had long ago disappeared into the mist. It was some time since we had last seen them and we took their continued presence at the head of the column merely on trust.

Porta, for once, was not talking of food. He had fallen back on his second subject of conversation and was relating one of his interminable tales about whores. The Old Man was bringing up the rear, marching stolidly onwards with his head sunk between his shoulders, the inevitable pipe protruding from the corner of his mouth, his helmet hanging by its strap from his rifle. We always called him, always had called him, the Old Man. Right from the start. In fact he was Feldwebel Willy Beier, our section leader. He hardly looked the Army's idea of the perfect soldier, crashing along in a pair of big black boots several sizes too large for him, with his shabby uniform and his week's growth of beard, but he was the best section leader I'd ever known.

We turned off the road and marched through what had presumably, a few days back, been a fairly extensive wood. But now the trees were flattened, the earth churned up by a succession of tank chains; the remains of burnt-out wrecks, abandoned jeeps, overturned trucks, lay scattered thickly over the whole area. No less thick were the piles of human debris.

'Jesus, this lot copped a packet!' muttered Little John, for once in his life sounding almost awestruck.

Porta paused for one merciful second in his tale of drama and whoredom.

'Heavy shells,' he said.

'It's a new type of mortar grenade,' contradicted Heide, always up to date with the latest information. 'They evaporate on your uniform and burn you.'

'Oh, lovely, lovely!' said Porta, clapping his hands. 'I can't wait to try one!'

Charred bodies were certainly thick underfoot. And there were other sights, too, to give you a thrill. Propped against the trunk of a tree was a naked body minus its legs. Stray limbs abounded. Little John came across a severed head, still encased in its helmet, and took a hefty swing at it as if it had been a football. The Legionnaire, not usually the most impressionable of men, put a hand over his mouth and turned the other way.

'There are some things,' he told us, 'that just turn my stomach. And the sight of human heads bouncing along on their own like that happens to be one of them.'

'It's like a butcher's shop in here,' remarked Gregor, with a rare flight of imagination. 'Joints of meat hanging everywhere.'

'More like hell's kitchen if you ask me,' said Porta. 'I bet you there's enough roasted meat lying about here to feed half the German Army for a week.'

'Shut your filthy mouths!' snapped the Old Man, suddenly.

We fell uncomfortably silent. Porta was just beginning to

inquire whether he had 'ever told us that one about——'
when the earth rumbled and shook beneath our feet and
there was the shattering sound of an explosion. Instinctively, we fell as a body on to our knees.

'Fags out! Company scatter!'

Hastily, we scattered. A spout of flame shot brilliantly
into the sky over our heads. It must be coming from the
Dora batteries, the batteries of rockets with twelve cannons.

In single file, bent double, we crept along in the shelter
of one of the drystone walls that abounded in that part of
the country. The enemy were making life more difficult
than was strictly necessary by changing their position
after each fresh salvo, laboriously towing the guns to a
new spot and blasting off at us from some unexpected
vantage point.

'Get a move on, can't you?' hissed the Old Man.
'They're still coming closer. They'll be on us any moment.'

There was every justification for his remark: immediately behind us rose a cloud of dense smoke, shot through
with leaping crimson flames. Judging from the ghastly
howls and shrieks that came to us from the other side of
the cloud, it seemed that many poor devils had copped
it.

We scuttled along by the side of the wall. The protection it gave was more psychological than actual, but fortunately one didn't stop to think about that at the time.
A front-line observer, an artillery lieutenant, suddenly
emerged from a shell hole and angrily confronted us. He
was covered in mud and blood and had a raw open
wound on his forehead.

'What the devil's going on here?' he demanded. 'Who's
in charge of this load of cretins?'

Oberleutnant Löwe, who had replaced our late Lieutenant Brandt, shook with anger in his shoes.

'Who are you calling a load of cretins?'

The Lieutenant raised both hands in a gesture of despair.

'Your bloody company, of course! Can't you get the

hell out of here, you're drawing the enemy fire on us!'

Crouched down behind our drystone wall, we followed the discussion with our usual interest.

'He wants a good kick up the arse,' declared Porta, in loud tones. 'What's he think we're doing here? Playing bleeding tiddlywinks?'

The rocket battery was in position a few hundred metres away, over on the far side of the road. The missiles were coming across thick and fast, and the umbrella of fire lit up the misty air for kilometres around.

We remained in the illusory shelter of the wall, huddled together, each man pressed close to his companions. The flames were not far off us, now. They were gathering force on the opposite side of the road and would doubtless soon be swooping across and engulfing us. Lieutenant Löwe passed the word along that we were moving again, single file; by which he stressed that he meant one by one and not an undisciplined scramble for front-line places.

Obediently we moved off. We had gone only a short distance when, glancing back, I saw the billows of flame rolling across the road and settling themselves down to beat against the wall that had been our shelter. For a moment the figure of a man was outlined against the glare; then slowly it threw up its arms and fell back into the blaze. It was the arrogant lieutenant of artillery. Had he not wasted so much time attempting to put Lt. Löwe in his place, he might yet have been alive. But that's the way it went, as Porta cheerfully reminded me.

I recalled another occasion when things had gone well for us and badly for someone else, through the purest chance, and Porta had made the same remark. Our group had been sheltering in a wood in company with some men from one of the engineering corps. It was pouring with rain and after a bit we were as wet as we should have been out in the open. And Little John, as usual, grew impatient with prolonged inactivity.

'I've had enough of this!' he declared. 'Can't we get a move on?'

And so we had got a move on, and before we had gone fifty metres there had been a loud explosion and both trees and engineers had been blown to fragments.

And another time, I remembered, we had installed ourselves in an abandoned house in some village or other, I forget where it was, and were playing a round of cards with a group of anti-tank boys. It was sheer luck that had caused Porta's eye to wander to that particular corner of the room where two wires could be seen running along the skirting board.

'Hang on,' he said. 'What's that over there?'

Being both by nature and experience a suspicious-minded lot, we at once downed cards and began tracing the path of the wires. The anti-tank lads remained in their seats, cursing us for interrupting the game. Seconds later we were following the wires out of the back door; and seconds after that, before we had traced them to their source, the house went up in a sheet of flame.

But that's the way it goes.

We reached position 112 at last and duly took over from the company we had been detailed to relieve. They were S.S. men, belonging to the division of Hitler Jugend, 12th Panzergrenadieren Division. None of them, apart from the officers, was more than seventeen years old, but in the last three days these silent, stiff-backed boys had become old, old men, their faces shrunken, their shoulders hunched round their ears, their eyes glazed and withdrawn. Over half their company had fallen in battle.

At our arrival, without a word they packed up their belongings and stood waiting for the signal to depart. They had even cleared up their spent cartridges. They were a model of perfection, and it was the saddest sight in the world. We watched them as they went, and wonderingly shook our heads. Only Heide was favourably impressed.

'There's discipline for you!' he said, admiringly. 'What soldiers those kids are! Mind you, they should be with the officers they've got ... Did you see? They all had the Iron Cross, 1st Class, every man jack of them ... God, what I wouldn't give to be a section leader with that lot!'

'You're welcome,' said Porta, laconically. 'It's downright uncanny, if you ask me.'

48

'To hell with bloody heroes,' added Little John, for good measure.

We stood staring after them as the column of old men stepped out, two by two, over the hill and out of sight. Their uniforms were immaculate, their bearing was military, their equipment glistened and gleamed through the mist—all this, after three days of hard fighting! To all of us except Heide the sight was almost unbearably pathetic. To Heide, it seemed perfection itself. His eyes shone with fervour and he seemed unable to grasp how the rest of us were feeling.

'Oh, go and tag on behind them, if that's what you want,' growled Porta. 'Who the hell's stopping you, you bloody warmonger?'

Heide remained unmoved by Porta's words. In all probability, he never even heard them. He was lost in his own private dreams of glory. In his imagination he already was an officer with a crack regiment. I saw his hand wander up to his throat, doubtless feeling for the Croix de Chevalier that should one day adorn it. Little John shook his head in disgust. Impatiently he snatched up a couple of twigs and bound them together into the shape of a cross.

'Here! Try this for size!'

Heide stared at him with vacant eyes and gave him a rather beautiful, if totally vacuous, smile. Little John turned and spat.

It began to rain and the cold drops trickled forlornly off our helmets and dribbled down our backs. What a bloody awful climate it was, in this part of the country! Fog, rain, wind, mud—mud in particular. You couldn't move without getting covered in the stuff. It was a thick, sticky, red clay and it clung stubbornly to uniforms and equipment and left a crimson pall over everything.

Shortly before dawn, the enemy attacked. They were unaware that the S.S. troops that had held the position for the past three days had been relieved and we didn't let them come near enough to find out. We had our own obstinate discipline when under fire, bitterly learnt on the Russian front.

49

The opposition seemed to consist mainly of a Canadian regiment. We had an especial loathing for the Canadians and their sadistic ways. We had heard tell that they used to tie up their prisoners with barbed wire and attach them to tanks, and we knew for a fact that if you fell into their hands the very best you could hope for was a bullet through the back of the neck.

After a bit the Canadians were joined by the Gordon Highlanders, but we didn't hold any particular grudge against the Scots. We even went so far as to go out and rescue three of their wounded who had got themselves entangled in our barbed-wire entrenchments. The poor devils were terrified and evidently under the impression that we were going to shoot them out of hand. God only knows where they got that piece of information from. Propaganda, I suppose. Rumours spread by evil-tongued journalists, who, if I had my way, would be butchered out of hand and no questions asked.

The whole day was passed under heavy fire. The British were launching an air attack on Caen and the sky was full of bombers and shrapnel and flying missiles.

'I hope to Christ they don't think of sending us over that way,' muttered Porta, jerking his head in the direction of Caen. 'You remember how it was in Kiev, with the Russians only two paces behind all the time? Bloody hell! I can't stand being in towns.'

'What about Rome?' challenged Little John. 'You had a bloody good time in Rome, if I remember rightly. It's a wonder they didn't end up by making you into a cardinal!'

'Rome was different,' said Porta.

An enemy machine-gun tore up the ground in front of us with a spurt of bullets. Barcelona's helmet was blown off and rolled to the bottom of the trench, and he screamed in fury as he bent down to retrieve it.

'Load of Scotch bastards! You come over here and I'll show you a thing or two!'

A sudden lull in the fury of the onslaught. We spread mackintoshes over the mud at the bottom of the trench and settled down to a game of cards. Porta's little bright eyes gleamed beneath his bushy eyebrows, darting this way and that in an attempt to see other people's hands. Heide, always mistrustful, held his cards close against his chest and squinted awkwardly down at them. Probably a wise precaution: Porta had been known to cheat before now, and his eyes were veritable X-rays. I saw from the expression on Gregor's face that he was contemplating at least a five-card trick. I turned to look at Little John, but he was far away, leaning back with his stinking feet propped on someone's gas-mask case, picking his teeth with his tongue. God, how his feet stank! It must have been weeks since they had seen water, and heaven alone knows when soap had last come in contact with them.

Barcelona took a quick glance at his hand, declared, 'Hombre! I'm packing!' in tones of disgust and slammed his cards down on the ground. Barcelona was getting more Spanish than ever, these days. He was for ever dreaming of the years he had spent in Spain, fighting in the Civil War. He even carried a dried orange in his pocket as a memento.

'Straight from Valencia,' he used to tell us, fondly.

The Legionnaire picked up his hand and surveyed it without emotion. There was never anything to be gained from studying the Legionnaire's face. Years spent in the French Foreign Legion had left their mark on him and his grey eyes were always steady and cold, his mouth always pursed in a grim line. I found it hard to recall if I had ever seen him laugh. On the whole I thought I probably hadn't, because if so I should surely have remembered the occasion.

The Old Man made a noise in the back of his throat and threw in his cards, turning for solace to his beloved pipe. Somehow, the Old Man always put me in mind of Erich Maria Remarque's 'Kat'. It was the Old Man who'd taught us all to recognize various grenades by the sound they made, just as Kat did for his section. It was the Old Man who had taught some of us almost everything we now knew, and God knows that many of us would not have been alive today had it not been for him. He had pulled the section out of many and many a sticky situation in his time. And there were many new young officers, fresh from the military training school at Potsdam and thrown only half prepared into the thick of the front line, who had cause to thank him. And never should I forget the S.S. Obersturmführer who was sent to us for a spell of punishment duty. It had taken him no more than half an hour to lose an entire company, which the Russians had silently encircled right under his eyes. The Obersturm-führer had been one of the few to break out of the net and survive, and had it not been for Major Hinka's for-bearance he would undoubtedly have been hauled up before a court-martial. As it was, he became suddenly very humble and turned out to be one of the Old Man's best pupils.

I overheard a conversation once between the Old Man and one of the M.O.s attached to General Staff, who fer-vently declared that we should win the war because we were better than our enemies.

'Unfortunately,' said the Old Man, rather dryly, 'it's not always the best side that wins, not by a long chalk.'

'Ah well,' said the doctor, 'perhaps you're right. I wouldn't know about these military matters ... But tell me, when do you reckon we shall be getting these splen-did new weapons they've been promising us for so long?'

'New weapons?' The Old Man scratched the lobe of his ear with the stem of his pipe and laughed to himself. 'I don't place too much reliance on these mythical new weapons, you know. I'm willing to go on fighting with the old ones...'

And he turned and gestured towards the rest of us. To-wards Porta, with his long scraggy neck and his knock knees; towards Little John, a man the size of an ox with a large heart and a small brain; Barcelona, pitifully flat-footed, me with my weak eyes that couldn't stand the light; Gregor, who had lost half his nose, and Major Hinka, who had lost his right arm.

'A sorry-looking lot, if you like,' admitted the Old Man, when the Major was well out of earshot. 'But believe me, I'd rather have them by my side than any number of new weapons. It's men like them who keep the enemy at bay, not your rockets or your flying bombs.'

The doctor sighed.

'Ah well,' he said, again, and this time it was a positive sigh of despair, 'perhaps you're right. I wouldn't know about these military matters . . .'

Two days later we heard that he had put a bullet through his head. I often wondered if the Old Man's remarks had perhaps been too much for him to take. At first sight we weren't exactly a bunch to inspire much confidence. It must have shaken him pretty badly to think he was reliant upon men like us to win the war.

The alert sounded, shrill and anxious. They were coming at last. A horde of khaki-clad soldiers, leaping over the barbed wire, showering us with grenades, preceded by rolling waves of fire. Through the flames we could see their bayonets glinting. Their objective was to take position 112. An order from General Montgomery, who was bent on capturing Caen at all costs, even if it meant losing a whole Scots division. Position 112 was soon to become a second Hill of Golgotha.

The Scotsmen came on at the head of the attack. On either flank were armoured divisions. Gregor was manning the 81-mm. mortar, which he used like a machine-gun. He had lost his helmet and his face was black with smoke, marked here and there by channels of sweat. Major Hinka, his empty coat-sleeve stuffed into his pocket, had taken over a heavy machine-gun and was sending off salvoes of bullets into the oncoming mass of infantrymen. He was assisted by one of the medical orderlies. Neither man said a word; their mouths were set in hard lines, their uniforms caked with mud.

Little John was preparing two hand-grenades at the same moment. Both exploded the instant they reached their destination. Little John had never yet been known to fail where hand-grenades were concerned. As for me, I was having trouble with my machine-gun. It was a model I particularly disliked. In my experience you inevitably spent more time tinkering with the wretched thing than actually firing it. On this occasion, as on so many others, a bullet had become jammed in the loading device. With a

53

shrill curse I yanked the bayonet out of my rifle and began jabbing it at the offending bullet. It had no effect whatsoever, except, perhaps, to push it further in. Fortunately Porta came to my rescue.

'Get out of the way, you silly sod!'

He elbowed me to one side, and seconds later waved me back to a gun that was now in perfect working order. During those few seconds the suicidal Scotsmen had made headway and were now a swirling mass of colour before us. Red, green, blue, yellow ... so pretty, and so dangerous! They were all yelling like maniacs, hurling themselves forward over the barbed wire, regardless of the relentless hail of grenades and machine-gun fire. Montgomery evidently wanted Caen very badly indeed. The Scotsmen died in their hundreds on the barbed wire. The armoured divisions were crucified in their burning tanks. Yet still they came on, because Caen had to be taken.

The section holding the ground on our immediate right flank was in danger of being wiped out. There was hand-to-hand fighting in the narrow trenches. Our neighbours were putting up a desperate battle for their lives with bayonets, rifle butts and knives, and if they fell we knew that we should be next on the list. Major Hinka turned for a moment from his machine-gun. He waved his arm, imperiously, and shouted something that was lost in the general uproar. We knew what was required. He didn't have to repeat himself. Barcelona turned his gun towards the trenches and sent a steady stream of fire into the midst of the fighting mob. Friend and foe alike were slaughtered. There was no room for sentiment on the Hill of Golgotha. From somewhere a little further up the line we saw a white flag raised: an old grey vest waving uncertainly from a rifle. We saw a small group of Canadians move in upon it. Saw them motion to the surrendering Germans to leave their shelter and to line up along the edge of a trench, drop their weapons, place their hands behind their backs. We heard the order given to fire. A sergeant raised his Sten-gun and the men in grey fell one after another to the ground.

'Bastards!' screamed the Legionnaire, at the top of his

voice.

With a quick jerk of the head to Porta and Little John he called them up to a quick and apparently decisive conference. Next moment, Porta had dragged a tattered vest off the nearest dead body, attached it to his rifle and was slowly crawling out into no-man's-land towards the group of Canadians, now victoriously sheltering in their victims' burial trench. Behind Porta crept Little John and the Legionnaire, pulling the flame-thrower with them. Porta agitated his grey flag and called out to the Canadians. I saw the sergeant with the Sten-gun stand up, smiling, in the trench. I saw him prepare to fire. Before his finger could press the trigger, two events took place almost simultaneously; the flame-thrower went into action and Porta hurled a grenade into the trench. The Canadians were wiped out within seconds.

'That'll teach the bastards,' muttered the Legionnaire, as he arrived back at my side. 'They won't try that trick again in a hurry.'

I had no time to congratulate him: enemy tanks were bearing down upon us. A tight formation of Churchills and Cromwells, which had already broken through our front line. We did our best with the anti-tank guns, but all round us men were abandoning their positions and scattering before the oncoming tanks. Major Hinka shouted to us to use the Goliaths. These were a type of mini-tank, radio-controlled, each containing 100 kilos of explosive. Willingly we hurled these useful little weapons into the midst of the enemy. They had evidently not come across them before. The first two Goliaths, looking small and harmless pulled to a halt before an advancing company of soldiers. It must have seemed that owing to some mechanical fault they were unable to proceed any further. The enemy were plainly puzzled. At first they treated them with some caution, and then, as nothing happened, they grew bolder and began to move in upon them. Someone pulled out a camera and took a photograph; someone else, very daring, put out a hand and touched; from there it was but a short step before some foolhardy spirit put out a boot and fetched one of the Goliaths a hearty kick.

55

A few of the men at once dived for cover, but the company clown sat squarely on top of a second mini-tank and started vigorously on the chorus of 'Tipperary' ... It was at that moment that Barcelona pressed the plunger. The Goliath exploded in a vast spout of flame, roaring its way into the air and carrying a motley assortment of humanity with it.

'Stupid buggers,' grumbled the Legionnaire. 'Like a load of kids, have to go and touch at everything ... Never mess about with unidentified objects ... You'd think that would be elementary, wouldn't you?'

Seventy enemy tanks went up altogether. And seventy tank crews were burnt to cinders. But Caen had to be taken, and always there were more tanks in reserve. The fighting went on for eighteen hours, with the usual hideous losses on both sides. At the end of that time we neither knew nor cared what was happening to Caen. Did it stand, or had it fallen?

'I couldn't give a tinker's cuss,' said Barcelona.

'And who the hell wants it, anyway?' complained Porta. 'I certainly don't!'

Within seconds of speaking they had both fallen to the ground and were sound asleep. The rest of us dropped down beside them like a house of cards collapsing. Who the hell wanted Caen, anyway? Porta didn't. I didn't. Only Montgomery wanted it, as far as I could see. And for all I cared at that moment, he could have it.

CHAPTER FOUR

Many unknown Frenchmen, members of the Resistance, gave their support to the invading forces, and the exact number of those who lost their lives was never known.

Some while before the invasion took place, London had quite coolly requested that the head of the Resistance network for Caen, an engineer called Meslin, should furnish them with detailed information regarding the German fortifications in that area. They knew full well the enormity, one might almost say the impossibility, of the task they were setting him, but still they expected him to turn up with the right answers. Meslin heard the request in silence; merely put his head in his hands and wondered how the hell he was going to work the necessary miracle. Each road, major or minor, each lane, each pathway leading to the coast was heavily guarded and under constant surveillance. Anyone fool enough to be caught wandering about without an official pass was shot out of hand.

The more Meslin pondered the way and means at his disposal, the more he came to the realization that those ways and means were limited indeed. Non-existent, he was tempted to say. Even if he found himself work with the Todt Organization he would see no more than a minute section of the beach. And there were 160 kilometres of shoreline altogether. Plainly it would require several hundreds, if not thousands, of agents to cover the entire area.

The task was plainly ludicrous. Meslin looked at the situation from every possible angle and decided to pass on this piece of information to London. He couldn't tell them much about the German fortifications but he could tell them what to do with their lunatic requests in the future.

It was at this point that chance intervened, brought about a change of plan. One of the members of the group was a painter and decorator, René Duchez, nicknamed 'Sang Froid'. He was walking the streets of Caen, pondering the same problems as Meslin, when a notice pinned outside the police station caught his eye:

'The Todt Organization is looking for an experienced painter.'

For a few moments Duchez stood staring, turning over in his mind the pros and the cons and eventually deciding in favour of the pros. He turned and walked off to the offices of the Todt Organization, where a sentry pushed him roughly away before he had even the time to open his mouth. Duchez stood his ground and demanded to be taken to see an officer. The sentry, speaking no French, also stood his ground, and thus they remained, glowering at each other, until an N.C.O. arrived to sort the matter out. His French was minimal, but it served its purpose, and Duchez found himself led past the sentry box and into an office marked 'Civil Buildings and Works Controller'. The Controller took a note of his name and address and promised to let him know within eight days whether the Organization would be taking advantage of his offer. Duchez was well aware of the purpose behind the eight-day period: during that time the Gestapo would be shaking the details of his life, past and present, through a sieve of the finest mesh. Anything the least questionable, anything that could possibly give them a lead to his Resistance activities, and not only would they turn him down but his life would be endangered.

All, however, went well. On the eighth day Duchez presented himself for work with a range of sample materials and was shown into the office of an Oberbauführer. He had been there only a few seconds when the door opened and one of the engineers walked in. He greeted both Duchez and the Oberbauführer with a pleasantly impartial 'Heil Hitler!' and flung down a roll of blueprints on the desk.

'Not now, for Christ's sake!' The Oberbauführer waved a hand, impatiently. 'Come back later, I'm too busy to bother with them now.'

'Just as you like. I'm in no hurry.'

The engineer hunched an indifferent shoulder and left the room. The blueprints remained on the desk. The Oberbauführer grudgingly unrolled them, and behind him Duchez craned his neck to see. He was hardly able to believe his eyes: the blueprints were none other than the precious plans, coveted by London, of the German fortifications all along the Atlantic wall from Honfleur to Cherbourg.

The Oberbauführer seemed uninterested in fortifications. The very presence of the blueprints was apparently sufficient to anger him. He rolled them up and tossed them into a corner, then turned once more to Duchez and to the question of which paint and which paper he was to use. Seconds later they were again interrupted, this time by an overbearing officer who brushed aside all other claims on the Oberbauführer's attention and ordered him into an adjoining office to talk on 'matters confidential'.

Duchez, left alone in the room, instantly and as a reflex action snatched up the blueprints. Not until they were in his had did he pause to consider what should be done with them. Useless to attempt hiding them anywhere about his person. His frenzied gaze stopped short at a large painting of Hitler that was fixed to the wall behind the Oberbauführer's desk. It seemed highly unlikely to him that the painting would ever be moved, and equally there seemed no reason for anyone ever to look behind it. Feverishly he stuffed the roll of blueprints between the portrait and the wall and stepped back to his pile of paints and papers as the Oberbauführer returned.

'Idiots! Idiots the lot of them! They're all bloody idiots round here!' He glared at Duchez, as if to imply that he need not consider himself exempt from the charge. 'Some fool's mixed a load of sugar with the cement. What the hell am I supposed to do about it? Dig

the stuff out with my fingernails?' He made a noise of
disgust in the back of his throat. 'Let's have another look
at those samples of yours.'

The paint and the paper were finally settled. Duchez
was told to report for work at eight o'clock on the Monday morning, his task to be the redecoration of the Organization's offices. Duchez took himself off, after a fervent
salute and a knowing smile at the portrait of the Führer.

It was then Friday. He spent the entire weekend in a
state of ferment, suddenly appalled by the idiocy of the
thing he had done, expecting the Gestapo to drop down
on him at any moment. It seemed quite obvious to him
now, in cold retrospect, that the blueprints were certain
to have been missed within at the most twelve hours and
that the Oberbauführer would very naturally have laid
the blame at his door. Not only was he a Frenchman, and
therefore automatically suspect, but inescapably he had
spent several vital seconds alone in the room with the
wretched blueprints. He was as good as dead already.

Sleep was impossible. He roamed the apartment from
wall to wall while his wife lay snoring in happy ignorance. Fear, the damp, sweating fear of anticipation, drove
him almost mad. He cursed himself and he cursed the
English, smug in their island across the Channel. The
crashing of heavy boots on the pavements took him with a
puppet-like jerk to the windows. A police patrol, armed
with light machine-guns. The beam of a powerful torch lit
up the flat and he shrank back into the shadows by the
curtains. The patrol went on its way. Duchez snatched up
a bottle and passed the rest of the night in a drunken
haze, racked with waking horror dreams of the Gestapo.

But the Gestapo never came. And in any case, by
Monday morning Duchez had grown almost indifferent to
his fate. He set off for the Organization with his paint
pots and his brushes and he found that he had grown
accustomed to his fear and that it no longer troubled him
so much. He showed his pass, was searched by the man on
guard and sent on his way. The Oberbauführer had been
transferred over the weekend to a different service. No
one else, apparently, had the least idea what was going

on, and Duchez found himself greeted by gaping mouths and raised eyebrows when he presented himself, whistling, in the first office to be decorated. Finally they dug up a Stabsbauführer who confessed vaguely to having heard of the project. However, the Stabsbauführer was at that moment occupied with heavy artillery and with shelters, both of which he found a great deal more interesting than office decoration.

'Just get on and do the job as you were told,' he said, loftily. 'Don't come pestering me about it. I have other things on my mind, I can't be bothered with petty matters of this nature.'

For two days Duchez worked hard at his painting. People grew used to seeing him about the place and for the most part ignored him. Not until the afternoon of the third day did he risk a look behind the portrait of the Führer. The blueprints were still there. He had not expected them to be, and the sight of them threw him into a state of renewed panic. He decided to leave them there, but at the last moment he snatched them up and hid them in a roll of wallpaper.

As he was leaving the building, he was called to a halt by the sentry. It was a new man, one he hadn't met before; one who didn't know him and didn't trust him. Duchez felt suddenly, violently sick. The man patted his pockets, looked inside his canvas bag.

'O.K., you can go.'

Duchez walked out of the gates.

'Wait a minute! What have you got in those buckets?'

'Paste,' said Duchez, meekly.

'Paste?'

'For the wallpaper.'

Duchez jerked his head at the paper, rolled up beneath his arm with the blueprints hidden in the centre.

'Ah-huh?' Suspiciously the sentry stirred the thick mess in the buckets with the tip of his bayonet. 'O.K., I just wanted to make sure. Can't always trust Frenchmen, unfortunately.'

Duchez gave an unhappy laugh and walked away on tin legs. As soon as he could, he presented himself at the

Café des Touristes, the headquarters of the Resistance in that area, and handed over the wallpaper and the blue-prints. He was heartily glad to be rid of both: by now even the wallpaper had come to seem incriminating.

From Caen the blueprints were smuggled to Paris, to a Major Toumy in the Champs-Elysées. Major Toumy, on realizing the full significance of the coup, declared himself to be both stunned and staggered. He added almost immediately that that was an understatement but that words failed him.

'Fantastic! Brilliant!' he declared, when speech returned. He tapped the blueprints with one finger, rather nervously, as if they might crumble to dust. 'This man—what's his name? Duchez?—this man has brought off the most magnificent coup of the whole war ... And that,' he added, thoughtfully, 'is another understatement.'

BILLETING

The little amphibious V.W. lurched past the first few straggling houses that marked the start of the village, and Gregor pulled her to a halt with an unpleasant squealing of brakes. Sub-machine-guns at the ready, we peered out at the apparently deserted street. The least sign of a suspicious movement in the shadows, from a doorway, at a window, and we were fully prepared to shoot. We were beasts on the prowl. We could not afford to take any chances. Too often you took a chance only to discover that quite suddenly the tables had been turned and it was you the prey and the unknown the hunter.

The silence was thick and unnatural. It hung over us like a heavy blanket. Porta was the first to leave the car, followed by the Old Man and by me. Gregor stayed behind the wheel, his gun resting against the windscreen, his finger resting on the trigger.

The road was rough and winding, meandering through the village between the sad grey houses and the devastated gardens and finally disappearing in the distance into fields and woods. The village itself was little more than an obscure cluster of dwelling-houses, marked on only the smallest scale maps. Thirty kilometres away, few people had ever heard of it.

With guns at the ready we bore down upon the nearest houses. We knew from experience that people would protest, and sometimes quite violently, against these incessant demands for billets for the German troops. We sympathized with them, but you couldn't afford to waste time arguing or explaining: it was our job to arrange billets for the companies now on their way to the village, and if the job wasn't done by the time they arrived we should find ourselves in the dog house with both officers and men.

Stealthily, with shifty eyes and padding footsteps, the village was returning to life. Doors half opened, curtains crept back. We went from house to house, checking up on rooms and deciding how many men it was practicable to quarter there. On the whole, the village had come through the war pretty well unscathed. Convoys had churned up the road and made a mess of the gardens, but otherwise it was undamaged: not a single shell had landed there.

As we left one house and prepared to cross the street to the next, a small girl, perhaps seven or eight, came rushing towards us and flung her arms round the Old Man's waist.

'Papa! You've come back! I knew you would! I said you would!'

She pressed herself hard against him and the Old Man stood there, awkward and helpless.

'Hélène!' A woman's voice came harshly from inside a cottage. 'What is it? What are you up to?'

'It's Papa! He's back! Come and see, grandmère, he's back!'

An elderly, large-boned woman, her black hair pulled hard back from her thin face, her eyes deep down in their sockets, appeared at the cottage door. She barely glanced at the Old Man.

'Don't be foolish, Hélène. It's not your father. Come back indoors.'

'It is, it is! This time it really is!'

With what seemed to me unnecessary brutality, the woman jerked out a sinewy arm, tore the child away from the Old Man and tossed her through the cottage door. I noticed she was wearing mourning, like so many French women at that time. She spoke stiffly and ungraciously.

'You'll have to excuse her. She's mentally unbalanced. Her father fell at Liège in 1940 but she persists in thinking he's still alive. Her mother's dead, too. Killed by a Stuka. It's not easy to know how to cope.'

'Of course not,' muttered the Old Man. Rather timidly, he held out the piece of chalk we used for marking the houses. 'I have to decide about billets ... Do you mind? I'll write it up on the door ... 1st Section, 3rd Group...'

'Do what you like,' said the woman, sourly. 'You always do, don't you?'

In the cottage next door, we were offered wine to drink. The lady of the house was wearing a long silk dress that must have been in vogue half a century earlier. The room smelt strongly of naphthaline. Our host hovered at our elbows, replenishing our glasses each time we took so much as a sip, reiterating over and over that we were welcome, always welcome, very welcome, and all the time eyeing our uniforms with a manic gleam in his eye. They were the ordinary black uniforms of the tank corps, with the death's head insignia on the collars.

'I see you are the Gestapo,' observed the man, at last. 'There are things I should tell you about this village. Peculiar happenings take place here. For instance, and for a start, it's swarming with Communists. With the Maquis ... Call them what you will, they're all tarred with the same brush.' He bent down, tapped me on the shoulder and pointed through the window at a neighbouring house. 'Over there—see it?—right over there? Well, that's where five of your Gestapo men were murdered. Murdered! You understand me? They did it in cold blood.' He straightened himself up. 'I just thought you ought to know.'

A man wearing a farm labourer's smock rode slowly past on a bicycle. Hanging from his cross bar was a dead chicken. Our host pointed excitedly.

'See that man? That's Jacques. Brother's in the local police force. Jacques's in the Resistance. I know it for a fact. Not only that, if the truth were out he's responsible for all the crimes ever committed in this place ... And I shouldn't be surprised if his brother weren't hand-in-glove with him. In fact I'm pretty sure of it.' He refilled our glasses. 'You ought to be made aware of these things. I'm only trying to be helpful.'

His wife nodded vigorously, her pale, pinkish eyes suddenly gleaming with satisfaction. We set down our wine glasses and took our leave. '1st Section, 4th Group' was chalked up on the door.

'Slimy sods,' growled Porta. 'Anything to save their own precious skins.'

'None of our business, anyway,' decided the Old Man. 'We're not here on Gestapo business. I couldn't care if they'd knocked off a round dozen of 'em!'

Further on in the village we came across Pierre, the suspect brother of Jacques. He had a soiled *képi* pushed far back on his head and as he caught sight of us he at once leaped to his feet, almost emerald green with fear, knocking off his *képi* and tumbling a bottle of calvados to the floor. The calvados was retrieved and reverently offered to us. Pierre himself drank our health several times in quick succession, shouted a few enthusiastic Heil Hitlers! and began to pour out a flood of incoherence.

'German soldiers are the best in the world, let me refill your glasses, gentlemen, I always say so and besides it's been proved, everyone knows it and you will win the war.' Here he giggled nervously, slapped the Old Man on the shoulder, gave vent to a few more Heil Hitlers to relieve his feelings and showed us a picture of his wife and family. 'Have another drink ... your health, gentlemen! You will win the war. The war was engineered by the Jews. Here——' He pulled out a sheet of paper and earnestly pressed it upon us. 'This is a list of all those I have arrested. If I had my way, the whole country would be cleared of Jews. They bring us nothing but trouble. Look at Dreyfus!'

'Dreyfus was innocent,' protested the Old Man. 'It was a

legal error.'

'Ah, but it doesn't alter the fact that he was a filthy Jew!'

'A Jew, at least,' I muttered.

Porta suddenly jerked up his gun in a way that terrified even me. Pierre stared at him with saucepan-lid eyes.

'They tell us,' said Porta, menacingly, 'that you work for the Resistance and that a great many rather peculiar things go on in the village. What do you have to say about that?'

'Say? Say?' cried Pierre, wildly. 'What should I say? It's a pack of filthy lies! I've been pro-German from the beginning and everyone knows it!'

'They don't know it down there,' said Porta, jerking a thumb towards the house we had recently left. 'If I were you, pal, I'd keep an eye on them. They don't seem over-fond of you.'

'But that woman's my cousin!'

'Cousins can be as vindictive as anyone else.'

We left Pierre to chew his fingernails and marked up '2nd Section, 1st Group' on the door. I smiled, happily, and wondered if Pierre would still love the Germans as much when he'd met Little John. Pierre saw me smiling and came reeling to the door to promise us the best of food and drink for the men who were to be billeted with him. We looked back as we left and saw him polishing off the Calvados at a quite astonishing rate.

'Almost shit himself with fright,' observed Porta, in disgust. 'Bloody cardboard heroes, the lot of 'em!'

'Not so easy,' murmured the Old Man, 'living in an occupied country.'

In the next house, an old peasant with the Croix de Guerre pinned to his chest gave us a very glacial welcome. As we looked over the house we could feel his little cold eyes glittering malevolently upon us.

'Hah! A bath!'

Porta pulled his find clattering and banging into the middle of the room. An old tin bath, small and a bit battered, but a bath nevertheless. Baths of any description were rare in the smaller villages.

'Better chalk it up for some of the brass,' advised Porta. 'They're the ones that seem most addicted to water.'

66

We moved on to visit the Mayor, a round man with a big hairy moustache. He greeted us most cordially and straightway informed us that he was a member of the Party.

'Good,' said Porta. 'Let's give him Hauptfeldwebel Hoffmann. I doubt if anyone could stay in the Party after meeting him.'

Further up the street, set on a slope a fair way back from the rest of the village, was a small house that seemed at first glance to be deserted. We approached it cautiously but no one answered our hammering at the door and we finally abandoned it and went on with the search for billets elsewhere.

Late in the afternoon the battalion arrived with all its usual fuss and bother and noise and clouds of dust. We'd managed to fix everyone up, but fortunately we'd been at the game long enough to know that we should not expect any gratitude. Just as well, because we had none—except from Little John, who was met by a beaming Pierre and the sight of a well-stocked cellar.

Leaving the rest of them, I slipped back to take another look at the deserted house at the top of its lonely slope. I had a curious feeling about that house, and I approached it cautiously, not by the gate and the front path but through a gap in the thick hedge, round at the side. It was like an enchanted garden in there. Flowers grew in unregimented masses, scarlets and blues, golds and purples; the grass was ankle deep, a bright wet green, slightly darker beneath the apple trees. Half overgrown with moss and ivy was an old well with an upturned bucket and a broken chain. I stood for a few moments mesmerized.

'What do you want here?'

At the sound of the voice, floating imperiously towards me from the flowery depths of the garden, I instinctively wrenched out my revolver and took cover behind the thick trunk of a nearby tree. It was an automatic reaction, but the voice was a woman's and it was not unfriendly. It came from the far end of the garden, where I now saw a young girl, about twenty-five years old, lying in a hammock that was slung between two apple trees. She raised herself on an elbow and stared at me out of suspicious, almond-shaped eyes.

'What are you looking for?'

'Nothing,' I said, moving towards her but keeping the revolver in my hand. 'I thought the place was deserted. We called here this morning and got no reply ... We were finding billets for the troops down in the village.'

'I see.'

The girl swung her legs gracefully out of the hammock. She was wearing a Chinese-style tunic with a high neck, two slits up either side revealing well-shaped thighs.

'I'm about to have a cup of coffee. You want to join me?'

'You live here?' I demanded.

A stupid question, really. At the time I was rather knocked sideways by the sight of so much leg and could think of nothing more intelligent to say. She gave me a slow smile, as if realizing my confusion.

'Sometimes I live here. Sometimes I live in Paris ... Do you know Paris?'

'Not yet. I hope to soon!' I laughed, and then thought that perhaps I was being tactless. 'Are you married?' I asked, maladroitly.

'In a manner of speaking. My husband is in a Japanese prisoner-of-war camp somewhere in Indochina. I last heard of him three years ago.'

'I'm sorry,' I muttered.

She shrugged.

'Why be sorry? Where else is there for a man to be, these days? Either behind barbed wire or behind a machine-gun. You don't get much choice, do you?'

I remained silent. What she said was so obviously true that there seemed little point in even agreeing wth her.

'Do you think,' she said, suddenly, 'that the war will finish soon?'

I lifted an apathetic shoulder. Of course I thought the war would finish soon. I've been thinking it for some years now. Ever since it had started. It was the only way I could manage to keep sane.

'It's marvellous up here,' she told me. 'You can almost forget what's happening in the rest of the world. But at the same time it scares me. It's so isolated from

68

people. It's so cut off from reality ... I'm going back to Paris tomorrow. It's better there. Conditions are worse, but you're not so much alone ... Do you suppose they'll make Paris an open city, like Rome?'

I had no idea. I wasn't even aware that Rome was an open city. No one ever told us anything, in the Army. We were only soldiers; machines that obeyed orders. Why should we be told what was going on?

The girl moved up close to me. One of her hands touched mine. It was soft and gentle, and a tremor of excitement ran through me as forgotten senses came suddenly to life. She raised her other hand and removed my dark glasses, but the light was so obviously painful to me that she promptly replaced them.

'I'm sorry.' She smiled at me, apologetic and uncertain. 'I didn't realize ... I thought you were just wearing them for show. To make yourself look interesting——'

'I wish I were,' I said, bitterly. 'I spent three months lying in bed as blind as a bat and working out ways of killing myself after I copped this lot.'

'Where did you——' She waved a hand. 'How did it happen?'

'A phosphorus grenade got me when I was jumping out of a blazing tank. I suppose I'm a lot luckier than some. There are thousands of men back home who've been blinded in the war. I at least haven't lost my sight. It's just that I can't stand any sort of light in my eyes.'

'I shouldn't have thought you'd still be asked to go on fighting!' she said, indignantly. 'It's disgusting!'

'One arm, one leg, one eye ... that's all you need for this war,' I said.

She looked at me a moment.

'How long are your soldiers staying here?'

'I should know! A few hours, a few days ... Only the officers are told things like that.'

'Of course,' she said, as if realizing it for the first time, 'you're not an officer, are you? I never notice these things ... Where do you come from, in Germany?'

'The barracks, in Paderborn ... Actually I'm from Denmark.'

'Ah, so you're not a German?'

'I am now, yes. If I still had Danish nationality I'd be serving in the Waffen S.S. Sort of foreign legion.'

She leaned against a tree trunk, solemnly regarding me.

'Why on earth did you join up?'

'To earn myself a daily meal and a roof over my head, basically. There didn't seem any other way of doing it at the time—and besides, *All Quiet on the Western Front* was my bedside book when I was a kid. I thought your actual ordinary German soldier the most romantic figure in the whole world. I never quite got over it.'

'Really? But I always thought the book was *anti* all that sort of thing?'

'Maybe it is. Try telling that to a small boy! No one's ever going to convince *him* that peace is more exciting than war, or that a man out of uniform can ever be as heroic as a man dressed up with a rifle over his shoulder and a helmet on his head ... And then there's no getting away from the fact that there's a great comaraderie in the Army. You know what I mean? You're all in it together, in peace or in war; it gives you somewhere to belong, it makes you feel a part of something.'

'But why the German Army?' she persisted. 'Why not the Danish Army?'

I laughed.

'Because there hardly was one! And soldiers weren't popular in Denmark. People used to spit on them in the street. Officers as well as men. Even the police used to turn a blind eye.'

'I suppose that was why Denmark fell so quickly in 1940?'

'They couldn't have done anything, anyway. Germany's the biggest military force in the whole of Europe. Even the French Army couldn't hold out for very long.'

The almond eyes narrowed.

'France hasn't given up the fight yet, don't you worry! As long as England stands we shall go on fighting. And England won't fall, you can depend upon that; and she won't let us down, either!'

I laughed, genuinely amused by her naïveté.

'You want to know who England's fighting for? She's fighting for herself, and only for herself. She couldn't give a damn about France. She already let you down once. Remember Dunkirk? You remember what happened there?' I shook my head. 'Nations never do anything for other nations. Only for themselves.'

'That may be,' she said, 'but you know quite well that Germany's as good as lost the war. Why don't you get out while you've still got the chance?'

'Desert, you mean?'

'Why not? Others have done it. The Maquis would look after you if you worked for them over here.'

'I couldn't desert. I may be fighting for a lost cause, but that's beside the point. If I backed out now I'd be letting down the friends that were left behind. They count on me, just as I count on them. None of us could ever desert in cold blood. We've been together far too long.'

Growing enthusiastic, I placed my hands on the tree trunk, one on either side of the girl's shoulders, leaning towards her and looking down at her as I spoke.

'The five of us, we've lived through hell together ... in the trenches, in tanks, under fire ... When you've done that you can't just walk out on people.'

'But the war is lost!'

I made an impatient clicking sound with my tongue.

'Of course it is! We've known that for months. Long before the politicians knew it.'

'Then why don't you all desert? All at the same time?'

How simple she made it sound! I shrugged my shoulders.

'Why didn't they desert in the First World War? It's something to do with companionship, I suppose. Even if you all deserted you'd have lost that sense of—of belonging. You'd be out on your own again. I can't explain it too well ... Remarque does it a damn sight better in his book. Try reading it again and perhaps you'll understand a bit better, though it's difficult to have the same sort of feelings when you don't know what it's like to have been totally alone in the world.'

She stretched up her arms and locked her hands behind my neck.

'I'm alone in the world,' she said. 'I know how you feel.'

'I doubt that,' I murmured.

I took her in my arms and for a long while we stood there, straining against each other, kissing greedily and blindly as if we were starving. Which perhaps, in a sense, we were. It was so long since a woman of this quality had wanted me; so long, indeed, since an opportunity of any kind had offered itself. I found her encouragement as heady as a bottle of wine on an empty stomach.

The earth trembled beneath the weight of a column of tanks moving into the village below. We felt the breath of their exhaust hot on our cheeks, and hand in hand we wandered towards the house for the promised cups of coffee. Real coffee! I had forgotten how it tasted. I sipped it slowly, eager for the pleasures still to come yet loth to waste a drop of the precious stuff without savouring it to its fullest.

'What sort of man are you?' she said. 'I mean, really?'

'Just an ordinary soldier,' I said. 'Does it matter—really?'

She laughed and shook her head. Slowly she embraced me. Slowly, luxuriously, she began shedding her clothes, emerging slim and lovely as from a chrysalis.

'Look at me,' I said, ruefully. 'Look at my clothes—sodden heaps of oil and mud! I tell you, I'm just an ordinary soldier. Trained to kill and nothing else. At times I disgust even myself.'

'If you could choose, what should you care to be?'

I shrugged my shoulders. The question of choice had never arisen, probably never would arise.

'Difficult to say. I've been a soldier too long to think for myself any more. I'm so used to carrying out orders, so used to a strict discipline and to other people running my life for me, I doubt if I could live any other way.'

'I'm sure you could if you really wanted to,' she said, pulling me down on to the bed.

And so, for a while, I did. The war went on without me and we never missed each other. Tanks rumbled past beneath the windows and I never even noticed them. My companions down in the village drunk and swore and gambled, and I never even thought about them. The coffee cooled down in its pot, until finally it was cold.

How many hours, I wonder, did we manage to snatch from the dreary round of death and destruction? One, perhaps; or two. Certainly no more. But enough to give me a taste of a different life from the one that I was forced to live; enough to make me resentful when we were roused from a sweet semi-sleep by the sound of fists and boots hammering at the door. I became aware that the road leading out of the village was full of sound, whereas before it had been calm and silent. I heard shouts and curses, the squealing of brakes and the grinding chains of the tanks, heavy boots crashing on the gravel, harsh voices shouting orders.

We sat up, the two of us, and she threw me my shirt and herself pulled the sheet to her chin. Whoever was at the door grew tired of knocking. There was a sound of splintering, then heavy steps in the hallway. It was Porta who burst in upon us, red faced and indignant.

'So this is where you've been! What the bleeding hell are you up to? I've been looking everywhere for you, you stupid sod!'

'Piss off,' I said. 'Get out, scram, shove off! We don't want you. Go and find someone else to play games with.'

Porta stepped forward, picked my clothes off the floor and hurled them at me.

'Get yourself inside of that lot, and better make it snappy! I'm not here to play games, chum—not when the Yanks are on their way!'

I fought my way through a heap of pants and shirt and battledress and stared up at him.

'Where are they coming from?'

'Christ knows! And who the bleeding hell cares, anyway? They're just coming, ain't that good enough? They're coming, and we're going . . .'

He turned to the girl and gave her his grotesque parody of a charming smile, his lips drawn back over his gums, his tooth gleaming like the fang of a uni-dentoid vampire.

'You'll have to excuse me, darling. I hate to spoil anyone's fun, but like I said, the Yanks are coming. If you play your cards right you'll be able to find a replacement for him soon enough.'

He turned to the table, picked up the coffee pot and

stuck his large nose deep inside. It came out again with nostrils flared in excitement.

'Coffee!' he said, in strangulated tones.

He poured it down his throat, cold as it was, and snapped his fingers at me.

'If you don't get a move on, mate, they'll be after you for desertion. Almost everyone else has cleared out already. We're just about the last lot to go ... Little John's pissed as a newt, by the way, I left him roaring and ranging down the village ... Lt. Schmidt was dragged out of his sick bed and told he'd be court-martialled if he didn't make an immediate recovery, and Feldwebel Mann —you know Feldwebel Mann?—first thing he did when he got settled in was lock the bog door behind him and shoot himself ... Oh yeah, and Obergefreiter Gert's done a bunk. Not surprising. He always was a stupid cunt. They're out looking for him, they're bound to pick him up in a couple of hours—well, not as long as that, I don't suppose——'

During Porta's seemingly inexhaustible torrent of words I had been hastily dragging on my clothes. The girl now suddenly flung herself across the bed at me and burst sobbing into the midst of Porta's latest piece of vital information.

'Sven! Don't go! It's madness to keep on fighting. We all know you've lost the war ... Stay here and I'll hide you! Please, Sven!'

'I can't,' I said. 'I've explained to you once. It doesn't hurt indulging in dreams now and again, but don't ever get them mixed up with reality.'

'Reality? What is reality?' she demanded, the tears streaming down her cheeks. 'Blood and dirt and cruelty, and dying for a cause you don't believe in?'

'I guess so,' I said.

Porta, who had been digging out the wax from his ears with the wrong end of a teaspoon, now flung the spoon on to the table and gave me a look of genuine bewilderment.

'What's she blarting her eyeballs out for? She's still got a house that's in one piece, ain't she? And enough food to fill her belly, and enough money to get black market coffee?' He spat, contemptuously. 'Makes me sick,' he said.

'Think she'd be content with what she'd got, wouldn't you?'

'Shut up or get out!' I told him, curtly.

I turned to the girl, but she refused to say goodbye. I left without a backward glance, wishing that dreams could sometimes have a sweeter ending, yet not prepared to shed any tears about it.

The Company was already formed up in the town square and it was impossible for me to slip unnoticed into my place. Major Mercedes caught sight of me immediately.

'Where the blazes have you been? You think we're all going to hold up the war just on account of you?'

'Don't go on at him too much,' begged Porta. 'If you'd been up to what he's been up to——'

A loud and ribald cheer burst from the ranks of assembled men. I assumed a Don Juan smile and the Major turned in a fury upon everyone in general.

'Stop that bloody racket! What d'you think this is, a bloody pantomime? A bloody magic lantern show? You——' He swung back to me again. 'You're under arrest! Get back in the ranks and don't let me catch sight of your stupid face again until I call for it ... Oberleutnant! Get them out of here, at the double!'

The Major ducked into his car, the door slammed, and he disappeared in a whirling cloud of dust. Oberleutnant Löwe pushed his helmet back and nodded to me.

'Get fell in, you filthy whoring son of a bitch ... Company! 'Ten shun! Company ... right ... turn!'

For a moment he stood critically surveynig us as we stood stiff and correct in our ranks. Next second he was hard put to keep his feet as one hundred and eighty men in wild disorder threw themselves towards the waiting tanks. We had quite a fight luring the drunken Little John inside with us. He showed a sportive inclination to climb up the side of the tank and crawl about the top of it shouting, and it took three of us to cram him head-first down the hatch. Once inside, he fortunately passed out and we were able to kick him into a corner and forget about him.

With a roar as of approaching thunder, twenty-five

Tigers moved out of the village.

'Straight ahead,' said the Old Man. 'Just keep going till we pick up the main road. Get the cannons loaded. Check all systems.'

With startling suddenness, I found myself overcome with a sharp pang of nostalgia for that dream world I had been so rudely dragged away from. Apathetically, I began carrying out the Old Man's orders, pressing buttons, checking equipment. My thoughts were full of civilization. Of women and houses and hot baths and real coffee. Bed and gardens and bath salts and sugar. Soft pink flesh and the scent of roses——

'That's my eye, you stupid sodding bastard!'

'Sorry,' I said, and I removed my finger from Porta's eye and placed it firmly on the button it had been searching for.

I stared down at the dark interior of the tank. It stank of oil, of hot metal, of human sweat and bad breath. This was reality. Like it or not, this *was* reality. Sweet dreams of any other way of life would surely drive you mad.

Little John opened an inflamed eye, caught sight of me and leaned confidentially towards me. He belched, and fumes of stale drink rose up and stifled me.

'Hey, Sven!' He grinned and poked a lewd finger into my groin. 'I heard what you were up to! What's she like, eh?'

I stuck my face close to his.

'Fuck off!' I said.

When we reached the point where the village street went straight on and the slope leading to the house branched off to the left, I made no attempt to stop myself looking out of the observation slit. I was glad I took that last glance. Jacqueline was there, standing by the hedge, waving as we went by.

The village was still in sight when an enemy tank was reported as being 700 metres away at two o'clock. We swept into action and I was jerked back with a sickening thud into the midst of reality. It was, as it happened, a false alarm—a burnt-out wreckage at the side of the road, with two charred bodies beneath it—but once and for all it put a stop to my day-dreams.

Soon it was night, the sky lighted fitfully by a pale phantom moon. The tanks ploughed onwards, shaking houses to their very foundations. All along the route people were woken by the noise, curtains were twitched back, nervous eyes appeared, glinting in the moonlight, to watch our passage, find out who we were—because from this stage on, who knew? It could be friend or foe; American or German.

Three battalions of heavy tanks ploughing through the darkness to take the British by surprise. The lumbering Tigers stretched across the whole width of the road. Bright flames, a metre long, flickered from the exhausts. The reverberations of the engines crashed and boomed through the stillness of the night, and more than one house had its windows blasted out as we passed by. Some buildings were even more unfortunate: they stood directly in our path and were simply demolished and left behind as heaps of rubble.

'Come, sweet death,' intoned the Legionnaire, cheerfully, behind his periscope.

Little John shuddered and turned to Porta.

'Gives me the perishing willies,' he complained. 'Got any booze on you?'

Porta obligingly handed over a bottle of the best Schnapps, which he had nicked from a supplies depot a short while back. The Schnapps had been originally requisitioned for a divisional commander, but unluckily for him Porta had arrived there first. According to Porta, he had smelt alcohol several miles off and had followed his nose along the trail.

Little John, attacking the Schnapps as he did everything else, with full verve and gusto, poured half the bottle down his throat. He then belched, spat through the observation slit against the wind and received the whole lot back in his face, whereupon he swore hideously, and wiped himself on a piece of oily rag. By such little excitements were our journeys habitually enlivened.

We went on, hour after hour, towards the enemy lines. The road was more congested, now, with the debris of war. Burnt-out cars, the wreckage of other tanks, English and German, the charred remains of human beings sprawled over, under and beneath them. An entire column of infantry lay scattered at the side of the road in the grotesque attitudes of death.

'Jabos,' said Porta, unemotionally.

You couldn't get too worked up about the slaughter: we'd seen it all before, so many times.

'Remember the old tank song they used to put out on the radio?' said Barcelona, suddenly and for no very apparent reason.

He turned to the rest of us and began softly chanting the song that we'd all heard so often, back in 1940. The words no longer seemed very appropriate:

'Way beyond the Maas, the Schelde and the Rhein,
Advancing upon Frankfurt, a hundred tanks in line!
A hundred German tanks and the Fuhrer's Black Hussars
Gone to conquer France, cheered on by loud huzzahs!
With a hundred throbbing motors, a hundred grinding
   chains,
A hundred German tanks are rolling o'er the plains!'

A banal song at the best of times, it now seemed utterly absurd. There was a burst of scornful laughter, both from our own tank and from others in the column: we had left the radio switched on and the whole company had enjoyed Barcelona's moment of nostalgia.

'Belt up!' came Heide's raucous voice, over the radio. 'What's wrong with you stupid buggers back there? It's not the time for that sort of thing!'

Poor Heide! He was taking it very hard, the way the war was going. The rest of us merely laughed until we felt sick. The hundred German tanks and the Führer's Black Hussars were no longer rolling triumphant o'er any plains but desperately fighting a rearguard battle against the advancing enemy.

Our laughter was cut short by the sight of a strange, straggling group along the roadside. I couldn't at first make them out. Prisoners, perhaps? No, prisoners would not be guarded by nuns, and I suddenly saw that the weird, batlike figures running hither and thither were members of a nursing order trying in vain to restore order

78

to their group of—what? I screwed my eyes up behind my dark glasses.

'Nuts!' hissed Little John, in my ear. 'Bleeding nuts out of the nut house, that's what they are!'

He was quite right: an asylum near Caen had been evacuated and the arrival of our long column of tanks had created panic in their already confused midst. They darted about in all directions, some clapping their hands and grinning, others raving and howling like wild beasts. Some just stood vacant in the middle of the road, heads rolling limply and arms hanging. One poor idiot hurled himself under a tank and was crushed. The nuns called out despairingly and threw their arms into the air, but the demented horde seemed bent on self-destruction. Suddenly, out of the gloom, a man wearing the white coat of a doctor advanced threateningly upon us.

'Stop!' cried the Old Man, foreseeing disaster. 'Stop, for the love of God!'

The radio was still turned on. Three battalions heard the order, and slowly the entire column of tanks came to a halt. Almost at once Major Mercedes' car came tearing along by the side of us, going full speed ahead and sending showers of nuns and lunatics scattering into the ditch. His voice came furiously over the radio.

'What cretin gave the order to stop? Whoever he is, he can expect to be court-martialled for sheer bloody stupidity! Get started again, we stop for no one!'

With groans of agony the heavy tanks lumbered once more into movement. One of them ploughed straight through the group of lunatics. The driver obviously panicked and lost control, and the vehicle shuddered to a halt in the middle of the road, once again bringing us to a standstill. Bodies lay crushed on either side of the offending tank. One old nun advanced furiously upon it and began beating against the metal with clenched fists.

'Murderers! You're nothing but murderers, the lot of you!'

No one took any notice of her. The Major's car drew up with an ill-tempered screeching of brakes, and the Major's head appeared through the window, scowling and hideous in its anger. The black patch gleamed nastily over his right eye.

'That idiot's not fit to drive a toy car, never mind a bloody tank! Get someone else on the job, for Christ's sake! And as for you'—he glared at a luckless lieutenant nervously inching himself up through the hatch—'we'll see about you later! Of all the crassly stupid things to do——' Words happily failed him. He turned back to the rest of us and waved the column onwards. 'Get going and keep going! I don't care if you see Christ himself walking down the road, we stop for no one—and I mean no one! Is that quite clear? Anyone gets in the way, he's had it. Teach him not to be so damn careless in future.'

At that moment, before the Major had had time to move off again, a group of vehicles marked with red crosses attempted unsuccessfully to overtake us. In spite of their demands for passage we stood firm and let them sink themselves in the ditch. The Tigers stopped for no one; the Tigers gave way to no one.

An infantry lieutenant came storming past us on foot, followed by an officer for the Feldgendarmerie, his half-moon badge glinting evilly through the gloom. He had snatched out his revolver and seemed disinclined for any civil form of conversation. I heard him shouting as he walked.

'This is sabotage! Someone's going to suffer for this! Who's the fool commanding this load of morons?'

He was very sure of himself. The members of the Feldgendarmerie were, in general, scared of neither man nor the devil; nor even, for that matter, of the Führer himself. An ordinary major was mincemeat to them. Happily, Major Mercedes was no ordinary major. He didn't give too much for man or the devil himself, and I don't believe the Führer roused any particular feelings of reverence in him.

'Tigers!' His voice bellowed along the length of the column, rolling and echoing from one side of the road to the other. 'I gave you an order: get started! We stop for no one! And as for you, sir'—he turned towards the two men, pushing the Feldgendarme out of the way and addressing himself to the Lieutenant—'I advise you to get your miserable little pushchairs well off the road if you don't want them crushed. I should also,' he added, as an afterthought, 'proceed back via way of the ditch. I think you'll find it safer.'

The Tigers rolled onwards. We managed to get some way before we ran into yet another column of men, almost as bizarre to behold as the group of lunatics from Caen. For a start, although the column wore the uniform of the German Army, it was comprised of half the peoples of Europe. There were Russians, Ukrainians and Cossacks; Bosnians of the Muslim division, Bavarians, Alsatians; Hungarians, Poles, Italians. And not only that, the entire column had obviously but one thought in its multiracial mind, and that was flight. They came pell-mell up the road towards us, a strange mixture of panic and determination on that strange mixture of faces. We raised a great cheer as the vanguard of the fleeing hordes flashed past us.

'The German Army!' shouted Porta, exultantly. 'God bless 'em! If only Adolf were here to see it...' He pointed at a fast-moving knot of men from a parachute regiment. 'If only Hermann were here to see it!'

'Can it be,' said Barcelona, very solemnly, 'that we are losing the war?'

'Never!' shouted Porta.

Our laughter echoed wildly inside the tank.

'Hallo!' said the Old Man, peering out again. 'What's this lot coming up?'

It was a cavalry unit. They approached at a furious gallop, slashing with sabres at the deserting hordes, spreading out in a wide fan shape to engulf the whole mass. We recognized them by their red collars as General Vlassov's Cossacks, specialists in this kind of work. They rode like demons, standing upright in the stirrups, with the foam flecking the nostrils of their sturdy little horses. Harsh commands were shouted in Russian; sabres flashed and glinted. In a matter of minutes they had rounded up the whole column and were encircling them, yelling like savages all the while. Some of them dismounted and waded into the midst of the heaving mass of bodies, slashing and cutting at random until we could see the rivers of blood from some distance away. No one put up any fight.

81

Possibly they were too cowed, or possibly they had abandoned their weapons in their initial panic to escape.

It was impossible for the Tigers to keep moving. We watched the scene, filled with disgust and hatred. Such brutality was all that could be expected from the Cossacks. As far as we were concerned, the German Army could well have done without their help. We saw an officer of the Feldgendarmerie clap a Russian captain on the shoulder, evidently congratulating him on a job well done, and our anger grew apace. Many of the Russians had led their horses to a nearby stream and were now lying on their bellies, drinking up the water side by side with their mounts. The sight was not very surprising: in a Cossack regiment a man and a horse are as equals.

The tanks had of necessity been brought to a temporary halt. The Cossacks now advanced towards us, their small black eyes glitteringly manically, the red star of Russia gleaming on their fur hats. A thick-set corporal, stinking of vodka, stopped by the side of our Tiger. He wore his sabre slung across him, and in one hand he carried a nagajka, the whip beloved of all Cossacks.

'Salut, Gospodin!'

He looked up at us and laughed. I could feel the others prickling with hatred at my side.

'Hey, tovaritch!' Porta suddenly leant out towards the man. 'You ever had your fortune told?'

'No. Why do you ask?'

'Because I tell 'em, that's why! Want me to tell yours for you?'

'What for?'

Porta shrugged.

'It could be interesting.'

'Why?' demanded the Russian again, in that maddeningly stolid way they have.

'Scared?' sneered Porta. 'It wouldn't surprise me. Lots of people are. Haven't got the guts to face up to the truth, in case it turns out to be unpleasant.'

The Cossack scowled. He stepped forward and held out one broad, stubby hand.

'I am not scared. But it's not always good to know the future.'

'Try it and see.'

Porta seized the hand before it could be withdrawn, and his face took on a faraway expression of what to me looked like sheer vacant imbecility. It seemed to impress the simple corporal, but then, of course, he didn't know Porta as I did.

'Hm ... ah ... mm ... Yes! I get the picture.' Porta sucked his tooth, thoughtfully. 'You were a corporal with Uncle Joe Stalin, right? You wore a helmet with a red cross on it. Right? And you were stationed in a garrison at ... Majkof. Am I right?'

The man nodded, his jaw dropping open. Anyone could have made the same lucky guess who'd fought on the Russian front and met as many Cossacks as we had in the German Army, but Porta's initial success brought a little knot of staring soldiers, their faces puckered and a vaguely apprehensive gleam in their eyes.

'So! I'm right!' said Porta, triumphantly.

The man crossed himself and made a move to pull his hand away, but Porta held on to it.

'Wait! I'll tell you what I see for the future ... I see a long dusty road, leading to nowhere and going on for ever ... No machorkas, no water, no food ... A long column of men, all wearing the same uniform as what you are ... They all belong to General Vlassov's regiment. There's a coincidence, now! Are you strong enough to hear the truth?' He glanced down at the man and gabbled on before he could be stopped. 'I see many American generals seated at a table with many Russian generals. They're drinking whisky ... and vodka ... they're smoking big fat cigars ... Now they're signing papers and shaking hands with each other.' Porta closed his eyes as if he were in immense pain. 'I see something else! Adolf has fallen and all the Cossacks are being taken back to their homeland ... I see—I see ...' Porta gave a great cry of agony. 'Tovaritch! You know of Dalstroj,* of course? Well——' He nodded his head in sage satisfaction. 'That tovaritch, is what I see! Not so good, eh?'

The Cossack snatched away his hand and jumped back, rage and doubt mingled on his face. He hissed savagely in

* A prison camp in Siberia.

a stream of Russian that was too fast for me to catch, but in a flash Little John was out of the tank and on top of the man. He picked him up in one immense paw and shook him vigorously to and fro.

'Filthy Russian peasant, you'd better change your tone pretty quick or I'll thrash you half-way to Dalstroj myself, and I'll use your own nagajka to do it, as well!'

Another stream of Russian. Obviously abuse, almost certainly obscene. There's no language quite like Russian when it comes to swearing. It would be worth taking it up for that alone.

Little John just jeered and threw the man contemptuously away from him. The Cossack bolted for his horse, leaped into the saddle and shot off after his companions, who had prudently disappeared at the first mention of the word Dalstroj. He turned to raise his sabre in a menacing gesture and to hurl a few more obscenities at us, but it had small effect on Little John.

'Get knotted, filthy peasants!' he roared.

The regiment of Cossacks, driving the would-be deserters before them, faded slowly into the distance, and Lt. Löwe came up to our tank with disapproval written all over him.

'Obergfreiter Porta, I will not allow men under my command to make fools of our allies ... particularly when they're voluntary allies! One of their damned officers has just been and complained to me about you.'

'I beg your pardon, sir,' said Porta, very earnestly. 'The man wanted his fortune told, so I told it, that's all.'

'Oh? I didn't know you were gifted with clairvoyance? What did you tell him?'

'Only the truth,' said Porta, hurt.

'Which is?'

'I told him he'd be ending his days back home with Uncle Joe, stewing out at Dalstroj. Any fool could foretell that.'

'I wish to God you'd keep your big clanging mouth shut just once in a while!' snapped Löwe, irritably. 'You'll end up in Dalstroj yourself one of these days, if you're not very careful!'

'Ah, very likely,' agreed Porta, with a sigh.

The Lieutenant stalked away, evidently displeased. The column moved forward again, accompanied by the screeching of owls somewhere in the woods near by. The night gradually wore itself out and began mistily to merge into day. Inside the tank, we prepared a sort of breakfast, brewing ersatz coffee over a spirit stove, at grave risk of setting ourselves alight and blowing the Tiger sky-high. We carved hunks of bread off the tough rubbery block that passed for a loaf in the Army, and to make it more palatable than usual we smeared it inches thick with some beetroot jam that Porta had casually picked up at the same time as the Schnapps.

Day at last arrived, grey and unpleasant. The column came to a temporary halt. A regiment of grenadiers arrived from somewhere, all of them cursing roundly and in thoroughly bad humour, and a battery of Flak was set up. Porta made matters worse than was strictly necessary by taunting them that they couldn't even hit a formation of bombers five metres away at ground level. Fortunately, before a fight could break out, we were once more ordered on our way.

The heavy Tiger ground protestingly forward, nose to tail with her immediate neighbours. A couple of enemy planes appeared overhead, scattered a few bombs at random throughout the length of the column and flew off again, completely unharmed despite the ferocious efforts coming from the Flak batteries.

At last we reached the positions we had been making for. The signal for attack was given. The Tigers moved into formation, killers once again. Beneath every stone, behind every bush, every tree, every fold in the landscape death was lying in wait for the unwary in the shape of tanks and bazookas, cannons, magnetic mines and flame-throwers. Through the periscope we were able to make out the enemy positions. For infantrymen, a full-scale attack by heavy tanks is an atrocity pure and simple, and the enemy observers had had their eye on us for a long while. Grenades were already raining down on us, but we were plunging forward at the rate of forty kilometres an hour and nothing could stop the attack.

'Fasten down the hatches,' ordered the Old Man. 'Turret at two o'clock. Range seven hundred. Pak heavily camouflaged.'

Lines and squares danced in a blurred vision before me. The Old Man tapped me on the shoulder.

'Got it?'

'Not yet. All I can see are a few bushes and a heap of ruins.'

'That's where it is,' said the Old Man, grimly.

A sudden flash from a cannon revealed the camouflaged anti-tank guns. A grenade missed us by a matter of centimetres. I set hastily to work again and the figures leapt and jerked: 600, 650 . . . the points met, the lens cleared.

'Get a move on,' said the Old Man, nervously.

I fired. The pressure of air hit us like a clenched fist, the red-hot cartridge case fell to the floor. A sound of clicking and the cannon was ready again. But not needed for the moment: we could see from the debris rising into the air that we had achieved our target. The anti-tank gun had been put out of action and whatever might have been left of it was very soon crushed to pulp beneath our tracks.

'Turret at two o'clock! Range five hundred. Fire straight ahead.'

The motor purred, the turret swivelled, and I saw the target at once: Churchills, which were always easy to identify with their long bodies and low turrets. There were six of them, standing stationary and in line.

We drew to a halt. Only the inexperienced fire while moving, but yet an element of speed was essential if we were to take full advantage of the situation. A stationary tank is, so to speak, a sitting duck. Little John threw open one of the side panels to watch the fun and instantly had the Old Man roaring down his neck.

'Shut that flaming thing up!'

'No need to panic,' said Little John, equably. 'And just please to remember that I am an Obergefreiter and the backbone of the German Army.'

The Old Man swore and turned towards me as being more malleable.

'Pick off the last of the buggers to begin with, then try the leader. O.K.? . . . Fire!'

The long cannon leapt in my hands. A spout of flame

86

shot out and I had time to see the Churchill rocking beneath the blow before the turret swung round and I fired on the leader of the column. This time I had the satisfaction of watching the target disintegrate completely and go skywards in a whirling mass of metal.

'Change position!'

Porta backed down into a fold in the ground and I followed the remaining four Churchills in the periscope. I chose one of them, got it in my sights and fired. This time I was not so lucky, the shot glanced off the turret. They must have had a nasty few seconds inside her, but already they were opening up the hatches and jumping out. Heide instantly let rip with the machine-gun and we received an answering salvo of grenades. Fortunately they fell short, but it was enough to send Little John reeling back inside the tank with sweat pouring off his brow.

I concentrated the next of the Churchills in the periscope. The long grenade flew swift and sure to its target, yet the tank remained in place. For a moment I was puzzled, and then we saw a thin white spiral of smoke rising from the stricken vehicle. Seconds later there was an explosion. Flames burst their way out, leaping voraciously upwards in search of anything else that might be combustible.

'Change position! Over by the ruins. Turret at two o'clock. Range 300 ... Fire!'

The remaining two Churchills were easy prey. Little John insisted on jumping out of the tank there and then and painting the six rings of victory on the turret. The Old Man's wrath was dreadful to behold, but Little John had no idea of discipline and threats were a mere waste of breath. He and Porta must have held the joint record for disorderly conduct.

Behind us, the field artillery were opening up and we were beneath a protective umbrella of fire. The enemy were mopping up the whole of Beach 109 and the Canadian infantry were fighting like fanatics with anything they could lay hands on. One sergeant, for want of anything more lethal, even tried hurling rocks at us.

As usual, we lost all sense of time. We might have been in the battle for one hour or twelve hours. It always seemed to us neverending. But at last we were done with it, the Tigers came to a welcome full stop and a strange silence fell over us. The crackling and spitting of flames were all that could be heard.

We climbed stiffly to the ground, our throats and lungs raw with the constant inhaling of fumes. Porta, with his face as black as a coal-hole, almost instantly spotted a promising ruin not far off. Possibly that same morning it had been an inhabited house: now it was little more than a tumbled heap of broken bricks and charred wood. But Porta set off towards it with as much enthusiasm as if it had been the Ritz Hotel—and, as usual, his faith was justified. Porta's instincts never let him down where food and drink were concerned: he returned minutes later with his arms full of canned beer. He let the tins fall clattering and clashing at our feet, and without even pausing to recover his breath turned on his heel and set off again, shouting as he did so.

'There's a whole crate of it up there! It's Victory Beer, and you can take my word for it it's bloody good stuff ... I've already downed a couple of pints!'

Little John gave a great war-cry of triumph and ran off after Porta. They came back carrying the crate between them, but before we had time to enjoy the results of their pillage we found that some trigger-happy fool was ploughing up the earth at our feet with machine-gun bullets.

'Bastards!' yelled Little John, as we dived for cover.

Heide yanked the pin from a grenade and flung it over the ridge towards the unknown attacker. Almost immediately following the explosion a khaki figure appeared on the top of the ridge, paused for a second, then rolled down towards us in a mass of flames. He was dead by the time he reached us, and he seemed to have been alone for we were not troubled again. Unfortunately, he had done the maximum amount of damage before he died: our precious cans of beer had all been punctured by bullets and the stuff was wasting away into the ground even as we looked at it. Porta walked over and gave the crate an almighty kick.

'That's the bloody war for you!' he snarled.

CHAPTER FIVE

The Resistance workers of Caen had received an order
to assassinate the Chief of the Militia, Lucien Brière, who
not only worked in direct liaison with the German police
but also had the effrontery to be a personal friend of the
Head of the Gestapo for that area, Commissar Helmuth
Bernhard. Brière had been responsible for the execution
of a large number of Frenchmen.

It was a man called Arsène who volunteered to carry
out the assassination. With three helpers he managed to
enter Brière's house and offices in the rue des Fossés-du-
Château and lob a handful of grenades into the living
quarters of the building. Unfortunately the attempt
failed to cause any serious damage and the four men were
themselves lucky to escape without being identified. From
that point on the house was guarded day and night by
members of the Waffen S.S., making any further attempts
to assassinate Brière in his own home well-nigh impossible.

For the meantime the Resistance stayed their hand, endlessly discussing and endlessly rejecting new ways of carrying out their mission, until finally Arsène grew impatient
and announced that he would do the job alone. When
questioned as to the method he intended using, he merely
shrugged his shoulders and declared that he would trust
to luck.

In the event, he killed Brière in the simplest way possible, by walking up to him in the street and shooting him
twice through the head. Brière obviously sensed danger
the moment he saw Arsène coming towards him, but
Arsène had no intention of failing a second time and the

man was dead even as he turned to run. The street was fairly empty at the time. Those passers-by who saw the assassination take place prudently melted into the shadows. Of those who witnessed the deed from behind their bedroom curtains the vast majority were probably in favour of it. At any rate, Arsène had the time to take out his camera and calmly photograph the dead man before strolling off down a side street and disappearing from the scene.

Three days later Brière was given a martyr's funeral by his friends of the Gestapo. The whole of Caen turned out to jeer and cheer and to sing the Marseillaise. Arsène, although anonymous, was definitely the hero of the day.

IN THE STYLE OF HEMINGWAY

There was no continuous front line in Normandy. You could go out on reconnaissance trips for several hours and not catch a single glimpse of the enemy. You could still, at that late stage in the war, come across unspoiled villages where the inhabitants seemed almost unaware that only a few kilometres distant fierce fighting had wiped out a whole community and half an army.

It was night time when we drove into the village of Montaudin. We approached cautiously, because you never knew when you might be driving into a hornet's nest of enemy troops, but the main street was dark and deserted and there was no sign of anyone, either villagers or soldiers.

'Hey, look, a boozer!' hissed Porta, excitedly pointing ahead towards the one lighted building in the street. 'Let's stop off and see if they've got any grub going. I'm so bloody starving my belly's in knots.'

Porta was pretty persuasive once he got on to the subject of food, and besides, we were too tired to argue with him. We parked the Puma in the middle of the village square, like any peacetime tourists, and then, weary, dirty, and in incredibly bad tempers, we unwound our stiff arms and legs and staggered out into the night air. We had been on reconnaissance for two days and it was weary, tedious work.

'I'm knackered,' grumbled Heide. He opened his mouth in a loud, crackling yawn, then turned and kicked one of the Puma's heavy tyres. 'Bloody car drives you bloody mad.'

'Where are we?' I said. 'Are we behind the lines?'

'Which lines?' said Porta, sardonically. 'Ours or theirs?'

'Either, so long as I know.'

The Old Man scratched the back of his neck, then pensively rubbed a finger up and down his nose.

'Your guess is as good as mine, but to be on the safe side we'd best leave our caps in the car. They're the only things that give us away.'

'I shall take my naga,' announced Little John, lovingly picking up the heavy Russian revolver that he had mysteriously acquired at some stage during the war. 'People aren't so friendly these days.'

'Let's all stock up,' I suggested.

We crammed our side pockets with hand-grenades and stuffed revolvers in to our breast pockets, and then the Legionnaire, gun in hand, kicked open the door of the inn and led us through. One dim light was burning, high up in the ceiling, and the place seemed as deserted as the street outside.

'Salut, patron!' cried the Legionnaire, in his best French. 'Y a des clients!'

I became suddenly aware that Heide was clutching my arm and pointing ahead with trembling finger. I followed his gaze and swallowed a yell of horror. Through the gloom, I could make out the shape of a vast figure slouched at the bar, one arm flung out, its head resting on an overturned whisky bottle. It was, unmistakably, an American. Drunk as a lord, but still an American. Heide's fingers twitched nervously on my arm.

'Let's get out of here!' he hissed.

'Balls!' said Porta, loud enough to wake the dead.

'But it's a Yank——'

'I don't care if it's bleeding Eisenhower himself, I ain't leaving this place till I've had some grub!'

'But we're behind the enemy lines——'

91

'How do you know?' demanded Porta, fiercely. 'How do you know that great lump of fat over there isn't behind *our* lines?' He took hold of Heide and shook him till his teeth rattled: Porta could be very touchy when he thought his food was in jeopardy. 'Chances are it's him that's gone wrong, not us.'

We looked at the American. Our shouting and mumbling had disturbed him and he was now snoring lustily with his mouth drooping open.

'I'm going to eat,' said Porta, very firmly.

The Legionnaire nodded and called once again to the patron. Creaking stairs away to our right marked the passage of the landlord from his bed. A stout, middle-aged man appeared, yawning and red eyed with a greasy dressing-gown draped round his shoulders. He took one look at us and raised his eyes heavenwards in supplication.

'More Americans! God grant me patience!'

'Patron,' said the Legionnaire, smoothly, 'excusez le dérangement, mais est-ce qu'on pourrait avoir une soupe genre bouillabaisse? Si vous manquez de personnel, on est là pour le coup de main.'

(Forgive us for disturbing you, but have you any food going? Perhaps a thick soup, something on the lines of bouillabaisse? If you haven't any staff available, we don't mind giving a hand.)

The man stared at him with open mouth.

'You're French? I thought you were more of those damned Yankees.'

'I'm French,' lied the Legionnaire, blithely. 'My friends are German members of the Foreign Legion, all of us. We're *en route* for Paris.'

The landlord thrust his feet into a pair of tatty bedroom slippers and padded towards us down the creaking staircase, his face a-beam.

'Vlà des Français!' he shouted, to those on the floor above. 'Vive la France! Come on down, everybody!'

With the swift movements of a professional barman, the landlord produced a row of venerable and dust-covered bottles. Instinctively, the sleeping American opened an eye and looked round, his nose evidently hot on the trail of more drink. His moustache was soaked in whisky, and if you'd thrown a lighted match at his uniform he'd have gone up in a sheet of flame faster than any petrol tank. He caught sight of us and lifted a limp hand.

'Hiya, Mac! Got n'y Scotch on ya?'

He didn't wait to hear our reply; merely gave us a charming smile and fell back among the pools of whisky.

'Completely stoned,' said the landlord, indifferently. 'He spent the entire afternoon and half the evening drinking with a couple of his mates. They arrived here yesterday morning and I don't think they stopped drinking once.'

'Disgusting,' said the Legionnaire. 'What—er—happened to his friends?'

'Gone. Got into a jeep and went off without him. This one's been flat out ever since.'

We all solemnly regarded the American. He lay grunting and snuffling like a walrus, but the combined weight of our disapproval evidently penetrated his fuddled brain. He opened his eyes. Both were bloodshot and horrible to look upon. Very slowly, and with immense dignity, he rose to his feet and began pounding on the bar.

'Landlord! Where's that damned Scotch I ordered?'

The landlord shrugged his shoulders.

'What did I tell you? I think all Americans are alcoholics.'

'It's disgusting,' said the Legionnaire, again.

We all solemnly hypocritically agreed. The American began lurching puppetlike towards Barcelona.

'You know something, Mac? You've got a damned ugly face . . . looks like a Kraut face to me. You know that? You look like a lousy Kraut.'

He gave a deep bellow of laughter and fell to the ground, where he rolled over on to his back and commenced singing 'My Old Kentucky Home'. The landlord beckoned us past him and up to the bar.

'A case of D.T.s, I shouldn't wonder. He's a war correspondent. They're always the worst kind. Anyway'—he laughed, darkly—'he won't be doing any more corresponding yet awhile. He smashed up his typewriter after he'd gone through his first two bottles of whisky. Said it couldn't spell, I ask you! Said his typewriter couldn't spell ... And they cost money, you know, typewriters do. I tried to put it back together, but he's a big bugger, he made a thorough job of it, I'll say that for him.'

He was a big bugger. Almost as big as Little John. I shouldn't personally have cared to cross him, and I smiled ingratiatingly as he sat up and waved towards us.

'Have a drink, pal! Have a dozen drinks! Have 'em on me ... Say, Mac, you know who I am?' He swivelled round on the Old Man. 'Not giving away any secrets, mind, but I'm a pretty important guy ... just pretty damned important, that's all, and I have to get to Paris before the war comes to a lousy end ... Did anyone ever ask you, pal, whether it's difficult to die?' He cocked an inflamed eye in my direction. I shook my head, mesmerized. 'Well, I'll tell you, 'cos I've been wondering 'bout it quite a lot these last few days and I reckon I've come up with the answer.' He leaned forward, confidentially. 'The answer is simply: no. Just no. How's about that? It's more damn difficult to live than to die, that ever strike you? You bet your sweet life it didn't, I'm the only thinking guy in this whole damn outfit ... Hey, you over there! Big boy!'

He beckoned urgently at Little John and Little John stood staring, fingering his naga and doubtless wondering whether it would be a good idea to give this tiresome Yank a bat over the head and be done with it.

'Come here and I'll tell you a secret ... C'mon, I mean it! I know a man from Alabama when I see one and don't you try to tell me you're not from Alabama 'cos I won't believe one damn word of it ... come on over here and I'll take you into my confidence.' Little John moved a few paces towards him, his hand in his pocket. 'You ever eaten a Negro for dinner?' asked the American. 'I'll bet you have, you old nigger-hater, you! Now, you just listen to me and I'll tell you where to get the hard stuff from.' He dropped his voice to a loud, stern whisper. 'Behind the bar, third shelf to the left of the looking-glass.'

Little John jumped round as if stung, made a sudden

dive over the counter and swept a vast paw along the bottles on the third shelf.

'Whisky!' he shouted, as if he had discovered a gold mine. 'Enough to float a battleship!'

'Never mind the drink,' grumbled Porta. 'What about my food?'

A couple of disgruntled women had appeared at the foot of the stairs. The landlord beckoned to them and pointed towards the kitchens.

'Out there. Come and tell me what you want.'

Porta was out in the kitchen like a shot, and after a moment's hesitation I followed him, interested to watch the preparation of his famous bouillabaisse which he was always on about.

'Let's see what you've got,' he said, tersely.

The landlord beamed.

'Lobster,' he said. 'Several tins of it. I got it'—he waved a vague fat hand—'from the Americans. We've been waiting for the Yanks ever since the war began, and now that they're here, what do they do? Drink themselves senseless in every town and village from Caen to Paris. You call that war? I call it——'

What he called it we never knew, because he was interrupted by a savage howl from the bar and the sounds of shattering glass.

'Mille diables!' The landlord snatched up a rubber truncheon from the kitchen table and waved it over his head. 'All the same, you soldiers! Nothing but drink and fight!'

We surged back into the other room, leaving Porta busy with a tin opener. We found Little John and Heide locked together on the floor in a death grip. The Old Man was resignedly drinking whisky in a corner; Barcelona and the American were sitting at the ringside, cheering. The Legionnaire, as usual, was aloof. Two accurate swings of the rubber truncheon, straight between the eyes, were sufficient to part the fighting couple. They fell back insensible and the spectators loudly applauded.

'That's pretty good,' I said, admiringly. 'But I should keep out of Little John's way when he comes round.'

'Merde!' said the landlord and marched stolidly back to the kitchen with me at his heels.

Porta, dressed up on a chef's cap and a butcher's apron, looked up and waved a floury hand at us.

'What was all that about?'

The landlord unleashed a stream of French, and Porta and I exchanged puzzled glances.

'I suppose you don't speak German?' asked Porta, casually. 'My French is none too hot.'

'What?' The man glanced at him, suddenly suspicious. 'How long have you been in the Legion?'

'A couple of years, but I don't have any gift for languages. Besides, we all tend to stick to our own tongue. You don't find you learn too much of other people's lingo.'

'Well, it's true they call it the Foreign Legion,' agreed the landlord, scratching his crutch. 'All the same, it seems odd, somehow——'

'Very odd,' said Porta, briskly, 'but I can't be bothered with that sort of thing at the moment. I'm more interested in getting this bouillabaisse under way. Vegetables, please!'

Distractedly the landlord began handing them up to me. Tomatoes, carrots, onions, potatoes. I passed them over to Porta in his new role of chef. He was plainly enjoying himself.

'I shall want thyme and bay, as well. And then lemon and parsley, if you've got it.'

While the landlord and I and the two disgruntled women ran about the kitchen, fetching and carrying, cutting and scraping, Porta happily mixed things in a vast saucepan and sang in a foreign language at the top of his untuneful voice.

'Hungarian sailors' song,' he explained, in the face of our total lack of enthusiasm. 'They're mad about bouillabaisse in Hungary. That's where I got the recipe, years ago.'

'What's the bloody sailors' song got to do with it?' I said sourly.

I had scraped my thumb on a nutmeg grater and cut off half a finger with a carving knife and was beginning to resent my role of skivvy.

96

Five minutes later, the landlord found it necessary to separate the two of us with his rubber truncheon.

'Gentlemen, please! Should we not continue with the bouillabaisse?'

'You're quite right,' said Porta. 'This is a matter of the utmost importance. It needs peace and quiet and great skill ... Either stop interfering, Sven, or go back to the bar and get pickled ... landlord, give me some white wine! Two bottles at least!'

He not only wanted the wine, and the lobster and the shrimps, and the vegetables and the herbs and the lemon, he also demanded saffron and cinnamon and fish and rum. What was more surprising was that he actually got them.

Fifteen minutes later, boiling furiously and stinking to high heaven, the mixture was pronounced ready for consumption. I preceded it through the doorway and found everyone sitting up at the bar like a row of school kids waiting for dinner. Little John and Heide had regained consciousness. Even our drunken American had dragged himself on to a bar stool and was making a determined effort to remain there. His nostrils twitched greedily as Porta began serving out his bouillabaisse.

'I'm darned if this isn't the best damn thing that's happened to me since I arrived in this country.' He gave us a slow, sly smile. 'But I have to tell you boys something: I been watching you pretty closely and I reckon I've just about got your number ... Foreign Legion, for crying out loud!'

He swayed guffawing on his stool and probably never knew how close he was to death. I saw Little John's hand go to his pocket and Barcelona half rise from his seat.

'What do you mean by that remark?' asked the Legionnaire, coldly.

The American slewed round on his stool and nodded in a knowing fashion.

'I got your number, Mac ... I got your number!'

There was a strained silence. Then Porta, very casually, pulled out his heavy P.38 and fired two shots into the ceiling. The landlord screamed and thumped on the counter in a fury.

'No harm done,' said Porta, dipping into his bouillabaisse. 'Just a warning, that's all.'

'I've had my eye on you,' continued the American, with the obtuse persistence of the dead drunk.

'Give it a rest!' snarled Heide. 'You're canned!'

'Canned, stoned, pissed, what the hell, I still been watching you. I come to the conclusion you're a load of queens ... don't know how to hold your liquor, that's your trouble.'

The Legionnaire raised a frosty eyebrow. Little John rose up with a great roar of anger. The rest of us, realizing that the American was in fact too drunk to talk sense and had no suspicion at all of our true identity, returned with relief to the bouillabaisse.

'Who's calling me a queen?' shouted Little John, advancing upon the hapless American with clenched fist.

'Oh, for Christ's sake!' snapped Porta.

Picking up an empty whisky bottle, he gave Little John a businesslike blow on the head and for the second time that evening he was laid out cold. For a while we existed peaceably enough, eating our way steadily through the stinking stew, which tasted slightly better than it smelt, drinking our way through the landlord's supply of whisky. The Old Man was quietly sick through an open window, Barcelona and the American lay with their heads resting together, the Legionnaire had a glazed expression on his face. They had all obviously been drinking hard while we were preparing food in the kitchen, and I lost no time catching up with them. Porta soon lost ground, being distracted by the sudden reappearance of the less middle-aged of the two disgruntled women. He sat her on his knee and began experimentally sliding a hand beneath her skirts. His expression changed suddenly to one of surprise and gratification.

'Hey, she hasn't any pants on!' he yelled.

The American woke up and held out an empty glass.

'Here's to women that don't wear pants! Here's to America! Here's to the war! Here's to dead Krauts, and thousands of 'em! Here's to——'

He was interrupted by a roar of baffled rage from Little John, who had again recovered consciousness.

'What shit clobbered me?'

'Here's to the Frogs! Here's to the British!'

Porta went into a huddle with his captured lady. Barcelona spewed up his ring down the back of the landlord, who was himself too drunk to notice. Heide let his head fall into the stewpot and half drowned before the Legionnaire lifted him out. The American turned hopefully towards me.

'Say, Mac, are you guys going to Paris by any chance?'

'Did you ever hear of a journey through France that didn't end up in Paris?' I parried.

'I have to get there before the lousy war ends,' he told me, stertorously breathing whisky fumes over me. 'I have to make sure those damned Krauts haven't blown up the Ritz bar. I'd surely appreciate it if you guys could take me along.'

Fortunately his attention was distracted by the sight of Little John pouring a mixture of rum, whisky and cognac into the stewpot, and for a few moments it was touch and go whether any of us would survive till morning: the concoction went screaming down your throat like a tongue of flame and lay simmering in your stomach like red-hot coals. Little John snatched up a soda syphon and sprayed himself with it, and the landlord fell sobbing and screaming beneath the counter. Only the American seemed unaffected. He returned, annoyingly, to the subject of Paris.

'If any of you guys have a jeep you'd care to sell——'

'We've got a tank,' said Porta, suddenly tiring of feminine company and tossing his rejected lover into a heap on the floor. 'It's outside, parked in the square.'

'Parked in the sq*uay*er?' The American rose to his feet with surprising agility and moved across to the door. 'Jesus, I sure hope it's still there. The local gendarme's awful hot on parking offences. Two shakes of a duck's arse and he'll have you towed away.'

We followed him out to the street. The Puma was still there and the American gazed at it enraptured. It took him a long while to notice what had struck me instantly.

'Say, what's the idea of that damned Kraut cross painted on it?'

All eyes turned to the incriminating swastika.

'Someone's idea of a joke,' said Porta, bitterly. 'It may surprise you, Yank, but not everyone over here likes the idea of being liberated by the Americans.'

'Well, to hell with that, we'd better get some white paint and do something about it. I can't drive around the country looking like a damned Kraut.'

The landlord was picked up from beneath the bar and ordered to produce white paint. He did so. Porta and the American solemnly obliterated the offending swastika, then sat side by side in the gutter, smoking cigarettes and smugly surveying their handiwork.

'O.K.,' said the American. 'That's settled: you take me along to Paris with you. The minute we get there, I'm going to send off a dispatch to my newspaper. Know what headline I'm thinking?' He raised his right arm and spelt out the words several metres high in the air. '*War Correspondent and Tank Driver Liberate Paris: A Million Krauts Surrender*. How's about that? You know how to take pictures, brother?'

'Of course,' said Porta, boastfully.

'Fine. In that case we'll line up all the Kraut generals and snap them in the Ritz bar before kicking them out into the gutter head-first. C'mon, kiddoes, let's get going!'

He bounded to his feet, took two strides towards the Puma, then collapsed in a final and definitive heap in the middle of the square. His capacity for alcohol must have commanded anyone's respect, but even Americans, it seemed, had their limitations. We left him lying there and ourselves climbed stiffly back into the tank. Porta took us on a crazy zig-zag course across the square and up the village street. I wasn't too sure whether it was me or the road that was lurching up and down; whether the brightly spinning Catherine wheels before my eyes were illusions or a new type of enemy weapon. Barcelona was snoring with his head on the Legionnaire's knee; the Old Man was pressing his hands to his temples, Little John was alternately belching and bellowing unmusically. To begin with I thought Heide was also attempting to sing, although he was not a singing sort of person, and it wasn't until we were some way out of the village and he suddenly doubled up with his hands clutched to his side that I begin to have doubts.

'What's up with him?' demanded Porta, impatiently.

Heide groaned a few times, then noisily deposited the entire evening's intake of food and drink over the floor of the tank.

'It's that damned American whisky,' he muttered.

The stink was so hideous that sympathy was quite out of the question. We turned on him, cursing, and Heide doubled himself into a ball and screamed a few times.

'Ignore him,' advised Little John.

We did our best, but the man was persistent and it's difficult to ignore someone who's screaming down your left ear every few seconds.

'You don't think he's really ill?' I ventured, at length.

Everyone turned and critically regarded the huddled figure.

'Stop the car,' said the Old Man. 'Let's have a closer look at him.'

Porta brought us to a halt beneath the shelter of some trees at the roadside and it took four of us to extricate the screaming Heide and lay him out on the grass.

'Put a bullet through his head,' suggested Little John. 'Put him out of his misery. Far simpler in the long run:'

'Shut up,' said the Old Man. 'Help me get his clothes off.'

We tore his jacket open, wrenched his trousers down. The Old Man prodded cautiously here and there and Heide gave a great yell of pain and began to use abusive language.

'Appendicitis,' said the Old Man, dryly. 'He needs an immediate operation if the thing's not going to burst open ... Trouble is, the only place they'd operate is behind the American lines. How do you feel about it?'

'Risk a bullet for that shit?' asked Porta, horrified. 'Not bleeding likely! I say balls to his appendicitis!'

The Legionnaire shook his head.

'It's naïve to think the Americans would go to the trouble of operating on a German soldier. They're too busy winning the war, they can't spare the time or the men. Chances are they'd shoot the lot of us.'

'Put him out of his misery,' urged Little John.

We stared down at the twitching Heide. Porta found a marijuana cigarette in one of his pockets and stuck it between the blue lips. Little John fingered his naga, Barcelona looked uncomfortable. The Old Man was rubbing his nose, a sure sign that he was worried. Heide began muttering feverishly to himself and we caught the word 'God' once or twice.

'It's a bit late to start thinking of him,' said Porta, severely.

The Old Man came to a decision.

'We'll try to get in radio contact with one of our units. There must be one somewhere within reach of us, though God alone knows where. Just keep on trying until we get hold of someone.'

The Legionnaire hunched a shoulder, picked up the headphones and began twiddling the knobs on the radio receiver. A series of spits and crackles and then a voice spoke:

'Hallo, hallo. This is Betty Grable here.'

'I don't think so,' said the Legionnaire.

He tried again. A new voice spoke:

'This is Hella 27. This is Hella 27. In urgent need of a doctor. Hella 27, Hella 27.'

Someone else in a bad way, but that was no consolation to the pain-racked Heide.

'Keep trying,' said the Old Man, grimly.

It took us about five minutes to make contact with someone from our own side.

'Wild Cat 133. We're listening to you.'

'We need a surgeon,' said the Legionnaire, briskly. 'Got a case of appendicitis on our hands.'

'All right, keep in contact. Where are you?'

The Legionnaire swore.

'What do you take me for? Mind your own business and find that surgeon!'

At the other end, the unseen operator chuckled.

'All right, keep your hair on. Here's the medico now. Good luck, pal!'

There was a pause, then a new voice spoke.

'This is Lt.-Colonel Eicken here. How do you know it's

appendicitis?'

The Legionnaire swiftly reeled out a list of Heide's symptoms.

'Fair enough, you're probably right. I don't know where you are, but in any case I couldn't reach you so you'll have to manage it on your own. I shall give you the instructions step by step, it's up to you to follow them—and no messing about or you'll have a corpse on your hands. Is that understood?'

The Legionnaire glanced at the Old Man and nodded.

'O.K., we're ready.'

'Right. First thing to do is wash your hands in alcohol. Next, smear the patient's abdomen with iodine and make sure he's tied down securely.'

To Little John's horror, Porta at once began covering Heide with neat whisky. There was no iodine in the medicine case and whisky seemed as good as anything by way of substitution.

'When you've done that, sterilize the instruments in alcohol. You should have a litre of it.'

'We have,' said Barcelona, in surprise. 'Now if I'd known that, it wouldn't still be there!'

'Lay out the pads of cotton wool ready for staunching the blood. Hold the scalpel firmly but lightly. Make the incision on the diagonal, cut through to about ten centimetres.'

The voice went on to give cold, precise details as to where the incision should be made. The Old Man did his best to carry out the instructions. I noticed that his hand was surprisingly steady, though his forehead was awash with perspiration. It had been impossible to anaesthetize the patient and Heide's demonic screams cut shrieking through my head like a dentist's drill. We had tied him down with the straps on our gas masks but it still needed four of us to keep him still.

'There's an awful lot of blood,' reported the Legionnaire, who was following the operation from his post at the radio.

'Don't worry about the blood. Use the cotton wool pads and try to keep the working area clear. Hold back the skin on either side of the incision with the clips provided.

Now cut a bit deeper, but take great care not to go through the intestines. How is the patient's breathing?'

'Good enough for him to keep screaming,' said the Legionnaire.

'Well, stand by with the rubber mask and oxygen you've got in case it becomes necessary. Can you see the appendix yet? It's about the size of your little finger, slightly curved.'

The Old Man nodded. Heide was still yelling and Little John closed his eyes at the sight of the welling blood. The Old Man wiped the sweat off his face and shook his head.

'You'll have to shut him up somehow, I can't stand it much longer.'

Little John opened his eyes and raised one enormous, clenched fist.

'You'll have to forgive me, Julius. I'm doing it for the best, there's nothing personal about it.'

Two blows were sufficient. The nerve-racking screams ceased and we put the oxygen mask over his face.

'We've anaesthetized the patient,' reported the Legionnaire.

'How?'

'Knocked him out.'

There was a silence.

'Is he still breathing? How's his pulse?'

'Pretty fast.'

'All right. One of you keep an eye on it and report to me the minute anything goes wrong. Have you found the appendix?'

'Yes, we've got it.'

'What does it look like?'

Intrigued in spite of ourselves, we all craned over and peered into Heide's open abdomen.

'Large and inflamed,' said the Old Man.

'Large and inflamed,' relayed the Legionnaire.

'Very well. Take the long, curved instrument out of the medicine case. Hold the intestine out of the way and cut off the appendix at the lower end. Take your time and don't panic. Just make sure you don't cut the intestine. When you've removed the appendix, bathe the stump in alcohol.'

The Old Man said afterwards that for him personally Heide's appendicectomy was the worst moment of the whole war. I can well believe it. If you've never seen the inside of someone before it's pretty difficult to find your way around, and to this day we're not too sure that what the Old Man eventually cut out was indeed the appendix. But he cut something out, and he sewed up the wound just as the doctor told him, very neat and natty with six stitches, varying considerably in size but tied off with good tight knots, and we then smothered the area with sulphonamide powder and swathed the patient in bandages. And the wonder was that at the end of it all he was still alive.

'You'll have to stay put for the next couple of hours, the patient can't be moved before then. If anything at all happens, anything you're worried about, call me on the same wavelength and let me know. I shall be here all the time, but you'd better close down now before we have the enemy getting too interested in us. At the end of two hours try to make your way back to base and get the patient into hospital as soon as possible. The best of luck—and whatever you do, don't try anaesthetizing him again!'

The Legionnaire took off his headphones. The soothing voice of authority was no longer with us and we felt alone and helpless with the mummified figure of Heide. We made him as comfortable as possible, camouflaged the tank and sat tensely with weapons at the ready. Heide slowly returned to consciousness, his face white and pinched, his pulse scarcely discernible.

'Am I dying?' he muttered.

'No such luck,' said Porta, bracingly. 'If you can survive that butchery you can survive anything . . . Look what we took out of you!'

Heide looked, and promptly swooned away. Barcelona turned round with a finger to his lips.

'Enemy convoy coming up the road.'

From the scanty cover of the trees and our own camouflage we watched a procession of armoured cars filled to the brim with American infantrymen. At the same time, three Jabos swooped down from the sky, so low that we could see the bombs slung under their bellies.

'If that lot catches sight of us we'll all be dying,' grumbled Porta.

The column passed by, the Jabos flew on. For an hour we were left in peace and then there was another load of traffic to disturb us. We spotted them when they were still some way off, a couple of Shermans with their distinctive white stars at the head of a column of jeeps and armoured vehicles. As they passed us their crews hung out of the turrets, singing and shouting, sublimely unaware that they were within striking distance of our heavy Puma, which could easily, had we felt aggressively inclined, crushed them beneath her like eggshells.

'Why don't we have a bash at 'em?' demanded Little John, who nearly always was aggressively inclined. 'I bet their mouths are full of gold chobblers.'

'Not worth it,' said Porta. 'There are far too many of 'em.'

Little John watched fretfully as the end of the column disappeared into the distance. Our two hours were up and it was time to turn the Puma into an ambulance for Heide. We threw out the front seat and with immense difficulty and many groans from the semi-conscious patient managed to get him through the hatch.

'Shut up beefing!' snapped Porta. 'You're not sick any more, we yanked out the bit that'd gone rotten. You're just making a fuss over nothing, so shut up!'

We avoided the main road, it was too full of traffic, and instead went by the more tortuous side roads that the Americans tended to ignore.

Shortly before nightfall we arrived back at base and Heide was promptly transferred to a field ambulance. As for the rest of us, we were hauled up before the medico and given a long lecture on the shortcomings of our medical case. It appeared that not only had the iodine been missing but also a vital roll of sticking plaster and a couple of clamps.

'Unless, of course, we sewed them up inside Julius?' wondered Barcelona.

It was always a thought.

106

CHAPTER SIX

A certain Robineau, a Resistance worker in the Port-en-Bessin network, had had the misfortune to fall into the hands of the Feldgendarmerie, who lost no time in subjecting him to the particular brand of torture they reserved for those of his kind. They beat him, burnt him, half drowned him; broke his arms in several places and taught him how to lick up his own vomit. He confessed, in the end, that the man who gave him his orders was a Dr. Sustendal of Luc-sur-Mer.

The doctor was called in for what was euphemistically termed 'questioning'. To begin with, he hotly denied all the accusations levelled at him, which was a source of great joy to his interrogator: the longer a suspect held out, the more fun it became. They subjected him to the same treatment as Robineau, and still the doctor held out. They decided at last to confront him with the battered and almost unrecognizable form of Robineau and to judge his guilt from his reactions.

The two victims were accordingly brought face to face. The doctor at first remained impassive: this cringing object with its face swollen to the size of a full moon, its bruised and toothless mouth hanging open, its useless, dangling arms and its blood-caked body, bore no resemblance to the man he had known as Robineau. Robineau had been a proud young man on the threshold of life, broad-shouldered, straight-backed, bending the knee to no one. Unfortunately, the miserable Robineau recognized the doctor. He fell sobbing at his feet, begging for forgiveness in a voice as feeble as a child's. And it was then that the doctor broke. Personal torture he could

107

stand, but the realization that this broken wreck of humanity was none other than the defiant Robineau of a few weeks back was more than he could take. He confessed everything and was accordingly sentenced to death.

The following day, Robineau reasserted his rights as a human being and succeeded in hanging himself in his prison cell.

A LOST MACHINE-GUN

Our combat group, together with Oberleutnant Löwe, were billeted in a large house that stood near the entrance to the village. The occupants of the house were an old couple who had barely managed to grasp that there was a war going on, and almost certainly had no idea what it was about. During the whole period of the occupation so far they had had a German officer quartered on them—an officer of the old school, who still believed he was serving his emperor. Before his departure he had thrown a magnificent dinner party for all the notables of the village, civilians and military alike, at which the crowning glory had been the aristocratic von Holzendorf with his constant, contemptuous references to Hitler as 'the little Bohemian corporal'.

As far as M. and Mme Chaumont's experience went, therefore, German officers were a breed of supermen, possessing immense elegance, exquisite manners, extravagant tastes and the very best connexions. Their confusion on being confronted by Oberleutnant Löwe was a joy to behold. Could this rough-looking creature with his filthy uniform and dusty boots be a genuine Prussian officer? From the expressions on their faces, I gathered that they had strong doubts on the subject.

Löwe saluted briefly and told them their house had been requisitioned.

'I beg your pardon, sir?' said the old fellow, indignantly.

Löwe raised an eyebrow.

'I said that this house has been requisitioned for use by the Army ... I'm sorry if it disturbs you, but there is a war on, you kmow.'

Monsieur Chaumont indignantly drew himself up and stretched both arms protectively across his doorway.

'I suggest, sir, that you produce your requisition order!'

Oberleutnant Löwe stared at the man in cold amazement. Behind me someone sniggered, and behind M. Chaumont his wife opened her eyes wide in horror and disbelief at the sight of Porta, with his one fang and his villainous visage.

'This is an outrage!' she said—and she then saw Little John striding up the path with his arms full of telephone wires and equipment, and I thought for a moment that she was on the verge of a fit.

Of course, Little John wasn't exactly a reassuring sight for an elderly lady.

'What's that?' she demanded, pointing to him.

Löwe jerked his head round.

'One of my men carrying out his orders,' he said, briefly. 'I repeat, Madame, I'm sorry if it disturbs you but we all have to suffer a certain amount of inconvenience.'

Little John trundled peaceably on his way, round to the back of the house. He was followed by Heide, fit once more after his traumatic experience under the knife, busily unwinding lengths of cable. They were following instructions and preparing to set up the central telephone post in the kitchen.

'I really must object, sir,' said M. Chaumont, shaking in every limb. 'Our last officer was a very fine gentleman, he would never have behaved in such a manner. I warn you, if you persist in forcing your way in I shall carry my complaints to the very highest authority!'

'Do,' said Löwe, cordially. 'Might I suggest you get in touch personally with von Rundstedt? If he gives you no satisfaction, I'm sure General Eisenhower will be only too glad to help.'

The old chap fell back, baffled and silenced, but when it came to setting up a machine-gun on the roof he burst forth again in a fresh stream of protest.

'You call yourself an officer, sir? I am astounded! The Count would never have conducted himself in such an uncouth fashion. He was a perfect gentleman in every respect, it was a pleasure to have him here. He was a guest in our house, he——'

At this point, Little John blew a loud raspberry. Oberleutnant Löwe, by now thoroughly exasperated, turned on him in a temper, but before he could speak Gregor Martin had burst in from the road, and flung himself, mud and all, on to the sofa.

'Enemy troops,' he gasped. 'Several columns of 'em—approaching the village——'

Löwe snatched up his field-glasses and rushed to the window.

'We must warn the Regiment . . . Where's Holzer? The fool's never around when you need him!'

'I know where he is,' said Little John, soothingly. 'I'll get him for you.'

He was back within five minutes—minus Holzer but carrying several bottles of calvados.

'Too late,' he said, mournfully. 'He's gone—so I brought the booze instead.'

Löwe made an impatient noise in the back of his throat and turned irritably to the Old Man.

'Feldwebel Beier, I'm leaving you in charge here. Hold the position at all costs. You two'—he turned to Barcelona and me—'you come with me. We've got to get a message through somehow.'

We followed him out of the house, up the main street and out across the open fields. The enemy troops were already attacking the village and we had to twist and turn beneath a constant shower of grenades and tracer bullets.

General Staff had set up its headquarters in a castle, and the first sight to meet our eyes was the ordnance officer sprawled in an elegant armchair drinking champagne. He greeted us cheerily enough.

'Lieutenant Löwe, by all that's wonderful! You don't have any ice on you, by any chance? It's apparently impossible to get any in this place, the champers is almost red hot . . . Still, apart from that one not inconsiderable annoyance I find the spot reasonably tolerable. Have you seen the curtains? Exquisite, are they not? The French do have good taste, that I have always maintained.'

'To hell with that!' snapped Löwe. 'Where's the C.O.?'

Even as he spoke, Major Hinka came into the room. He was dressed in shirt and breeches and he also was nursing a bottle of champagne.

'Well, Löwe! What brings you here? Anything up?'

'And how!' Löwe pulled a crumpled map from his pocket and spread it out on a table. 'The enemy are approaching the village, sir. This is the position: we're here—the English are about there. They're attacking in force and I need more troops if I'm to hold them off.'

The ordnance officer finished off his bottle of champagne, selected another and began a lewd drinking song to go with it. Löwe threw him an irritable glance.

'Fat lot of good he'd be in an emergency!'

Major Hinka had set down his champagne bottle. He lit up a cigar and leaned thoughtfully over the map.

'All right, Lieutenant. No need to panic. Dig yourselves in just here, behind the hill, and hold the position. After all, what are a few English troops? Think yourself lucky they're not Russian bastards!'

He chuckled merrily and puffed out a thick cloud of cigar smoke. The ordnance officer swung his legs over the arm of his chair. I could see that Löwe was near to losing his temper, and I was in all sympathy with him. What, indeed, were a few English troops when you were safe and comfortable, shut up in a castle with a supply of champagne and fat cigars? Löwe drew himself up stiffly.

'I should still like at least one company of tanks brought up in support, sir. I consider it the least I could manage with.'

'My dear Lieutenant,' said Hinka, with heavy sarcasm, 'I accept that your wisdom and experience are probably very much greater than my own—I only wish it were in my power to promote you on the spot to be in charge of the entire Regiment. I could then retire to Cologne, as I have long wished to do. Doubtless we should all be far better off. Unfortunately, it is not in my power and we must both bow to a superior authority and fulfil the roles that have been assigned to us. I suggest, therefore, that you confine yourself to the task of commanding the 5th Company and carry out the orders that are given to you. Leave me to do all the rest.'

Löwe raised a hand in sullen salute.

'Just as you say, sir.'

'All right, Löwe, all right, let's not be touchy about it! I daresay we're both a bit on edge. Trouble is, the tide's turning against us and there's not a damned thing we can do.'

'We still have the best army in the world!' said Löwe, swiftly.

'That I do not dispute. But what do they have to fight with? Bare fists and bows and arrows!' Major Hinka shook his head. 'It's a hell of a position to be in. The only damn thing that's still going great guns is the High Command of the Wehrmacht.'

There was a silence. Even the ordnance officer seemed to have lost some of his joie de vivre. The Major sighed.

'Hold the position as long as you can, Lieutenant. At 21.15 we'll pull out of here and reform fifteen kilometres to the west.' He turned to the map and stabbed a finger on it. 'At this point here. I don't really see that we've any choice in the matter ... At 22.30 you pull out in your turn. Leave a section behind to cover you, the best one you have.'

'That's Feldwebel Beier's section, sir.'

'I'll leave it to you. Make sure the bridge is out of action before you leave. If it falls into enemy hands intact there'll be hell to pay for someone.'

'Yes, sir.'

Löwe sounded depressed, and we guessed what he was thinking: the rest of the Company were to make their retreat at the expense of the Old Man's section. Major Hinka must also have read his thoughts. He rested a hand on Löwe's shoulder.

'No misplaced camaraderie, Lieutenant. You're not saving your own skin, remember, you're saving a regiment, a division, maybe even the whole sector. I know it's hard, but I don't need to tell you that we're at war, I think we've all realized that by now ... You can't afford to worry about one single section, any more than I can afford to worry about one single company. It's the overall picture that matters.'

The ordnance officer suddenly burst into loud guffaws.

'You should be proud, Lieutenant! The whole of the Fatherland will fall about your neck in gratitude, even as the Führer has promised.'

This time, Löwe was unable to contain himself. He walked across to the man and knocked the champagne bottle from his hand.

'One of these days I'm going to let Little John loose on you!' he said, threateningly.

'Just as you like, old boy, just as you like.'

Major Hinka intervened, checking his watch against Löwe's.

'Right . . . Well, good luck, Lieutenant. Remember that the future of the entire division is in your hands.'

As we left the Castle and passed beneath the windows of the room, I heard the ordnance officer's high-pitched voice raised in a bleat of protest and I naturally paused to listen, waving to Barcelona to shut up.

'It's a good company, the fifth. I wonder if they realize they're being thrown to the dogs?'

'You know,' remarked the Major, dryly, 'you are beginning to irritate me just a little. The constant cynicism——'

'I suppose it's a form of self-defence, sir. My family has already sacrificed fifteen of its sons and daughters for the Fatherland. I shall be the last to go. After me——' He paused. 'Simply and plainly, there aren't any more left after me. And I'm beginning to wonder what I should put on the family vault, an eagle or an iron cross . . . I've never been a particularly religious man, and I can't say I go too much on this "Gott mit uns" kick. It doesn't seem to me as if Gott——'

'Captain,' said Major Hinka,' I regret the necessity for interrupting you, but I have more important matters on my hands than arranging the details of your family burial place! Please excuse me.'

I shrugged my shoulders and ran off after the other two.

It was no news to me that we were being thrown to the dogs. We had all realized it right from the start, and, besides, we had been thrown to them often enough before and managed to survive.

A fine, cold Normandy rain had begun to fall long before we had dug ourselves in for the night behind the shelter of a hill. By the time darkness fell we were all soaked to the skin and thoroughly disgruntled. We could hear the unmistakable sounds of digging coming from the other side of the hill.

'Let the bastards come!' roared Little John. 'I'm ready for 'em!' He fingered the M.G. with one hand and with the other gave me a jab in the ribs. 'Best get prepared, chum. They could come any time.'

I edged him irritably away from the M.G. It was my gun, I was in charge of it. Little John was merely responsible for the loading. I was the best machine-gunner in the company and there was nothing Little John could tell me that I didn't already know. I checked the loading mechanism and the firing mechanism, though I knew that both were in perfect working order because I'd already checked them three times within the space of half an hour. But machine-guns are pretty sensitive creatures, they need a lot of coddling if you're to get the best out of them.

The enemy came at us in full force at dawn. Porta had just brewed up some coffee—real coffee. I couldn't imagine where he had obtained it and I couldn't help recalling the girl Jacqueline and wondering if a little sleight of hand had been practised while he was there. At all events, real coffee it was and the scent was carried away on the breeze and must surely have set men's mouths watering many kilometres off. Little John always swore it was the lure of the coffee that brought the Scotsmen over the ridge towards us so promptly.

We watched them advancing, marvelling at their text-book precision. They ran for ten metres, dropped to the ground; jumped up with unnerving enthusiasm, ran another ten metres, fell to the ground again. They might almost have been on exercises. It was beautiful to behold, but completely idiotic in the present situation. Little John began loudly cheering them on, and Gregor nodded sagely as he positioned himself behind the heavy gun.

'Recruits,' he said. 'They shouldn't give us too much trouble.'

'Never underestimate the enemy,' said Heide, who was given to that sort of remark. 'They wouldn't be such fools as to send a regiment of greenhorns at us. They'll have something nasty up their sleeves, don't you worry.'

With my right thumb I flipped back the safety catch and took a firm hold on the grip, at the same time setting my feet against a large rock. It was essential when you were using a 42: the recoil was so powerful that you could never keep your balance unless you were firmly wedged.

The Scots were about 200 metres off and were approaching the area that we had mined during the night. We waited, tensely. The air was soon alive with the shouts and groans of wounded men and the first wave fell back, disconcerted. It's unnerving, to say the least, when you find yourself on the edge of a minefield with half your companions lying broken and limbless all about you. The bloody fool officers could be heard yelling at the men to come on. Little John nudged me and jerked his head in the direction of one of them. He was racing towards our trenches, his kilt swirling about him. It was picturesque but foolish. The man was obviously one of those blind, unthinking heroes who throws away his own life because he's over-excited and out of control and provokes hundreds of other poor sheep into following him. I waited until he was about 150 metres off. My finger curved round the trigger. I made a move to fire—and abruptly found myself the victim of a sensation that I had known once or twice before. I seemed suddenly paralysed. I found myself trembling, sweating; I felt sick with fear, my finger refused to move. I knew that when I did fire, it would be short. Little John gave me a furious shove in the small of the back.

'Fire, you bastard!'

I fired. The shot fell short, just as I had known it would. It was only the first shot that affected me like that.

It had happened before, I never could understand why. The moment was over now and I was in full control once more. Lieutenant Löwe came storming up to me.

'What the hell are you playing at? Get a grip on yourself or you can expect a court-martial!'

They had crossed the minefield, the first of them were only a hundred metres away. Any moment now and the hand grenades would start coming over. My right eye, which had been more seriously affected than the left by the phosphorus grenade, began to play up, burning and aching and generally giving me hell. I pressed myself hard up against the machine-gun, concentrating on the hundreds of legs that were racing towards us. My muscles tensed. The gun began spitting out its hail of bullets almost of its own accord. Men fell like flies before it. The moment of weakness had passed, I was back in my stride, feeling myself to be an integral part of the machine-gun. Löwe passed behind me, giving me an approving pat on the shoulder.

Little John fed in belt after belt. The gun became brutally hot, my lungs were filled with acrid smoke. All fear had long since disappeared, I was carrying out a well-known, routine action and was scarcely aware of the general course of the battle. A light drizzle began to fall, but now it was welcome because refreshing.

The first assault was repulsed. I wondered if the idiots were not aware that to wipe out a nest of machine-guns you need artillery and not merely men with rifles and hand-grenades. They were more stubborn, more persistent than the Russians, these crazy Scotsmen, but we had an hour's respite before they came at us again.

'Why don't they send the bombers over?' demanded Little John.

'Search me,' I said. 'Perhaps they're out for the Victoria Cross? Want all the glory for themselves?'

'Who wants glory?' sneered Little John.

At H hour we began silently to withdraw, according to Major Hinka's instructions. It was fortunately during a lull, while the enemy were lying low and licking their wounds, and we took care that they should have no hint of our movements. The last thing we wanted was a horde of maddened Scotsmen pouring after us and catching us at a moment when we were particularly vulnerable and almost defenceless. An impatient group of engineers were waiting for us at the bridge.

'You the last?' demanded an Oberfeldwebel.

'As usual,' confirmed Little John.

The man nodded and turned back to his waiting engineers. The moment the bridge had blown they could make their escape and the hell with everyone else. They cared neither for what had gone before nor what would come after. We hid ourselves among the trees at the road-side and the Oberfeldwebel took one last look about him.

'O.K., take her away!'

His men flung themselves towards a parked car further up the road. The Oberfeldwebel pressed the plunger of the detonator. There was an ear-splitting explosion and the bridge plunged down into the water below. The Oberfeldwebel was gone like a shot and we saw the car haring off along the road.

'Wait for it,' said the Legionnaire. 'That'll bring them running ... I give 'em two minutes to get here.'

He was accurate almost to a second. Before we had even finished setting up the M.G. the first of the enemy troops had appeared on the opposite bank of the river. The more impulsive of them threw themselves into the water and began to swim across. Little John waited patiently until they reached the bank and then lobbed a succession of hand-grenades into their midst.

'O.K., that's enough!' shouted the Old Man. 'Let's get out of here.'

We struggled back to the road, dragging the heavy equipment with us. We were just in time to see the last of our trucks disappearing in a shower of dust, swaying and bumping over the uneven surface.

'Bastards!' roared Porta, hurling a stone after them.

Already the Jabos were coming over, swooping low across the backs of the departing column of trucks and lorries. As it happened, we probably owed our lives to the fact that they had gone without us. The road was jammed

117

with burning vehicles and wounded men, and as the Jabos hurled in for a second attack we heard Lt. Löwe yelling at everyone to get the hell out as fast as they could, which of necessity meant abandoning the wounded.

'The Tommies'll take care of them!' Löwe waved vigorously towards us, beckoning and pointing ahead. 'It's more important we get to the rendezvous, I can't afford to lose the whole damn Company!'

We took up a new position in a bombed-out village a few kilometres away. Whoever had destroyed the place, whether British, American or German, or more likely all of them together, had certainly made a very thorough job. The streets were a sodden mass of rain-filled holes and craters. Not one building remained intact. There were only ruins. Heaps of rubble and charred wood; piles of stinking garbage, wrecked motor vehicles, gaping holes where once there had stood a row of houses. There was nothing left to damage any more. Everything destructible had been destroyed; everything that could burn, had burned. And over the whole empty ruin of a place hung the sweet stench of death and the swarms of hovering flies, bloated on their diet of rotting human flesh, that inevitably accompanied it.

Our section installed itself within a heap of rubble that had once been part of the village school. On two sides of us were the remains of brick walls; before and behind us were great hillocks of debris, roof beams, iron girders, shattered glass, bricks and mortar and plaster. And people. For the most part, thank God, they were buried out of sight beneath the rubble. We could only guess at their presence. But the half-rotted corpse of a small child could plainly be seen, and it was Porta alone who had the necessary sang-froid to remove it. He slung it out into the street, and I involuntarily turned away and retched as I saw one leg detach itself from the rest of the body. Almost at once a rangy yellow dog slunk out of the shadows, snatched up the spare limb and loped away with it. The Old Man was more upset than any of us. He retired into his shell and spoke to no one for the next forty minutes. You could get used to almost anything in the Army, in wartime, but most of us still had at least one vulnerable spot that refused to grow insensitive. With the Old Man, it was children. God knows we had seen enough of them killed or maimed over the past few years, and the rest of us had come to accept it with a certain detachment, but with the Old Man it was different. We knew how he felt on the subject and we respected his feelings and left him alone until he'd come round again.

Surprise, surprise, we had a delivery of letters round about mid-day. Most were several weeks old, but the novelty of receiving any mail at all was sufficient to cause a flutter of excitement in the ranks. Barcelona was handed a large brown envelope containing the papers for his divorce. The solicitor wrote to say that his wife had been granted custody of the children.

'Infidelity,' read Heide out aloud, peering over Barcelona's shoulder. 'Alcoholism ... Whoever would have thought it of you?'

Porta spat disgustedly.

'Everyone's an alcoholic in this flaming war, just as everyone's flaming unfaithful. It shouldn't be allowed as a cause for divorce in wartime. By that reckoning the whole flaming Army could be had up for it.'

'Custody of the children of the marriage is granted to the wife,' continued Heide, 'the husband being judged unfit to give them a proper upbringing.'

'Jesus Christ, it's a bit bloody much!' snarled Porta, as if Heide himself were responsible for the order. He turned indignantly to Barcelona, who was staring ahead with a moody, vacant expression on his face. 'I ask you! You fight all the way from the bloody Ebro to bloody Stalingrad, and what do you get for it? A kick in the bloody teeth, that's what!'

'And a bullet in the head,' added Little John, helpfully.

'And a bullet in the head,' agreed Porta, remembering the occasion when Barcelona had come very near to dying on us. 'Even got the scar to prove it, and much bleeding good it does you! Not fit to bring up his own bloody brats! And who says so? I'll tell you who says so! Some po-faced old git who couldn't tell a hand-grenade from a new-laid egg!'

We all turned solemnly to look at Barcelona and see how he was bearing up. He shrugged his shoulders, evidently resigned and probably past caring.

'What can you do?' he said. 'You can't really blame her, can you? Trouble is, you get home on fifteen days' leave and it just goes straight to your bloody head. Before you know where you are you're drinking beer with every Tom, Dick and Harry in the neighbourhood. You leave the old girl behind with the kids—'I'm just going up the local to see the lads, I won't be more than an hour'—and you mean it, you really mean it! Only six hours later you're still there, pissed to the eyeballs and telling 'em all how you've helped win the war. That's the trouble,' said Barcelona, plaintively, 'they flaming *encourage* you. They buy drinks for you, they treat you like a ruddy hero, you don't know whether you're on your arse or your elbow ... And then there's the birds,' he said, with a sombre expression on his face. 'All them birds just hanging about waiting to be had. See a soldier in uniform and they go berserk ... It was never that easy before the war. You just couldn't get it for love or money before the war. They just didn't want to know ... But you go home on leave and walk down the street in uniform and they're yours for the asking. So of course,' he said, simply, 'you take 'em. Who wouldn't?'

None of us, at any rate. We nodded, in complete sympathy and understanding.

'And these birds,' continued Barcelona, 'they're young and single, they don't give a damn, you have a bleeding good time and you forget all about the old cow waiting up at home with curlers in her hair, moaning at you to shut up or you'll wake the kids, nagging at you because you're pissed, won't let you have it because she says you stink, going on at you because she thinks you've been having it off with some other bird...' He sighed, deeply. 'You can't really blame her, can you? Even if she is an old cow ... But believe me, by the time she's finished with you you're only too glad to get back to fighting the flaming war again!'

We sat silently brooding for a while.

'What it is,' said Little John, sagely, 'they don't understand us back there at home. We've been away too long, I reckon.'

The Legionnaire opened his mouth to add his opinion, but what it was we never knew: a sudden loud explosion somewhere in the stricken village sent us all flying for cover. Other explosions followed in quick succession. The two remaining walls of our shelter collapsed in a heap of dust and rubble. In front of us the earth was torn up and heaved itself into the air in a solid geyser of mud. The enemy had obviously located us. It was a full-scale barrage and it continued non-stop for two hours. The moment it showed signs of letting up we crawled out of our hiding-places and began feverishly to assemble hand-grenades and machine-guns. The barrage had been but a preliminary: we could now expect the attack.

Sure enough, it came. Eight Churchills advanced upon the ruins, followed by swarms of infantrymen. I saw Gregor and Barcelona dash across the street with their bazookas. Barcelona knelt calmly behind a pile of bricks and took aim: the nearest Churchill lurched in its tracks, came to a halt and blew up. Gregor hit the turret of the one behind. The tank remained intact, but I doubt if any of the crew survived. Further up the street a Churchill had come to a full stop. Heide coldly and precisely made his way up to it, slapped a limpet mine on the turret and hurled himself to safety in a shell hole seconds before it exploded. We covered his return with the machine-guns.

The remaining Churchills seemed undecided. They made a half turn and began returning the way they had come, and Little John rushed after them with a bellow of rage, hurling grenades as he did so. One of the Churchills blew up even as we watched it. That made it the twenty-ninth tank that Little John had personally demolished with either hand-grenades or Molotov cocktails—an astonishing record. It was, generally speaking, a foolhardy thing to attempt, and most people counted themselves lucky to destroy one, or at the most three tanks and get away with it. Little John had the devil's own luck, although he personally attributed it to the charm that he wore round his neck. It was the skin of a cat that he had caught in Warsaw and turned into a quite palatable stew, and his faith in it was such that if ever he had lost it I believe he would have lain down and died simply to prove his point.

There was a second's breathing space and then a new wave of infantry arrived. The English were obviously determined to take possession of the village, heap of rubble though it was. Almost immediately three of our machine-guns were put out of action, but Little John had a nest of grenades at his side and the M.G. was safely camouflaged and still in perfect working order.

'Hold your fire,' murmured the Legionnaire. 'Let 'em come a bit closer.'

Softly, under his breath, he began chanting the celebrated song of the Legion: 'Come, sweet death...' And the enemy came, closer, closer, until we were able to recognize them as one of the famous regiments of General Montgomery, the 9th Grenadier Guards.

'Hold it, hold it,' breathed the Legionnaire, laying a restraining hand on my arm. 'All in good time ... Wait till they're on top of us.'

We waited. We could hear them laughing and calling out to each other as they picked their way through the debris. They seemed very sure of themselves.

'Plenty of dead Krauts about!' I heard one of them shouting. 'I reckon all those that could still walk must have pissed off by now!'

'That's all you know,' I muttered, and my finger twitched impatiently on the trigger of the M.G.

I pressed my shoulder hard against the gun. The Legionnaire's steely fingers were still closed about my wrist. At our side, Little John had prepared a heap of grenades, tying them together two by two. The first of the enemy troops were no more than thirty metres away.

'Fire!' hissed the Legionnaire.

All hell was promptly let loose about their unsuspecting ears. Those that survived the first salvo at once scattered themselves in shell holes and behind protective heaps of bricks and began furiously to return our fire. The M.G. rattled out continuous streamers of bullets, and I reflected that if she should suddenly choose to give up the ghost then we should probably be done for.

Out in the street the bodies were piling up, one on top of another. Most of them were young boys, green recruits with no experience of full-scale fighting. The only ones to survive in this sort of warfare were the old hands like ourselves; those who had learnt to use all their senses automatically and simultaneously, who could sense danger seconds before it manifested itself, who could read the enemy's mind and anticipate his next move. It was a game of cunning and brutality, and it was not for novices. We mowed them down even as we pitied them.

The constant kick of the heavy M.G. had bruised my shoulder so badly that I was in real pain from it. I tried wedging my cap underneath my shirt but it did little to cushion the blows. My eyes were burning and watering, my throat was parched and cut like a knife edge each time I swallowed. Worse than all that, the ammunition was running dangerously low.

A moment's respite, which prolonged itself minute by incredible minute until at length it had stretched itself into a whole hour. And then they came back again, in force this time. It began with the aeroplanes screaming overhead and dropping napalm bombs. Hot on their heels came the artillery, closely followed by more tanks. Little John snatched up a T mine and dashed out with it towards an oncoming Churchill. He was not so lucky on this occasion. The mine exploded with no harm to the tank and Little John himself was blown off his feet by the blast. Furiously he picked himself up and glared round. The Churchill was still there, intact, grinding its way down the street over the piles of bodies. With a manic yell Little John bounded after it, hauled himself up to the turret and discharged a whole round from his machine-gun down the open hatch. Not content with that, he then lobbed a couple of hand-grenades down there before leaping off into the road and rolling into the nearest bomb crater. The heavy Churchill turned ponderously on its axis, reared into the air, slewed round in a semicircle, crushing several infantrymen beneath its chains as it did so, reversed into a couple of sturdy oak trees and finally ended up on its nose with burning petrol spouting out of it.

Lieutenant Löwe, his face awash with blood, yelled the order to retreat. In small groups, one by one, the Company pulled out. Our turn came, and in my excitement and confusion I began firing rapidly from the hip, totally forgetting that you just couldn't do that with a 42. Barcelona and Porta narrowly missed death and I myself was knocked to the ground by the fierce recoil. The machine-gun lay only a short way off, firing manically of its own accord, and I found myself in the ludicrous position of having to take cover from my own weapon. Unhappily one of the bullets gouged a hole through Little John's calf. It would have to happen to him, of all people. Little John was not the man to take a personal affront of that nature lying down. He turned in a fury, aimed an almighty kick at the machine-gun, hurt his toe, gave a loud howl and suddenly went completely berserk.

'You stupid murdering sod, I'll get you for this!'

It was me, and not the machine-gun, he was addressing. As a sign of good faith he hurled his last hand-grenade in my direction and followed it up with a volley of shots from his naga. Believe me, when that unthinking monument of bone and muscle lost his temper you didn't stop to argue. I turned and ran but slipped on a patch of oil and went sprawling. Little John was on me in an instant, I could feel his breath hot on my face and his huge hands closing round my neck. I was no match for him in size or strength, but sheer terror heaved my body from under him. I wrenched my ankle in a shell hole, tripped over a heap of bricks, stumbled up a slope on hands and knees and came face to face with a Churchill that had pulled to a halt by the side of two wounded soldiers. Hot on my heels came the maddened bulk of Little John. Dazed with fear, I pulled out my revolver and fired two crazy shots that flew harmlessly into the void. I took a step forward and promptly fell head-first into a ditch of muddy water. Somewhere close at hand I heard the voice of Lt. Löwe furiously shouting orders, but much I cared for Lt. Löwe at that moment. A field-marshal himself could not have stopped me. I staggered dripping from the ditch, hared across an open field and crouched panting behind the cover of some bushes.

Enemy troops began appearing from nowhere, running like the clappers alongside the bushes where I lay hidden. Compared with Little John they were harmless as babies. I wondered where the devil he was, whether he was spying on me from behind a tree, and I began fervently praying that a grenade would blow his head off for him.

Suddenly I caught sight of him away to my right, blundering through some bushes with a flame-thrower in his hands. With a yelp of panic I hurled myself into the nearest ditch and scuttled along it, scrambled out again about half a kilometre further on, vaulted over a gate into a side road and ran head-first into Lt. Löwe and the rest of the section. They were not, on the whole, very pleasantly disposed towards me.

'I'll have you up before a bloody court-martial, so help me God!' yelled the Lieutenant.

The others stood by, sullen and hostile, while he tore strips off me. I tried to explain about Little John and his blood lust, but it impressed no one.

'Serves you right if he catches up with you!' snarled Löwe, unfeelingly.

Heide looked me up and down and curled his lip in a contemptuous sneer.

'Where's the M.G.?' he demanded.

'Yes, where's the M.G.?' agreed Löwe, seizing upon a new grievance.

'I—ah—lost it,' I said.

'Lost it?' repeated Löwe, incredulously. 'What d'you mean, you lost it? Nobody loses machine-guns in this outfit! Bloody well go back and get it and don't let me see you again until you have!'

'But I——'

'Don't make futile excuses, man! You'll get that M.G.

125

back even if it means asking Montgomery for it personally!'

'Stupid sod,' hissed Heide. 'You nearly killed off the whole bloody company!'

Porta hawked a disgusted gout of spittle in my direction. As if this were a signal for the enemy to start up again, grenades began raining down upon us and the rest of the section dived for cover. It hardly seemed tactful to join them. I jumped back over the gate and sought shelter once more in my ditch. When I dared again to raise my head they had all disappeared, leaving me to my fate. I heard the sound of heavy boots and English voices and at once doubled up and held my breath. They passed so close I could smell the new leather smell of their belts, and it was another ten minutes before I could bring myself to venture out into the open.

Soon I was back at the spot where the Churchill had pulled up beside the two wounded men. The Churchill had gone, and in the interval one of the men had died. The other stared at me out of dull eyes. He looked too weak to do me any harm, but I cautiously circled round him, fingering my knife and prepared to finish him off at the least sign of trouble.

'Water!' he muttered, urgently.

I regarded him with continuing suspicion, but he was too badly wounded to be dangerous. Half his belly had been torn away, presumably the work of a shell or a grenade, and blood was trickling from the side of his mouth and down his chin. I stretched out a hand to him, forgetting that I was clutching the knife, and he drew back piteously, evidently under the impression I was about to slit his throat for him. I stuck the knife back in my belt, wiped the blood from his mouth and held out my packet of field dressings as a sign that I meant him no harm. Carefully I pulled open his uniform, some of which was embedded in the open wound. There was nothing I could sensibly do for him. I patched him up as best I could, more as a gesture than anything else, and when the bandages ran out I tore the tail off my shirt and wound that round his belly. He was still feebly moaning for water. He shouldn't have had any, wounded in the guts as he was, but it was obvious that he was dying and I supported his head in one hand and with the other held my water-bottle to his lips. I had no cigarette to offer him, only a handful of chocolate. I crammed one or two pieces into his mouth and he munched them with apparent pleasure and attempted a smile. If I could have been sure he would die within the next few minutes I would have stayed with him, but he could well linger on for another half hour and that lost M.G. was preying on my mind. I didn't need to be told that a machine-gun was of far greater importance than a shoulder. I could have lost my life with honour, but not a machine-gun.

I put a gas mask over the man's face, stuck a rifle into the ground near by him, with a helmet slung on top of it to help the stretcher-bearers spot him when they came to clear up after the slaughter was done. What else could I do? Not very much. Only leave him the rest of the chocolate and put into his hand a photograph of his wife and child that I had found in his pocket. That way, at least, he would not be alone when he died.

Three enemy fighter-bombers screamed past, skimming the ground. I waited until they had gone, then cautiously retraced my steps through the ruined village. Miraculously, the M.G. lay where I had dropped it. In my relief I forgot to take the elementary precaution of spying out the land. I ran straight up to it and was almost immediately engulfed beneath the bodies of two English soldiers. I didn't stop to ask myself where they had come from, and in any case there were enough shell holes to hide a whole army. I reacted instinctively, as we had learned during training and as I had put into practice many times since: I doubled myself up, rammed home a knee into the groin of one of my attackers, gave a quick chop in the throat at the other. Thank God they were not veterans or they would have been prepared for it. I was in too much of a hurry to finish them off, I simply picked up the M.G. and ran for it, back up the road, over the slope, into the field.

The wounded soldier had died in my absence. I could see at a glance that he was dead, but I had no time to take a closer look. A hail of bullets splattered into the earth at my feet, and turning I saw a group of English soldiers, led by a sturdy sergeant, clambering up the slope after me. I turned and ran, set up the M.G. with bullets sizzling round my head, managed to get her working just in time. I saw the sergeant go down and the rest of them fall back. By now I was pretty low on ammunition: two belts for the M.G., three hand-grenades. I snatched up the gun and dashed off across the field, bent double, until I reached my old friend the ditch. Bullets followed me all the way, ripping up the earth and my boots as well. The entire sole was torn off one of them and I finally tripped over it and fell head-first into the muddy water. Panting and trembling, I tore the pin out of a grenade and hurled it towards the oncoming English. One of them snatched it up but before he could return it it had exploded in his face. I hurled the other two after it and set off once again on my mad flight. I was by now no means certain of the direction I was taking. I was just running blindly, away from one danger and headlong into another.

Round a bend in the road I came face to face once more with the enemy. But this time only one of them. A small man with a dark skin, wearing a grey turban wound about his head. It was one of the dreaded Ghurkas, who, so rumour had it, would slice off your ears as soon as look at you. It was hard to tell who was the more terrified, him or me. We hurled ourselves upon each other, fighting like wild beasts. I gave him a swift chop across the throat, which sent him flying, but quick as greased lightning he was up again with a vicious-looking knife in his hand. He raised his arm and I hurled myself at him; we fell to the ground, turn and turn about on top of each other, biting, clawing, kicking. With the kriss in his left hand he aimed a blow at the top of my head, at the same time giving me a kick which sent me rolling away from him. Then he was coming for me, and instinctively I lowered my head and butted him in the belly like an enraged billy goat. He staggered back. I seized him by both ears and began bashing his head hard against an outcrop of rocks until he was a senseless mass of blood and pulp and my own hands were red and sticky. Even then I was too terrified to let him die in peace: I picked up his fallen kriss and plunged it into his chest, just to make sure.

Pausing only long enough to catch my breath, I picked up the M.G. and staggered off with it, my legs trembling beneath me. It was one hell of a journey, over fields, through woods, paddling across streams, hiding in ditches, late into the night, until at last I stumbled upon a section of our own engineers and thought maybe I could relax. No such luck: their C.O. treated me with the contempt that I no doubt deserved.

'Don't tell me! Just don't tell me! You've lost your unit and you don't know how to get back to them ... Well, all I can say is, no soldier worth his salt would ever get himself into such a degrading position! If I had my way you'd be court-martialled for desertion!' He looked me up and down a few times, as if I were a peculiarly nasty specimen fresh out of its bottle. 'All right, let's have it! Which regiment?'

'Twenty-seventh Panzer S.B.V., 5th Company, sir.'

They had positioned themselves in a hamlet about four kilometres away to the west. My arrival provoked a general outburst of jeers and catcalls, but by then I was past caring. I presented myself wearily to Lt. Löwe, who was in conversation with Hauptfeldwebel Hoffmann.

'Fahnenjunker Hassel, sir, reporting back with the lost M.G. 42.'

'About time, too,' said Löwe; and left it at that.

I trailed back to my own section and discovered Little John now in excellent humour.

'Bloody good job for you I didn't catch up with you! Remind me to ram your teeth down your throat for you some day when I'm in the mood.'

'What's more to the point,' said the Old Man, sourly, 'is what the hell you've been up to all this time?'

I shrugged my shoulders and made no reply. Just sank to the ground and began mechanically to clean the cursed M.G. that was the cause of all my troubles. Porta at once sat down beside me and jabbed me humorously—and painfully—in the ribs.

'Well? What was she like?' he demanded. 'Why didn't you bring her back so's we could all have a go?'

'Give it a rest,' I said. 'Do you mind?'

Seconds later, whistles were blowing and Lt. Löwe was bawling at us to get cracking, we were moving on again. Major Hinka came up to inspect us, and as Löwe saluted I noticed for the first time that he had a bandage round his forehead.

'Fifth Company ready to move, sir. We've lost one officer, three N.C.O.s sixty men. One N.C.O. and fourteen men hospitalized. Four men missing . . . Oh yes! And one machine-gun lost and now recovered.'

Hinka, apparently indifferent, returned Löwe's salute and cast an eye upon us.

'Thank you, Lieutenant.'

He moved slowly along the line surveying each man in turn. He saw nothing to excite either his wrath or his admiration until he came to me and almost threw a fit.

'Lieutenant Löwe, why is this man in this disgusting condition? Button up your jacket, tuck your shirt into your trousers! Let me see that machine-gun.'

Fortunately the M.G., at least, was clean and beyond criticism. The Major grunted and thrust it back at me.

'Take a note of this man, Lieutenant. I will not tolerate slovenliness!'

Löwe nodded resignedly and made a sign to Haupt-feldwebel Hoffman, who at once took out his notebook and officiously wrote my name in capital letters on a blank page.

The Company moved off along the road, boots pounding in unison on the tarmac. Someone started up a song, the rest quickly joining in:

> *'Weit ist der Weg zurück ins Heimatland*
> *So weit, so weit!*
> *Die Wolken ziehen dahin daher*
> *Sie ziehen wohl übers Meer*
> *Der Mensch lebt nur einmal*
> *Und dann nicht mehr . . .'*

'Sing!' urged Little John, marching on my left.

'I'm knackered,' I said, petulantly. 'Piss off and leave me be!'

I was too tired to march, too tired to sing. Too tired to do anything but lie down and die. My eyelids drooped and I felt myself swaying on my feet.

'Sing, damn you!' hissed Little John. 'Bloody open your mouth and sing or I'll ram your teeth right down your flaming throat!'

'Long is the path to home, long is the road to the sea,
And the clouds in the sky are restless and wild
And they lead me far off from my home, from the place
        where I'm longing to be.
And a man has one life
And when that is done
He's vanquished for ever—
One life; just one . . .'

Hesitantly at first, then louder as my spirit grew stronger, I began singing with the rest.

CHAPTER SEVEN

In the north, in the south, in the east and in the west, German soldiers were dying the deaths of heroes; and back home in the Fatherland, German mothers were thanking God with tears in their eyes and going into mourning with heads held high and a proud smile on their lips ... At least, that's what the 'Völkischer Beobachter' said they were doing.

History was repeating itself. It seemed that the youth of Germany was fated always to be in the throes of sacrificing its life for some cause or other, and that it never died without some patriotic jingle coming from its lips. Long live the Emperor, long live the Fatherland, or simply Heil Hitler. Men were falling thick and fast on all four quarters of the globe, and the sound of drums and trumpets sped them on their way; and no mother, no wife, nor sister or fiancée would have disgraced herself by sitting down to weep over her lost hero. The womenfolk of Germany were proud to have given such sons to their country in the hour of her need.

Such were the trappings of war. No one ever spoke of the hard realities. The womenfolk of Germany must never hear tell of the men that screamed in agony with their legs blown off, or hung in lumps of charred and stinking flesh out of the turrets of their burning tanks, or crawled blindly over the battlefield with skulls split open and their brains exposed. No one ever spoke of these things save traitors or madmen. All German soldiers died a hero's death, and no hero ever died like that, repulsive to behold and stripped of all human dignity.

The German heroes of the history books were men in

shining uniforms their chests ablaze with medals; they sang as they marched, to the blood-stirring sounds of the trumpet and the drum, and the flags waved bravely as they went off to war and a million German mothers dressed up in black with their heads held high.

Heroes never lived in the mud and the filth of the trenches; heroes never spoke of defeat or cursed those men at the top who had engineered the war; heroes never died while sobbing like babies for their mothers and trying to shove their spilt guts back into their bellies ... Yet that was war as most of us knew it, and I suppose I knew it as well as anyone.

DISCOVERY OF AN AMERICAN DEPOT

All along the road, for a kilometre or more, the crowd were throwing themselves panic-stricken into the ditches or pressing themselves in terror against the hedgerows. It was as if an unseen hand had suddenly unzipped them, straight down the middle, leaving a gaping hole where once there had been people. The irony was that they were Germans fleeing for their lives from other Germans. The oncoming column of trucks and cars were moving at a dangerously high speed, impatiently sounding their horns and making it clear that they intended to stop for no one, friend or foe.

'Someone's in a bleeding hurry to get home!' grumbled Porta, falling into the ditch at my side.

'All the brave heroes getting the hell out of it while there's still time,' I sneered.

Two large Mercedes limousines approached us, accompanied by outriders of the Feldgendarmerie on motorcycles, clearing a passage by means of brute force and sheer speed. From the windows of the Mercedes well-groomed officers with long noses and thin lips and plenty of gold braid regarded us with an air of slightly disgusted condescension. By their side sat mistresses or whores, or what you will, plump and sleek and staring proudly straight ahead. One was foolish enough to glance in our direction. Porta promptly made an obscene gesture and she turned in confusion, scarlet to the roots of her hair. We gave a great jeer of delight, as if we had scored a personal victory over the class that we hated. Seconds later we were covered in dust as a couple of heavy transports flashed past us, gleaming pennants fluttering defiantly.

'Sod the lot of them,' snarled Heide, in agony with an eye full of dust. 'Bloody backroom heroes sitting on their bleeding arses while we do all the fighting for them! They're the first to pull out when danger threatens, and shit to everyone else!'

'That's nothing new,' said Porta, sourly.

We dragged ourselves out of the ditch and trailed resentfully in the wake of the disappearing column of motors. We began to catch up on those who were ahead of us, and slowly we realized how it was that their progress was so erratic and uncertain: they were all either lame or blind, some of them very seriously wounded. It appeared that an entire ambulance crew had suddenly panicked and dashed off without them, leaving them to fend for themselves. The poor devils were now moving along the road like a pack of sheep, so certain of death that they had passed into a state of deep, unshakeable apathy. Two men with bandages over their eyes were carrying a companion who could see but not walk; a column of six blind men stumbled hand to shoulder behind their leader, who hobbled on crutches; three men with no sight and a man with one arm carried a litter on which lay a still, mummified figure, bandaged from head to foot. They had no idea how far they had walked. Several kilometres, according to one of them, and judging from the pitiful state they were in he was probably correct. Many dozens of vehicles had passed them, full not of fighting troops but officers and their ladies. One and all they had ignored the column of wounded. When he heard this Lt. Löwe went quite mad. I thought I had seen him in all his varying stages of anger, from heavy sarcasm to screaming fury, but this was evidently at the top end of his range and I think it took us all by surprise. He shot out into the middle of the road and waved his arms furiously at an oncoming convoy of vehicles. To my surprise, they actually squealed to a bad-tempered halt. A bristling colonel stuck his head out of the leading car and shook a fist in Löwe's direction.

'What the devil's going on here? Get out of the way before I put you on a charge!'

A major of the Feldgendarmerie jumped off his motor-cycle and ran up to Löwe, jerking his revolver out of its holster.

'Clear the road, you filthy scum! We're in a hurry!'

He waved an arm above his head, jabbing his finger in the air as a sign to the driver of the first vehicle to start up again. Löwe had barely the time to spring back into the ditch before the convoy shot forward. One of the wounded men was not so agile. He was struck a glancing blow on the head and must have died almost instan-taneously. Löwe pursed his lips in a thin, determined line and turned to the Old Man.

'Feldwebel Beier, get your men stationed on either side of the road with the S.M.G. a few metres further up. Sergeant Kalb, take charge of the bazookas. Feldwebel Blom, wave down the first vehicle that comes along. If it refuses to stop'—he looked round at us, meaningly—'it's up to you to make it.'

Porta gave a great shout of joy and spat on his hands. I think we all shared his sentiments.

We took up our allotted positions. The group of wounded crouched down in the safety of the ditch, Barce-lona made his stand in the middle of the road. The Legionnaire thoughtfully cleared away the corpse. We had only a few minutes to wait before a grey Horsch appeared in the distance, going like a bat out of hell as if the entire British Army were at its heels. Barcelona waved his arms. The Horsch screamed to a full stop when it was almost on top of him and a lieutenant-colonel jumped out.

'What do you think you're playing at, Feldwebel? What the devil do you mean by standing out there prac-tising semaphore in the middle of the road?'

Lieutenant Löwe scrambled out of the ditch and walked up to the colonel, his machine-gun pointed directly at the man's beribboned chest.

'I have orders to requisition the transport that I need for conveying my wounded to the nearest first-aid post or hospital. As you can see, I have no transport of my own or I should obviously have put it to use. I must therefore ask you to hand over your vehicle to me.'

The Colonel swelled up like a balloon and went on swelling, until I thought he must surely burst out of his uniform.

'Are you aware of my rank, Lieutenant?'

'Perfectly, sir. But I think you'll agree that seriously wounded men must take priority over mere rank.' Löwe ran his eyes over the Colonel's vehicle. 'If you'd be good enough to ask the three ladies to get down—they can continue their journey on foot, they look young enough and healthy enough. They'd better bring their gear with them, we shall need all the room we can get. Some of my men need to lie down flat.'

'Have you gone mad?' roared the Colonel. 'I have an important engagement to keep!'

'In deference to your rank, sir,' said Löwe, heavily polite, 'I shall not insist that you join us on the road. I assume that you are capable of driving the vehicle? If so, you can tell your chauffeur to get down and you can take his place. Just make sure that my men are taken good care of and then you're perfectly free to keep your important engagement.'

Löwe smiled slightly and jerked his head towards our two most belligerent members, Little John and Porta.

'Get everyone out of there and see how many of the wounded it'll take.'

Little John and Porta went joyously about their task, covered by the rest of us. The driver and the three women stepped down on to the road with sullen faces but no resistance, and ten of the wounded were installed in the back of the vehicle. Only the Colonel continued his futile protestations.

'I'll have you up on a charge for this, Lieutenant! You can't get away with this sort of thing, you know!'

He made a move towards his revolver, but quick as a

flash Barcelona had stepped forward and snatched it out of his hand. Löwe shook his head, regretfully.

'I'm sorry you're taking it like this, sir. I didn't know the spirit of the Army had deteriorated so badly. Of course'—he smiled at the Colonel—'one does get a bit out of touch being in the front line all the time. However, I do know there's one thing that hasn't changed, and perhaps you'd care to be reminded of it: according to the orders of the Führer himself, the commanding officer of a fighting unit is the man who says what goes in his own sector. I think you'll find that's still current policy ... I should be quite within my rights to have you shot if you attempted to threaten me.'

'We shall see about that, sir!' said the Colonel.

He placed himself in silent sulkiness behind the steering wheel. Löwe nodded.

'One last word of warning, just for the record: I shall send a signal to my commanding officer explaining the situation. I have also taken a note of your number and I shall personally check on the safe arrival of my men.'

The Horsch lurched forward up the road. The grateful shouts of the wounded men were still ringing in our ears when we heard the roar of approaching motor-cycles and saw a Mercedes hurling itself towards us with the usual accompanying outriders roaring ahead and shouting at us to give way.

'Stop that car!' shouted Löwe.

Barcelona positioned himself gallantly in the centre of the road, but this time the driver continued straight for him and he had to spring to safety at the last moment.

'Stop that car!' screamed Löwe, in a frenzy.

There was a burst of machine-gun fire from further up the road. The large Mercedes skidded, slewed round in a semicircle and came to a halt. We stared in gloating triumph at the occupant of the rear seat: a major-general in all his glory, gold braid, red silk tassels, shining silver buttons and decorations in all colours of the rainbow.

'We've bagged a good 'un this time,' hissed Porta in my ear.

Very slowly, very imposingly, the Major-General stepped from the car, aided by two obsequious Feldwebels. His leather boots glittered and creaked. From the way they hugged his shapely calves I guessed they had been made to measure. He walked arrogantly up to Lt. Löwe, and then, to our intense delight, screwed a monocle into his left eye.

'Well, Lieutenant!'

His voice was low and deceptively gentle. He paused some distance off from Löwe and he spoke with authority.

'I have to presume, in your own defence, that at the moment of committing this outrage you were unaware of the person with whom you would have to deal?'

Löwe walked smartly up to him and saluted with two fingers.

'I very much regret the inconvenience, sir. Naturally if your man had stopped the car in the first instance we should not have found it necessary to shoot.'

'I imagine you have a good reason for this piece of insolence?'

'Yes, sir, I think you'll find it a good enough reason when I've explained the situation to you. I have a number of seriously wounded men back there and not enough transport to take care of them all. They're quite unfit to walk and some of them are almost certain to die if they don't get medical aid pretty quickly.'

'That's hardly any concern of mine, Lieutenant.'

'Excuse me, sir, but that vehicle of yours is large enough to accommodate several of my men quite comfortably.'

The Major-General readjusted his monocle.

'You must be out of your right mind, Lieutenant. I shall be charitable enough to put it down to a nervous condition, but it occurs to me that you are yourself in urgent need of medical attention. Think yourself very lucky that I'm prepared to forget the incident.'

He made to turn away, but Löwe at once moved up to him.

'Sir! I repeat that some of these men are sure to die if they don't get help quickly.'

'This is wartime, Lieutenant. Many thousands of men are dying every day. I really cannot afford to have my vehicle cluttered up with blood-stained bodies. The provision of transport for the wounded does not fall within my sphere of duties. In any case, I happen to be *en route* to join my division. I have far more pressing affairs on my hands than giving free lifts to relatively unimportant soldiers.' He cleared his throat. 'Unimportant in the overall scheme, that is.'

'May I inquire which is your division, sir?'

'No, you may not! Kindly get out of my way before I'm forced to give my men orders to shoot!'

I saw Löwe turn very pale. I prayed that he would not back down at this point. I think if he had, Little John and Porta would have taken matters into their own hands, but Löwe could be very stubborn when a matter of principle was involved.

'Are you or are you not going to take my wounded along with you?' he demanded, in the sort of voice that not even one major-general would use to another major-general.

There was a pause, I saw the two Feldwebels exchange glances, and instinctively I tensed myself for a showdown. Before a shot was fired, however, a new vehicle had appeared on the scene, a light troop carrier. It pulled up near by and we saw, sitting next to the driver, a brigadier-general of the S.S. He climbed lazily from the cab and walked towards Löwe. He was very tall and very lean, with broad shoulders and a thin, arresting face. His uniform was old and faded, covered in the dust of the road, with no distinctive marks on the collar. Nevertheless we all recognized him as the commanding officer of the 12th Tank Division, 'Panzer Meyer', the youngest general in the German Army.

'What's happening here, Lieutenant?'

Rapidly, Löwe put him in the picture. His grey eyes narrowed, his firm jaw set itself aggressively.

'Refuses to take your wounded?' he said.

'Refuses to take our wounded,' confirmed Löwe, still very pale. 'In his own words, the Major-General cannot afford to have his vehicle cluttered up with blood-stained bodies.'

Panzer Meyer turned his cold, clear gaze upon the Major-General, now uncomfortably twitching.

'I am on my way to join my division,' he said, hurriedly; 'This fool of a lieutenant has not only damaged my car with machine-gun fire, he's also held me up with insolent talk for the past fifteen minutes.'

'Which division are you joining, General?'

'The 21st P.D.'

'Really?' Panzer Meyer pursed his lips and raised a thoughtful eyebrow. 'Strange you should say that. I have just this moment parted company with General Bayerling, who, as you should presumably know, is the commanding officer of the 21st Panzers. All I can say, General, is that you're heading in quite the wrong direction if it's your intention to rejoin the division.'

The Major-General clawed anxiously at his monocle.

'Are you accusing me of desertion, sir?'

'Yes, I suppose I am,' murmured Meyer, as if the idea had only just struck him. He nodded towards Löwe. 'Take care of him. You know what to do.'

Löwe in turn jerked his head at Little John, who needed no second invitation. Under the startled gaze of his two Feldwebels the Major-General was manhandled towards a telegraph pole at the side of the road and there secured with his own shining leather belt. Löwe glanced towards Panzer Meyer, but he merely gave a slight shrug of the shoulders and turned away.

The Major-General died badly. All arrogance gone, he was screaming for mercy even as the shots from Little John's naga entered his heart and brought his life to an end. His two Feldwebels had deserted him at the first propitious moment, and we let them go and concentrated instead on installing the rest of the wounded into the comfortable Mercedes. The convoy moved off, and Panzer Meyer stayed only to shake hands with Löwe and then he, too, was gone, disappearing up the road in a cloud of dust.

We followed behind on foot, feeling suddenly despondent after our initial glow of exaltation. We were not left long alone. A motor-cycle came belching up the road and pulled in beside us. It was Werner Krum, one of the dis-patch riders. He brought us the news that enemy tanks had been sighted and that our orders were to hold the road to the last man and the last round of ammunition. Lieutenant Löwe readjusted the bandage round his fore-head and muttered something beneath his breath.

'Second section, form up single file behind me,' com-manded the Old Man, shouldering his machine-gun.

We arrived at a small hamlet, consisting of no more than a few scattered houses. The first sight that met our eyes was the decomposing corpse of a young boy. His uni-form was still new and relatively unspoiled but the flesh was turning putrid on the bones.

'Let's get him buried,' suggested the Old Man. 'I can't live here with that lying about looking at me.'

It was easy work digging a grave in that rich, soft soil. In a nearby field we could see beetroots and cauliflowers growing, and the sight so entranced me that I stood star-ing long after the others have shovelled the dirt over the young corpse and disappeared. When at last I wandered back I found them in a state of mingled consternation and excitement over the activities of two S.S. men who had been seconded to us. They seemed to be brewing something in a vast stewpot, but what it was I could not make out. They had fixed the lid so it was hermetically sealed, and as I approached I caught sight of Heide crouched behind a wagon with his head peering caut-iously over the top.

'What's up with you?' I said.

'Nothing. I've just got a bit more sense than some people!' he told me, irritably.

'Why? What's cooking over there? Dynamite?'

Heide curled his lip at me.

'When that lot goes up you won't find it so damned funny!'

I went up to Barcelona, who was hovering on the perimeter.

'What's in there?' I said.

'Liquor!' he replied, briefly.

'Liquor?' I said. 'What's it in a stewpot for?'

'It's simmering. Elderberries and sugar, in a state of ferment ... We're waiting for it to explode.'

'Hey!' yelled Little John, suddenly. 'What's that thermometer rigged up for?'

The S.S. men glanced at it indifferently.

'If the temperature goes above the red mark,' explained one of them, 'the thing's liable to blow up.'

'You're bloody mad!' screamed Little John, diving for cover with the rest of us. 'It's been past the red mark for the last ten minutes!'

The man shrugged his shoulders.

'Very likely, but we haven't got much time. Don't you want a drink before the Yanks arrive?'

We did, but not at the expense of having our heads blown off our shoulders. We prudently remained under cover until the danger was over and the mixture was pronounced fit for consumption. Considering our behaviour, I thought it pretty generous of the two cooks to let us even taste it, let alone help them finish it off. By the time it had gone we were all perfectly willing to risk our necks to brew up a second lot, but we were interrupted in the task. Little John suddenly pointed across to the field of beetroots.

'Here come the liberators! The Yanks certainly have a good nose for booze!'

We sprang up in a panic but there were only two of them, unconcernedly tramping their way through the mud, quite unaware of our presence.

'We'll have to take them,' said the Old Man.

'You're joking!' protested Porta. 'Who wants to start working after that little lot?'

Nobody wanted to, but as some fool was always sure to remind us, there was a war on. Full of drink and rather uncertain on our legs, we hid ourselves in a spinney and watched the unsuspecting Americans draw near. One was a corporal, the other a private. They came up laughing and talking together and jumped into the trench that we had earlier on dug for ourselves. Nonchalantly, we strolled out of our hiding-place and confronted them.

'You're under arrest!' shouted Heide.

They jumped out of the trench as if a live grenade had gone in after them.

'What in hell are you doing here?' demanded the corporal.

'Breathing the air,' said Porta. 'Any objections?'

'I sure as hell *have*. They told us there weren't any damned Krauts in the area!'

'They'll tell you anything if it makes 'em happy.'

'Sit down and make yourselves at home,' suggested Barcelona. 'We've got some liquor on the stove.'

The two S.S. men, having completely lost interest in the proceedings, had already set up another elderberry brew. We watched the thermometer eagerly enough this time, urging it on with loud shouts every time it moved up a degree.

'Your friends,' suggested Heide, hopefully, 'must be some way off from here?'

'Friends!' shouted the corporal, in a sudden rage. 'Don't ever mention that load of shits to me!'

We never did discover where they were, nor what they had done to offend. It seemed to be bound up, in some intricate and unfathomable way, with points of origin. We gathered that the corporal and the private came from Georgia, while their erstwhile friends were New Yorkers.

'And I love a lousy Kraut better than a damned New Yorker!' cried the private.

We thanked him warmly and felt quite pleasantly disposed towards him.

'Damned New Yorkers are damned cretins!' he shouted.

By the time the elderberry mish-mash was ready once more we were all on the best of terms. Two hours later we were sitting in one another's laps and fawning on each other.

'Where—were you going—when we—jumped on you?' asked Porta, his eyes round and owlish with the effort he was putting in to the enunciation of each word.

The corporal looked at the private for support.

'Where wuz we going?'

The private shrugged.

'I dunno. I didn't know we wuz goin' any place.'

'You're right. We wasn't goin' no place.' He turned back to Porta. 'We wasn't goin' no place. We wuz lost.'

Porta belched sympathetically.

'You can't help getting lost in this damn country. Every damn road looks alike.'

'It's the goddamn hedges an' all that get me. How's in hell you supposed to tell one goddamn hedge from another goddam hedge?'

'Hey!' said the private, suddenly. 'How come you and me's not dead yet?'

The corporal scratched his cropped head.

'I dunno. They always told us the goddamn Krauts didn't take no prisoners.'

'They always told us that the bastard Yanks didn't, either,' retorted Barcelona.

'That's a lousy, goddam lie!'

'You know what we came across one day?' demanded Barcelona, challengingly. 'One of your Churchills with a German soldier tied to the turret with barbed wire. I'm buggered if I'd call that taking prisoners!'

'I'll just tell you something,' said the corporal, with feeling. 'I'm willin' to bet you any sum you care to name that that tank crew was a bunch of lousy New York perverts!'

I suddenly heard footsteps approaching: Lt. Löwe. I made a hasty signal to Porta, who unceremoniously pushed the two Americans out of the way at the foot of the trench. The Old Man staggered to his feet, swayed slightly and remained in an upright position with a very obvious effort.

'Nothing to report, sir.'

His voice rang with sincerity; his face was bland and open.

'Get your section installed in the village,' commanded Löwe. 'One man posted outside with a machine-gun should be sufficient guard for the night. I advise the rest of you to catch up on lost sleep and——' Löwe stopped short, his nostrils twitching. 'Feldwebel Beier, I smell alcohol!'

144

One of the S.S. men, doubtless intending it for the best, appeared at Löwe's elbow with a mess tin full of liquor.

'Care to try some, sir? It's elderberry wine.'

'Elderberry wine?' said Löwe, peering at the sticky black mess in the tin: 'It looks more like machine oil to me.'

'Well, it tastes all right, sir.'

Löwe glanced at the man suspiciously.

'You're drunk!' he looked round at the rest of us. 'You're all drunk! Get to your feet this instant ... Second Company, present arms!'

Needless to say, the task was beyond us. We crawled miserably to our feet, all supporting each other and frail as a house of cards. Gregor was in a drunken coma and couldn't even open his eyes.

Lieutenant Löwe was in another of his rages. I suppose, on the whole, it was justified.

'You load of drunken imbeciles! Look at you—so pissed you can't even stand! Surely to God you can be left alone for a couple of hours without making brutes of yourselves? Jesus Christ, you ought to be locked up in a home for the criminally insane, the whole drunken pack of you!'

He walked up to Gregor and flipped him lightly in the chest. Gregor instantly fell to the ground and lay there like a corpse, with his legs stretched stiff before him.

'Look at that!' roared Löwe, growing over-excited now that he had proved his point. 'What the hell would you have done if the enemy had suddenly appeared?'

'Shot 'em,' said Little John, hopefully.

'Hold your tongue, Creutzfeld! What's more to the point is, what would you have to say for yourselves if Major Hinka suddenly decided to come round on inspection?'

'Skol,' said Little John.

I don't believe he intended to be funny. He was so drunk that to him it doubtless seemed a perfectly apt remark with which to greet a superior officer on a tour of inspection. Löwe, however, interpreted it as a piece of sheer impertinence. He advanced upon Little John in a fury, and Little John, by now thoroughly confused, dropped his rifle to the ground.

'God in heaven!' screamed Löwe, who was shaking with rage. He turned furiously upon the Old Man. 'Feldwebel Beier, this is the most ill-disciplined section in the whole company and I hold you entirely responsible! Get these men sobered up immediately. I don't give a damn how you do it, I don't care if you have to run up and down through the bloody beetroots all night, but if I find a single man from this section suffering from drink in half an hour's time I'll put the whole damn lot of you on a charge!'

He stalked away with his back held rigid and his head high in the air. Little John sighed lustily.

'I don't get the feeling he loves us any more,' he said.

'Who can blame him?' retorted the Old Man, sourly.

He bent over the unconscious Gregor and began slapping his cheeks and flipping his head from side to side. Porta, who had quietly made himself scarce during the Lieutenant's tirade, now appeared from the shadows of a nearby house triumphantly waving a banjo and an accordion.

'I've found an orchestra!' he shouted.

'Well bloody put it away again!' snapped the Old Man. 'You start playing that lot, they'll hear us fifty kilometres off. And I'm warning you, any more trouble from this section and we'll all be facing three days in the cooler when we get back.'

'If we get back,' said Porta, unmoved.

The Americans had crawled cautiously out of the trench and were staring wonderingly after the departing figure of Lt. Löwe.

'Gee, they sure are tough with you boys,' said the corporal, feelingly.

He took the banjo from Porta and strummed a few chords on it. Barcelona at once snatched up the accordion, Porta pulled out his flute and Little John his mouth organ.

'Jesus,' said the Old Man. 'Don't you people ever learn?'

146

'Too old to pick up new habits now,' said Porta. 'Let's try "Three Lilies" ... Ready? One, two, three——'

> '*Drei Lilien, drei Lilien* [we sang, loudly],
> *Die pflanzt' ich auf mein grab* ...
> *Three lilies, three white lilies,*
> *I shall plant them on my grave* ...'

Far away in the distance a battery of artillery burst into action, as if in response to our song. We followed the blazing trails of the rockets, doubtless heading for Caen. Seconds later we heard the explosions. And seconds after that the whole sky was lit up and the air was full of shrapnel. Porta, his flute at his lips, danced gleefully round the trench like some wild creature celebrating midsummer rites. The rest of us more prudently took cover. The American private flung himself flat, Barcelona dived head-first into a pile of farmyard manure, Winther, one of the S.S. men, attempted to seek shelter in a chicken run and became wedged fast in the doorway, half in and half out. He was set free by Little John, who tugged at one of his legs and brought the whole flimsy construction down about his ears. Chickens flew hysterically in all directions.

'What the hell's going on here now?'

It was Lt. Löwe again. I crouched trembling beneath a pile of empty grain sacks and prayed that I was invisible. Porta was still dancing and playing his flute, and now the American corporal and Little John had joined him, with the banjo and mouth organ, all three crazily cavorting round the trench.

'What's that Yank doing here?' demanded the Lieutenant.

He fought his way forward through a demented flock of chickens, but before he had gone very far the situation had abruptly and incredibly altered. Loud bursts of machine-gun fire ripped the night apart. I felt a stream of bullets tearing the grain sacks off me, and in a panic I dashed forward towards the ruins of the chicken run. As I did so, the American corporal gave a loud shriek, spun in a circle and collapsed at the bottom of the trench. I saw running figures silhouetted against the skyline, and realized with horror that the English were almost on top of us. I could see their bayonets gleaming and their arms already raised to start showering us with grenades. It was no use seeking for shelter, it was every man for himself in hand-to-hand fighting.

We defended ourselves with whatever weapons were most readily available, knives, pitchforks, shovels, naked fists. It was difficult, in the turmoil, to keep any sense of purpose other than just staying alive, but at last I managed to fight my way over to the spot where we had the M.G. camouflaged, Little John joined me, and together we set it up. A few paces ahead of us we saw Winther stoop to pick up a grenade that was rolling innocently towards us. Before he could hurl it back at the enemy it had exploded in his face. The next second it was Winther's severed head, and not the hand-grenade, that was rolling towards us. Barcelona stopped a bullet in his right lung, and Gregor, panting and gasping and bleeding like a pig from a head wound, dragged him to comparative safety behind the M.G. Concerned though we were about Barcelona, we had no time to pause and inquire as to his state of health. His life and our lives, and the lives of the entire section, if it came to that, now depended upon the M.G.

As soon as it was set up, Little John yelled at me to start firing. I needed no prompting on this occasion. The English were victorious, and they knew it, but they momentarily fell back before the rapid firing of the M.G. and we were able to pull out, with heavy losses of men and equipment, making our way across the open fields under cover of the dead American's goddam hedges. We took up a new position in some ruins about a couple of kilometres off. Barcelona was alive but in a bad way. It was obvious he needed urgent medical attention, and while transport was being arranged we gathered round his stretcher and began piling him up with all the cigarettes and all the money we had on us. Barcelona was sobbing rather querulously, weak from loss of blood, and moaning at us not to send him away.

'What do you think I am?' he maundered. 'A bleeding baby?'

'You're certainly behaving like one,' said Löwe, sternly. He laid a hand on Barcelona's shoulder. 'You know perfectly well that hospital's the only place for you. Why don't you just thank your lucky stars you're still alive and can look forward to a nice long rest? There are many of us who'd be only too pleased to be in your shoes right now.'

'The war will be over by the time I get back,' he complained, feebly.

'No such bleeding luck,' commented Little John.

Löwe smiled.

'Don't be ridiculous, the war couldn't end without you! I'll tell you what, you'll be back with us again inside a month. Here——' He searched his pockets, found an empty cigarette packet and his gold lighter. Heroically, he handed over the lighter. 'Take this. It's a good luck charm. That'll see you through all right.'

The only transport available was a motor-cycle combination. We wrapped him up in blankets and a ground sheet and installed him as comfortably as possible in the side-car, with a machine-gun on his knees, just in case he should need it, then stood sadly waving as he was borne off into the darkness.

'All right,' said Löwe, wearily. 'Get fell in and let's see what our losses are.'

Each section leader took a count and reported the number of men dead or wounded or missing. A dispatch rider was then sent off to the Regiment. Five minutes later, the enemy was on us again. Porta had his field-glasses to his eyes at the time. A bullet tore them from his hands and he regarded the shattered pieces with stupefaction. Had it not been for those field-glasses, Porta would almost have certainly been a dead man.

Enemy troops were coming at us from two directions at once. Again we were forced to retreat. I stumbled after the rest of the section, the M.G. doing its best to trip me up. There were times when I wished I was not the best machine-gunner in the Company. There were times when

I wished someone else could drag the perishing thing about with him in the teeth of enemy fire. A hand-grenade came rolling towards me. I kicked it savagely out of the way and had the satisfaction of seeing it explode at the feet of two soldiers dressed in khaki. Serve 'em right, the bastards! They didn't have to contend with a damned heavy M.G.

I caught up with the rest of them sheltering behind a high ridge of ground. Lieutenant Löwe was yelling at them again for some misdemeanour or other. He was threatening, for probably the thousandth time in the past week, to put them all on a charge. It appeared that Little John was missing, that no one had seen him fall, and that Löwe, knowing Little John, was inclined to think that he had disobeyed the order to pull out.

'He was here a while ago,' said the Old Man, defensively.

'I don't give a damn where he was a while ago! I want to know where he is now! Don't you have *any* control over your section, Feldwebel Beier?'

'Over some of them,' said the Old Man. He looked hard in Porta's direction. 'Not over others.'

'I've a good mind to put the whole lot of you on a charge!'

The Legionnaire hunched a cold shoulder.

'If it amuses you,' he said, and turned away.

'What did you say?' screamed Löwe. 'You dare to talk to an officer like that, you—you French rat!'

The Legionnaire gave one of his superior smiles.

'Excuse me, sir,' I said meekly.

He swung round on me.

'Well? What is it now, Hassel?'

'I just thought you'd be pleased to know that I've still got the M.G. with me, sir.'

'For God's sake!'

The Lieutenant raised one clenched fist in exasperation and went storming off again. We passed the rest of the night in comparative calm, untroubled either by enemy or by officers.

Towards morning, Little John showed up. He came

whistling over the hill towards us, as unconcerned as a hiker out for a dawn stroll. Under each arm he carried a large tin of jam. We sat up and stared at him, our mouths sagging. He began bawling at us when he was still some distance away.

'Why did you all go tearing off like that? You should have hung around a bit. I ended up with the place to myself ... Thirty-one gold teeth I got! There was one sergeant, he had a whole denture made out of the stuff ... You should have been there, it was some sight!'

'We'll go halves?' said Porta, greedily eyeing the two bulging sacks that hung from Little John's belt.

'Drop dead!' said Little John, prudently buttoning up his combat jacket.

We had time only for a quick coffee and some bread and jam, and then a fresh lot of orders came through: the second section were to go out on reconnaissance towards the north-west, to the forest of Ceris. The Regiment required to know whether or not it was in enemy hands.

For once it was not raining. The sun was high above us before we had been out more than an hour, and on the whole I think I should have preferred the usual downpour. Clothes that stuck to your back with sweat were even worse than clothes that stuck to your back with rain. The Old Man, taking a firm line with us, refused even a five-minute break until we had reached our objective.

We entered the forest and began moving cautiously through it, weapons at the ready for the first sign of trouble. Suddenly, away to our right, we heard unmistakable sounds of human activity. The Old Man held up a hand. We listened, but were unable to make out what was happening. Stealthily, we moved forward—and stopped in astonishment at the sight that met our eyes. It was an entire corrugate village in the middle of the forest. We saw half a dozen men in Yank uniform busily working among drums of petrol and vast heaps of grenades. Four trucks stood by, each attached to a trailer piled high with boxes of ammunition.

'Bloody hell!' said Porta. 'It's an arms depot!'

'What do we do?' I hissed.

'Wait and see what happens. We don't know how many of them there are.'

'If it's only those six, I reckon we ought to have a go at 'em right away,' urged Porta, shouldering his machine-gun.

'I don't care if it's sixty-six,' said Little John, with his usual thirst for blood.

'Put that thing away!' snapped the Legionnaire, jerking Little John's arm as he saw him reaching for his revolver.

One of the Americans left his companions and began walking towards us. He appeared not to have noticed us, and was obviously making for the trees for some reason of his own. At my side, I could feel the Legionnaire tensing his muscles, ready for action. The man had not even the time to cry out before the Legionnaire, practising the skills of his Foreign Legion days, had one arm round his neck and a knife in his back.

The remaining five men were hard at it loading drums of petrol on to one of the trailers. The Old Man jerked his head at us. Silently we crept forward, moving stealthily across the clearing, placing our feet with care as the Legionnaire had taught us. One man turned his head at the last moment. The others were taken by surprise. We bounded forward like so many panthers and had silenced them probably even before they knew what was happening. It was an art we had acquired, of necessity, when fighting in Russia.

The Old Man glanced round and jabbed a finger towards a long, low, prefabricated building. We crept up to it and cautiously peered through the windows. Inside, men were seated at two large tables eating breakfast. Outside, doubtless, there were sentries patrolling the entrance to the hut. The Legionnaire and Little John went off in opposite directions to deal with them. The rest of us grimly pulled out hand-grenades.

A series of explosions. The men seated round the tables jerked into the air, fell forward with their noses in their mess tins. We saw Little John and the Legionnaire burst through the door on the far side, saw a startled group of men come running out of the showers, clutching damp towels round their naked bodies. They were mowed down by the Legionnaire's machine-gun, and at a signal from the Old Man we hauled ourselves up and made our entry through the windows.

'All right, hold your fire! There's too much petrol lying around this place for my liking.'

'Here, take a gander at this!' yelled Little John, who had opened another door and found a provision cupboard behind it.

'Food!' shouted Porta, making a dive for it.

The Old Man attempted to hold him back, but it was too late. Little John had already cracked the first bottle of whisky; Porta had already plunged his bayonet into the first tin of pineapple.

'Leave that stuff alone!' roared the Old Man.

'Have a heart,' said Gregor. 'I haven't seen so much grub since the food started.' He rushed to join the two rebels and gave a great shout of joy. 'Champagne!'

Really, it was too much. I darted forward with the others and snatched up a bottle. The floor was soon awash with corks bobbing jauntily on a sea of champagne. While the rest of us drank, Porta was feverishly stuffing a large saucepan with every particle of food he could lay hands on, corned beef, meat balls, potatoes, tomatoes, bacon, eggs, butter, cheese...

'Why wasn't I born a Yank?' he sighed, blissfully stirring the mess with a wooden spoon.

The Old Man gave a howl of indignation, but Little John seemed to be of the same mind as Porta. He pulled an American tunic off the back of a chair and forced his way into it, splitting all the seams as he did so. A champagne cork hit him smartly in the nape of the neck.

'You're dead, you're dead!' chanted Heide, drunkenly reverting to the days of his youth.

He giggled stupidly as Little John hurled an empty bottle at him. The air was soon full of flying missiles.

'Stop arsing about and come and eat!' screamed Porta, above the din.

153

It was like some marvellous Bacchic dream. Only for a wonder it was reality.

'Such a pity old Nuts had to miss it all,' I murmured, thinking of the wounded Barcelona and absently pouring champagne down my ear instead of my mouth.

'I'm warning you,' said the Old Man, seriously. 'I disclaim all responsibility for this debauch. You have openly opposed me with guns in your hands.' He belched and tried to pretend that he hadn't. 'I'm warning you,' he repeated. 'I've written it all down in my notebook.'

'That's easily settled,' said Porta. He seized the notebook and promptly dunked it in the stewpot. 'Have another glass of champagne, it'll take your mind off things.'

Little John beamed happily at everyone. His face was shining with grease and goodwill.

'Adolf never gave anyone a spread like this,' he said. 'I'm going to write to Mr. Eisenhower and ask to join his gang.'

The revels continued. The Old Man joined in willy nilly. Heide discovered a barrel of cognac and we drank our way stolidly through it. After that we began to play games. Silly, childish games accompanied by much hysterical laughter and horse play. I clambered up a tree pretending—and doubtless thinking—that I was a monkey. The only nuts I could find were hand grenades, so I sprinkled them at will over the ground below. By some miracle, no one was killed. Little John and Porta set light to a drum of petrol and began leaping in and out of the flames, until Little John sat down in the middle of it and was nearly burnt to a cinder. We rushed at him with the extinguisher and sprayed him liberally, by which time he looked like a giant snowman. The Legionnaire, in his solitary way, was gravely mixing together every possible combination of drink, rum and cognac and whisky, brandy and vodka and crème de menthe, and Gregor ran about barking like a dog and tripping people up.

Suddenly, out of the trees, came a well-known voice. In an exceedingly bad temper.

'This time you've really gone too far! Where's Feldwebel Beier?'

We stopped our revels and stood gaping, as Lt. Löwe appeared like a black cloud in our midst, with the rest of the Company agog behind him.

'Where is he?' he repeated, grimly.

A long search revealed the Old Man flat on his back, snoring like a pig, with a grenade clutched in either hand.

'He tried to stop us,' I said, with a vague, befuddled feeling of loyalty towards the Old Man. 'We opposed him—we openly opposed him—with guns in our hands.'

'He wrote it all down in his notebook,' added Heide, helpfully.

'His notebook's in the stewpot!'

Gregor screamed with laughter and once again began barking like a dog. Lieutenant Löwe roared. Just opened his mouth and roared. No words were necessary.

'Sh!' cautioned the Old Man, opening his eyes at last. 'You'll bring the enemy down on us.'

'Have a Foreign Legion special,' offered Little John.

He held out a glass containing God knows what mixture of drinks. The Lieutenant slapped it ungraciously from his hand and the liquid splattered itself over his uniform.

'Now look what you've done,' said Little John.

Out of his pocket he dragged a filthy piece of rag. He leaned forward to wipe down the Lieutenant's uniform, gave a drunken lurch and put out both hands to steady himself. He and Löwe crashed to the ground, locked in a far from loving embrace. Löwe, being sober, was the first to reinstate himself. Little John clutched anxiously at one of his legs, trying to pull his vast bulk upright, and Löwe kicked out and sent him flying.

'Got his knickers twisted,' observed Gregor to me, very solemnly. 'In a bad mood.'

'Filthy temper, more like.'

Little John staggered to his feet, fell into the Lieutenant once again, and once again they disappeared earthwards in a flying tangle of arms and legs.

'Look at that!' said Heide, reprovingly. 'An officer

lowering himself to brawl with one of his own men. I'd like to hear what a court martial would have to say about that.'

While the Lieutenant and Little John were rolling about the ground in each other's arms, the rest of the company, with loud whoops of delight, had flung themselves upon the debris that we had left behind. We heard the familiar and beloved sound of champagne corks popping; we heard bottles being smashed, we heard the clatter of knives and forks. Clearly our companions had no intention of missing out on the feast. I saw one of them firing his revolver into a barrel of rum and gulping the stuff down as fast as it spurted out. A tin of corned beef came flying out of a window, followed by an empty vodka bottle. The third section was pelting the fourth with eggs. I felt moved almost to pity as I contemplated Lt. Löwe, standing helpless in the midst of it all. I didn't hold it against him, getting mad at us.

'I don't hold it against you, sir,' I said, kindly. 'Getting mad at us, I mean. I understand how you feel.'

The look he turned upon me was one of pure hatred. I was a bit taken aback, I admit, but nevertheless I persisted.

'If you just had a little drink yourself, sir, it might make you feel a bit better.'

Löwe raised both fists high above his head.

'You'll swing for this!' he said. 'The whole damn lot of you, you'll swing for this!'

Gregor at once rushed to the nearest tree and began hanging from a branch, throwing his legs up and down and chattering like a monkey. Little John promptly began pelting him with stones, and I, feeling slightly jealous, because after all it was me that had played the monkey game first, took a rugger dive at his legs and tried to dislodge him. We were soon all three in a fierce rough and tumble on the ground and had forgotten Lt. Löwe's very existence.

It was probably Porta who brought the final and annihilating blow down on our heads. It was certainly Porta who ran berserk with a bulldozer and caused the entire prefabricated hut to collapse. I heard Lt. Löwe screaming his head off somewhere and caught the words 'loot and pillage', and I heard Porta braying like a donkey and declaring that he was now a member of the U.S. Army and had reason to believe there were Krauts in the camp. After that, I got my face in the way of someone's boot and didn't know any more until I was jerked awake by an earth-shaking explosion and discovered the whole camp in flames about my ears.

Considering that at least 99 per cent of the Company were almost totally insensible with drink, it doubtless says something for army training that not a single life was lost nor a single man injured, apart from the black eyes and broken teeth that are the inevitable aftermath of any debauch.

'Not a bad binge, that,' said Little John, as we marched back to base. 'We'll do it again some day.'

CHAPTER EIGHT

In the offices of the Gestapo on the Avenue Foch, Commissar Helmuth Bernhard, section IV/2 A, was interrogating the journalist Pierre Brossolette. Brossolette had been picked up on a beach in Normandy, attempting to make his way to England and there reveal the plans for the insurrection of Paris. Helmuth Bernhard was merely the latest in a long line of interrogators.

The Gestapo were well aware of Brossolette's intentions on reaching England. What they required to know was the names of his collaborators, and they worked towards this end with all their usual diligent brutality.

Bernhard himself was more subtle in method than his predecessors, and in any case, by the time Brossolette came into his care it was fairly obvious that any more physical torture would probably kill the man before he could be of any use to them. Already they had smashed both his legs in several places, so that now he could only drag himself painfully along the ground on his hands and elbows. Bernhard, viewing him with a practised eye, decided that the moment was ripe for a more refined form of persuasion. Given the right treatment, the man would soon break.

Unfortunately for Bernhard, Brossolette himself was equally well aware that he was nearing the end of his resources. In a final burst of defiance, therefore, he succeeded in hurling himself from a top-floor window during a moment of inattention by his guards. His fall was broken half-way by a stone balcony. The Gestapo rushed outside in time to see him bouncing off the balcony on to the ground below. He was dead before they reached him.

That night, eight hostages were shot by way of reprisal.

GENERAL VON CHOLTITZ VISITS HIMMLER

S.S. Reichsführer Heinrich Himmler had installed himself and his staff in a castle not far from Salburg. Tall, grim S.S. men mounted a rigid guard day and night all round the perimeter. They were the men of Himmler's own special S.S. company, the fanatical 3rd Panzers of the Totenkopf Division—the only S.S. division to wear the silk-embroidered death's heads on their collars.

They had been in existence now for ten years, and during that time four commanding officers, having fallen foul of the Reichsführer, had disappeared without trace. The 'T' Division received all its orders direct from Himmler, and from Himmler alone, and they owed allegiance to none other. Hitler both hated and mistrusted them.

Three large staff vehicles were drawn up before the entrance to the castle. A general of an infantry division was slowly and ponderously climbing the steps, to be met at the top by an S.S. Sturmbannführer and promptly relieved of his briefcase.

'Sorry about that, sir,' said the S.S. man, officiously. 'New orders, as from the twentieth of July . . . The Reichsmarschall himself would even have to submit!'

'Perhaps you'd care to take my revolver, as well?' suggested the General, sourly.

'No, you can keep that, sir . . . If you'd care to follow me?'

The visitor was ushered into the palatial office of the Reichsführer, and the two men saluted each other in accordance also with the new regulation of 20th July.

'General Dietrich von Choltitz, sir,' announced the Sturmbannführer. 'Here to make his report.'

'Ah yes.' Himmler rose from his chair and held out a hand. 'Consider yourself welcome, General. I'm pleased to make your acquaintance . . . May I congratulate you on your promotion? From lieutenant-colonel to general in three years! That's not bad going. Not bad going at all.

Even our own S.S. officers don't usually progress at that rate!'

General von Choltitz smiled faintly in recognition of the Reichsführer's praise. Himmler took him confidentially by the arm.

'Well, tell me, how are you finding things in Paris? You're managing to keep the French in their place all right?'

'I'm managing,' said von Choltitz, grimly.

'It's a tough job.' Himmler nodded his encouragement, then flipped a finger towards the cross that von Choltitz wore at his neck. 'A souvenir of Rotterdam, I take it?'

'A souvenir of Rotterdam ... yes.'

Himmler laughed.

'Eighteenth of May 1940!'

'You have an outstanding memory, Reichsführer.'

'Just so. One needs it, in my job.' Himmler disengaged himself from the General and walked up to his desk, which was covered beneath piles of papers and folders and trays full of documents. 'As you will see, I receive plenty of mental exercise! The work piles up day by day. It's been the same ever since I began to occupy myself with matters of the Interior ... We are surrounded by enemies and traitors! Enemies and traitors! What do you make of this one?'

He thrust a document at von Choltitz, who calmly accepted it and read it through with no indication of any kind as to his feelings.

'In the name of the German people, Mme Elfriede Scholtz, *née* Remarque, is accused as follows:

'That she did over a period of months hold defeatist views, demanding the removal of the Führer, declaring that our soldiers were no longer anything but cannon fodder, etc. That she had conducted a fanatical propaganda campaign against the Third Reich. The person who denounced her, and who is, in fact, her late landlady, adds the information that Mme Scholtz had never believed in ultimate victory and had on many occasions said so. Madame Scholtz is said to have been much influenced by the famous novel written by her brother, Erich Maria Remarque, *All Quiet on the Western Front*. This can hardly be taken into account as a mitigating circumstance, however, since by her own admission the accused had not seen her brother for thirteen years.'

General von Choltitz silently, with no comment offered or even implied, handed the document back to the Reichsführer. Himmler tossed it furiously on to his desk.

'Death is almost too good for people like that!'

He searched among his papers for another example to show the General but his eye was caught by a document labelled 'top secret', and he picked it up, frowning, and glanced through it. It was a detailed list of all the watches, bracelets, fountain pens, spectacles, rings, chronometers, etc., that had been 'collected' from the deportation camps. Himmler cleared his throat, folded the document carefully into three and hid it away from the glances of the curious. This was one piece of information he would not show von Choltitz, no matter how meteoric had been his rise from the rank of lieutenant-colonel.

'General'—he swung suddenly round on him—'as the Führer has already told you at Wolfsschanze, he wishes Paris to be razed to the ground. I have called you here to inquire why you have not, as yet, put this order into execution ... My agents tell me that life is pursuing its normal course in Paris, apart from one or two little—episodes, shall I call them?—that can be laid at the doors of the so-called Resistance Movement.'

Von Choltitz gave an almost imperceptible shrug of the shoulders.

'Reichsführer, I have neither sufficient men nor sufficient arms. The heavy guns have failed to arrive, nobody even knows where they are ... And not only that, I've never yet received the new units I was promised.'

'You shall have whatever you need,' said Himmler, magnificently. 'I am at this moment in the course of re-constituting two regiments armed with rocket batteries.

Tor and Gamma are *en route*, and I've already given orders to Model to send you a regiment of ZBV tanks—they're hard nuts, I can promise you! They'll do anything you like, go anywhere you wish ... I'm relying on you, Choltitz, one hundred per cent, and there are very few other officers I could say that to. I hope soon I shall be seeing you in the uniform of an S.S. Obergruppenführer!'

At dinner that evening, von Choltitz found himself seated to the right of Himmler. The splendid silverware came straight from the court of Rumania, but the meal itself was comparatively spartan, and the faces of the assembled officers betrayed only too clearly what they thought of it. It was Himmler himself who decided which of the guests should be entitled to second helpings. A large cavalry general, who was allowed only one meagre portion, was heard to mutter his regrets at having been dragged away from the pleasures of his own table for the undoubted honour but rather more doubtful pleasure of being a guest at Himmler's. A major pulled a cigar from his pocket and held it lovingly beneath his nostrils, but a sharp glance of horror from his host caused him at once to replace it. Himmler had a hatred of tobacco. Coffee (ersatz) was served in the next room. One cup for everybody, and only the privileged had the right to a glass of cognac. As they rose from the dinner table, the Reichsführer made a sign that he wished to exchange a few words with a general who had been given the task of taking up the struggle against the underground movement in Jugoslavia.

'Oberführer Strauch, I understand that you recently granted a reprieve to a group of enemy resistance workers. This is the second time this has occurred since you were appointed to your post. This is the second proof of inexcusable weakness on your part ... Why?'

'Reichsführer, the group in question consisted of six women and two twelve-year-old boys——'

'My dear Strauch, you quite take my breath away! Six women and two twelve-year-old boys! And are not women and boys just as capable of acts of sabotage as grown men? Particularly if they know they're liable to get

162

away with it? You really must rid yourself of this absurd sensibility! I don't care who it is, men, women or children, nuns or priests or babes in arms—if they dare to raise so much as a finger against us, wring their necks! You understand me?'

There was a pause.

'How many prisoners do you have in Belgrade?' asked Himmler, suddenly.

The miserable Strauch looked down at his feet.

'Two thousand nine hundred, Reichsführer.'

'You are misinformed,' said Himmler, dryly. 'I would seem to know more about your affairs than you do ... There are exactly 3,218 people held as prisoners in Belgrade. Your courts are dealing with only fifty cases per day. It's not enough. You'll have to double the number at least.'

Strauch opened his mouth to protest, but Himmler cut him short.

'If you're short of judges, then enrol some more! Drag them off the streets, if necessary ... They don't have to be qualified in any way, for God's sake! Just remember, my dear Strauch, that a certain amount of harshness is necessary if we are to win this war. And we shall win it, never doubt that. But in the meantime it's our existence that's at stake. The Allies will show no mercy, and they've made no secret of the fact. Just remember that, in future, when you're tempted to be sentimental over women and children.'

When, later on, Himmler and von Choltitz returned to the large conference room, an ordnance officer presented himself with a large map of Paris, which he spread before them on a table. The two men leaned over it.

'According to my experts,' said Himmler, 'the entire town could be paralysed by blowing up the bridges. We've managed to lay hands on an old report which speaks of various ammunition dumps that everyone's conveniently forgotten about. We've uncovered one or two of them and obviously they'll have their uses, but before we can actually do anything it's essential that we crush the Resistance Movement ... Essential, do you hear me? After the Jews, the French people are our worst enemies. They have been for centuries.'

Himmler straightened up and stood by the table, regarding von Choltitz.

'In Paris, we know, there are two Resistance organizations. One is Communist, run by a dreamer who decks himself out in a uniform and ribbons to which he has no right. My men have run into him several times. The Communists, by the way, are by far the more dangerous of the two groups ... The other is under the command of a group of intellectuals who claim they're working for de Gaulle. Our aim must be to turn these two groups against each other, set them to destroy each other and save us the trouble of doing it. You understand me?'

'Perfectly.'

'Good ... In fact, the Communists are half-way there already. They can't stand the intellectuals and they won't take much pushing to do our job for us. We'll use them as long as we need them, then get rid of them.'

'What units am I going to have?' demanded von Choltitz, bluntly.

Himmler gazed across at him.

'Ah yes ... your units ... I'll give you the 19th S.S. Panzerdivision "Letland" and the 20th S.S. Panzerdivision "Estland". They're both in Denmark at the moment. And in addition to them you can have two regiments of the Feldgendarmerie from Poland and the 35th S.S. Polizei-Grenadierdivision ... My experts have estimated that it should take you approximately twelve days to mine the town. I'll let you have the 912th Engineers and the 27th Panzer Z.B.V. for the job. How does that suit you?'

'Very well indeed, Reichsführer ... so long as they actually arrive. If they don't, then I regret my task will be impossible.'

'General von Choltitz, don't speak to me about impossibilities! Twice already in this war you have achieved impossibilities—at Rotterdam and at Sebastopol. What you have done once before, you can do again. Remember I am relying on you one hundred per cent.'

Von Choltitz turned away and discreetly slipped a tranquillizer into his mouth. His previous exploits hung like millstones about his neck. He could foresee that if anyone had to go short of men it would be him, on the grounds that he was a proven miracle worker and what he had done once, he could do again.

In May 1940 von Choltitz had been a lieutenant-colonel, commanding the 3rd battalion of the 16th Infantry Regiment with their transport planes, the JU 52s, in the marshy hinterlands of Holland. He took over the command of various combat units of the 2nd Luftland-division and began the struggle in the Woolhaven–Rotterdam region. The roads and railway bridges leading to Rotterdam were immediately taken over, although at no small cost in personnel: for every few metres gained, a new river of blood was shed. Sixty-seven per cent of the officers were lost. When, after five days' hard fighting, the battle came to an end, seventy-five per cent of the division had fallen. The Dutch must have been in similar case, or even worse, but General Lehmann stubbornly refused to think of capitulating. He was given three hours for an unconditional surrender and at the end of that time, when he had received no reply to his message, von Choltitz knew that the only course left open to him was the bombardment of Rotterdam.

Two thousand four hundred bombs and incendiaries were dropped on the city. Thirty thousand civilians lost their lives. When the bombardment came to a halt it was exactly 15.05 hours, and out of the burning ruins the remnants of the Dutch Army came running, bayonets at the ready, to avenge themselves on the enemy who had destroyed their city. It was a resistance that was both glorious and unexpected; a sudden mad burst of heroism from not one man but hundreds. The Germans were taken by surprise. A young Dutch lieutenant, mortally wounded, managed to wipe out an entire combat group before he himself collapsed and died. A boy recruit of perhaps eighteen years ran amok with a flame-thrower and created stark panic among soldiers with more than twice his experience. From out the ruined streets appeared the dark hulk of Dutch tanks, advancing majestically over the rubble. A panic seized hold of the Germans. They faltered and fell back, and it was then that Lt.-Colonel von Choltitz, minus all his officers and half his men, was himself seen to plunge into the heart of the chaos and vigorously set about restoring the flagging morale of the troops. Men on the verge of flight were pushed back into the battle. Others found their faith renewed simply by the sight of an officer. With his own hands von Choltitz helped set up a machine-gun and stayed long enough to see that it was properly manned before rushing off to give aid in another quarter. Metre by metre he moved forward, dragging his men with him. He himself was seen to wipe out a nest of enemy machine-guns with a shower of grenades, and so long as he was there men found themselves for very shame unable to turn and run.

Exactly two hours after the end of the bombardment, General Lehmann surrendered 'to avoid further excessive loss of life'. At 17.00 hours the order went out to the Army, over the radio, to cease fire, and it was at that moment that the Dutch Colonel Scharroo presented himself to Lt.-Colonel von Choltitz in his temporary headquarters on the Willemsbrucke. Von Choltitz was cold and unforthcoming. When, after some five minutes of conversation, Colonel Scharoo held out his hand, the German refused to take it: in his opinion an officer who surrendered was no longer worthy of being treated as an officer.

At the head of his triumphant troops, von Choltitz entered into Rotterdam and received the unconditional surrender of that town. He was the first German governor of Rotterdam, and a very harsh ruler he made. It was on 18th May 1940 that he received the Iron Cross from the hands of the Führer in person.

Other urgent tasks were lying ahead of this triumphant officer, and he took them all in his cool, unruffled stride. In the front line of the 2nd Infantry Division, his own old regiment of Oldenbourg, he mounted the attack on Krim and was brought to a halt only by the formidable cannons of Sebastopol. But the Führer knew his man. The conqueror of Rotterdam was now given the means by which to become also the conqueror of Sebastopol; the 60-cm. 'Thor' mortar, which weighed over 120 tons; the 43-cm. 'Gamma', weighing 140 tons; and a whole battery of Doras, 80-cm. cannons of 55 tons.

Even before the battle began, Hitler had removed one of the little red flags from the map in his office, indicating to all the world that von Choltitz had already as good as taken what was then the most powerful fortress in the world. Von Choltitz duly took it. Both town and fortress fell to him after a bombardment that can surely have had no equal in the history of warfare.

Von Choltitz received the Führer's personal thanks, and the German radio blared forth his name by day and by night to his grateful countrymen. Himmler offered him a high-ranking position in the S.S., but von Choltitz was a Prussian and preferred the Army. Himmler hid his wrath behind a charming smile of regret, and von Choltitz shot onwards like a comet, overtaking even Rommel in his quest for glory.

Himmler turned his back upon the map of Paris, and upon von Choltitz. Unlike his visitor he was not armed, but he had no fears that the General would run suddenly mad and make an attempt on his life. The General was by way of being some thing of a national hero. Himmler picked up his cognac and stood calmly with the glass held below his nostrils, savouring the fumes. Already, locked away in his desk, were the papers approving the nomination of the General to the rank of Obergruppenführer of the Waffen S.S. It was to be his reward following upon the total annihilation of Paris, and this time there would be no question of preferring the Army.

'Von Choltitz,' said Himmler, slowly turning to him, 'I trust you have no doubts as to our final victory? Because if so, I do assure you that they are ill-founded. Another two years is all we need. Let us just hang on for that length of time—and you know as well as I that we are perfectly capable of it—and I swear to you that victory will be ours ... This latest stunt of the Allies, this invasion of Normandy——' He dismissed it contemptuously. 'The final fling of a dying man! Believe me, Choltitz, they've really had to scrape the bottom of the barrel to pull off this little trick. We have only to hold out against them, and purely and simply they'll have nothing left to fall back on. They've used up all their resources, they're staking everything on the belief that we'll collapse—which, of course, we shall not do. But in the meantime, General, while we're hanging on we must be hard; we must be brutal. We must be inhuman, if necessary ... the destruction of Paris will be a demonstration of our power and a psychological blow from which the enemy will never recover ... Are you with me?'

General von Choltitz took a deep, slow breath before replying.

'Reichsführer, you must allow me to point out that Paris is not Rotterdam ... Paris is not Sebastopol. There will be a world outcry if we destroy her—and God help us if we lose the war!'

A dark smile of pleasure spread itself across Himmler's face.

'Nero fiddled while Rome burned. And all the world still talks of it ... One day, my dear General, the world will talk of you and me. In a thousand years they will still talk of us. We shall have outstripped Caesar and Attila the Hun! And if, contrary to all my expectations, we lose the battle—at least we shall lose it in a blaze of glory.' He threw back his head and gave a great, delighted guffaw. 'The world will shake in its shoes at the mere sound of our names! Himmler and Choltitz! Children shall cry and women shall scream and the strongest of men turn pale!'

Himmler's voice raged onwards in a great surge of anticipated glory. Von Choltitz took another sedative and ran two fingers round the inside of his high Prussian collar. Boldly he interrupted the Reichsführer.

'And what if Patton's armoured divisions get to Paris before I have a chance to destroy the town?'

'Ah! You're thinking of your family! I knew something was on your mind!' Himmler extended a cordial hand and gripped von Choltitz hard beneath the elbow. 'Never fear for their safety, I shall personally guarantee it. Keep in contact with Model and Hausser. Don't bother with von Rundstedt. He is nothing but an old woman, you can forget him. And as for Speidel, he's already got one foot in Gemersheim.'*

'Gemersheim? General Speidel?'

Von Choltitz jerked his head up in quick amazement and Himmler gave a secretive smile.

'My agents are quite au courant, I assure you ... We shall strike when the hour is ripe.'

'But Speidel——!'

Himmler smirked. Von Choltitz distractedly pulled out a cigarette and lit it, and the hated smoke curled up into Himmler's face.

'You can rely on me, of course,' said von Choltitz. 'The destruction of Paris shall be carried out just as soon as I have the troops and the arms that have been promised me, but for the moment I don't even have enough men to defend the Hotel Meurice ... I was told I could have a regiment of heavy tanks. The only trouble is, they no longer have enough tanks left to supply even one to each company. The exact number, I believe, is seven Panzers, all in a deplorable condition and quite unfit for active combat, and a couple of Tigers. Besides that they have enough ammunition for approximately twenty minutes' fighting. At the moment the tank crews are simply wandering about the countryside on foot with rifles over their shoulders ... I have no wish to end up in Gemersheim or to be hanged at Plötenzee like a common criminal, you understand, Reichsführer, but unless I receive the necessary troops and the necessary weapons, I really cannot guarantee that I shall be able to carry out my orders to the fullest.'

Himmler nodded gravely, one hand over his mouth against the cigarette smoke.

'You shall have all that is necessary,' he said. 'Now let us turn back to the map and see in detail what is to be destroyed.'

* Military prison in Koblenz.

Throughout the whole of the Third Reich the telephones were ringing. In Jutland, where the 9th S.S. Panzergrenadierdivision 'Letland' was stationed, they were ringing through for them to reassemble. Hundreds of heavy vehicles were leaving the military camp of Boris. At Flensborg and at Neumunster six hundred armoured cars of every description were being assembled. The engineers laid down roads, of a sort, overnight. Commanding officers worried and nagged at their men to get a move on. There had been no advance warning of the departure of the armoured divisions, and the result was a monstrous bottleneck. Jutland became one enormous military camp.

In the middle of the chaos, the 20th S.S. Panzergrenadierdivision 'Estland', which had only just been ordered to Jutland, received counter-orders to about turn and make their way back again. Obergruppenführer Wengler at once performed a remarkably good imitation of someone having an epileptic fit. His men watched admiringly as he went through his antics and waited in some anticipation for the invectives that would surely follow.

'What short-arsed cretin thought that one up?' he roared, into the grey and rainy night. 'How the bloody hell am I supposed to turn round on these filthy flaming roads?'

'I don't know how, but as to who,' replied the liaison officer, sitting laughing on his heavy motor-cycle with the rain dripping off his black cape, 'your short-arsed cretin was none other than the Reichsführer himself.'

Wengler spat and swore, and then spat again as the liaison officer roared back up the muddy road in a spray of black droplets.

'All right! Orders to all commanding officers: head back again in the direction of Neumunster. Exact destination not yet known. And don't take all bloody day about it!'

Officers at once skidded off in all directions shouting orders. Wengler stood sourly watching. He was one of the toughest of the officers commanding the armoured divisions, and he had small patience with any situation that did not place him firmly in the front line of the fighting.

Even as he watched, the scene disintegrated with astonishing rapidity into a state of demented confusion. Vehicles were reversing blindly into each other, into ditches, into trees, into fences. Several had arbitrarily broken down and were now blocking the road. Everywhere men were shouting and swearing. Someone had uttered the word 'sabotage', and the idea was now firmly fixed in most people's heads as a proven fact.

Slowly, very slowly and very unsurely, the enormous column lurched forward in a southerly direction. The leading vehicles had reached the crossing of the Haderslev –Tënder roads before matters went irretrievably wrong. An innocent Oberstabszahlmeister approached with his munitions column, making for the heavy coastal batteries. His tiny vehicle narrowly escaped a head-on collision with a tank. The car skipped dexterously out of the way, but the tank careered into its neighbour, there was an ugly squealing and grinding of caterpillar tracks, the clang of metal upon metal, and both tanks came shudderingly to a halt. The cries of sabotage, which had never entirely faded, were now taken up again and reached a pitch of frenzy, to such an extent that the unfortunate Oberstabszahlmeister was hoisted from his car, pinned against a tree, and summarily shot. It was almost certain that the wretched man had merely mistaken his way, but if so he paid very dearly for his error. The munitions column never reached the coastal batteries. They were sent off instead to an infantry division being held in reserve in Fionia, and several weeks later there was intense consternation when it was discovered that the 21-cm. shells could by no means be fitted in to the 10·5-cm. field-guns. Conversely, the artillery batteries on the coastal cliffs were exceedingly amused when their 21-cm. guns began spitting out 10·5-cm. shells.

'Sabotage!' cried the staff officers.

'It's that bloody Resistance again!' screamed an apoplectic colonel.

As a matter of form, a few miserable hostages were executed. Someone had to pay the penalty, after all.

It was dawn when the leading vehicles of the 20th

Armoured Division entered into Neumunster. They had learned now that their destination was Paris, and that the matter was one of the greatest urgency. It came, therefore, as something of a surprise to reach Neumunster and discover that the only form of transport awaiting them at the railway station was a dozen French goods wagons of an extremely venerable vintage. The roads were blocked for kilometres around by the 19th Tank Division, also on its way to Neumunster. And coming up strongly from the east was the 233rd Panzerdivision. Every road in Jutland was crammed to overflowing with tanks and soldiers and armoured cars. All bound for Neumunster, all needed in Paris, and a dozen French goods wagons to take the lot of them.

'Sabotage!' screamed the Reichsführer's frantic dispatches.

More hostages were executed. The officials responsible for the running of the Neumunster railway station were executed. The Reichsführer was temporarily appeased, but meanwhile the problem continued. Two armoured divisions, 14,000 vehicles and their full complement of men, stranded in Jutland with twelve French goods wagons!

CHAPTER NINE

For three weeks, a boy of twelve years, condemned to death, had been confined in the prison of Fresnes awaiting execution of his sentence. The crime that had placed him there might well have been no more than a piece of childish high spirits. It might, on the other hand, have been a premeditated act of resistance against the enemy. The Germans naturally preferred to believe the latter. The boy had stolen a revolver from a German soldier at the corner of the Boulevard Saint-Michael and the Place de la Sorbonne, and for this he must die.

The frantic mother tried all she knew to have the sentence repealed, and she finally reached the highest authority of all: General von Choltitz. Not that she herself was allowed to pester the General. The liaison officer, Dr. Schwanz, presented her case for her. He met with no more success than might have been expected.

'Why come to me with this trivia?' cried the conqueror of Rotterdam and Sebastopol, angrily tossing the documents back across the desk. 'There are proper channels for this sort of thing: use them! Presumably if the boy's been sentenced to death there's a very good reason for it? At any rate, I have far more pressing matters to deal with. Take it away and don't waste my time.'

There was no one else to whom the woman could turn, and the following day a child of twelve years died at the hands of the firing squad out at Vincennes. Why should a man of the stature of General von Choltitz concern himself with the fate of a mere child? That was not the way to fame or glory. Posterity would not remember a general who saved a child from the firing squad. It would, on the

173

other hand, remember a general who had destroyed one
of the most beautiful cities in the world...

CAN PARIS BE SAVED?

General von Choltitz returned to Paris. The city was
sombre and sullen; beneath the smooth surface of life
there lurked an air of brooding menace. The number of
desertions from the German Army was assuming catas-
trophic proportions. And accordingly the number of re-
prisals was stepped up. In one evening alone over forty
people suspected of working for the Resistance were lined
up before the firing squads. The Communists were the
first to die.

One morning at dawn, two officers of the front line
presented themselves to von Choltitz. One was a major-
general, who wore a patch over one eye and the black
uniform of the tank corps; the other was a young captain
of the engineers and an expert in the laying of mines.
Both men were specialists in the art of destruction. As
soon as they had entered the General's room, a large
notice was hung on the door: ENTRY STRICTLY FORBIDDEN.
Behind that door the future of Paris was being decided.

At the same time as this most secret conference was
being held, another, even more secret, was taking place in
an apartment on the Avenue Victor-Hugo between a certain Hauptmann Bauer, an officer in the service of
Admiral Canaris, and a diplomat who went by the pseu-
donym of 'Farin'. Hauptmann Bauer was earnestly putting the diplomat in the picture, as he saw it, and the
diplomat was as earnestly listening.

'Monsieur Farin,' declared the officer, speaking very low
and very rapidly, 'this whole town is going to go up in
smoke and come down in ruins unless something very
unexpected happens to put a stop to it. It's absolutely
essential that you get to see von Choltitz before it's too
late.'

The diplomat mopped up a few genteel pearls of perspiration from his forehead. He swallowed two glasses of
cognac before replying.

'Who is this General von Choltitz? Where has he come from? Why have I never heard of him?'

'You have heard of him—you simply haven't remembered the name. You've heard of Rotterdam, I suppose? You've heard of Sebastopol? Well'—Hauptmann Bauer nodded, grimly—'that is General von Choltitz!'

'You mean——'

'I mean that the man's a past master in the art of destruction! Why else do you suppose they picked him for the job? He belongs to the same school as Generalfeldmarschall Model: blind obedience, no matter what the circumstances. Give him an axe and tell him to chop off his right hand and he'd do it, provided your rank was higher than his.'

The diplomat scraped his throat a few times.

'What—ah—what do they have to say about it in the Bendlerstrasse?'

'Nothing, for the most part.'

'Then why ... why are we—why are you——'

The Hauptmann's eyes glinted behind his dark glasses.

'The only reason they say nothing is because the few that are still left are too damned scared to open their mouths! The others have—gone.'

'Gone? Gone where?'

'The same place you and I shall be going, unless we're very careful—to Plötenzee.'

The diplomat opened his mouth.

'Hanged?' he said, hoarsely.

'Certainly hanged! Now listen, Monsieur Farin, and tell me what you think of this: a new tank regiment has just arrived in Paris. They're stationed at the Prinz-Eugen barracks out at Versailles. Their commanding officer is a man typical of the type we shall have to deal with: a major-general, twice demoted, in charge of the toughest group of tanks in the world. And I don't say that lightly. I can promise you that if word ever reached Berlin that they were on their way Admiral Canaris would be gone so fast you wouldn't see him for dust. He wouldn't even stop to pick up his grandmother, that one ...'

'So what do you suggest?' asked the diplomat, nervously. 'What can I do about it? And why have they been brought here, anyhow?'

Bauer hunched a shoulder.

'What could be more destructive than a tank? Especially a tank from the 27th Z.B.V.... Let me tell you a bit more about them. The regiment consists of six battalions under the command of Major-General Mercedes. He himself, as I already explained, has had cause to be demoted twice in his career. The men under him have all, at some time or another since being in the Army, served prison sentences. Rape, robbery, thuggery, buggery—you name it, they've done it. They are, to say the least, a thoroughly undisciplined bunch of roughnecks ... You can imagine how it would be if they were let loose in the streets of Paris?'

'Yes.'

'Wholesale massacre——'

'Yes.'

Farin moved slowly to the window, another glass of cognac in his hand. He stood for a while, silently staring down into the street.

'A blood bath,' he said, at last. 'You're right, of course. Something must be done to prevent it.'

'I'm glad you agree.'

'How would it be——' Farin hesitated. 'How would it be if we were to organize police barricades? Look down there, Hauptmann Bauer.' He pointed out of the window, at a police sergeant strolling down the street. 'The defence of Paris—and why not? The police, aided by members of the Resistance ... it could be arranged.'

'I'm sure it could, Monsieur Farin. But at the same time, I rather fear we might be playing straight into Hitler's hands. I happen to know that at this very moment a battalion of the Dirlewanger Brigade is on its way to Paris. Every single man of that force is a reprieved criminal—reprieved not because his case has been considered in a new light, but because the Führer suddenly decided that even criminals might have their uses. My information is that they're being sent here for the express purpose of provoking action of just the type you mention.' Bauer shook his head, regretfully. 'The police and the Resistance ... It's a tempting idea, but just how long could they hold out against the might of the German Army? Just how much resistance *could* they put up? Not enough, I fear. Not enough.'

'So what do you suggest, Hauptmann?'

'As far as I can see, we have only two courses of action open to us. One is to hold up for as long as possible the men and vehicles that von Choltitz is waiting for; the other is to get the American armoured divisions to Paris as quickly as possible.'

Farin sighed.

'I could wish I were in London at this moment!'

'I believe you,' agreed Bauer, with a short laugh. 'Paris isn't the most comfortable place on earth, is it? Mind you, Germany's no bed of roses, either. The Admiral's already burnt all his papers. And you know who's been appointed Oberbefehlshaber for the West? Generalfeldmarschall Walter Model! None other. There's a man who can sniff out treachery a hundred kilometres off. I believe even Hitler himself is none too keen on the fellow.'

'The man's an uncivilized brute,' said Farin, very feelingly. 'You heard the tale of von Rundstedt's champagne, of course? Model's spies discovered he had sixty cases of the stuff in his cellar. Five minutes later—five minutes, mark you!—the whole lot had been poured down the drain. What a waste! How unnecessary!'

'They say he sleeps with a copy of *Mein Kampf* beneath his pillow. I can well believe it. He and von Choltitz are not so much men as military robots.'

The two conspirators stood brooding a while, and then at last the diplomat finished off his cognac and picked up his coat and brief-case with a new air of determination.

'We must see what can be done. Paris must be saved at all costs. I shall present myself to von Choltitz straight away and try to judge what chance we stand with him. It would help if we could only find something against him—some hold over him—something that might interest friend Model.'

'I doubt we could ever do that. The man's the very

model of perfection. Nevertheless, I wish you the best of luck.' Bauer held out a hand and the other grasped it firmly. 'I'll keep in touch through the usual channels, of course—always assuming that I'm still around to do so.'

'I shall trust that you are.'

Farin stood listening at the door for a moment before opening it.

'I think it best if we leave separately. The very paving stones have eyes these days . . . Au revoir, Hauptmann!'

'Au 'voir.'

CHAPTER TEN

Normandy had become a second Stalingrad. Fifty thousand men had been taken prisoner; forty thousand men had lost their lives. The 27th Panzer Regiment was reduced to one-fifth its original strength, and the remaining fifth was sent to Paris for reasons that had not as yet been divulged to it.

With a glum satisfaction that he took no pains to conceal, Generalfeldmarschall von Rundstedt reported that 1,800,000 Allied troops had landed in Normandy; and that against these 1,800,000 were pitted a mere 200,000 Germans. No armoured division now possessed more than ten tanks; many had as few as five; some had even less. Regiments had dwindled to the size of companies. The situation was desperate, as von Rundstedt frequently pointed out to his colleagues.

But the situation went on being desperate and even old man Rundstedt lost patience in the end.

'What's the use of ringing me up forty times a day?' he screamed down the telephone. 'I can't tell you what to do! I can't produce troops out of a top hat! I can't make tanks out of pieces of cardboard! The only sensible course is to surrender, I've said so time and again but the cretins in Berlin won't hear of it! They ought to be locked up, the whole damned lot of them! I tell you, we're run by a bunch of lower-grade morons!'

He slammed the receiver back on to its cradle. The telephone slipped and crashed to the floor. Von Rundstedt merely snorted, snatched up his coat and stormed from the room. His coat was as bare of ribbons as that of the lowest private, and yet he was the most decorated man in all Germany. Through some quirk of his own, General-feldmarschall von Rundstedt never wore his decorations unless specially ordered to do so. He crammed his helmet on to his head, marched through the outer office and briskly saluted.

'I bid you farewell, gentlemen ... By this time tomorrow you will have a new officer commanding you. I have the feeling that I am about to be removed!'

THE GUARD-ROOM AT THE HOTEL MEURICE

Two civilians wearing leather coats and with hats pulled well down over their eyes were sitting in the guard-room at the Hotel Meurice. They had no particular business there, but nevertheless they had made themselves at home. One sprawled in a chair, hands in pockets, legs stretched out, ankles crossed. The other leaned back with his dirty shoes resting on the table, his hard grey eyes flickering about the room and resting momentarily on each object as if it were his own personal property. The man on guard duty was for the most part ignored.

'Hey, Heinrich, you know what?'

The man sprawling in the chair shifted position slightly and jerked his head at his companion, who merely grunted and raised one eyebrow.

'What?'

'I'm pissed off with this place. This town bores me.'

'Ah-huh.'

'It does. It really does. We were better off at Lemberg. Things really moved in Poland, eh?'

'Ah-huh.'

'You remember that bird Tamara at Brest-Litovsk? What a woman!' He turned condescendingly towards the man on guard duty. 'You know what? That girl had a whole battalion of partisans under her command! Killed two of our generals with her own hands! Some girl, eh?' He shook his head. 'Seemed almost a shame to shoot her.'

'In Moscow,' said the grey-eyed one, suddenly, 'they brainwash you. Turn you into a different person and say you're cured. That's worse than shooting.'

'You know what?' demanded his companion, for the third time. 'If we lose this cursed war I've a damned good mind to join the Reds. I have really. When you get down to basics, their programme hardly differs at all from ours. I really think I shall become a Communist. I have an instinct in these matters. That's why I've managed to keep my head on my shoulders all these years. I was at Dirlewanger, you know. I was——'

'I'm not interested where you were before. You're in Paris now, that's all I know, so stop beefing and make the best of it.' Heinrich suddenly swung his feet off the table and turned accusingly upon the guard, an Oberfeldwebel of the artillery. 'I take it you realize that all conversations held in here are top secret?'

The Oberfeldwebel lifted an indifferent shoulder. He had never heard of the Japanese proverb 'see nothing, hear nothing, say nothing', but it was, nevertheless, the creed that he instinctively held—and to which he added, for good measure, 'think nothing'. Just to be on the safe side. It often was better not to think, when you were in the Army. Thinking could be uncomfortable, and thinking could get a man into trouble. Particularly like now, when you were stuck through no fault of your own with a couple of lousy Gestapo types who were quite likely to turn nasty for no better reason than that your face happened to displease them.

The Oberfeldwebel heaved a sigh and glanced involuntarily towards the clock. With any luck, the relief would arrive within minutes. He began laboriously to write out his report. What rotten luck it was to have been born in Germany just in time for the war? What did he care about Lebensraum and the like? As far as he was concerned, he had had all the living space anyone could require back home in Dortmund. Not very exciting, perhaps, but he asked nothing better than to go back there. Why had he had the rotten luck—— He abruptly switched off his thoughts and made his mind an obedient blank. Thinking was a dangerous occupation. Better not to encourage it.

The door suddenly clattered open. The Oberfeldwebel

and the Gestapo looked up in alarm, but it was only the arrival—admittedly somewhat unorthodox—of the new guard. Twelve soldiers of a tank regiment crashed noisily into the room.

'Hallo-allo-allo!' roared the first of them, Obergefreiter Porta, in a voice that caused the very walls to shake. 'What have we here?'

He pointed a finger at the Gestapo, who remained in their chairs, staring insolently up at him. Behind Porta crowded Little John. He immediately seated himself on the top of the desk, with his usual scant regard for discipline.

'O.K.,' he said, cheerfully. ' We've come. You can tell 'em we're here and then you're free to scarper.'

'How dare you?' said the Oberfeldwebel, indignantly. He may not have thought much, but he did believe in discipline. 'Stand up and salute and announce yourselves properly! Where do you think you are? In a Biergarten? This is a Prussian guard-room, I would remind you!'

'Oh, get lost,' drawled Porta.

'If you're here to relieve the guard, why the hell don't you get on and do it?'

Everyone turned, slowly, to regard the Gestapo. It was Peter, the would-be Communist, who had spoken.

'Who's them?' demanded Porta.

'I have no idea.' said the Oberfeldwebel, coldly.

'In that case, they'd better bloody well get the hell out of here! We don't want civilians cluttering up our guard room. Unless, of course'—a thought suddenly struck Porta —'unless, of course, they're under arrest?'

'Obergefreiter!' roared Peter, leaping angrily to his feet. 'I am an Untersturmführer!'

'Really?' said Porta, looking bored. 'Why tell me about it? I'm sure it's very hard on you, mate, I'm very sorry for you, but what do you expect me to do for you? I'm an Obergefreiter, like you said, and for the next twenty-four hours I'm on guard here keeping the bogeymen away from the old General upstairs. That's all I know, and I can't have civilians cluttering up the place.'

Heinrich suddenly yawned, pulled his hand out of his

pocket and held out a card.

'Secret police,' he said, wearily.

Porta remained unmoved by this revelation.

'I don't care if you're secret police or secret road-crossing sweepers,' he told Heinrich. 'We still can't have you cluttering up our guard-room. Regulations is regulations, even for the Gestapo.'

'Has it occurred to you,' asked Heinrich, darkly, 'that we could be waiting here for the express purpose of arresting you?'

'Frankly, no.' said Porta. 'To me that seems most unlikely.' Porta in his triumph put a hand in a pocket and pulled out a white armband marked with the letters Z.B.V. 'Ever heard of us?' he murmured.

The two Gestapo men glanced at the armband and then at each other.

'What the devil are you doing in Paris?' demanded Peter.

Porta tapped the side of his large nose and said nothing. The door burst open again. This time it was Barcelona. He marched up to the Oberfeldwebel and smartly clicked his heels together.

'Feldwebel Blom, 27th Panzers, 5th Company, reporting for guard duty.'

The Oberfeldwebel returned the salute, evidently relieved to find someone who conformed, however sketchily, to regulations.

'Oberfeldwebel Steinmache, 109th Artillery Regiment, handing over the guard.'

Barcelona relaxed out of his regulation stance.

'What about them?' he said, jerking a thumb towards Peter and Heinrich. 'What right have two civilians in a guard room? What are they doing in here?'

This time, the Oberfeldwebel lost all patience.

'Ask them, not me, mate! If you don't like the look of 'em, boot 'em out! You're in charge here now, not me, thank God.'

He snatched up his helmet, sketched another brief salute and left the room.

'I see,' said Barcelona, thoughtfully.

He seated himself in the Oberfeldwebel's chair and looked about the room. His gaze returned at last to Peter, who had been growing obviously more and more uncomfortable since his exchange of words with Porta. Or was it only since Barcelona's entry? The man was certainly very unhappy about something. He nodded his head at Heinrich.

'Let's go. Who wants to stay where they're not welcome?'

He pulled his hat further down over his eyes and buttoned his leather coat right up to the chin. Heinrich frowned.

'What's the hurry? I move when I'm good and ready.'

'I am ready,' said Peter.

He moved towards the door, and immediately, with the instinctive awareness that characterized so many of their actions, Little John and Porta moved with him and arrived there first.

'Hold it a minute!'

Barcelona sat with eyes narrowed, tapping his teeth with a fingernail, staring across at Peter. Suddenly he slapped a hand on to the desk.

'Señor Gomez, by all that's wonderful! After all this time! The world's a small place and no mistake—or did someone already say that? Never mind, I'll say it again ... Well, well!' He whistled softly between his teeth. 'I must admit, your new skin suits you quite well, Comrade!'

Peter turned imperiously towards the door.

'Kindly let me pass.'

Little John and Porta stood immovable. For a second the three men formed a frozen tableau, and then Heinrich, evidently sensing danger, joined his companion at the door.

'There's liable to be trouble,' he said, 'if you lay your hands on a member of the Gestapo.'

'Open that door!' demanded Peter, sounding a trifle hysterical.

Very slowly, Porta stretched out an arm, swivelled the man round to face into the room, and pointed at Barcelona.

'Maybe you didn't realize the gentleman was talking to you?' he said. 'Maybe you'd like him to repeat it all?'

'I demand that you open the door!' screamed Peter.

'You don't demand anything,' contradicted Porta, with a broad smile on his face. 'You just pipe down, little man, and do as you're told.'

'*Un*less, of course——'

Little John left the sentence unfinished; merely pulled out a vicious-looking knife and stood toying with it. Barcelona had assumed a musing expression.

'Twenty-second of June 1938,' he murmured. 'Rambla de la Flores in Barcelona ... I remember you gave us drinks in your suite at the Ritz ... You remember that, comrade? I do. I remember it very well. Only'—Barcelona narrowed his eyes as he regarded the man—'in those days, as I recall, you swore allegiance to the Communist Party. What's happened to the red stars, comrade? Your eyes used to be full of them!'

'You're mad!' Peter struggled once more against Porta's large, restraining hand. 'You're raving! Can't you see I'm an Untersturmführer with the Secret Police? You've got eyes in your head, haven't you? I suppose you have seen an Untersturmführer before?'

'Oh, many times,' agreed Barcelona, smoothly. 'But I think you'll admit that it's not easy for someone who's known you as Comrade Gomez to suddenly begin calling you "Untersturmführer" ... What was your rank in Spain, Gomez? Captain, was it? Or was it major? Hombre! I still remember that fine speech you give us in your suite at the Ritz Hotel! You remember that speech, Gomez? Real soul-stirring stuff!'

Barcelona tilted back his chair, swung his legs on to the desk, clasped his hands across his chest and stared up, trancelike, at the ceiling.

'Comrades, the time for speech has come and gone! Now the time has come for action! Action, comrades, for the common good! That is why I am here—to advise you, to encourage you, to give you whatever help you need, whatever help I can ... Be secure in the knowledge that we are behind you, now and for always!'

There was a silence. Peter began twitching rather nervously. Heinrich was staring at him with wonderment in his eyes. Barcelona suddenly swung his legs to the ground and laughed.

'That was the biggest con trick of all time, wasn't it? Or did you have a sudden genuine change of heart?' He looked across at the rest of us. 'After pushing us all into a position of no-return the bugger suddenly upped and left us ... the very same day! Didn't even have the grace to carry on the pretence for another twenty-four hours! And where did he go?' Barcelona glared at the twitching Peter. 'Where did you go, eh? I'll tell you, in case you've forgotten that as well! You went off all smug and safe on board a ship with a load of other Commie bastards! And just to add insult to injury you spent the whole night boozing and whoring and gorging yourself sick with the sort of food the rest of us hadn't seen for years! What was the name of that Russian general? The one who laid it all on, as a reward for being good little cat's-paws and inciting other people to fight the Party's battles for them? What was his name? Malinovsky? Was that it? Or do you prefer Manolito? I think that's what you used to call him in those days, wasn't it? Or can't you even remember that?'

Peter suddenly pulled off his hat, wiped an arm across his brow and fell limply into the nearest chair.

'Yes, yes,' he said, rather wearily. 'I remember ... I thought I recognized you when you first came in, only I wasn't quite sure.'

'But now you are?'

Peter nodded.

'I suppose so.' He looked up at Barcelona and a smile flickered uncertainly across his lips. 'Yes, I remember now. You were a crack shot, weren't you? Are you still just as handy with a revolver?'

Barcelona did not return the hopeful smile. Porta stood like a statue at Peter's elbow and Little John still guarded the exit. The rest of us pricked up our ears and looked with new interest upon this member of the Gestapo who had been a member of the Communist Party in

186

Spain. There was a rare phenomenon indeed!

'I'm reckoned to be just as handy as ever I was,' said Barcelona, slowly. 'Some might even say more handy ... I've put in quite a lot of practice since last we met, Comrade! It's a pity I can't give you a demonstration, but I think our General upstairs might not like it too much.'

'Don't worry,' said Peter, hastily. 'I'll believe you without a demonstration.'

'You'd better!'

'And as for that business in Spain'—he shrugged his shoulders, carelessly—'surely that's long since dead and buried? I'd already done my share of the fighting when I met up with you. I was more vulnerable than you realized. You know what would have happened to me if the Phalange had ever got their hands on me?'

'Twelve bullets in the back of the neck,' said Barcelona, simply. 'And I can still think of many other people who'd be only too willing to give you the same treatment ... including myself!'

Peter leaped to his feet in a panic. He was promptly pushed back into his chair and held there by Porta. Barcelona waved a hand.

'Forget it for the moment. I may return to it later. But before then, there's a question I want to put to you. Was it you who killed Conchita? We found her lying in the gutter in an alleyway behind the Ronda de San Pedro. Her throat was cut ... Paco nearly went out of his mind. He always swore it was you who'd done it.'

Peter bit his lip.

'She was a whore. She deserved to have her throat cut.'

'Simply for being a whore?'

'She was a double agent. She'd been working for us for several months and we suddenly discovered that she'd been playing the same game for the other side.'

'So you cut her throat?' Barcelona walked across the room and stood looking down at the white-faced Peter. 'Just like that?'

'She was a double agent, I tell you——'

'So you say! I've no one else's word for it. And even if she was, she should have been brought before the tribunal of the Calle Layetana, not slung into a gutter with her head hacked off.'

We stared in amazement at Barcelona. He was usually a sentimentalist on the subject of Spain; even on the subject of the Civil War. It was a land of sunshine and orange groves and perpetual siestas, and the Civil War had been an episode of youthful romanticism, a time of valour and idealism. We had never before seen Barcelona so grim and bitter.

'If Paco ever catches up with you,' he informed Peter, 'it'll be a knife in the back before you know where you are.'

'The woman was a double agent,' protested Peter, for the third time. 'And anyway, I was acting on orders.'

'Crap! You killed Conchita for one reason and one reason alone: because she preferred Paco to you. Because she refused to sleep with you.'

Peter held out both hands in a helpless gesture.

'That's enough, Blom! Let's call it a day, can't we? Why rake up the past like this? We've all done things we'd rather forget about—including you, my friend! I could think of one or two little incidents you'd probably rather I didn't mention. And although you've an excellent memory, it's not always wise to recall too much from the past. We're both on the same side now, so let's bury the hatchet.'

Barcelona raised a sceptical eyebrow. Peter stood up and laid a hand on his arm.

'Listen, Blom. I'm a good friend of Obergruppenführer Bergers and I've had a bit of success one way or another. There were things that happened in Poland and the Ukraine ... only that's top secret, I can't tell you any more. You'll just have to take my word for it——'

'What's all this soft soap leading up to?' asked Barcelona.

'I was thinking that a leather coat would possibly suit you as well as it does me. How about it?'

'You mean, join your lot?'

'You could do worse.'

Barcelona shook his head and laughed.

'No, thank you! I took your advice back in 1938 and I've been regretting it ever since. I don't get caught the same way twice ... and besides, I never did care for leather.'

There was a sudden movement from Little John at the door.

'Look sharp, someone's coming!'

We sprang smartly to attention as the door opened and a captain from an engineering regiment came into the room. He was very small, very dapper; his uniform fitted like a second skin, his boots gleamed and winked like precious stones. More genuine authority emanated from that man than from a dozen generals. Even the Gestapo were visibly impressed.

His glance swept coldly round the guard room. His face, although young, was hard and lined, with high cheekbones and a strong jaw. He commanded your rather reluctant respect before even he opened his mouth. But he was a type—a type spawned by the war. Hard as a diamond, brilliant, precise, and flawlessly efficient. You didn't have to know the man to know what he was like.

'Sir!' Barcelona saluted with such verve that his arm looked as though it were on a spring. 'Feldwebel Blom, sir. On guard duty at the Hotel Meurice with three N.C.O.s and twelve men.' He paused. 'There are two civilians in the guard-room for interrogation,' he added.

From the corner of my eye I saw Peter's adam's apple working itself into a frenzy, but neither he nor Heinrich made any comment. The officer nodded.

'Anything to report?'

'No, sir.'

We waited for the order to stand at ease, but it didn't come. He kept us at attention while his ice-chip eyes roamed about the room, taking in every detail.

'Have the two civilians been interrogated?'

'Yes, sir.'

'Any charge to bring against them?'

'None, sir. They're free to go.'

'Then what the devil are they hanging about for? Get out, before someone thinks up a complaint against you!'

He turned ferociously on Heinrich and Peter, who left the room so fast you could almost see the dust clouds rising behind them. I noted, with satisfaction, that there was no question of their attempting to stand on their Gestapo rights when they met up with someone of this man's calibre. He now turned his frozen gaze upon Barcelona.

'What's happened to your uniform, Feldwebel?'

Barcelona glanced down at himself and hastily did up the two top buttons of his tunic. The Captain nodded.

'Never let me see you in that state again. Carelessness in dress leads to carelessness in other things. Kindly anounce my arrival.'

'Yes, sir. What name shall I say, sir?'

'Captain Ebersbach. I am expected.'

Barcelona disappeared. We continued to stand to attention during his absence, until at last he returned with a young lieutenant galloping anxiously behind him.

'Captain Ebersbach, sir! The General is waiting for you. If you'd care to come this way——'

He did care, thank God, and the moment he had gone we fell into postures of exaggerated relaxation. Seconds later, there was another interruption. It was Peter and Heinrich again. They looked cautiously round the door.

'Psst! Has old chisel features gone? We've brought you a present. Just been down to the kitchen and found it in a cupboard. We thought you might like it.'

'We thought we might share it,' added Heinrich, closing the door behind him.

The present they had 'found' in a cupboard was a bottle of cognac. It was good to know that even the Gestapo could be human on occasion.

'We'll all get five years in Torgau if we're caught boozing in a guard-room,' protested Barcelona, avidly wrenching open the bottle and raising it to his lips.

'I'll risk it,' offered Little John.

Needless to say, we all risked it. When there's the immediate and definite prospect of a drink, as opposed to the mere possibility of a five-year prison sentence, a sensible man really has no choice. The bottle was passed from hand to hand, from mouth to mouth, while one of us kept an ear at the keyhole in case of approaching trouble.

'I'm buggered if I know why we've been sent to this place,' complained Porta. 'They do nothing but talk of explosives all day long.'

'So what?' demanded Peter, ripping open a packet of Yank chewing gum and doing his best to look like an American. 'Doesn't concern you what they talk about, does it? They've still got to be guarded, haven't they?'

'Explosives aren't our cup of tea,' said Porta. 'If they're planning to blow the bleeding town up I wish they'd do it without us. Mines give me the willies.'

'They wouldn't blow Paris up,' said Little John. 'Not Paris, they wouldn't.'

'Why not?' asked Peter, challengingly.

He leaned back in his chair, his leather coat falling open, his thumbs stuck beneath his armpits. Before Little John could put forward any very convincing reason for the preservation of Paris, Porta had bent forward and snatched out one of the revolvers from the two shoulder holsters that Peter was wearing.

'They just wouldn't,' repeated Little John, doubtfully.

'That's all you know! Why, when I was in Katya——'

Heinrich suddenly screamed.

'Don't keep on talking about when you were in Katya! I can't stand it, you're worse than a belly ache!'

'But they haven't heard about it before——'

'Well, I have!'

'What happened in Kayta?' asked Little John, with annoying obtuseness.

Fortunately, before Peter could launch into a long and probably very boring tale, Porta had caught his attention by waving his revolver beneath his nose.

'Hey, Comrade! Want to swap this for a Glicenti?'

'I might,' said Peter, cautiously. 'Let's have a look at it.'

The Glicenti was produced, examined, considered, and finally approved. The exchange solemnly took place. I wondered if Peter realized that although he was now the possessor of one of the finest revolvers in the world, he would have the most extreme difficulty in finding any bullets for it. I was on the verge of pointing this out to him, but reflected just in time that Porta probably wouldn't thank me for interfering.

'I still didn't hear about Katya,' complained Little John.

'Later,' said Heinrich. 'We have to go now.'

'No, we don't,' said Peter.

We were saved once again; this time by the arrival of Julius Heide, who burst into the room in his usual flurry of efficiency, his uniform, as always, correct down to the most insignificant detail, his face consciously alert and scrupulously shaven.

'Who's this gorgeous creature?' demanded Peter, his eyes contemptuously following Heide across the room.

'That's our Living Rule,' explained Barcelona, as if Heide were not actually present in person to speak for himself. 'He's in training for a military sainthood. Every last hair on his body has been taught how to stand to attention.'

Heide glared at Barcelona and treated Peter and Heinrich to one of his most scathing of looks. From their leather coats and their general sinister demeanour he must presumably have guessed their identity, but he gave no signs of being at all impressed. Instead, his eyes flickered away in the direction of the circulating cognac bottle and he turned to Barcelona with a frown of displeasure.

'You know perfectly bloody well it's forbidden to drink when you're on guard duty!'

'Why don't you give your arse a chance?' suggested Barcelona, amiably.

'You'll find yourself in Torgau before you're very much older!' snapped Heide.

'Yeah? Who's going to put me there?'

Heide inflated his chest like a rubber life raft.

'It may interest you to know that the new C.O. is a personal friend of mine. We were in Rotterdam together. You drunken load of imbeciles are probably not aware of the fact that I started my service career as a corporal in a parachute corps. I have many influential acquaintances.'

'Get that!' said Porta, admiringly; and ruined the effect by adding in robust tones: 'What a shit!'

Frigidly, Heide turned on his heel and regarded Porta. His eyes were glacial, his jaw set very firmly. I had always known that Julius was destined to travel far along the paths of military hierarchy, but never until that moment had I realized quite how far. Looking at him, I had a sudden vision of the man wearing the uniform of a lieutenant-colonel, and I knew, with a strange certainty, that this was no idle daydream but a clear vision of his future.

'Obergefreiter Porta,' he said, in the cold tones of authority, 'we may be comrades in arms at the moment, but I can promise you that one of these days I'm going to make it my bounden duty to put you on a charge and have you up before a court martial.'

A sudden raspberry from behind made him wheel sharply upon Little John, who was grinning all over his ugly face and raising one ape-like arm as if to strike.

'You lay so much as a finger on me and you'll be in trouble!' threatened Heide, pulling out his revolver. 'Just one little finger and see where it gets you ... It's a punishable offence, to offer physical violence to an N.C.O. You know that, don't you? You're dispensable, you people: I'm not! Furthermore, I intend to survive this war. I very much doubt if you will.'

With a gloating cackle, Little John kicked the gun from Heide's grasp and closed his two enormous fists round his neck.

'Comrades in arms!' sneered Heinrich. 'What a touching sight!'

Little John shook Heide to and fro a few times.

'Well, little man? Now what do you have to say for yourself?'

'You let me go!' panted Heide, aiming a misplaced kick at Little John's shin. 'You want to strangle me, you bloody fool? You want to end up in Torgau along with Barcelona?'

'Why not?' agreed Little John, beaming down upon his victim. 'It might be a pleasure to die for such a cause.'

Heide's face began to turn puffy and purple.

'Oh, let the bastard go,' said Porta, in disgust. 'His hour will come, don't you worry ... But when it does, we'll do the job all fair and square and according to the rule book, just as he'd like it.'

Little John tossed Heide carelessly to the floor. Heinrich politely applauded.

From outside came the welcome sound of heavy boots along the passage and we knew that we were about to be relieved by the new guard.

'Ten minutes bloody late,' grumbled Barcelona, finishing off the last of the cognac and hurling the empty bottle at Heide.

CHAPTER ELEVEN

Bleeding and broken, the parachutist Robert Piper was taken away to the Feldgendarmerie in the rue Saint-Amand.

'You have twelve hours in which to speak,' Oberleutnant Brühner tersely informed him.

What was to happen at the end of twelve hours, if he chose not to speak, was not revealed to him. Possibly his captors themselves did not know. Possibly it never crossed their minds that the problem would arise. You could, after all, make anyone talk in twelve hours. S.S. Untersturmführer Steinbauer, Gestapo agent, smiled so broadly in anticipation that his face split almost in two. Twelve hours! It was child's play.

He glanced contemptuously towards the tattered wreck of the parachutist. That one wouldn't last thirty minutes. If that long. Some of them broke after the first twenty; almost all were subdued by the ice baths that followed. By that time a man was liable to be no more than a lump of meat, raw and bleeding and insensible. But just occasionally, when they were stubbornly bent on continuing the farce, the brain would endeavour to remain active. At that point, one could always resort to a good old-fashioned whipping, or if one felt really energetic one could work off one's excess spirits by sending a few well-aimed kicks into the groin or the belly. The only trouble with that method was that one must needs be an expert if the patient weren't to die before divulging his information. On the whole, a more favourite pastime was to turn on a jet of water at full pressure. That was fun, and never failed in its effect.

Twelve hours! A piece of pudding! The Untersturmführer rubbed his hands together and set about the task
with his accustomed zeal.

The tortured parachutist broke after twenty-seven
minutes. He provided a list of thirty-one names and
addresses, and during the course of the night thirty-eight
people were arrested.

General von Choltitz calmly signed thirty-eight death
warrants.

ESCAPE FROM THE PRISON OF FRESNES

The barracks at Prince-Eugène seemed perpetually to
be in a state of confusion: shouts, screams and oaths filled
the air; men ran round in circles, officers yelled themselves hoarse with streams of contradictory commands.
Yet the apparent confusion masked an order that was
strict, a discipline that was never questioned. Everywhere
there were eyes that watched and ears that listened. The
sentries who lounged in the sun, apparently asleep, were
in reality very much awake and ready for action at the
least sign of trouble.

For the moment the barracks were quiet. They seemed
half deserted. A heat haze hung over the courtyard, and
from one corner came the muted sound of regimental
music, drums and trumpets echoing lethargically into the
general stillness. Over the far side of the courtyard a company of sweating recruits were being put through their
paces by an evil-tempered N.C.O. In general he followed
the school of thought which states that the louder and the
longer a man shouts the more he is likely to achieve
results. But today it was too hot, and he conducted the
exercises in a grim and sullen silence.

On the whole, in spite of the harsh discipline, it was a
fairly cushy billet. The duties weren't too strenuous, and
as for the executions, in which we were required to par-
ticipate every three days—well, a man became used to it
after a while. When all was said and done, there wasn't so
very much difference between pressing the trigger as a
member of a firing squad and pressing the trigger when

you were a member of a tank crew. Either way it spelt death for some poor devil.

'That's war,' said the Legionnaire, every time it happened.

That afternoon we were on guard duty outside the courthouse. Those unfortunate enough to be on trial had to form a queue and wait their turn, as if on a visit to the cinema. Inevitably one or two of them begged cigarettes from us, and inevitably we provided them.

'Here you are, chum.'

Porta handed over a half-full packet, and an S.D. man turned to glare at him.

'Don't give anything to that bastard! He killed one of our boys!'

He was only a boy himself. Porta, suddenly afflicted with acute deafness, held out a light and grinned companionably. The S.D. man turned crimson.

'Just make the most of it,' he said, between his teeth. 'You won't be alive to enjoy it this time tomorrow.'

The boy hunched an arrogantly indifferent shoulder.

'You're mighty proud,' said Gregor, with a shake of the head. 'Great big ships at night, son ... little paper boats in the morning, eh?'

'You think I care? The whole damned lot of you can go to hell!'

'Why us?' demanded Porta, with a grin. 'Why not your jolly red brothers in Moscow? Honestly, it beats me what a kid like you sees in 'em!'

'I happen to be a Communist,' said the boy, very stiff. 'Freedom for the workers is the only thing that interests me.'

'Oh, sure,' agreed Porta, soothingly. 'And tomorrow you'll be dead, and where will it have got you? Apart from a stone slab over your head, if that's any comfort ... And all the time that you're lying six foot underground they'll still go on persecuting the poor bleeding workers. You think it's any better in bleeding Moscow?' Porta turned and spat. 'Don't make me laugh! You just go there and try it, mate. You'd change your idea quick enough after a few days.'

197

'So? Is it any better in Nazi Germany?'

'Did I ever claim it was?'

'Well, is it?'

'Of course it isn't! But here in France it is, and you'd see it if you only stopped to think about it. You want to speak out against authority—right? You do it—right? Because you're in France, and you can do things like that over here. You try doing it in Moscow and I wouldn't give a couple of lousy kopeks for your chances.'

'That's beside the point. I'm fighting against Fascism.'

'Come off it!' said Porta. 'Fascism, my eye! You know what you've done, don't you? You've gone and killed one of your own poor bleeding workers that you're fighting so damned hard to save! He may have been a German, I grant you that, but he was still a worker. Before the war, he was a worker. And you've gone and clobbered him. For what?'

'For France! I'm fighting for France like any other good Frenchman!'

'Well, make your mind up,' said Porta, disgustedly.

'And just see where it gets you, in any case,' added the Legionnaire. 'That's what comes of carrying out orders given by the English. They tell you to go out and kill someone or go out and blow up a bridge, or go out and put a bullet through your head, and you all run about bleating like a flock of sheep, falling over yourselves to do what they say.'

'That is not true! I'm fighting for liberty!'

'Liberty? Or Communism?'

'They're one and the same!'

'Balls,' said the Legionnaire. 'Why don't you get yourself sent behind the Russian lines as a German spy? Kill two birds with one stone that way. Save yourself from the firing squad and learn a bit of the truth about life.'

The boy turned sullenly away. From somewhere further down the line a melancholy voice wailed out a question.

'What is it they're accusing me of?' A paper-thin man in the overalls of a French railway worker spread out appealing hands. 'I haven't done anything!'

'Well, for God's sake,' warned Gregor, 'whatever you say to them when you get in there don't keep repeating that you haven't done anything. They won't believe you and you'll just make 'em mad.'

'But I haven't done anything!'

'Maybe not, but there's no place for innocents in this world, believe me ... Confess whatever they want you to confess. Tell 'em anything you like, if it'll keep you from the firing squad.'

'But what am I to confess? I haven't done anything! It's all a mistake!'

One of the S.D. guards came out with a sound piece of advice.

'Invent something—something small, something they'll believe in. But make sure it's not something that'll carry the death sentence. For instance, firearms. Don't even mention the subject. They'll all go berserk if they think you've been nicking guns. You'll be condemned out of hand if you so much as hint at it.'

'But what *have* I done?' bleated the melancholy man.

'Oh'—the guard pulled a face—'bashed a soldier over the head with an iron bar?'

'What for?' said the man, bewildered.

'Oh Christ, how the hell should I know? Because you felt like it, I suppose!'

'But I wouldn't—I mean, I couldn't——'

A fellow-prisoner came to his aid.

'My group pinched a truck. Don't know if that's any use to you. You can come in on the job if you like ... Only trouble is, the shits are bound to check up on it. They always do. That's their whole damned trouble, they're too damned thorough!'

'How about the black market?' suggested Porta. 'That's always a good one.'

'But I don't know anyone—anyone who does that sort of thing——'

'Of course you don't know anyone!' agreed the S.D. man. 'That's one of the first rules of the game: never admit to knowing anyone, or they'll keep you in prison till you rot.'

'Trying to drag names and addresses out of you,' explained Porta. 'Best to say you were alone.'

Helplessly, the man shook his head. We watched him walk into the courtroom, and we didn't give much for his chances. Then minutes later he reappeared. To our amazement, he was full of smiles.

'I did it! They believed it!'

'Did what?' said Gregor.

'Believed what?' demanded Porta.

'I'm a black marketeer,' said the man, happily. 'Three months in prison!'

He went off to serve his unjust sentence with tears of gratitude in his eyes. We discussed the phenomenon for a few minutes until one of the S.D. men started up again, poking the young Communist in the chest and generally doing his best to goad him.

'If I had my way, I'd hang you! Hang the lot of you! Bloody Reds! You killed my father back in 1933—you'll say you were too young to remember that, I suppose, but you're just as guilty as the rest of 'em! You're all bloody Commies, aren't you?'

'Leave him be,' growled Porta. 'He's only got a few hours left, for God's sake! Leave him in peace, can't you?'

'He's a Jew,' said the S.D. man, doggedly. 'I can smell 'em half a kilometre off ... You're a bloody Jew, aren't you, little red brother?'

The boy tilted his head.

'I am a Jew,' he acknowledged.

'Good! That's good! They'll be pulling your eyes out this time tomorrow, and I'll be right there, helping 'em.'

Seconds later, the boy was called into the courtroom. He did not reappear for a full half hour, and when he did he had no cause for smiles: he had been sentenced to death, as we had foreseen. They had even added a rider that there was to be no right of appeal.

'You see?' said Porta, sadly, as we accompanied the boy back to Fresnes in the prison van. 'It doesn't do to be so proud. Why the hell did you get mixed up in all this Communist business? You probably mean well, but people like you aren't going to cut the war short—not even by one bleeding minute, you aren't. And it just ain't worth it.'

'How old are you, boy?' demanded the Old Man, gently.

'I shall be eighteen tomorrow.' He corrected himself. 'I would have been eighteen tomorrow. Maybe I still shall. It depends when they decide to murder me.'

'Too young to die,' grumbled Porta. 'Why didn't someone put the young idiot over their knees and wallop some sense into him while there was still a chance?'

'Eighteen?' said the Old Man, thoughtfully. He turned to regard Heide. 'Who's on guard duty, Julius? Is it you?'

'Ah-huh.' Heide nodded, vaguely, his thoughts plainly elsewhere. 'It's me all right. Twenty-four hours of bloody boredom...' He suddenly jerked his head up and looked at the Old Man. The light of suspicion dawned in his eyes. 'Why? What's it to you who's on guard duty? Listen, Old Man'—he leaned forward, earnestly—'don't try getting mixed up in this business. We don't want any trouble.'

The Old Man remained silent; just rubbed a finger up and down his nose a few times and said nothing.

At 18.00 hours we relieved the guard on Block 4. At that time of day a prison is always at its busiest. The evening meal is being dished up, prisoners have to be escorted to and from dining rooms, cells and lavatories. The Hauptfeldwebel took his usual evening tour of inspection, heavy keys turned in locks, hinges squeaked, doors rattled and slammed. The place was a madhouse of activity.

I stuck close behind the large door at the end of the main corridor, peering out through the grille. Close by, Barcelona was finishing off a game of cards in the cell of three condemned men, and elsewhere in the prison, under cover of all the general six o'clock activity, Little John had taken the opportunity of gaining illegal entry to the Hauptfeldwebel's office.

He ushered Porta into the room with him and closed the door behind them, whereupon Porta, very calm and very casual, sat down at the Hauptfeldwebel's desk, and with the Hauptfeldwebel's pen, signed the Hauptfeld-webel's signature upon an exit permit for the young Jew who had been sentenced to die. The exit permit was granted on the grounds of 'further interrogation by the Gestapo at 19.00 hours'.

'Sounds good?' said Porta.

'Sounds fine to me,' said Little John.

As a house-breaking and forgery team, Little John and Porta almost certainly had no equals in the German Army. The lock had not yet been discovered that Little John could not pick; the signature had not yet been written that Porta could not reproduce. The firm, upright hand that flourished so boldly at the foot of the exit per-mit was later to be instinctively claimed by the Haupt-feldwebel as his own. Only by sheer process of deduction was it subsequently recognized as a piece of blatant forgery.

Porta tossed the square of cardboard across to Barce-lona, who had arrived to supervise the operation, and leaned back with his feet on the polished desk.

'I never realized it was that comfortable, being a Hauptfeldwebel ... What a cushy number those idle bastards have! Look at this——'

He prodded the soft seat of the swivel chair, but Little John was more interested in testing the qualities of the sofa, and Barcelona was hovering nervously by the door with the sweat pouring off his face.

'For Christ's *sake*! You've got no more nerves than a pair of bloody oxen! Get off your fat arses and get out of here!'

'What's all the fuss about?' protested Little John. 'We're only carrying out orders, aren't we?'

'That's what bugs him,' said Porta, idly opening a drawer and peering inside it. 'It was him that gave the orders ... Break into the Hauptfeldwebel's office and forge his name on a bit of paper, he says. Then when you do it, he gets cold feet. Never happy, some people aren't.'

'I didn't say lounge about in his flaming chairs and ransack his desk!' snarled Barcelona.

Slowly, and with maddening precision, Little John and

Porta went about the room eliminating all possible trace of fingerprints, while Barcelona stood watching with his brow ploughed into furrows. Fortunately he was too busy watching Porta wipe the Hauptfeldwebel's pen with his handkerchief to notice Little John stuffing a fistful of cigars into his pocket.

'Come *on*, for Christ's sake, that's *enough*!'

Barcelona jerked his head viciously at them and flung the door wide open. Porta reluctantly replaced the pen and followed him into the corridor. Little John came last. He closed the door behind him and carefully inserted a piece of broken matchstick into the lock.

'What the blazes are you doing now?' hissed Barcelona.

'Saving your bleeding neck for you!' retorted Little John. 'Never open a door without examining the lock first, see? I only did that once in my life and it got me nine months in the nick: the bastard that owned the door had stuck a bit of wood into it and I hadn't noticed. So now I always have a quick gander before I do the job. You can bet your sweet life if the Hauptfeldwebel got back and found his precious matchstick missing there'd be hell to pay. As it is, he won't know a thing about it, will he?'

Barcelona shook his head, reluctantly admiring.

'All right, you win! You know what you're doing, I'll grant you that.'

He and Little John went their separate ways about the prison. Porta came to give me the O.K., and together we paid a visit to the young Jew in his cell.

'Here.' Porta flung a coat towards him. 'Get that on and come with us.'

'Why?' The boy leapt up, white-faced. 'I thought it wasn't until tomorrow?'

'What wasn't?'

'The execution.'

'It's been put off indefinitely,' I said.

'I don't believe you! Why should they?'

'Oh Christ,' said Porta. 'Get a move on, can't you? We've come to get you out of this place, we haven't got time for idle chit-chat. You'd think the least you could do would be to co-operate.'

'But——'

'But nothing! Belt up and flaming listen! I'm only going to tell you once, so make sure you take it all in. Soon as we've gone, get the hell out of here and make for the stairs. If anyone stops you, say you're going to the shithouse. If you don't see anyone, get down to the ground floor as quick as you can, and don't make any bloody noise about it. O.K.? When you reach the ground floor take the first door on your left. That'll bring you out behind the bog. Stay there, out of sight, until the lights go out. As soon as that happens, make a dash for the far side of the courtyard. Got it?'

'Yes, but——'

'Unless peace breaks out in the meantime,' continued Porta, ignoring the interruption, 'we reckon you'll have about two minutes to do it in. They'll have the lights back on again by then, and the sentries'll just about have reached you. They'll be expecting you. Fall into line with 'em, and then it's up to them to do the rest. O.K.? Just do what they tell you and you can't go wrong.'

'It's a piece of piss,' I said—I being the one convinced pessimist who could see no possibility whatsoever of the plan working.

'Course,' said Porta, 'if anything does go wrong it's only right to warn you that we should have to shoot you. Know what I mean? You get caught in the act, so to speak, we can't risk our skins more than what we're already doing.'

'Best of luck, anyway,' I said.

We returned to the guard-room to follow the course of events. Porta said he couldn't care less, anyhow, he didn't hold any brief for Communists even if they were only kids of eighteen, but when I pointed out that he could in that case have refused any part in the night's proceedings he replied by threatening to push my teeth down my throat for me if I didn't shut up, and after that the conversation tended to peter out.

The boy left his cell as soon as our footsteps faded into the distance. He closed the door quietly behind him, ran to the head of the stairs, stood listening. No one came. Seconds later he had reached the ground floor and discovered the door on his left. It squealed like a cat in ecstasy as he pulled it open, and Barcelona put both hands over his ears and raised his eyes heavenwards.

'Sweet Christ! If anyone hears that we're done for!'

'Probably are in any case,' I muttered.

The Old Man, who had been hanging about outside, pushed open the door of the guard-room and nodded towards us.

'O.K., he's out there.'

According to plan, Porta and I went off to lock up the trail of doors that had been left open. As we reached the guard-room again, all the searchlights went out in the courtyard. That was Gregor's doing. He had told us to leave it to him, and it seemed that we had left it to good advantage.

The searchlights were out for just over two minutes, and then once more they began sweeping the grounds from corner to corner. But the shadow of the fugitive was no longer to be seen hiding between the latrines and the walls of the prison. He had put the two minutes to good use and was now out of sight, lying flat on his stomach in the angle of the far wall.

Heavy footsteps approached him. He guessed that this must be the sentry patrol that was to lead him on the next stage of his journey. The raw glare of the searchlight flashed above him, along the top of the wall, into the dark recesses of the courtyard. He saw the patrol marching towards him, led by the Legionnaire and Gunther Soest. Their helmets, the hated German helmets that would have transformed the face of a saint into the grimacing mask of a gargoyle, glinted menacingly in the harsh light. The boy must have had his doubts as to the supposed friendliness of the patrol.

As they approached the spot, Gunther swore nervously under his breath. This was the second time he had assisted at a break-out, and after the first he had called vigorously upon all the saints to bear witness to the fact that he, Gunther Soest, would never be taken as a mug again.

'It just isn't worth it,' he said. 'Nothing's worth anything in this flaming war, least of all risking your life for a flaming prisoner.'

And Gunther should have known, if anyone did. He had driven a tank for eight years. During that time he had seen thirty-seven of his closest companions fried to death, and had on nine occasions narrowly escaped a similar fate himself. But on the tenth occasion his destiny had caught up with him: he had escaped with his life but left nearly all his face behind. Burning oil had eaten away eyebrows and lips, his flesh had fallen off in chunks like a well-done joint of meat. He had spent seven months in a water bed. They had wrenched him back from the edge of death, but death had nevertheless left an indelible mark on him. His hands were like parchment claws, his face a bloated purple mask. This was the man whose fiancée had been unable to conquer her horror at the sight of him, who had run off shuddering; and this was the man who for the second time was risking his life to smuggle a condemned prisoner out of Fresnes.

A Frenchman, at that. And a Jew and a Communist besides. Who knew but one day, after the war, that same Jew, that same Communist, would pass him by in the street and turn to stare in pity and disgust at that grotesque purple mask? When even your fellow countrymen were unable to conceal their feelings, what chance of a foreigner doing so?

And after the war, what would men like Gunther do? Live in a home with others of their kind? Exhibit themselves as freaks in a side show? Hide away and live in the dark where no one could see them? It seemed unlikely that normal people would ever be able to look upon them without shuddering. Yet Gunther had been handsome, once. He was used to adulation, to girls falling about his neck and vying for his attentions. Now, even his own sisters could scarcely bear to be in the same room with him, and on his last leave he had been home only two days when his mother had a nervous breakdown—on account, so the doctor said, of the the constant stress of being reminded what the war had done to her only boy.

Gunther had left home then. He had spent the rest of

his leave in an army convalescent home at Tols. There, at least, he could be with others of his kind; a whole new generation of Frankenstein monsters created by the war. They were well treated at the convalescent home, although there was a strict rule about going into the village: you could go on crutches, you could go in a wheelchair, you could go without your arms, you could go without your legs; but on no account must you go without your face. It was bad, so they said, for the country's morale. Heroes were acceptable only provided they had heroic wounds, and it was not heroic to be burned alive in a tank and end up looking repulsive. But in any case, very few of the faceless monsters had any desire to go into the village. They were still sensitive at people pointing and staring, and well they knew that no girl would ever again kiss them on the lips. For the most part, they had no lips; only a shapeless hole edged with ragged purple tissue. Some of them spoke hopefully of having their faces re-modelled after the war. That was the only reason Gunther had remained in the Army and had come back to do more than his fair share. It was his one lifeline, the belief that if he saw the thing through to the very end the Army would surely reward him by giving him a new face? Provided, of couse, that Germany won the war. Men like Gunther could simply not afford to consider the alternative.

The patrol drew level with the young boy, crouched down in the shadows. Silently he rose to his feet and merged in with them, marching in step. Their rhythm never faltered. They smoothly swallowed him up and bore him along in their midst. At the end of the wall, where it turned sharply to the left, they drew to a halt. The Legionnaire spoke rapidly without looking at the boy.

'You'll find a rope ready secured up there. As soon as the searchlight's passed overhead, make a dash for it. You'll have approximately thirty seconds to get over the top and down the other side, so you'll have to move pretty fast . . . Take this and use it if you have to, but not other-wise. It's an identity card, but it was done in a hurry so don't place a hundred per cent reliance on it. It'll be all right for a casual check.'

The searchlight flashed across them. The patrol stood bunched together, hiding the boy from its gaze.

'Get across Paris as quick as you can. You've got about two hours to daylight. Make for the Sacré-Coeur in Montmartre. Go into the third confessional box and say you've stolen some flowers from a cemetery. When the priest asks you what flowers they were, you reply, myosotis. He'll take over from then on?'

'A priest?' muttered the boy, uneasily.

The Legionnaire raised an amused eyebrow.

'You prefer the Gestapo?'

'Of course not!' The boy flushed in the darkness. 'You know I'm very grateful to you for all your help——'

'Don't speak too soon, you've a long way to go yet. Here comes the searchlight again. You'd better make a bolt for it after this one.'

The beam swung across them. The Legionnaire gave the boy a quick shove, Gunther stood by to help, but he was as lithe as any panther and was atop the wall within a couple of seconds. The Legionnaire fingered his machine-gun, flicking back the safety catch and nodding at Gunther to be ready. If the searchlight should pick out the boy in the act of escaping they would have no alternative but to shoot.

It seemed that the finger of light was on them again almost immediately. The Legionnaire pressed his gun hard into his shoulder.

'This is it,' muttered Gunther.

The light swung over them and across the wall. They trained their machine-guns upon the spot where the fugitive was fumbling for the rope. At the precise moment when the light reached him, the boy disappeared from sight, slipping down the rope as if it were a greased pole and doubtless ending up with hands that were raw to the bone. But he had made it.

The Legionnaire casually replaced the safety catch and slung the gun over his shoulder. The patrol continued imperturbably on its way.

'Well, the Old Man will be pleased,' remarked the Legionnaire, a few paces further on. 'It was his lunatic idea.'

'Lunatic's the word,' grumbled Gunther. 'Where's the point of it all?'

'I'm not sure that there is any.'

'So why the hell do we do it?'

'Haven't the faintest idea,' said the Legionnaire, with a smile.

'Well, neither have I,' said Gunther. 'And I swear before God that's the last time anyone's taking *me* for a mug again!'

Half an hour later, the guard was relieved. And from all over the prison our voices came in chorus:

'Nothing to report.'

CHAPTER TWELVE

The commanding officer of the 103rd Cavalry, Colonel Relling, had of late been enjoying a general run of luck, which culminated in what was perhaps the greatest triumph of his career: the double arrest of Colonel Toumy, the head of the French Resistance, and of Yeo-Thomas, the British Secret Service agent. Thanks to the capture of these two men the Germans were able to set in motion an avalanche of arrests throughout the whole of France.

The man who succeeded Toumy was General Jussieu, and it was a toss-up whether the French general or the German colonel should receive the final accolade for general cruelty, brutality and total lack of scruple when it came to the taking of human life.

A wave of terror swept the country. People were knifed, shot, strangled, murdered in every conceivable way and in quite a few that were so bestial as to be almost inconceivable. Administrative offices were blown up, supply columns butchered, sentries killed in their dozens; bridges and trains were such common targets as no longer to cause any comment. A well-drilled group under the command of French officers launched a successful attack on the Gestapo headquarters at Bourg-en-Bresse and dispatched everyone they found with a bullet in the back of the neck.

And inevitably, after a time, organized gangs of criminals jumped on the bandwagon, attached themselves to the Resistance, and under their umbrella committed an appalling series of thefts, rapes and murders. They were soon being hunted down not only by the Germans but by the French as well. It was later maintained that the majority of the crimes could be laid at the door of deserters from the German Army or from the Italian Fifth Army, of Spanish Communists and of foreign agitators. Be that as it may, whatever their nationality they were shot without trial as soon as they were caught and their bodies buried without ceremony.

WITH 'REDCOAT' IN MONTMARTRE

'It's out at Malakoff,' explained Redcoat, earnestly. 'Getting hold of the thing is no problem. It's how to get it over here that bothers me. I've got to the stage where even just thinking about it gives me a belly-ache ... Yet there must be a way of doing it.'

'Why not borrow a truck and bring it over in that?' suggested Barcelona. 'We could always forge a transport pass.'

Heide shook his head.

'Far too risky. Never get away with it.'

'The best way is the easiest way,' announced Porta. 'And the easiest way is simply to walk it here.'

We looked at him dubiously.

'You must be raving mad!' gasped Heide. 'Some interfering busybody's only got to catch sight of us and ask us what we're doing and we wouldn't have a leg to stand on.'

The Old Man scratched behind his ear with the stem of his pipe.

'Julius is quite right. It's far too dangerous.'

'It's a shitty idea,' added Little John, to clinch matters.

Redcoat left us to attend to some new customers. He strode across the room with his long white apron flapping about his legs, his hair and his beard floating gently about his face. His body was short and round, incredibly balanced on two dainty feet. His face, in comparison, was large and heavy-jowled, tomato in colour, full moon in shape. It beamed with fat good humour and was usually glowing with grease.

The bistro, with its well-worn tables and chairs, its

greasy walls and torn oilcloth, stank of revolution; of informers, deserters and black marketeers. Porta, who had led us there originally, was in his element.

Redcoat settled the new arrivals and made his way back to our table, carried along on a strong smell of burning that came from the kitchens.

'I tell you what!' Little John greeted him. 'It's all a lot of hot air about nothing. Look here'—he picked up a salt cellar—'we take the thing—we bash it on the head'—he slammed the salt cellar on to the table, and it immediately shattered—'and we carry it away. Quite simple. I don't see why you're making all the fuss.'

Porta frowned.

'Are they armed?' he demanded.

'If not, they're bigger fools than I take them to be,' retorted Redcoat.

'So what?' Little John shrugged. 'Mere amateurs. We'll clobber anyone who draws on us.'

'Why don't you give your arse a chance?' said Heide, irritably. 'You've got no more brain than a flaming pea! There's already enough commotion about this damned Communist that escaped, don't let's stir up another hornets' nest for Christ's sake! I tell you, we haven't heard the last of that affair. The Gestapo's going over the whole of Paris with a fine tooth comb trying to get hold of the people responsible for it. Any moment now someone's going to sit down and put his brains to work and discover just what did happen.'

Porta gave one of his disgusting guffaws.

'The Hauptfeldwebel hasn't tumbled to it yet. He still swears blind it's his signature on the exit permit, even though he can't remember doing it. Then there's that fool of an N.C.O. who swears he saw the prisoner going off in the afternoon transport!' He cackled again. 'I could tell 'em different, if they asked me ... When the transport left, he was down in the bogs playing dice with me! Still, I should worry. They want to think he escaped somewhere between Fresnes and Gestapo headquarters, then let 'em. All the better for us!'

'Crap!' said Heide, angrily. 'They're not as bloody

stupid as you seem to think. That boy had already been tried and found guilty and sentenced to death. He didn't even have any right of appeal. There was less than fourteen hours to go before he was due for the chopper. So sooner or later some clever Dick's going to ask why the hell the Gestapo wanted him for further questioning. And once they start asking themselves that, it's only going to be a short step to discovering that the bloody Gestapo never did want him for further questioning. And then what happens?'

'The war'll be over by then,' said Porta, imperturbably. 'What've you done with the kid, anyway?'

'In the kitchen,' said Redcoat, simply.

'In the kitchen?' roared Heide. '*Here?*'

'Where else?' said Redcoat, simply.

'My God, that just about puts the tin lid on it!'

Heide made an agitated movement of disgust and banged the table with a clenched fist. On the whole, I sympathized with him. I must admit I wasn't too happy about the arrangement myself.

'What's up with him?' asked Little John, staring at Heide.

'I'll tell you what's up!' panted Heide, by now thoroughly over-excited. 'The Gestapo have got about nine million men scattered over Paris looking for that worm, that's what the matter is! And when they look for someone, believe me they really look! And once they've picked him up it's only a question of hours before the sod talks. My God!' He shook his head, violently. 'The idea of a rope round your neck might appeal to you, but it certainly doesn't do anything for me!'

Redcoat smiled kindly at Heide.

'No need to get worked up about it. They'd never recognize him in a month of Sundays ... Hang on and I'll show you.'

The transformation was remarkable. I certainly should never have recognized this cretinous country bumpkin of a kitchen hand as the bright, alert youth who had escaped from Fresnes. The black hair was now unpleasantly red; the smooth upper lip had suddenly burst into bloom with a wild moustache; heavy spectacles cut his face in half. He wore clumsy boots and trousers that ended way above his ankles.

'How's that?' said Redcoat, proudly.

'Bloody awful,' muttered Heide. 'He should have been got right away from Paris by now.'

'Easier said than done, my friend.'

'Here!' said Porta, suddenly thrusting out a hairy wrist and looking at his watch. 'Where the devil have the others got to?'

'Christ knows,' said Heide, eagerly seizing upon the opportunity for another mournful tirade. 'They should never have gone off in the first place. Gallivanting about Paris when the whole place is stiff with Gestapo. They're probably being interrogated even as we sit here——'

'Keep your hair on,' said Barcelona, with a grin. 'The Legionnaire knows Paris like the back of his hand, and in any case they've got Gunther with them. His face is an Ausweis (exit permit) in itself. Not even the Gestapo would have the nerve to stop Gunther.'

'That's all you know,' said Heide, bitterly.

Other customers were clamouring for Redcoat's attention. Some of the more vociferous were demanding a song, and Redcoat lumbered into the centre of the room, his face awash with grease and good humour, and prepared to oblige. Accompanied by Porta on an old violin and a girl with an accordion, he flung back his head and roared forth, in lusty tenor, a song in praise of Paris. His voice was not unpleasant and most of us had had a fair amount to drink. Even Heide so far forgot himself as to join in a chorus or two. The bistro was soon a riot of noise. The fat black cook, Janette (whom we knew to be an active member of the Resistance) stood shouting and clapping at the entrance to the kitchen. Feet stamped in unison, glasses and cutlery were thumped on table tops.

It was a shock when, about half an hour later, the doors were kicked open and through the gloom we saw the glinting badges of the Feldgendarmerie. They burst inside with their usual lack of manners, their heavy boots crashing on the floors, their inevitable guns at the ready.

The atmosphere changed on the instant. Janette fled back to her kitchen and we heard the sounds of frenzied activity, saucepans clashing and taps running. The rest of us fell suddenly silent. Men buried their heads in their glasses or became intensely interested in their fingernails or blank sections of the floor. If by chance you caught anyone's eye you saw nothing but fear, suspicion, hatred, and you both looked away in a state of confusion. Porta stood sullenly with the violin dangling from one hand. The girl with the accordion scuttled to a far corner of the room like a spider suddenly exposed to the light.

The leader of the patrol, a Stabsfeldwebel, stood for a moment by the doors, coldly staring round. He finally fixed his eyes upon Porta.

'You! Obergefreiter!'

He stalked across to him, and Porta watched him come, a brooding expression on his face.

'What are you doing here? Do you have a permit to be out at night?'

Reluctantly, Porta straightened up and produced his pass. We knew he was reluctant. It was not in Porta's nature than to be other than insolent to men such as the Stabsfeldwebel. But he knew, as well as the rest of us, that our position was far from secure. It was not the time to be drawing attention to ourselves, and Porta was no fool. Besides which, the Stabsfeldwebel was no ordinary Stabsfeldwebel. We knew him both by sight and by reputation. For four years he and his commandos had spent their nights in scouring every bar, every club, every brothel in Paris, and never a night passed by they hauled in some poor devil for questioning. And to be hauled in by Stabsfeldwebel Malinowski was virtually a death sentence. His success could be measured by the Knight's Cross that now hung round his neck.

'Who are you with?' he demanded, thrusting the permit back to Porta.

Porta waved a hand towards the rest of us, and we sat demure and upright at our table doing our best to look like model soldiers. Malinowski glanced contemptuously at us, nodded and passed on.

They searched the bistro from top to bottom. A young girl who was using the toilets and knew nothing of their arrival was commanded to open the door and show her papers. The kitchen was ransacked. Every box and every tin was opened and examined. The stove came under particular suspicion and they spent a good ten minutes raking out the ashes, while Janette looked on with arms akimbo and the nearest she could get to a sneer on her plump face. The boy was given one cursory glance and then ignored.

The whole of the top floor was searched. Clothes were pulled out of chests and cupboards and tossed to the ground. Blankets and sheets were ripped off the beds, mattresses and eiderdowns were prodded and poked, exploratory hands dived into storage tanks and cisterns.

At the end of an hour they gave up the search, but it seemed unlikely that they would leave the bistro without picking on someone as a scapegoat for the night's work. Malinowski stood by the bar, his gaze flickering from table to table. His men stood attentively by his side, waiting for the master to pounce. We all sat silent, wondering where the axe would fall.

Slowly, the Stabsfeldwebel pulled from his pocket a bundle of photographs. Slowly he looked through them; very deliberately he made his selection. In two strides he was across the room, standing before a group of young people who had been quietly drinking together most of the evening.

'Deutsche Feldpolizei. Ausweis, bitte.'

'(German Police. Your papers, please.)'

He was addressing an insignificant-looking boy, whose clothes were grey and crumpled and whose features were totally unmemorable. The papers were closely examined by the Stabsfeldwebel.

'Forgeries,' he said, grimly. 'We've been on the look out for you for the past two months. Now that we've found you we shall be able to demonstrate in some detail the way we treat deserters ... You must have had help! Who helped you?'

I imagine he did not seriously anticipate an answer. I

think most people in the room were astonished when one of the girls at the table immediately sprang to her feet and claimed the honour.

'Is she mad?' whispered Little John, in his usual audible fashion.

Malinowski turned to regard us. Barcelona aimed a vicious kick at Little John's shin and Heide hissed angrily between his teeth. This was not the time to be provoking a man in Malinowski's position.

Our warning came too late. Malinowski was a creature of instinct. His senses told him that there might, after all, be more to find in this particular bistro than a mere deserter and his girl-friend, and leaving a couple of his men busy with the handcuffs he led the rest of the dogs away with their tails in the air and their noses once again pressed into the ground. I guessed that Little John's whispered comment and our immediate reactions had set the Stabsfeldwebel off on a search that could continue throughout the night if he felt really vindictive. It was known that he loathed soldiers who had been on active service at the front, and there was a rumour that only two days previously he had actually arrested an Oberleutnant who had been decorated with the Iron Cross.

'That's it,' muttered Heide, gloomily. 'That's done it. I said it would happen. And all for a bloody Jew!'

'I think we shall try the kitchens again,' said Malinowski.

Redcoat moved anxiously to his elbow, protesting volubly about burnt soup and ruined dinners, but Malinowski, with a faint smile, pushed him out of the way.

'This is more important than burnt soup.'

'But my customers——'

At that moment, more customers arrived. Everyone turned instinctively to the door. The man who first entered seemed at a quick glance, to be wearing a stocking mask over his face, hideously distorting his features. Closer attention revealed that he had no features to be distorted. His eyes were slits, his nose little more than two slight indentations, his mouth a fringed and gaping hole. He had no eyebrows and the colour of his skin was mottled purple. Round the neck, which was supported by a stiff leather collar, hung the Knight's Cross.

'Well?' said Gunther, out of his parody of a mouth. 'Have you given up the habit of saluting, Stabsfeld-webel?'

Malinowski clicked his heels together and slowly brought his right arm up to his forehead. There was little else he could do. He might be Stabsfeldwedel Malinowski and he might have a Knight's Cross of his own, but a soldier with Gunther's disfigurement could make what demands he liked. If Gunther cared to bring out his revolver and shoot Malinowski dead, subsequently claiming that the man had insulted him, no one would hesitate to believe in the justice of his cause.

'Fahnenjunker!' Malinowski's tone just managed to be respectful. 'We are patrolling the 18th arondissement, according to orders. We've just picked up a deserter we've been searching for for two months, together with the woman who assisted him.'

'Good,' said Gunther, encouragingly. 'Thank you, Stabsfeldwebel. I take it you have now concluded your business here?'

Malinowski hesitated. Gunther turned casually away, as if there were an end to the conversation. Both his legs, from the knees down, were made of tin, but it was not immediately noticeable. It had taken him several weeks of superhuman energy and determination to learn to walk again, and also to cope with a left arm that was composed of four pieces of steel. He had wanted to die, at first, and no one really knew what it was that now gave him the will to go on living. He could have become an officer in the Waffen S.S., it was offered to him when he left hospital, but he had always served with the black hussars and it was to us that he returned when passed once more as 'fit for duty'. He felt at home with us. Not only were we his friends, but we were possibly the only people in the world who could look upon him with the same degree of detachment as we looked upon each other.

Again there was silence in the bistro. Everyone tense. Everyone staring at Gunther.

Calmly he drew out his cigarette case, extracted a cigarette and place it in his lipless mouth. Malinowski was no longer staring at Gunther, but rather at the cigarette case. It was gold, ostentatiously decorated with the red star of Russia and the hammer and sickle. Gunther held it out to him.

'Pretty, don't you think? A souvenir of Stalingrad, as you probably guessed.' He closed the case with a snap and pushed it back in his pocket. 'Were you ever in the trenches, Stabsfeldwebel? Three hundred thousand German soldiers died at Stalingrad, did you know that? Those of us that survived'—he spoke the words in quotes—'are entitled to some little bauble as a souvenir, don't you agree?'

Malinowski was seen to swallow, but he said nothing. Gunther's tone suddenly changed.

'If you've finished your business in here, I should be very glad to see the back of you!'

The Stabsfeldwebel really had no alternative but to leave. The doors closed on the last of his men and an audible sigh of relief swept the bistro.

'Looks as if we got back in the nick of time,' remarked the Legionnaire, dryly, as he left his post by the door and strolled over to our table.

'It's ridiculous,' said Heide. 'It's the height of lunacy. He should have been at the other end of France by now.'

No one took any notice of Heide. We were too busy filling Gunther with congratulatory drinks.

'Ah well,' he said, modestly. 'One has to make use of one's disadvantages or where's the point of them?'

The girl with the accordion came out of the shadows and began to play a dance tune. Porta took up his violin and Redcoat began to smile again. Gradually the tension died away. Heide happily drank himself into a near stupor and was incapable of doing more than grunt. Little John roamed about the room pinching girls' bottoms and telling dirty jokes to anyone who looked as if he might be even remotely shocked, and Gunther, full of strong red wine, stole a little girl in a yellow dress from under Barcelona's nose and began to dance with her.

'Vive la France!' shouted Porta, deliriously.

The Legionnaire was drinking steadily. He would soon join Heide in his stupor. Gunther was fast going the same way, and the little girl in yellow had stopped closing her eyes to avoid his face and was sitting on his lap giggling. There were occasional interruptions from the world outside, the sound of rifle shots, muffled explosions, the roar of aeroplanes overhead, but they were steadfastly ignored. The war had been going on too long for anyone to be bothered with it any more. Barcelona suddenly dug me in the ribs.

'Watch out. Door's opening.'

We stiffened automatically, half expecting it to be Malinowski returning. But this time it was Jacqueline, the girl I had met among the flowers in Normandy and who had given me real coffee to drink. There had been other things as well, of course, but somehow I always primarily connected her with the scent of flowers and the fragrance of fresh coffee.

I had seen a fair bit of her since we had come to Paris. These last weeks I had been meeting her in secret almost every day, but this was the first time I had dared make an open rendezvous with her here, in the café, and the moment she stepped through the door I regretted it. Porta, of course, recognized her immediately. He eyed her up and down as she, never doubting her welcome, walked towards our table. She was wearing a soft green muslin thing that made her look very pale and beautiful, but I wished I hadn't told her to come.

'So, you been having it off with that bird from Normandy?' said Porta, slyly. 'How long's that been going on, then? Some time, by the looks of things. You want to get rid of her, mate, before you get really tied up. That bird's in love, and women in love can be dangerous.'

'You don't know what you're talking about,' I said, coldly.

'Oh no?' jeered Porta. 'Remember how she blarted her eyeballs out that time in Normandy?'

'And what's that to do with you?'

'Everything!'

It was Heide, now, emerging from his stupor and joining in the battle. He glared across at Jacqueline, seized me by the collar and began breathing all over me, his small, bloodshot eyes staring with fixed maliciousness into mine.

'It's everything to do with us! You and your French tart! You can knock the arse off it all day and every day as far as I'm concerned, but *don't bring it in here!*' He took himself off my chest and pulled out his revolver. 'Porta's quite right, women like that are dangerous. They get jealous, they get emotional, they get too interested in what's going on. And worst of all, they talk.'

'What's happening?' demanded Gunther, from the far end of the table.

Barcelona whispered something to him. I saw Gunther staring across at Jacqueline, taking in every detail of her face and figure. Barcelona looked at me, and shook his head disapprovingly. The Legionnaire leaned back in his chair and began casually cleaning his nails with the point of his knife. Jacqueline smiled at me.

'What's up with you today? You're behaving very oddly.'

I took her across to the door and explained the situation. It was my fault entirely. I should have known better than to meet her in such a place. Paris was dangerous. Spies were everywhere and you had only to make one mistake and you could count yourself as dead. Jacqueline understood me perfectly. She asked no questions, raised no objections. We simply arranged a different meeting-place for the following day and she slipped quietly away down the darkened street. It was a relief to see her go.

Slowly the bistro began to empty, until at last we were alone. The doors were locked, Redcoat produced a map of Paris and we spread it out on the table.

'Obviously,' said Porta, 'the thing is likely to be bloody heavy——'

'I hope so,' said Redcoat. 'I shall be disappointed if it isn't.'

'How are we to get it over the bridge?'

'Carry it,' said Little John, brightly.

'Tell it to swim across the river.'

'They don't swim——'

'Course they do, don't be so bleeding stupid!'

'But it is a valid point,' said the Legionnaire, seriously. 'All the bridges are closely guarded.'

'Perhaps if you went in daytime?' suggested Redcoat. 'There'd be more people about. You could slip over unnoticed.'

Barcelona shook his head.

'No can do. I couldn't get the necessary passes.'

Porta suddenly jabbed a filthy finger on to the map.

'Here! We'll go right now and pick it up.'

'And how do we get over the bridge?'

'No idea until we get there. Can't be bothered with making plans all the time. That's what the flaming Prussians do, and see where it's got them. Eight days after the last war ended they all put their heads together and started plotting for the next one. It ain't worth it. Let things take their course, that's what I say.'

'And I say we ought to have a plan,' said Heide, obstinately.

'We don't need a plan. I've got a couple of rubber stamps in my pocket with "Top Secret" written on them.'

'What the hell good are they?'

'You'd be surprised,' said Porta. 'I can work miracles with a rubber stamp.'

'You make me sick,' grumbled Heide. 'You all make me sick. All this damn fool nonsense. If it's not Jews, it's——'

'Suppose they fire on us?' interrupted the Old Man, who had so far sat silent and frowning. 'Suppose we run into a patrol?'

'What sort of a patrol?'

'Malinowski's crowd, for a start!' snarled Heide. 'Rubber stamps won't be much help with those boys, no matter how top secret they are!'

'That's simple,' said Porta. 'We just make damn sure that we fire first.'

'Yes, and you've only got to let one of them get away and the game's up.'

'None of 'em won't get away!' Little John leaned forward with a belligerent expression on his face. 'We'll take bazookas with us.'

'Walk round Paris at the dead of night carrying bazookas?' sneered Heide. 'They'll think we're a load of bloody Commies!'

The Legionnaire stood up.

'I'm sick of talking,' he said, abruptly. 'We'll play it by ear.'

'Just what I said,' said Porta.

'So when do we go?' demanded Little John, eagerly. 'Right now?'

The Legionnaire raised a cold eyebrow.

'Certainly not. We'll go tomorrow night.'

CHAPTER THIRTEEN

The first of them appeared at the window. Climbed out on to the narrow ledge and balanced precariously for a few seconds, searching above and below for some kind of handhold. He found none. A sudden shot rang out and the man plummeted head-first into the void.

A second man appeared. He also climbed out on to the narrow ledge, then swung across like a cat and wrapped himself round a water pipe that ran the length of the wall. Cautiously he began to lower himself groundwards. Another shot ran out. The second man joined the first on the asphalt courtyard so far below.

The third man did not wait to be shot. His silhouette appeared briefly at the window; hung for a moment in space; then hurtled downwards in a swallow dive to share the fate of his companions.

But the incendiary bomb had done its work well. Flames poured forth from every window save for two small ones right at the top of the high building. Already a crowd of men could be seen up there. Two of them jumped at the same time and a hail of machine-gun bullets accompanied them all the way to the ground. The Gestapo were taking no chances.

It was at this point that we left our hiding-place and walked away. We had seen enough of the slaughter. It was the Gestapo revenging themselves upon a nest of Resistance workers for the recent death of fourteen secret police. But they were doing more than just revenge themselves: they were having a ball.

When the massacre was over they returned to their vehicle. Both the driver and the man left on guard were lying down in pools of their own blood, with their throats slit almost from ear to ear.

That was a scene that took place in Paris, one night in August 1944.

NIGHT'S JOURNEY ACROSS PARIS

The night was black. There was a pale slip of a moon, somewhere above the clouds, but the sky was generally overcast and not a single star was showing.

The parish of Malakoff was dark and silent. The cats, advancing warlike upon each other in the middle of the road, seemed the only living creatures there. They paused to consider us a while, with that look of contempt that seems the natural expression of all cats, then hurled themselves screaming upon each other. We gave them a wide berth.

Two members of the Feldgendarmerie suddenly appeared on bicycles. They turned their heads to look at us as they passed, obviously a trifle suspicious, and Little John raised his fist and shook it at them.

'None of that!' snapped the Old Man. 'Just remember that for once in a while we're out to avoid trouble, not go running after it.'

Little John gazed broodingly after the two cyclists.

'Any nonsense from those shits and I'll punch their teeth in for them.'

'For God's sake!' snapped Barcelona. 'Are you coming or aren't you?'

We caught up with Porta at the corner of the rue Bérenger and the rue du Nord.

'You sure you know where the bloody thing is?' demanded Gunther. 'Every damned hovel looks alike in this place. I don't feel in the mood for a circular tour.'

'I know where it is,' said Porta. He turned slowly round, taking his bearings in the darkness. 'It's not far from here. I remember we came in before by that road opposite. Over by the bistro, a man was shot. I remember the bistro. Let's see if there's any trace of the bullets on the wall.'

'Dozens of 'em,' said Gunther, having crossed over and examined the place.

'Really?'

Porta, too, had to cross the road and look. The Old Man made an impatient gesture.

'Can't we get a move on?'

'I'm not stopping you,' said Porta. 'Who invited you on this trip, anyway? Hang on a second.'

He ducked down, disappeared under a low archway and was gone for several minutes.

'Christ almighty!' Barcelona cast a nervous glance over his shoulder. 'Where's the fool gone now? I wish I hadn't been talked into this thing in the first place. Why can't we behave like everyone else? Why do we always have to be out looking for trouble?'

'Search me,' said the Old Man, glumly.

'Why doesn't someone go and drag him out?' I complained, having no intention of doing it myself.

Porta reappeared, grinning smugly.

'Just been casting my eye over the women of the district.' He gave Little John a lewd wink. 'Tomorrow evening, outside the cinema, place Clichy. You can think of me.'

'You bastard!' said Little John, automatically. 'I bet you never even asked her if she had a pal!'

'Look, are we going or aren't we?' I demanded.

'And what's more to the point is *where* are we going?' grumbled the Old Man.

'Right in here,' said Porta, ducking under the low archway. 'Follow me, lads, and keep your mouths sewn up. I've spied out the land, you can trust your Uncle Porta ... Come on, Sven, don't lag behind! Belt up and stick close.'

We followed him single file under the low archway, along a narrow muddied path and up to a ramshackle barn.

'In there?' hissed Barcelona.

'In there,' confirmed Porta.

He pulled out his torch and gestured to the rest of us.

'Come and have a gander!'

We pressed our noses against the grimy window. Gregor gave a low whistle of astonishment.

'Strike me, I didn't know they could grow to that size! It's like a bloody barrage balloon!'

Little John dug deep into his pocket and produced a large hammer.

'Right between the eyes,' he said longingly. 'It'll go down like a log. Never know what hit it.'

'Don't start going bloody berserk,' begged the Old Man. 'There are people sleeping all round us. We don't want to wake up the whole neighbourhood.'

'Where's the way into this place?' asked Barcelona.

'Round here.'

Porta led us up to the door, which was old and heavy and couldn't have been oiled for centuries. The sound of its creaking echoed and re-echoed through the night. Somewhere nearby a tom-cat began howling. We stood glued to the spot, ears pinned back, breath held. No one came to investigate. The tom-cat galloped past us in the dark and its howls gradually disappeared down the street. There was silence again.

'Come on!'

Little John led the way in to the barn, his hammer at the ready. The rest of us followed rather cautiously behind him. Quite suddenly, there was the sound of a thousand tin cans plunging down a staircase. Little John gave a loud yell and followed it up with a series of his favourite oaths. He surged into the torchlight and we saw that he was splattered from head to foot by some evil-smelling and repulsive-looking mixture.

'What happened?' I said.

Little John turned and roared.

'Some cunt left a bucket of shit lying around!'

He swung a foot angrily and sent the offending bucket, now empty, clattering across to the far wall. It rebounded and Little John aimed another almighty kick at it. We all yelled at him in chorus to shut up, but it was far too late, the damage had already been done. The Legionnaire whipped out his revolver and ran back towards the street. We could hear the sound of heavy footsteps.

'Wer da? Wer da?' came the cry, in the harsh accents of Saxony.

'Hell's bells!' bawled Little John. 'A bloody Saxon!'

He charged past the rest of us, caught up with the Legionnaire, elbowed him out of the way and crashed headlong into a couple of soldiers, armed with rifles, who were on their way down the narrow passage. Little John in a temper, covered in filth, wet and stinking, was no amiable proposition. The soldiers went down like ninepins before him. The Legionnaire and his revolver were unnecessary. Porta stood cackling as the two men were rolled this way and that in the thick mud and finally fled for their lives, black and unrecognizable, leaving behind them a couple of helmets and one torn collar.

'Now what?' said the Old Man, dryly.

Little John snatched up his hammer and turned back towards the barn. We stood grouped at the entrance as he plunged inside. We saw the flash of the hammer in the darkness. It was followed by a savage scream. Immediately we scattered. I flung myself flat to the ground, my hands over my head, but the sharp cries continued. Barcelona and Heide almost tripped each other up, heading back to the street. The Legionnaire leaped on to a low wall and at once jammed his gun into his shoulder and prepared to shoot down all-comers. The screams began to alternate with the sound of Little John steadily swearing. And now there were heavy footsteps and men running, and peering up from my hiding-place in the angle of the sloping roof and the floor I saw a couple of privates from an engineering corps burst through the door with rifles at the ready. They were closely followed by a corporal flashing a torch and shouting blue murder about saboteurs and thieves.

Renewed curses from Little John. The torch suddenly went out, someone yelled, there were thumps and thuds, the sound of a shot, general panic and confusion. Someone began shouting for help. I switched on my own torch and scrambled carefully to my feet. The barn seemed suddenly to be full of men. The corporal had disappeared and one of the privates was making a dive for the door. As I watched, a rifle came flying through the air and caught him on the back of the head. He fell like a stone, to the accompaniment of Porta's delighted cackle.

'What a load of shits!' said Little John. 'Beats me why some people can't mind their own business and keep their big noses out of things that don't concern them. 'He was seated astride a vast fat sow, which appeared to be dead. He tickled the creature tenderly behind one pink ear. 'Brave girl,' he said, approvingly. 'You put up a good fight.'

With no little difficulty and much loss of temper we managed to drag the animal out on to the road.

'You'll find it easier,' advised Porta, 'if you hold her by the hoof.'

'Belt up!' I said, fiercely. After only five minutes of battling with pig I felt a strong inclination to bash someone's head in. 'Why didn't we bring a knife and carve the flaming thing up here and now?'

'It's a skilled job!' said Porta, indignantly. 'You want to spoil the cut?'

'I wish my old General could see this,' said Gregor. 'He'd have died laughing. Did I ever tell you about the time he——'

'Yes,' said Little John, uncompromisingly.

'Did I? Did I really? Are you sure?'

'Bugger the General!' I snapped. 'Let's just concentrate on getting this pissing pig back home!'

In the end, three of us succeeded in hoisting the creature on to our shoulders. We held it as if it were a coffin and we proceeded single file along the road with measured steps like pall bearers. For some time we had the roads to ourselves, but as we neared the Porte de Vanves there was a fair amount of traffic and it was there that we had our first setback. It was tiring work, carrying that mountainous pig, and I suppose we had grown careless and slackened our hold, but Barcelona stumbled, the carcass slipped, and before we could stop it it had fallen from our grasp and gone rolling out into the centre of the road.

'You fools!' screamed Porta, with visions, no doubt, of his next six weeks' dinner being flattened beneath the wheels of a lorry. 'Get it back!'

He went dancing out into the traffic, waving his arms and yelling, as a Kübel pulled to a halt with its front bumper almost touching the pig. The door opened and a captain jumped out.

'What the devil's this?' he cried, prodding the pig with his foot.

It was Gunther, once again, who came to the rescue. He stepped out smartly and saluted. The Captain, like most people, was visibly taken aback at the sight of him.

'We're on street patrol, sir. It's our job to make sure the roads are kept clear and the traffic keeps moving. This—this carcass'—he jabbed a deprecating toe at our precious pig—'had been thrown down in the middle of a major road by French partisans. Doubtless hoping to cause a traffic jam and give us extra work.'

The Captain nodded, sagely.

'Doubtless,' he agreed.

He looked down at the pig. A slight furrow appeared in his brow.

'Where—ah—where are you taking the carcass?' he inquired, casually.

'Back to headquarters, sir.'

Gunther stared rather repressively at the Captain. Porta, sensing that he was not the only one who fancied roast pig, hastened to add the information that we had already reported the discovery of a carcass. A carcass, therefore, had to be produced.

'Of course.' The Captain stiffened his back. 'Of course ... Very well, get it cleared out of the way! Hurry up, man, you're holding all the traffic up!'

The pig was hastily dragged to the kerbside, hoisted back on to our shoulders, and we went on our way. It seemed that the journey would never end. A large pig is one of the least convenient animals to transport. By the time we reached the Boulevard Saint-Michel we were all tired and irritable, squabbling like kids, running with sweat and stinking of pig. The Old Man remarked every five minutes that you couldn't expect to carry a pig through the streets of Paris without drawing attention to yourself, and Heide kept up a non-stop monologue on the theme of 'we should never have tried to do it in the first place'. Since neither of them had to help carry the pig, their remarks were largely ignored.

'There's a couple of French cops ahead,' announced Barcelona.

I peered ahead, but couldn't see anything on account of the pig, and being the second of the pall-bearers with all Barcelona's bulk in front of me.

'What are they doing?'

'Waiting for us, by the looks of things. They're just standing there, waiting for us . . . One of 'em's undoing his holster. Not taking his revolver out yet, but he looks as if he's just itching to shoot someone.'

I grunted. If there was going to be any shooting, I decided, we must take shelter behind the pig. But it didn't come to that. The Legionnaire strolled forward towards the first of the policemen, very friendly and casually smoking a cigarette.

'Bonsoir, monsieur l'agent!'

The man raised an eyebrow at the sound of a French voice; then raised another eyebrow at the sight of the Croix de Guerre pinned on the Legionnaire's breast.

'Qu'est-ce que c'est que ça?' (What's that?) he demanded, pointing to the pig.

'Marché noir confisqué,' (Confiscated black market goods), replied the Legionnaire, smoothly.

The second of the policemen had dropped back a little, but was still fingering his revolver. The Legionnaire pulled out his cigarettes.

'Have a fag?'

The man hesitated, then leaned forward to take one. Quick as a flash, in one swift movement, the Legionnaire had flung him to the ground. His bicycle fell clattering after him. His colleague had immediately turned and ridden off, not stopping to use his revolver, but before he had gone very far his front wheel had skidded on a patch of grease, the man had gone head-first over the handlebars, crashed through a barrier of warning lights and signs saying 'Diversion', and gone straight down a hole in the road. He lay comfortably curled up at the foot of it and we placed a diversion sign across the top of the hole and left it there.

'While we're about it,' I suggested, 'can't we make use of the bicycles?'

After the usual arguments and displays of aggression we settled on a way of carrying the pig that would relieve our aching shoulders. We fixed a couple of carbines crossways between the two bikes, from crossbar to crossbar, and laid the pig over the top of them. It was then comparatively simple for two people to ride the bikes, holding the pig steady with one hand, and those following behind on foot would just have to run if they wanted to keep up.

Rue des Ecoles. A troop carrier, full to overflowing with field police, was slowly approaching. The Old Man groaned.

'I've had just about as much as I can take,' he muttered. 'This is all I needed!'

We merged discreetly into the shadows at the side of the road. The vehicle pulled to a halt some way further off. Why they had stopped there, whether they had caught sight of us, we had no idea. We could only wait and watch.

'They're out searching for something,' murmured Porta, as we took cover again.

'Us, I shouldn't wonder,' said Little John. 'I reckon it's those coppers gave the alarm. You should've let me finish 'em off when I wanted to.'

Somewhere close by we heard the clatter of a machine-gun. A group of the field police at once jumped down and went running off into the blackness. They returned a few minutes later with a couple of youths in handcuffs, tossed them into the vehicle and went on their way. This sort of scene was by now fairly routine in Paris. It was the nightly war fought by both sides, spreading terror throughout the city. Innocent or guilty, citizens were hauled from their beds and taken in for questioning and torture; German soldiers were found with their throats slit; small children were beaten and shot. It was the start of the reign of brutality that was to mark the liberation of Paris.

We hid the carcass in a darkened doorway and set off down a side road to take a look at the bridge. In two hours' time, as Heide repeatedly informed us, it would be day.

'And you're not thinking of carting that thing about the streets of Paris in broad daylight, I suppose?'

'Why not?' demanded Porta, aggressively. 'If you ask me, it looks a damn sight more suspicious running round with it at night!'

'My God!' said Heide. 'Anyone sees us with that whacking great lump of meat and we'll have half Paris at our heels. They'll knife you in the back for a bit of bacon rind these days, never mind a whole pig.'

The bridge, so far as we could ascertain, seemed to be unguarded. We walked back to fetch the pig and found an old crone staring at it, her eyes glazed, her mouth open, her hands clasped together on her stomach.

'Jesus Mary and Joseph!' she cried, as we approached her. 'Messieurs ... monsieur'—she clutched at Porta, who happened to be in the lead—'have pity on an old woman! Never a word have I said against the Germans! Never a one! My husband deserted in the first war and he's never fired a gun since!'

Her voice rose both in pitch and in volume. Porta began shouting back at her in his own brand of French. She had the edge on him in vocabulary but on the other hand his voice was louder. For a while they fought a running battle, until at last Porta shook himself free of her frenzied grip and roared loud enough for half Europe to hear him.

'Me chef! Pig my friend! You savvy? You no savvy, then you die!'

Porta began firing an imaginary machine-gun. The old woman spat at his feet, moved back a pace and stood malevolently gleaming at us.'

'Lovely French,' said the Legionnaire, admiringly. 'Couldn't do better myself.'

'Well, I think it's pretty good,' admitted Porta,

modestly. 'When you belong to an invading army I think you should take the trouble to master the lingo.'

'I quite agree with you,' said the Legionnaire, with a grave face.

There was a warning hiss from Gregor, keeping watch in the road.

'Careful. Trouble's coming.'

Porta instantly pulled out his revolver. Little John was already toying with the length of steel wire that never left his pockets these days. The trouble approached, in the shape of two youths, both in their early twenties, walking side by side with their hands in their pockets—a sure sign of the times. The Legionnaire stepped out suavely to meet them.

'Bonsoir, messieurs. Où allez-vous?' (Good evening. Where might you be going?)

'Prendre l'air. C'est défendu?' (To get some air. Is that forbidden?)

'Pendant le couvre-feu, oui.' (During the curfew, yes.)

The two youths stood eyeing us, seemingly unsure of their next step. Porta flicked back the safety catch of his revolver.

'Well?' said the Legionnaire, softly.

There came the sudden sound of men marching. Heavy boots on the paving stones. Harsh voices talking in German.

'Patrol!' hissed Barcelona.

We pressed back into the doorway. If a patrol found us red-handed with our booty we should have no choice but to shoot it out with them.

The two youths had crowded into the doorway with us, as anxious not to be seen as we ourselves. The old crone was suffocating somewhere in our midst, with Little John's hand over her mouth. The Legionnaire tucked the butt of his gun under his arm and prepared to fire a whole burst into the first person who tried interfering.

The patrol came in sight on the opposite side of the street. Eight men with the familiar steel helmets and the half-moon badges. At their head was an Oberfeldwebel. By the looks of him he was one of those who was unable to sleep easily in his bed if the night's work had not produced at least a couple of corpses.

The patrol passed by unsuspecting and Porta lovingly caressed the head of the dead pig.

'No doubt about it,' he said. 'They'd give a lot to get their hands on you, my fat friend!'

The Legionnaire turned back to the two youths. In the general emergency they had pulled out revolvers. That was no surprise: we had known they must be carrying them. But it was a matter of some interest that they should be P.38s—the revolvers used in the German Army.

'Nice weapons you got there,' remarked the Legionnaire. 'Where'd you pick them up? In a kids' toyshop?'

'We found them.'

'You don't say?' The Legionnaire's eyebrows went up. 'You're sure Father Christmas didn't bring them? They're very much in vogue just now, so they tell me.'

'What's it to you where we got them from?' demanded the youth, defiantly. 'What do you intend to do about it? Go running to the Gestapo?' He laughed. 'Not likely! You weren't too keen to get mixed up with that patrol just now, were you?'

The Legionnaire shot out a hand and caught him by the collar.

'Any more talk like that, pal, and you're for the high jump!'

'Why don't we get rid of 'em both and be done with it?' urged Little John, fingering his length of steel wire.

The second of the two youths, who had not so far spoken, now moved forward and spread out his hands peaceably.

'Surely there's no need for all this animosity?' he said.

In German. In a Hambourg accent. He smiled as we stared at him.

'Yes, I'm one of you. So I don't see the need for us to fall out. What you're doing here'—he glanced down at the vast pink body of the pig—'is strictly illegal and liable to cost you your lives if you're caught. Well, so what? I'm in the same position. I deserted from the Army. That's liable to cost me *my* life if I'm caught. So why can't we call it quits? And by the way,' he added, 'my name's Carl. He's Fernand.'

'So,' said the Legionnaire, narrowing his eyes. 'You're a deserter, are you?'

'A deserter and a saboteur!' Heide advanced upon them in one of his swift and menacing rages. 'You know what we do to your sort? The same as you did to four of our men the other day. They were shot with a P.38, now I come to think of it——'

'We've never fired on any of your lot,' said Carl, swiftly. 'That is one thing I couldn't do, I promise you that.'

'You expect me to believe the word of a deserter?'

'Shut up!' said the Legionnaire, curtly. He pushed Heide out of the way and turned back to Carl. 'What are you doing out here at this time of night, anyway?'

Carl shrugged a shoulder.

'Business ... You know how it is.'

'Hm. And suppose we let you go on your way, nice and peacefully, like you suggest? What guarantee do we have that you won't go running straight to the first patrol that comes your way?'

Carl laughed.

'You're joking, of course! You really think we'd risk our necks on account of a lousy pig? I couldn't give a bugger if you'd nicked a thousand flaming pigs! No, my friend. She's the one'—he nodded towards the old woman, who had been forgotten in the general commotion—'she's the one you want to watch out for. She's liable to start gossiping to her pals in the market place and before you know it the news will be half-way round Paris. I should kill her, if I were you. Life's cheap these days, no one's going to miss her.'

The old woman shrank back against the wall, shrieking.

'Stop that row!' snapped the Legionnaire. 'What's the matter with you? Anyone laid a finger on you yet?'

'She's the concierge over the road,' said Fernand. 'She's got no business to be out of doors at this time of night. We've been toying with the idea of getting rid of her for some weeks now.'

The old woman shrieked and threw herself sobbing at

Porta's feet, clutching him round the ankles. The Legionnaire caught her by the shoulder and pulled her up.

'Listen to me, old woman. You just watch your tongue if you want to stay alive, O.K.? One squeak out of you and you've had it. And don't forget that from now on you're a marked woman. Right?'

She scuttled away like a crab, back to her own building. Carl and Fernand accompanied us to the end of the road.

'How the hell do you expect to get back with that flaming great thing?' demanded Fernand. 'It's not exactly what you'd call inconspicuous, is it? You'll certainly never get over the Seine with it. Every bridge in Paris is guarded.'

We were still hoping that the little Notre-Dame bridge would be safe to cross, but we had left it too late.

'There was no one there half an hour ago!' complained the Old Man, bitterly.

Fernand shrugged.

'You must have been mistaken. Or else it was a fluke. You can see for yourself how it is.'

Sure enough, there were a couple of armed policemen guarding the far bank. We stood frowning, and from behind us came the sound of an approaching Kübel.

'Ditch the pig!' hissed Gunther.

With one quick movement Barcelona and I tipped up the bicycles and the pig went flying over the hedge into the square of Saint-Julien-le-Pauvre. There was a startled cry from the other side of the hedge. The pig had fallen on two sleeping tramps, who were now sleeping no longer but running as fast as their rags would allow down a side street. It was doubtless the first time in their lives that manna had descended from heaven upon their very heads, and they had been too terrified to take advantage of it.

We were stuck on the wrong side of that bridge for almost an hour and were no nearer to finding a solution to our problem. Heide was still obstinately repeating that we should never have come in the first place. The Old Man was monotonously moaning beneath his breath, and Fernand had pointed out not once but at least a hundred times that every bridge in Paris was guarded and the task was impossible.

'We could always swim?' suggested Porta.

'And tow the pig behind us?'

'Throw the pig away,' grumbled the Old Man. 'It's more trouble than it's worth.'

A fierce argument between him and Porta.

'One of us could swim across and clobber the guards,' I said.

And I looked hard at the Legionnaire, who was adept at that sort of thing.

'Anyone kills those bloody guards,' snapped Heide, 'and we'll all have our necks in the bloody noose.'

'So what do you suggest?'

'Dump the pig.'

'Dump the pig?' repeated Porta, dangerously.

'That's what I said. Dump the pig. I told you right from the start we should have had a plan, but as usual I was overruled. Oh no, they said, play it by ear. Leave it to chance. We can't be bothered with a plan. Well, look what's happened. Just what I said would happen. Here we are stuck with a monstrous great pig in the middle of Paris——'

'Here, where's Little John got to?' demanded Barcelona, trying to create a diversion.

'I don't know and I don't care,' said the Old Man. ' We should never have come on this trip in the first place.'

'Exactly what I've been saying all along, only no one ever listens to me. If you people occasionally took a bit more note of what I had to say——'

'It's obvious,' declared Fernand, as if he were about to come up with a new piece of information, 'that they're not going to leave a single one of the bridges unguarded. They're not fools. Leave one unguarded and you might as well leave them all. You'd have illegal traffic going over it all night long. It stands to sense——'

The conversation continued in increasingly irritable circles. I don't think any of us noticed the return of Little John until he suddenly tossed something into our midst with a loud 'Ha!' of satisfaction.

'What's that?' said the Old Man, gloomily.

Little John gave a proprietary beam.

'What's it look like?'

We all studied it closely, and the Old Man hunched an indifferent shoulder.

'A coffin.'

'Got it in one! It is a coffin. It's a coffin for putting pigs in.'

You had to hand it to him. He didn't have much brain but he certainly came up with some bright ideas.

'Where the devil did you get a coffin from?' asked the Legionnaire, admiringly.

'Oh, I just picked it up. I was walking round looking for things that might be useful and I saw this coffin in an undertaker's yard. So I picked it up and brought it along.'

'Will the pig fit?' I said, anxiously.

The pig fitted to perfection. We put it in and nailed it up, waved farewell to Carl and Fernand and set off at funeral pace across the bridge. The guards stood respectfully to attention as we passed. Porta took the opportunity to bare his one tooth and let a few tears trickle down his cheeks, where they left clean streaks among the grime.

It was growing light and Paris was waking. We received many sympathetic glances as we marched past with our coffin. Redcoat and Janette were waiting for us in the bistro, but at the sight of the coffin Janette gave a loud scream and rushed out to the kitchen. Even Redcoat looked a bit bothered.

'An accident?' he said.

He counted us up and wrinkles gathered in his forehead.

'Nobody's missing——'

'We thought it as well to be prepared!'

'Hang on,' said Porta, as we unceremoniously dumped the coffin on the kitchen floor. He turned to the Old Man. 'What was the name of that pig they had in olden times?'

'Who had?' asked the Old Man, patiently.

'The gods and things. Odin and Thor and all that lot.'

'I haven't the faintest idea.'

'Odin,' supplied Barcelona. 'It was Odin that had a pig. What was it called?'

'That's what I want to know. What was it called?'

Nobody knew. The question went the rounds and returned to Porta, and we became quite heated as to whether the pig had belonged to Odin or Freya or Thor. Little John walked out into the street and began stopping passers-by, and soon a whole group of strangers were disputing over the question.

'Somebody must know,' said Porta.

'The police,' I said. 'Try the police.'

The Legionnaire instantly picked up the telephone. He was very polite about it, quite apologetic, but we all heard the oaths that came down the wire towards him.

'I didn't intend to upset you,' said the Legionnaire, smoothly.

'Some bloody nut wants to know the name of a famous pig!' we heard the man shouting to a companion.

And we heard the answer, faint but distinguishable:

'The only famous pig I know is called Adolf!'

After that, we tried the Feldgendarmerie. More oaths, accompanied this time by the threat of arrest. We still hadn't settled the matter when an hour later we left the bistro, with the pig safely stowed away in Janette's care.

As we reached the Place Clichy we were stopped by a patrol. Mechanically they demanded our papers, but it was plain that for once they had no interest in them.

'Want to ask you something,' said the leader of the patrol, leaning confidentially towards us. 'You know that chap called Odin? You know he kept a pig?'

We nodded, breathlessly.

'Well—you don't know what it was called, do you?'

Regretfully, we admitted our ignorance.

We arrived back half an hour late at the barracks. To our amazement, no one batted an eyelid. They were all too busy talking about pigs.

'Hey, you!' An officer waved an imperative hand at us. 'You don't by any chance happen to know the name of the pig that used to belong to Thor, do you? We're having a little bet on it. We want someone to settle the question for us.'

It seemed that nobody in Paris knew. To this day I haven't found out.

CHAPTER FOURTEEN

One day at Suresnes, the Feldgendarmerie arrested a couple of kids in unauthorized possession of revolvers. The older of the two boys was fifteen; the younger only thirteen.

They were sentenced to death, but Major Schneider, either through unusual humanitarianism or because he feared the imminent end of the war, hesitated to carry out the execution. After some days of indecision he took the problem direct to General von Choltitz himself and asked for advice.

'Why come to me?' said von Choltitz, coldly. 'It hardly seems of the slightest importance.'

'But they're only children, sir.'

'They're old enough to know the law, aren't they?'

Major Schneider could not deny it. The two boys were executed the following day at Mont Valérien.

THE GESTAPO CAPITULATES

The news spread rapidly through the barracks: the Gestapo had arrived. They were out there in the courtyard, plainly visible for any masochist who cared to go and look at them. A large black Mercedes was parked outside the main doors, wedged between a couple of asthmatic DKWs.

It was breakfast time when we heard the news. Little John at once gulped down half a dozen mouthfuls in one go and hurried off to hide three bags of gold teeth under Hauptfeldwebel Hoffmann's rose bushes. All about us men were bustling to and fro in sudden frenzied bursts of activity. Very few people seemed to have any appetite left. Porta impassively went on eating, of course, but Barcelona always had claimed that that man had an extra stomach.

Out in the kitchens they were feverishly re-adjusting the scales. The French helpers disappeared into thin air and were gone for several days.

Major Hinka prudently removed himself. The M.O., who had been in the barracks only five minutes previously, had also gone to ground. It seemed that it was not only us ordinary soldiers that had a strong wish to avoid the Gestapo.

The order came through that we were to get fell in in the courtyard.

'This is it,' muttered Heide, gloomily. 'What did I tell you?'

Gregor, at my side, was sweating with terror.

'What do you think the sods are after?'

'How the blazes should I know?' I snapped, made irritable through sheer funk.

The Gestapo had installed themselves in the now empty dining hall. Eight men wearing the familiar leather coats and wide brimmed hats that had become almost a uniform. They had settled themselves importantly upon a raised platform at one end of the room—seated in high-backed chairs beneath the brightly coloured crowns that were still hanging on the walls after the 'Kraft durch Freude' fête that had been held three days ago.

We were called into the dining hall and stood at the far end while the Gestapo ran their cold grey eyes unblinkingly over our assembled ranks and waited for a face to take their fancy. Slightly in front of the others sat a small, heavy-jowled thickset man with bulging eyes like glass bubbles and long gangling arms like an ape's. In the middle of the room was a row of empty chairs; they stood there, menacing, waiting for the first victims.

The ape man picked up a carafe of water and took several gulps. In the silence, we could hear it gurgling and clanging down his throat. He leaned forward encouragingly and addressed us.

'Kriminalobersecretär Schluckbebier. Gestapo.'

There was a short pause, no doubt to allow the information to sink into our thick soldiers' heads.

'I am here,' said the Kriminalobersecretär, winningly, 'as your friend. I am here to help you. We of the Gestapo are men like yourselves. You must trust us and take us into your confidence.' He suddenly wiped off the smile and replaced it with a concentrated frown of hatred and ferocity. 'Only those who have guilty consciences need fear us! Only those who have transgressed, those who have betrayed their country and let down their Führer, need cringe away at the sight of us!'

Another pause. We remained impassive. One or two of us yawned.

Schluckbebier allowed the frown gradually to smoothe itself away and replaced it with the jolly smile of your simple Westphalian peasant.

'Come!' he said, encouragingly. 'Let us understand one another. Let us be frank. Those of you with clear consciences have absolutely nothing to fear. We of the Gestapo salute you. The backbone of the German Army! Let us rise together and sing our national hymn!'

The man beat the measure good-humouredly with his water carafe. The Gestapo sang lustily and a few thin, grudging sounds came from our end of the hall. Schluckbebier nodded approvingly as the hymn drew to a ragged end. Then he laid down the water carafe and placed his hands on his hips.

'I wish this were purely a visit of goodwill. Unfortunately there are serious—nay, deplorable!—matters that have to be discussed.' He took a step forward and threw out his hands towards us. His voice rose to a shattering crescendo. 'Jewish saboteurs have been staining your honour!'

I glanced at Porta, standing by my side, and we shrugged our shoulders.

'You know,' continued Schluckbebier, in the same hoarse shout, 'that black market transactions are punishable under the Criminal Code!'

He pulled a copy of the Criminal Code from his pocket and waved it triumphantly on high like the torch of liberty.

'Punishable by death!'

His voice rose another half octave. The hand holding the torch of liberty wiped itself swiftly across his throat, in a gesture that left no room for doubt.

'The black market is the new plague of Europe! Get rid of the black market and you get rid of your Jewish fifth-columnists!' He waved both arms, threateningly. 'And we shall get rid of them! We shall wipe Europe clean of this running sore! We shall wipe her clean of the filthy Jewish pigs that engage in this loathsome business!'

The Kriminalobersecretär fixed the front row of assembled men with his menacing frown. Unfortunately, by some mismanagement, the front row was us.

'You men there!' He jerked an arm and pointed towards the empty chairs.

We waited hopefully for someone else to obey the command, someone with a clear conscience, but it seemed that we had all betrayed our country and let down our Führer and had everything to fear from a confrontation with the Gestapo. No one moved. We had no alternative but to walk boldly forward and set ourselves in a semicircle in the isolated chairs. I told myself that it was purely fortuitous; the man had nothing on us, he simply wanted some scapegoats to sit in his punishment chairs and have strips torn off them. The trouble was I had a guilty conscience and couldn't be sure.

'Now then, you men.' Schluckbebier stood with straddled legs before us. 'I've already told you, we of the Gestapo are your friends. We're here to help you defend your honour against these sharks of the black market.'

He polished off the water in the carafe and gave a loud, rolling belch.

'Ten sacks of coffee have gone!' he cried. 'This coffee has been sold on the black market by the Jews! We of the Gestapo know this for a fact! There is nothing that is not known to the Gestapo! *Where is the coffee?*'

The question seemed pretty general, but we of the

second section, exposed in the centre of the room, felt ourselves to be particularly suspect. The rest of the men took the opportunity to direct their concerted gaze upon us until we felt that the sheer weight of public opinion would condemn us out of hand. From the corner of my eye I saw the Old Man distractedly shredding his notebook into long strips; I saw Heide stub out a half-smoked cigarette and instantly light another. Gunther had his head tilted back and was intently studying the blank ceiling, Barcelona was busily pulling a button off his uniform; Little John was examining the sole of one of his boots and Gregor was earnestly tapping his teeth with a fingernail, as if searching for hollow spots. Only Porta was unconcerned. He was staring straight ahead at Schluckbebier and the two pairs of eyes met and held.

There was a long silence. Shluckbebier seemed to be waiting for Porta to speak. To confess, perhaps. Porta kept his mouth rigidly closed.

'As you wish!' Schluckbebier transferred his gaze to the rest of us. 'Let us now turn to the second point. Three days ago a van full of bedclothes was stolen when it was left unattended for a few moments in front of the second company's quarters. Where are those bedclothes? I'm waiting!'

We all sat and waited with him. A full ten minutes passed. Not a sound was heard. No one coughed, no one blew his nose, no one shuffled his feet. We hardly dared even to draw breath lest it should make a whistling or a puffing sound.

'Fools!' roared Schluckbebier, shaking a fist. 'You needn't think you've got away with it! We of the Gestapo never let anyone get away with it! And you're not at the front now, you know. You may have been allowed to run wild in the trenches, but not here! Not when you're dealing with the Gestapo! I warn you! We shall have no mercy! Those who have betrayed their Führer must expect to be punished!'

Seven nods of approbation from behind. Schluckbebier was foaming at the mouth, little beads of spit pushing out between his lips. He did a dance round the table, banging

on it with his fist and sending the water carafe bounding
to the floor.

'Herr Kriminalrat!'

To my horror and consternation, it was Porta on his
feet. Addressing the maddened Schluckbebier with his
most charming of one-toothed smiles.

'You told us that the Gestapo were here to help us?'

General groans of disbelief from all over the room. The
entire Second Company glaring at Porta.

'So?' said Schluckbebier.

'Very humbly and respectfully, I wish to make a complaint. We are badly treated.'

With infinite sadness, Porta reached down and yanked
a bulky document out of his boot.

'For the last four months,' he said, 'we haven't had our
sugar rations.' He turned up a page and tapped a finger
on it. 'Two grammes per man every quarter, that's what it
says here.'

Schluckbebier regarded him with narrowed eyes, then
snapped his fingers.

'Get the quartermaster!'

Two of his leather-coated toughs left the room in search
of this unhappy soul. Schluckbebier watched every step of
the way as he was brought into the room.

'Quartermaster! I'm told that the men had not received their ration of sugar for the last four months! Can
this be true?'

The quartermaster shrugged, superbly indifferent.

'Certainly it's true. The Regiment hasn't received any
sugar to issue to the men.'

'I see. Thank you.' Schlückbebier turned triumphantly
to Porta. 'At this stage of the war, no one but a fool or a
traitor would be worrying about two miserable grammes
of sugar! We all have to make sacrifices. Your complaint
is negatived.'

'Then I should like to make another,' said Porta, very
firmly. 'For the past two months I have not received the
boot allowance that is due to me. I've already complained several times about this, and the last time I complained I was threatened quite violently. Now I don't

think this is right and just, and I don't think the Gestapo would think so, either, having our interests at heart like you said they did. The soldiers fighting for the Führer should be allowed to ask for their rights without being threatened. What would the Führer say if he came to hear about it? Look at the boots I'm wearing now!' Porta hoisted up a large foot and thrust it towards the man. 'I had to buy them myself.'

Schluckbebier regarded them with a mixture of horror and curiosity. Certainly they were not regulation army boots and had never been made in the Third Reich. At the back of the room, Hauptfeldwebel Hoffmann smiled impatiently to himself. It seemed as if Porta had pushed a bit too far this time. Who, after all, had ever heard of boot allowances?

'Who has ever heard of boot allowances?' asked Schluckbebier, wearily.

'But it's here!' Porta joyously plunged a hand into a pocket and brought out another booklet. 'Section 12.365, Paragraph IVa, 8th line: "Every soldier, non-commissioned officer and officer who undertakes the upkeep of his own boots shall receive 12 pfennigs a day, which are granted to him specifically for this purpose."'

Porta smiled amiably round. The inscrutable Gestapo faces were starting to twitch with irritation. They had come to the barracks to thrash out the important matter of stolen coffee, and here they were, bogged down by Porta's inanities. And seemingly no way out.

'How long?' said Schluckbebier, mechanically. 'How long is it since you received your money?'

'A very long time indeed! I've kept an account, though. As of this moment I'm owed seventeen Reichsmarks and twenty-four pfennigs. And in one hour's time that'll be thirty-six pfennigs.'

Hoffmann came suddenly storming down the room.

'This is ridiculous! I never heard such rubbish in all my life! Boot money, for God's sake! Here we are at war, and you're worrying over boot money! I'd like to know what General von Choltitz would have to say about it!'

'So should I, sir,' agreed Porta, earnestly. 'Unfortunately these little things that worry us ordinary soldiers never get taken to anyone in real authority. And they may seem trivial to you, sir, but they mean a lot to us, I can tell you.'

'Obergefreiter Porta, I'm ordering you here and now to stop wasting everyone's time! Another word out of you and I'm liable to do something we shall both regret—and you more than either of us! My patience is fast running out—and this time it's the Army that's talking not the Gestapo!'

Schluckbebier turned round and snatched away some-one else's water carafe. He drank avidly. The Army that's talking, indeed! And who did the Army think they were? A fine state of anarchy the Third Reich would be in if the Army took over. He finished off the water and looked round for some more.

'Time he went off for a slash,' muttered Little John.

'Excuse me, sir,' Porta was humbly saying to Hoffmann, 'but did you know an officer is expressly forbidden to threaten or intimidate a man of inferior rank while that man is voicing his grievances? It can lead to very serious consequences, sir. I was reading it just the other day. I made a note of it, somewhere ... Page 42, line 3 of the Regulations ... Signed by a lieutenant-colonel on General Reibert's staff. I thought I ought to tell you, sir.'

Hoffmann turned away, his face purple. I saw his fists clench and unclench, and I pitied him. I could almost have hit Porta myself when he put on that unctuous, treacly voice.

Schluckbebier seemed in two minds. Obviously it was annoying that this uncouth Obergefreiter should waste his time like this. On the other hand, there was no deny-ing the man knew the regulations back to front, he knew what his rights were, and had not Adolf himself said, 'the same law for those at the bottom as for those at the top'?

Over on the far side of the room, Lt. Löwe was leaning against the wall with a sublime smile on his face. He himself had many times been subject to the same treatment from Porta, and it was doubtless amusing to see others now undergoing it.

'Obergefreiter,' said Schluckbebier, quite friendly and pleasant, 'have you sent in a bill for the money owing to you?'

'Of course I have!' said Porta, indignantly.

Hoffmann spun round.

'That's a lie! That's an absurd lie! The oaf isn't even capable of signing his name properly, let alone making-out a bill! And as for those boots he's wearing, I can tell you where he got those from ... he stole them, the same as he steals everything else! And now he's trying to charge it up to the Army! I ask you!' Hoffmann strode excitably about the floor. 'I've had my eye on this man for the last three years. He's a psychopath, a swindler and a crook! You can take it for granted that it was him who stole the coffee! He should be put under arrest immediately, he's a disgrace to the Army!'

There was a delighted burst of laughter from Lt. Löwe, immediately echoed by Captain Gickel of the First Company. Slowly the ripples washed against the assembled body of men, and soon the whole room was shaking with hoots and guffaws. Porta smiled and clicked his heels together very smartly in acknowledgement.

'Herr Kriminalrat, have I your permission to defend myself against these slanderous accusations made by Hauptfeldwebel?'

Schluckbebier raised an eyebrow.

'Certainly, it's your right. And it seems as if you have any amount of witnesses to call on.'

'Let me begin!'

Hoffmann came up to our semicircle of chairs and pointed a finger at Little John.

'Creutzfeldt!'

Doubtless he felt quite safe with a buffoon like Little John.

'You're on oath, man, so don't try lying to me! Did this idiot or did he not steal the boots that he's wearing from a dead American soldier? And, incidentally, it's a serious crime to rob corpses!'

'I'm sure Obergefreiter Porta would never rob a corpse,' said Little John, looking very shocked. 'At any rate, I've never seen him rob one. And as for the boots, I know he bought four pairs off the sergeant-major of the 177th Infantry Regiment the day they set fire to the depot.'

Little John sat down again, looking pleased with himself. Hoffmann gnawed at his lower lip.

'That is a whole pack of lies and you know it!'

With perfect calm, Porta heaved a sheaf of papers from one of his pockets, sorted through them, and produced an account signed by Stabszahlmeister Bauser, 177th Infantry Regiment. Schluckbebier pounded on the table for some more water.

'Obergefreiter Porta, it would seem that you have—what was it?—seventeen Reichsmarks and twenty-four pfennigs standing to your account.'

'Very nearly thirty-six pfennigs,' corrected Porta. 'As a matter of principle,' he added, piously, 'I like to get things exact.'

'Quite right.' Schluckbebier nodded to Hoffman. 'Will you see that this man is paid straight away, Hauptfeldwebel? Better to keep the matter within these four walls. We don't want to trouble higher authority with it, do we?'

'I'll give him the money myself!' snapped Hoffmann, tossing a handful of coins at Porta.

Schluckbebier leaned forward, smiling.

'Any more complaints, Obergefreiter?'

'Yes, several,' said Porta, frankly. 'But I shouldn't want to trouble you with them now, Herr Kriminalrat. I know you have more important things on your hands—and we are, after all, fighting a war.'

'Cant!' muttered Hoffmann, and turned disgustedly away.

Schluckbebier remained thoughtful a while—doubtless wondering if he could now return to the vexed question of the coffee; how he could establish Porta's undoubted guilt, and, at the same time, come to terms with him by turning a blind eye in exchange for half the booty. Ten sacks of coffee! It was practically a fortune, and even half of it would make the prospect of a fifth year of war almost bearable. But Porta was evidently not such a fool as he looked. He had a measure of cunning and almost certainly a strong sense of self-preservation, and they would need to tread carefully.

'About this coffee,' began Schluckbebier, feeling his way. 'It pains me to return to the subject, but you have been accused of the theft, Obergefreiter.'

'Alas, yes,' agreed Porta, with a reproachful glance at Hoffmann. 'I wish I could help you, Herr Kriminalrat. Unfortunately I know nothing about the coffee. I never drink the stuff, you see.'

At this point, while Hoffmann's mouth was again dropping open at the enormity of Porta's statement, the door opened in a hurry and Feldwebel Winkelmann, who was in charge of the depot, burst into the room.

'Herr Oberinspektor!' He went galloping up to Schluckbebier, waving his arms excitedly. 'Good news, Herr Oberinspektor! I've just checked through the sacks of coffee again and found them all present and correct!'

'I beg your pardon?' gasped Schluckbebier.

'All present and correct,' babbled on the Feldwebel, blissfully. 'The missing sacks had been left behind the stocks of Jugoslav barley. They had no right to be there, one naturally never thought of looking. It's the men they give me to look after the stores, Herr Oberinspektor. They just don't care. Everything's jumbled up together, there's no order anywhere, I'm sometimes at my wits' end how to cope. These things will happen, you see, if I'm not given the men to do the job properly.'

Schluckbebier pursed his lips. He had by now settled firmly in his mind that five sacks of coffee were due to him. Whichever way you looked at it, therefore, it was still a question of theft.

'This is ridiculous!' declared Hoffmann, impatiently. 'You're lying, Winkelmann! You know perfectly well we counted the sacks together and went through all the stores with a fine tooth comb.'

Schluckbebier, Hoffmann, two other leather coats and the Feldwebel trooped off in a solemn line towards the depot. Seventeen sacks of Brasilian coffee, marked with the regulation army stamp, were lined up side by side.

Each sack was opened and the contents carefully passed beneath avidly quivering nostrils. Each sack unmistakably contained pure fresh coffee. It was obvious to Hoffmann that the Feldwebel had pulled a fast one, but how he had done it was beyond him. He considered, for a moment, the possibility that he had worked in conjunction with Porta, but reluctantly dismissed the idea. Porta was sufficiently adept at pilfering army stocks to scorn the help of an amateur such as Winkelmann.

'It seems,' said Hoffmann, reluctantly, 'that we were mistaken about the coffee——'

'Ha!' Schluckbebier pulled his hat down over his eyes. 'Now we're coming to it! False reports, slipshod work, deliberate waste of the Gestapo's time ... Paragraph 309 covers it, you'll find. It's by no means a minor offence, Hauptfeldwebel. It could get you into serious trouble. Very serious trouble indeed.'

One of his acolytes was already jingling the handcuffs in his pocket. The group, minus Winkelmann, walked slowly back to the dining hall. Hoffmann was obviously deep in thought, but he didn't look particularly worried. I wondered what he was hatching in that dark brain of his.

'Obersekretär,' he said, abruptly, 'while you are here, so as not to waste your time completely, I should like to demand an inquiry into an incident that took place three years ago involving the Fifth Company of the 27th Tank Regiment, 2nd Section, 1st Group. I accuse them of high treason, refusal to obey orders and cowardice in the face of the enemy ... Among other things,' he ended, darkly.

Schluckbebier raised a repressive eyebrow.

'Can you possibly substantiate such an accusation?'

'Certainly!' said Hoffmann.

It was an incident we all remembered. Two Tigers had broken down directly in front of the enemy lines. They had been abandoned and a colonel at staff headquarters had blandly given the order that they should be recovered. Lieutenant Löwe, knowing only too well the number of lives it would cost to rescue the tanks, had point-blank refused to do it. There had been a violent quarrel between the two officers, brought to an untimely finish by the explosion of a stray grenade in the Colonel's face. Porta had been sufficiently indelicate to stand laughing above the body of the dead officer, whereupon Löwe, thoroughly exasperated, had slapped him across the face. There had been no hard feelings between him and Porta, who frequently fell out on the question of discipline and accepted it as purely a matter of course, but the affair had somehow reached Hoffmann's ears and he had doubtless been hugging it to himself ever since, waiting for the chance to turn it to advantage. On two counts: refusal to obey orders, and the striking of an Obergefreiter by a superior officer. That chance had now come, and Hoffmann was making the most of it.

Schluckbebier listened with growing interest to the story. He belonged to that class of men who had no sympathy with officers, and particularly not with those who had been in the front line. This, then, was his chance as much as Hoffmann's. The affair was serious, and if the charge were proved it could well lead to promotion for the men who brought it to light. Strictly speaking it did not fall within Schluckbebier's province, but rather within that of the Feldgendarmerie, but he could almost certainly arrange matters with them.

He turned now to Lt. Löwe, standing pale and tense near by.

'Is this true, Lieutenant?'

There was a pause. We waited anxiously for Löwe's reply. He may have been an officer, but we were all in sympathy with him.

'Is it true?' repeated Schluckbebier. 'Did you strike a subordinate?'

'Yes,' said Löwe, very low.

Schluckbebier affected surprise and horror.

'You struck a subordinate? You, an officer? Laid hands on one of your own men? You have the effrontery to stand there and admit it?'

The tirade continued for almost ten minutes. It leapt from one pinnacle of astonishment to another. It gathered force and ran off into a mad crescendo of hysterical rage, pouring scorn and invective upon all officers in general and Löwe in particular. Half-way through it, Porta stood up and opened his mouth to speak, but Schluckbebier was unable to brake so suddenly and it took him another few minutes to grind to a halt.

'Herr Kriminalrat,' began Porta, in the horrible oily voice he reserved for such occasions, 'all that you say is only common sense. I quite agree with you. All officers are swine and should be hanged.'

An expression of faint alarm flickered across Shluck-bebier's face. Had he really said that? It was true, of course, but perhaps he should not have gone quite that far. It could be dangerous.

Porta slapped a theatrical hand on his belt, over the words 'Gott mit Uns'.

'God alone,' he said, piously, 'watches over the common soldier. Officers can behave how they like and get away with it. We all know that. If only the Führer knew it! But I'm sure you'll be able to drop a word in his ear now that you know how things stand, Herr Kriminalrat. A word from you would be very influential.'

Poor Löwe must have found it hard to believe that it was Porta who was speaking out against him. The two could hardly have been classed as friends, but there had always been an understanding between them, a certain sympathy and even respect.

'I have in my time,' continued Porta, 'received many blows from my superior officers. I usually accept them as part and parcel of serving in the Army. But this affair that the Hauptfeldwebel just told you of, I really saw red then. I admit it. I was so mad, to tell you the honest truth, that I took the matter up with some friends I have at the G.G.S.A. It was all settled long ago.'

'Just a minute, Obergefreiter!' Schluckbebier stretched out a shaking hand towards his empty carafe. 'You took it up with the—the G.G.S.A.?'

'That's right,' said Porta.

Schluckbebier's big red peasant face had turned pale. We were not surprised. We all knew what the G.G.S.A. stood for—Geheimes Gericht der Soldaten und Arbeiten

(Secret Administration of Justice for Soldiers and Workers). To this tribunal, any soldier or any labourer, no matter how humble, could take his complaints and know that they would be fairly dealt with. It was a powerful organization, and perhaps the only one feared by the Gestapo.

Schluckbebier, unfortunately for his peace of mind, had no means of knowing whether Porta's claim were true or not. If it were, then Schluckbebier had already said more than he should, from the point of view of his own security. And if it were not, he would never know, because he could not afford to run the risk of finding out. Any chance at all of the Geheimes Gericht being involved in the matter and it was best to get out and stay out while you still had the chance.

Schluckbebier began shovelling papers pell-mell into his leather brief-case.

'Very well,' he said, sternly. 'I shall make my report.' He looked menacingly towards Hoffmann. 'Next time you come running to the Gestapo with tales of Jews and black market and stolen coffee just make sure you've got your facts right or you'll find yourself in bad trouble. For the moment, you're lucky. We've let you off lightly. But don't think it will happen again—and don't think we shall forget it. My report will be in the files, and we shall have our eye on you. All right.' He nodded. 'Clear the hall. Get those men out. You—Obergefreiter—you stay here! I should like a word with you.'

The hall emptied far quicker than it had filled. Schluckbebier placed a benevolent arm across Porta's shoulders.

'Tell me, who is it you know at the Geheimes Gericht?' he asked, coaxingly.

'Top secret,' said Porta, with a grin. 'More than my life's worth to let you have their names.'

'Oh, come on, now!' Schluckbebier attempted a merry laugh. 'Off the record!'

'On or off, it's still top secret.'

'Hm.' Schluckbebier regard him for a moment, then jerked his head. 'Come up to the canteen with me. Talk things over.'

We heard afterwards of Schluckbebier's feeble attempts to uncover the truth.

'I, too, have friends at the Geheimes Gericht,' he began, very light and casual. 'I wonder if you know any of them?'

'Could well be,' said Porta. 'Do you visit them often? We'll probably meet up there one of these days.'

'Very possibly,' agreed Schluckbebier, and Porta noticed that he was beginning to perspire rather abnormally.

A short silence fell between them. Porta just sitting with a fatuous grin on his face, Schluckbebier turning his brains inside out to find a new method of approach.

'Have another coffee?' he tried, eventually.

'Why not?' agreed Porta. 'It seems to be in vogue at the moment.'

'You said you never drank it?'

'Thought I'd better give it a try and see what I've been missing all these years!'

Schluckbebier waited until the fresh cups were set before them, then leaned with a sly smile across the table.

'Man to man, comrade! Where have you hidden the stuff?'

'Stuff?' said Porta.

'You know what I mean! The coffee!'

'Ah ... yes. Yes, I'm with you now.' Porta nodded his head in an annoyingly imbecilic fashion. 'The coffee! Of course!'

'I have friends,' said Schluckbebier, 'who would pay a good price for real coffee.'

'I only wish I had some real coffee to offer them,' said Porta, regretfully. 'But in case I ever find any, who are these friends of yours?'

'Their names would mean nothing to you, but take my word for it, they'd pay well ... Fifty-fifty and we can do a deal! How about it?'

'You must be joking! You take ten per cent and I'll think about it.'

'Make it twenty. My friends are very influential people.

You could do yourself a lot of good by the transaction.'

Porta considered a while.

'Make it seventeen.'

'Seventeen?' Schluckbebier pulled one of his Gestapo faces, brow furrowed, eyes narrowed, mouth stretched out into a grim line. 'You're being very foolish, my friend. You don't seem to realize that the power of influential people can work either way—to your advantage or to your disadvantage, according to the service you render. We shouldn't want to anger them, should we?'

Porta rose to his feet without a word. Swallowed his coffee, tightened his belt, turned to leave. Schluckbebier was after him in one agitated bound.

'My dear fellow, there's no call to take offence! Perhaps my tone misled you? But I was merely having a little joke!'

'I can take a joke as well as anyone,' said Porta, with dignity. 'My grandfather was a celebrated clown, and a patriot into the bargain. He used to keep the audience in stitches with a spinning top in the national colours pinned on his backside. So you see, I have as good a sense of humour as anyone. I just didn't care for your particular joke. It sounded too much like a threat to be funny.'

'No, but listen!' Schluckbebier edged close up to Porta and whispered in his ear. 'I happen to know that one of General von Choltitz' ordnance officers is on the lookout for coffee ... And not for himself, mind! For the General, no less!'

'You're not suggesting I should go marching up to von Choltitz with a sack of coffee under my arm?'

'No, no, no, of course not! I should manage all that side of things. I should arrange the affair through various channels and neither you nor I would go anywhere near the General. He's hedged about by the spies of international Jewry and it's dangerous work approaching him unless a man knows his way through the tangle.'

'You know people who do?' inquired Porta, pleasantly.

'We of the Gestapo know everything ... And now'— Schluckbebier tucked his arm into Porta's and they walked out together—'seventeen per cent, I think we finally agreed upon?'

The deal was concluded that same evening. We all gathered in the kitchens of the Hotel Meurice for a drink, and were sufficiently mellow to invite Schluckbebier to join us.

'Tell me,' said Porta, suddenly, 'would you call yourself a man of culture?'

'A man of culture? Certainly I'm a man of culture! You don't suppose I should have reached my present position without a good background of learning, do you?'

'I didn't know,' said Porta. 'But being as you are a man of culture, perhaps you could help us with a little problem we have.'

'I shall do my best,' promised Schluckbebier, pompously. 'What is the problem?'

'Simply,' said Porta, 'we want to find out the name of Odin's pig.'

'Odin's pig? What *is* all this nonsense about pigs?' demanded Schluckbebier. 'That's the fourth time today someone's asked me about pigs.'

'The point is,' said Porta, 'do you know the answer?'

We waited breathlessly for the man of the Gestapo to parade his culture before us. We waited so long that our breath ran out. Finally, Schluckbebier shook his head.

'It's a funny thing,' he admitted, 'but even with my background and my education, I simply cannot recall the name of that damned pig!'

CHAPTER FIFTEEN

The guards in the transit camp known as La Rolande, near Beaune, were men who genuinely believed themselves capable of feeling pity. One among them in particular, Unterscharführer Kurt Reimling, claimed that he understood only too well the mental torments of his prisoners; and, indeed, that he went so far as to share them.

'Kill me with my children!' a Jewish mother one day pleaded with him.

She had three small children with her, and at the moment of death the prison guards wished to separate them. Reimling countermanded the order. Mother and children remained together until the last moment, and he dispatched the children first, quickly and neatly, so that the woman could see for herself that there was no suffering. Reimling was an expert with a revolver.

Some among the S.S. affirmed that their victims actually thanked them for the pains they took. Oberscharführer Carl Neubourg, attached to the camp at Drancy, was one of those. His humanity and goodness of heart prompted him to go so far as to allow one Jewish family to celebrate the Kaddisch (prayer for the dead) before forcing them to hang themselves, each in the presence of the others. And yet this generosity could have cost him dear. Had it been discovered by those in higher authority it could well have earned him three days of solitary confinement and a six-months' ban on promotion.

But to such lengths were some prison officers prepared to go. No wonder their victims were grateful.

The arms proposal had been put to us by a double agent called 'the Rat', who was employed as a member of a reception committee for men parachuted into France. The depot was in a disused factory behind the Gare du Nord. We met the Rat outside and he took us in and waved a hand towards three shelves full of arms.

'All the best quality,' he assured us. 'Straight from Churchill himself!'

We moved forward to examine them. As we did so the door opened and three men slouched in, each with a hand rather pointedly in the right pocket of his raincoat. They stood inside the door, staring past us at the arms cache.

'Dropped by parachute?' they asked, addressing the Rat rather than the rest of us.

'Word of advice,' drawled Porta. 'If you're enjoying life and want to go on enjoying it, I should get those hands out of your pockets ... Know what I mean?'

The three men turned to look at him.

'Are you threatening us?' demanded one of them.

'Not necessarily. Just depends on your behaviour.'

'Those arms are stolen. You realize that? You realize what happens to anyone caught with stolen weapons?'

'Not really,' said Porta. 'Try taking one, and then perhaps we'll see.'

'Don't bother yourself!'

A voice spoke from the doorway. Gunther, left outside for just such a purpose, had followed the three men inside. He was carrying a Russian M.P.I.

'Just do as we suggest and get those hands out of your pockets and we can all be nice and friendly.'

'Not very well managed,' remarked the Legionnaire, smoothly collecting three Colts. 'I suspect you must be amateurs. However, that's neither here nor there. Let's get down to business.' He waved his hand towards the weapons. 'You want to make an offer for this little lot?'

The youngest of the three men hunched a shoulder.

'We have need of the arms, yes. We're willing to buy them from you. But obviously we're not stupid enough to carry large amounts of money around. Send one of your men along with us and we'll come to an arrangement.'

'One of our men?' The Legionnaire laughed. 'Why not all of us together, I wonder?'

'It could be dangerous.'

'For whom?'

'A crowd of people attracts attention,' protested the youth.

'But there's safety in numbers!' retorted the Legionnaire, swiftly. 'Let's not waste time arguing, friend! We've got the arms, you want 'em ... We make the terms, O.K.?'

'But they're not yours!'

The Legionnaire raised an eyebrow.

'Who says they're not?'

'They were dropped by parachute from England.'

'So? Who's in possession of them? You or us? Us. So what do you intend doing about it?'

For a moment they looked mutinous, but the Legionnaire shook his head with a slow smile.

'Don't try it, pal! It's more than your life's worth. This is the German Army you're dealing with. We could put a bullet through your head whenever we felt like it and no questions asked by anyone. Not that we shall,' he added, magnanimously, 'if you're sensible about things.'

The youth shrugged his shoulders.

'All right, if that's the way it is. We thought it was a simple case of black market. If we'd known who we'd be dealing with, we'd never have come. How much do you want for the stuff?'

Porta promptly named a price that even I felt to be extortionate. The man turned on him in disgust.

'Look, you may be the bloody German Army, but we want arms at that price we can get them anywhere in Paris!'

'If other people are selling for that sort of money, why should we be expected to let 'em go cheap?'

There was a moment's pause. I began to feel that the price wasn't perhaps so extortionate after all. Why should we let things go cheap? Risking our necks as we were.

'Oh, don't bother,' said the Legionnaire, at last, in tones of supreme boredom. 'Why waste our time? We can sell this lot anywhere, any time we choose.'

'What'll we do with these three?' demanded Little John.

'Lock them in the bog,' suggested Barcelona. 'They can rot there till the end of the war.'

One of the men held up a hand.

'Just a minute. You're driving a hard bargain, but we're hardly in a position to argue with you. We can find the money all right. Enough for ten Sten guns, a thousand rounds for each and ten revolvers. O.K.?'

'O.K.,' said the Legionnaire. 'I suggest one of you goes off for the money and we'll hold the other two here until you get back.'

'You'—Gunther jerked his M.P.I. at one of the three— 'you go. And don't be all night about it.'

'How long shall we give you?' said Barcelona.

'Fifteen minutes should be ample. With any luck I'll be back in ten. Twenty at the outside.'

'All right,' said Gunther. 'We'll give you five ... And don't try any funny business or your two mates here won't live to tell the tale.'

'I'm not a fool.'

Gunther let him go. Little John had already prepared two lengths of steel wire with slip knots. Barcelona had set up a couple of chairs in a corner. The two hostages were pushed into them, their hands tied behind their backs, the loops of steel wire slipped over their heads and round their necks. The slightest kick on the chairs would be sufficient to strangle them.

We waited. Not quite ten minutes later the third man returned, panting. He was clutching two brief-cases filled with bank-notes and Porta snatched eagerly at them.

'It's all there,' said the man, sourly. 'What about the arms?'

We freed the two hostages and stood covering them as they picked their way expertly along the three shelves choosing their ten Sten guns and revolvers. The atmosphere grew gradually less tense. They smuggled the weapons outside and hid them beneath the back seat of an old tricycle carrier that they used for transport. We went on together for a drink in the nearest bistro, to discuss the question of hand-grenades. It appeared they wanted hand-grenades more than anything else. The Rat thought he knew where we might be able to pick some up, so half an hour later we set off in the old battered French truck, marked with the Letters W.L. (Wehrmacht Luftwaffe) that he had provided.

We had our sub-machine-guns at the ready and were prepared to use them on the first person who challenged us. This was war, our own war within a war, and we were talking no unnecessary chances. An amphibious vehicle containing four field police crawled along on our tail for a while, then finally decided the game was not worth the candle and disappeared after larger fry.

Porta brought the truck to a halt outside an old apartment block. We jumped out, cast a quick look round, pressed the buzzer that opened the front door and mounted the stairs silently and swiftly, four steps at a time. Porta rapped loudly on the door.

'Who is it?'

'Adolf and the Secret Police! Open up or we'll break the door down.'

There was a silence. Then, reluctantly, the door was edged open. Porta at once stuck a foot in the crack. Looking out at us was a Feldwebel of the Feldgendarmerie.

'Well, well!' he said, sarcastically. 'Secret Police, eh? That's your idea of a joke, I take it?'

'You take it quite right,' agreed Porta. 'And this is another joke...' He pressed the muzzle of his gun into the Feldwebel's chest. 'Come on, get your hands over your head, we don't have all night.'

The man unhurriedly raised his arms.

'This is going to cost you your life, Obergefreiter. You realize that?'

'Don't let it bother you. Doesn't bother me.'

Porta pushed him through the door. The rest of us followed, spilling into the salon and almost filling the small room. Porta turned and hit the Feldwebel in the guts. The man groaned and doubled over in agony, and Porta pushed him down into a chair. The room was lit by a small naked bulb. There was no carpet on the floor, and in the centre of the room stood a large box of ammunition carelessly surrounded by piles of rifles. Brooding over this horde was a man in the grey leather coat and soft hat of the Gestapo. In one corner of the room were four men, their faces turned to the wall, presided over by another field policeman. A second Feldwebel was sprawled in a chair drinking beer. He started up as we burst in, but we had the advantage of surprise and of numbers.

'Hands up!' demanded Porta, curtly.

The man in the leather coat obeyed immediately. The Feldgendarme standing guard over the prisoners hesitated, and had to be encouraged by the Legionnaire's knife suddenly flashing past his ears and embedding itself in the wall beside him.

'O.K.,' said Porta. 'Let's have a game of musical chairs ... You four'—he gave the Feldwebel a push that sent him staggering across the room—'change places with the other four. Noses to the wall and a bullet through the head if you so much as twitch.'

The exchange was effected. The four civilians stared in bewilderment, doubtless wondering whether they had been rescued or merely jerked out of the frying pan and tossed into the fire.

'Are there any more of the buggers out there?' demanded Porta, nodding towards the window.

'More than likely,' said Gregor. 'I'll go and check.'

Gunther sat down on a nearby chair, released the safety catch on his M.P.I.

'What are you doing here?' demanded Porta, of the three field policemen with their noses pressed into the wall.

There was silence.

'They came to arrest us, didn't they?' said one of the ex-prisoners, cheerfully. He was a little Frenchman, dark and thin with glittering eyes. 'Another second and we'd have been nothing but a dirty mess on the wallpaper.'

Little John dived into his pocket and brought out his steel wire.

'You want me to get rid of 'em?'

'Just a minute.' The Frenchman held out a detaining hand. 'We ought to find out who told them about this place. Someone must have tipped them off, they were waiting here for us when we came in.'

'Good.' Gunther walked across to the Gestapo agent and dug the barrel of his gun into the man's back. 'We'll soon get it out of them ... What's your name, ratface?'

'Breuer,' came the sullen reply. 'Max Breuer. Kriminal-obersecretär.'

'Then get ready to talk, Max Breuer. What you've done to others is about to be done to you ... see how long *you* can last out!'

'This should be fun,' said Little John, gleefully.

He stepped out to the kitchen, filled a bucket at the sink.

'We'll play the water game first,' he said.

He caught up the Kriminalobersecretär as if he were a rag doll, forced him to his knees, plunged his head into the bucket of water. Willing hands pinned the man to the ground. His struggles gradually ceased.

Little John flung him away and we stood watching as he slowly recovered his senses. He vomited all over himself and stared up at us with bloodshot eyes. The Frenchman promptly bent over him and rapped out a question.

'How did you know where to find us?'

No reply. Question repeated. The man closed his eyes and said nothing.

'How did you know where to find us?'

The Frenchman aimed a hard kick into his victim's abdomen, but he misjudged the distance, the blow was too powerful and the man passed out again.

'You haven't got the right technique,' said the Legionnaire, impatiently. 'Any more of that and you'll have a dead man on your hands before you've got the information out of him.'

With his eternal cigarette in the corner of his mouth, the Legionnaire bent over the Kriminalobersecretär, sponging his brow with cold water. The bloodshot eyes at last flickered open again.

'O.K.,' said the Legionnaire. 'That's better. You hear me now?'

Weakly, the man nodded.

'Who gave you this address?' demanded the Legionnaire. 'I advise you to speak, because much as I dislike using brutality I'm afraid I've only a limited supply of patience and we've already asked you the same question four times. If you don't give me the answer straight away I shall have to start applying a little of your own medicine.'

The silence continued. We stood round grimly, and at last the Legionnaire sighed.

'Well, I suppose it might be an interesting experience for you to be on the receiving end for once ... Little John, hold his head firm.'

Slowly the Legionnaire took the cigarette from his mouth and applied the glowing tip to the man's nostrils. There was a scream of agony and the unpleasant smell of singed flesh. The Legionnaire smiled.

'Done to a turn ... We'll grill the other side for you in a minute.'

'Has he got any gold teeth?' demanded Porta.

'What if he has?' said Little John, fiercely. 'I've just as much right to them as you!'

'Shut up! You can fight that out later.'

The Legionnaire pushed them both out of the way. With a sudden, adroit gesture he snatched up the man's right hand and deliberately snapped one of the fingers. I winced at the sound of it and the man screamed again and writhed upon the floor.

'Well?' said the Legionnaire, softly.

No response. Little John moved forward and pinned one hand to the floor beneath his boot. Slowly he increased the pressure until his victim's yells of agony filled the room. The Legionnaire made an imperious gesture, and Little John stepped away.

'Well, Herr Breuer?'

At last the man had had enough. Very faintly there came the murmured sound of a girl's name and an address.

'Mean anything to you?' asked the Legionnaire, turning back to the Frenchmen.

Three of them nodded very vigorously, turning wide eyes of accusation upon the fourth.

'It certainly does mean something! It's that girl Jacques has been going out with. We've told him time and again she wasn't to be trusted. Now we know for certain—and that explains a very great deal.'

One of the field police suddenly laughed. With an oath, Little John hurled himself at him and began pummelling his head to and fro against the wall. The Old Man, who had so far watched in grave silence, now stepped forward and grasped Little John by the shoulder.

'For God's sake, let him alone! Let's have done with all this violence.'

'All very well,' protested Porta, 'but we can't afford to let them go running back to headquarters, can we?'

'To hell with it!' shouted the Old Man, angrily. 'What are we? Common or garden murderers?'

'No, and we're not bleeding saints, either!' snapped Porta. 'I don't aim to put my neck in a noose for these miserable sods.'

The Old Man turned abruptly and left the room. We heard the front door slam behind him, heard his footsteps clattering down the stairs. We stood for a moment, uncertain, and then, at a sign from the Legionnaire, we followed him out. The prisoners were left alone with Gunther and the three Frenchmen. We had barely set foot in the street outside when we heard the sound of shots. I felt happier now that it was over, but glad it was Gunther and not me who had stayed behind with the gun.

We all met up again a short while later in a bar on the Boulevard Saint-Michel to conclude the second deal of the evening, and Porta stashed away a load of bank notes in his inside pocket, not bothering to conceal his satisfaction.

'What happened to our prisoners in the end?'

Gunther shrugged his shoulders.

'We stuck 'em in a cupboard. Locked the door on 'em.

They'll be quite safe until the end of the war, unless some busybody decides to go poking about in the meantime.'

'For my part,' said the Old Man, 'I'm through with this sort of thing. From now on you can count me out.'

'Me too,' said Heide.

The Old Man, of course, was troubled by the ethics of the thing; Heide merely worried in case his career should be put in jeopardy. Porta shrugged his shoulders.

'Just as you wish. Nobody's going to force you. And the less there are to share the proceeds, the more there is left for the rest of us. Leastways, that's how I see it ... And anyone else wants to follow 'em, that's O.K. by me.'

We parted company with the Frenchmen, and the rest of the section returned to barracks. I let them go on without me. I had an appointment with Jacqueline in her flat on the Avenue Kléber. She was there waiting for me. Her mood was sad and rather frightened.

'All this madness and killing,' she told me. 'It's getting worse than ever. Nobody trusts anybody any more. Everywhere you go you hear stories of people who've been shot down in the street, or knifed or strangled, for no reason at all.'

'It can't go on for much longer,' I said, reassuringly. 'The war's almost at an end. Our troops are pulling out all over Europe—even here in Paris most of the top brass are packing their bags.'

I told her the story of our previous night's adventures, of the black market deals, the shooting of the prisoners. She shuddered and shook her head in despair.

'You see what I mean? The whole world seems to have run mad. Even you. Selling arms that are going to be used against your own side! Arms that could be used to shoot *you*, in the end! Where's the sense in it? Killing people for money, killing people to shut them up, just killing all the time because there's been so much slaughter that human lives don't have any value any more.'

She poured me out a large whisky, disappeared for a while into the bathroom and came back wearing a Japanese kimono. She sat down beside me on the sofa.

'You know what I saw yesterday? Some of your troops

firing on a cripple out in the streets.'

I hunched a shoulder. What reply could I sensibly make, or what questions sensibly ask? Who knew or cared any more why people killed other people?

'Your friends don't like me,' she continued. 'Do you suppose they'll kill me?'

'Good God in heaven!' I said, shocked. 'Why the hell should they do that?'

'She smiled rather sadly.

'That's a silly question! People don't have to have a reason for killing any more. They just kill whenever they feel like it. And perhaps your friends do have a reason, anyway: you're in love, and I'm in love and people in love can be dangerous.'

I stared thoughtfully at her slim body beneath the embroidered silk of the kimono. Her eyes were cloudy and half closed, and I knew that she was ever so slightly drunk. She laughed, swung her long legs behind me on to the sofa and stretched out full length.

'Let's get stoned,' she said. 'Let's get absolutely stinking ... After all, what the hell else is there to do?'

She suddenly leaned forward and put her arms round me, rubbing her cheek against mine.

'I love you, Sven. Do you know that? I love you ...' And she added, inconsequentially: 'They threatened me because I keep having you round here.'

'Who threatened you?' I said. 'Porta and that lot?'

'Of course not!'

'Who, then?'

'Oh'—she pressed a finger against my lips—'nobody. Nothing. It was only a rather silly joke. Forget it for tonight.'

'But I want to know——'

'Forget it, Sven! I'm being silly.'

I didn't believe her. I should have had it out with her there and then, but she pressed herself against me with her kimono falling open and somehow the matter was pushed to the back of my mind.

'Oh, Sven, I wish you were a Frenchman!' she whispered. 'I loathe the Germans. I can't help it, I just loathe them!'

'But I wasn't born a German,' I reminded her.

'It's the same thing. You're fighting in their Army ... I suppose you hate the French?'

'Why should I?'

'You're fighting us, for God's sake!'

'I don't hate anyone particularly,' I said.

It was growing dark by the time we came back to consciousness. Jacqueline stretched out a hand for her cigarettes, but the packet was empty.

'I haven't any, either,' I said. 'I'll get dressed and go out and find some. You can always pick them up on the black market if you know where to look.'

'All right, but be careful.' She jumped out of bed and hopped naked into the kitchen. 'I'll get some coffee ready. Don't be long, will you?'

I wasn't long. I knew roughly where to look and I had returned with the cigarettes inside quarter of an hour. As I entered the building I passed two youths, who glanced in some consternation at my black uniform and pushed past me without a word. I watched them hurrying off down the street, wondered vaguely what they were doing out at that time of night and dismissed the matter from my mind. I climbed the stairs four at a time, anxious to get back to Jacqueline, to lie in bed with her, drinking coffee and smoking. She had left the front door of the apartment ajar. I guessed she was probably already in bed, waiting for me to come to her. I had a forty-eight-hour pass, we could spend one entire, glorious night together, and by the next day, or the day after, the war was almost certain to be over.

I called out to her as I entered the salon.

'I'm back! I managed to pick up five packets of twenty from a young kid just round the corner!'

There was no reply.

'Hey, I'm back!' I yelled.

Still no reply. The smell of burning came to my nostrils. By now thoroughly ill at ease I went through to the kitchen. The coffee had boiled over on to the stove, the gas was still burning. Jacqueline was lying spread-eagled across the floor. I knew at once that she was dead. For a moment I found myself unable to move, I just stood, staring down at her, saying her name dementedly over and over to myself.

When at last I found the courage to look at her, I saw that her throat had been brutally ripped open. It was now nothing but a gaping red hole with the blood still pumping out of it. Her face was already cold and waxen, her cheeks sunk. On her naked breast a note was pinned. It said, in crude lettering: COLLABORATOR.

Half an hour later, with a whole bottle of whisky inside me, I stubbed out my tenth cigarette and gently closed the door of the apartment behind me. I tightened my belt, checked the two heavy army revolvers, walked slowly downstairs to knock up the concierge. She appeared reluctantly, with a scared face, and I seized her by the throat and dragged her towards me.

'Who were those two boys that came here about forty-five minutes ago?'

'No one, Monsieur le soldat!'

'What do you mean, no one? Talk sense, women! I've just told you that a couple of boys were here!'

'But I don't know—I didn't see them—I can't spend all my time watching the people that come in and out——'

She was ashen-faced and shaking with terror. It was plain even to me that she was telling the truth. I tossed her into a heap in the corner and strode out into the Avenue Kléber. For the first time in my life I knew how it felt to want to kill and kill and kill again, for the sheer satisfaction of killing.

That same evening saw the start of the Liberation.

A child returned home after a visit to the cinema. He was late, and he ran most of the way in his case his father should be worried. But he laughed as he ran, the film had been so funny that his ribs still ached and his belly was still tied in knots.

'Papa!' The child went running up the steps, through the door and into the room where his father sat reading. 'I know I'm late, but it was so funny, I saw some of it again and I've run all the way home!'

The father smiled, put away his book and began quietly preparing the supper, while the child chattered like a magpie, following him about and too excited even to lay the table.

'Two eggs and a little milk,' said the father, at last, when he could slip in a word or two. 'A special treat for you. And there's a couple of slices of German bread, and a small piece of pudding. Will that fill you up, do you think?'

'You bet!' declared the child, stoutly. 'I don't feel half so hungry now as I used to. You know Jean, whose father is in the Resistance? He was telling me, when you feel hungry you should keep drinking lots of water and chewing bits of paper and soon you won't feel hungry any more. I tried it this afternoon and it works, my stomach doesn't rumble now.'

The father sat silently watching the child as he ate. He himself had had no food for two days now. It was more important to feed the child, and meanwhile it could surely not be long before the liberators arrived? There were rumours in Paris that two armoured divisions were *en route* for the city.

The child went on prattling.

'They killed an informer yesterday on the Boul' Mich. Did you hear about that? Raoul told me about it. Two boys came up on bicycles and shot him down right in the middle of the street, with people all about. Raoul said they were just boys like us, the same age and all. Jean wanted us to go out this evening and do the same, but one of the teachers gave us a whole long lecture about it to-day. He said we'd got to make sure and come straight home at night and not get mixed up in anything. All the teachers are scared stiff of the Boches, you know that?'

He pushed aside the empty egg shells and started on the milk. The bread had already vanished, pushed down an avid young throat into a stomach that was still more than half empty.

'I say, did you know, I'm the only boy in the whole class whose father's got the Croix de Guerre with three palms!

The others are all awfully jealous ... Did you know the Americans are coming Papa? All those Boches in their black uniforms, they're going to be killed pretty soon. A bistro was blown up yesterday. It was full of Boches. Afterwards, Raoul said, you could see blood running out into the gutters. Boche blood ... Gosh, I wish I could have seen it! Tomorrow I'm going to brush your uniform for you, Papa. You've got to put it on when the Americans get here. Did you know they've got thousands of tanks? Do you think they'll go all round Paris in them? Do you think——'

His father stood up.

'Time for bed ... Yes, yes, I know the Americans are coming, but they won't be here yet awhile. They've been a long time getting here, we can wait a bit longer.'

'When will they be here? Do you think they'll come in the night?'

'They might,' said the father. 'We'll have to see when we wake up tomorrow morning.'

The heat of the August night was heavy and oppressive. Tossing and turning in his bed, the child heard his father turn down the lamp and retire to his own room. He heard the door close. And immediately afterwards, the explosion came. The child was hurled out of his bed and across the room, ending up against the wall. Dust and bricks rained down upon him. He smelt smoke, and he saw the flames already licking round the edge of the door.

They pulled the child out first. He was bruised and shocked, but otherwise unharmed. It took them a while to find his father. They had to move piles of rubble, bricks and charred timber and broken glass. The man was laid gently on the pavement, but even the child could see that he was dead. There was nothing left of his face but a crushed and bloody mess.

The child was led away, sobbing, in the care of some nuns from a nearby convent. They gave him a tranquillizer and put him to bed, and before he fell into a troubled sleep there were men who came and questioned him whether he had heard anything, seen anything, before the explosion happened. He had seen nothing. A neighbour claimed that a motor-car had driven past, that it had slowed down before the building and a man had tossed something through the front window of the apartment. Someone else claimed that a couple of men had run out of the shadows. Some said they had been men in uniform, others that they were civilians.

The child was left alone in the world. His beloved Americans had arrived, but too late to save him from personal tragedy. It was never discovered who had killed the boy's father, whether Germans or Frenchmen, nor why they had killed him. Was the man a traitor, who had been summarily dealt with by his own countrymen? Or was he, like so many others, an innocent victim of terrorists?

No one ever knew. And he was typical of hundreds.

CHAPTER SIXTEEN

Bruno Witt had many friends in Paris—or at least, he thought he had. Where they were on this particular August day he had no means of knowing, but certain it was they were failing in their duties as friends.

With a hysterically raging mob close on his heels, he plunged down the rue du Faubourg-du-Temple. Leading the pursuit was a young girl, Yvonne Dubois, who had been a loyal member of the Resistance for the past twenty-four hours. Prior to that, she had been one of a select group of women who had had the entrée to the private rooms of the S.D. in the Hôtel Majestic. Today she prudently turned her back upon such privileges. Her duty lay clear before her and she would devote all her energies to the cause of the Resistance.

In his panic, Bruno Witt tripped and fell. The crowd were upon him in an instant. His faded grey tunic was soon torn to shreds, while two wild housewives fought each other for possession of his cap. Yvonne Dubois slashed open his throat with a pair of dressmaking shears and plunged her hands joyously into the hot, pumping blood.

'I killed a Gestapo agent!' she screamed, and she waved a pair of scarlet hands towards a crowd of people on the opposite side of the street. 'I killed a Gestapo agent!'

The newcomers took no notice. They were too concerned with their own patriotic deeds. In their midst were two naked girls, each with a swastika daubed on her chest. The crowd stopped, sat their victims upon a couple of low stools in the middle of the road, and amidst cheers and handclaps began shaving their heads.

They were all being dragged out into the open, now that the Liberators had arrived. Mothers of young children who had solved some of the problems of wartime by taking a German soldier as a lover; mild-looking shopkeepers and office workers who had denounced loyal Frenchmen to the Gestapo; harmless old concierges who had brought about the death of many a Resistance worker by poking their noses in where they were not wanted. They were all dragged out of their hiding-places and displayed in the streets, to the cheering and jeering of the hysterical crowds.

Seated in a wheelbarrow, a naked man was being paraded up and down one of the main streets with a placard hung round his neck. On it was printed the one familiar word: COLLABORATOR. A woman leaned out of an upstairs window and emptied the contents of her chamber-pot over the naked man. Unfortunately her aim was poor. The naked man was merely splashed a little, while one of the country's newly emergent heroes received the full force of it upon his head and shoulders.

'Liberté!' howled the mob.

Each man and woman was now suddenly only too anxious to prove his patriotism, to outdo his neighbours in acts of valour in the face of the enemy. Not a single person but had killed at least one German. Many people had apparently killed several Germans. The roads should by rights have been filled to overflowing with the bodies of the hated Boche, who had so foolishly crossed swords with the good and gallant Russians.

Accordions were played at every street corner. Banjos and penny whistles joined in. All the world was happy again. Democracy had returned to France.

'I was personally responsible for the preservation of Paris,' declared von Choltitz to the American general who was interrogating him. 'My orders were to destroy the town, but naturally, as soon as I realized the Führer had lost his mind, I had to make my own decisions.'

'I saved three Jews from the gas chambers,' said an officer of the Gestapo. 'I personally saved them. I have proof, I have witnesses!'

'I knew one of the colonels who took part in the attempt on the Führer's life on the twentieth of July,' claimed Lt. Schmaltz, of the N.S.F. 'I knew what was going on, yet I didn't denounce him to the authorities. I could have done. I should have done! It was my duty to do so. But I risked my own neck and kept my silence.'

Suddenly, all the French were patriots, all the Germans had been forced into carrying out orders that were distasteful to them. But Paris had been liberated!

REFUSAL TO OBEY ORDERS

It was gone midnight. In General Mercedes' room, the officers were taking counsel. They were all in combat uniform and each held a sub-machine-gun. Mercedes was leaning over a map.

We were to leave Paris that day, crossing the frontier at Strasbourg, with the Second Battalion at our head.

'I think we'll have to reckon on attacks from Resistance groups,' warned Mercedes. 'They're all out in the open now and hellbent on taking their revenge. Our orders are to regroup as quickly as possible. Nothing, repeat nothing, must be allowed to stand in our way. Any attacks must be repelled by whatever means are available to you ... We have to get through! Do I make myself clear, gentlemen?'

The officers nodded, gravely. Mercedes straightened up, readjusting the black patch that he wore over his empty right eye socket. At that moment the telephone rang. The General's aide-de-camp took the call, listened for a moment and then held out the receiver.

'For you, sir. General von Choltitz. It seems to be pretty urgent.'

Mercedes pulled a face.

'Hallo? Major General Mercedes speaking.'

'Ah, Mercedes! Choltitz here. What the devil are you doing, man? I've heard rumours that you're packing your bags and getting out. I hope it's not true?'

'I'm afraid it is, sir. In approximately two hours from now we shall have left Paris and be on our way to

Strasbourg.'

There was a loud explosion at the other end of the line. Mercedes held the receiver well away from his ear, and the assembled officers grinned.

'I forbid you to do any such thing! I am still your superior officer and I believe my authority is still good. I order you to remain where you are until such time as I decide you shall withdraw.'

'I'm sorry about this, sir, but as it happens I'm no longer under your command. I received the order to pull out direct from General Model. My instructions are that we should set off a couple of hours from now, taking all equipment with us.'

The sound of the General's heavy breathing could be heard all over the room.

'Equipment? What precisely do you mean by that? Arms, ammunition, tanks?'

'Yes, sir. All arms, all ammunition—and all nine of my tanks.' Mercedes smiled rather grimly. 'You may remember, sir, that I command a tank division with virtually no tanks.'

Von Choltitz snorted down the line.

'What is the object of this futile exercise, may I ask?'

'My orders are to cross the frontier at Strasbourg, where we shall re-group and take delivery of four hundred tanks that are straight out of the factory. The Generalfeldmarschall has allowed me a whole fortnight in which to get the men accustomed to the new machines.' Mercedes laughed again, and the assembled officers shook their heads and began muttering among themselves. 'He's not over-generous with his training period, but we shall do the best we can. You can expect to see us back in Paris by the end of a month.'

'General Mercedes, I repeat, I absolutely forbid you to leave France! I'm countermanding the orders of Feldmarschall Model, do you understand me? You can ignore them! I accept full responsibility for it. I shall be in touch with G.H.Q. immediately, informing them of my action. But I insist that you and your men remain here until I give further orders!'

'I'm sorry,' repeated Mercedes, with a heavy sigh. 'Unless I receive a direct counter-order from General Model himself we shall be leaving in two hours' time.'

'You seem to forget, General, that it's I and not Model who is in command! Your division was sent to me specially by the Reichsführer himself! If you dare to go against my orders, I'll have you up before a court martial, I swear to God I will!'

There was a silence over the line; broken only by an occasional gasp from the outraged von Choltitz.

'Are you still there, Mercedes?'

'Yes, sir.'

'I trust I've made myself clear?'

'Perfectly clear.'

'You take your men out of Paris before I give you the O.K. and I'll have you up for sabotaging the orders of the Führer himself! God help me, so I will!'

'I believe you,' said Mercedes, smoothly.

A pause. Von Choltitz took a grip on himself and tried a more reasoning line of approach.

'The thing is, man, that without your troops I'm in no position to hold out for even a day against these damned Resistance people. They're killing my soldiers in broad daylight now! They've even shot one of my own ordnance officers! I tell you, Mercedes, that the situation is desperate.'

'I appreciate that, General. However, I repeat that I can only obey the orders I've been given by General Model.'

'You'll face the firing squad for this, Mercedes! I shall send in my report, never fear! To General Heitz, no less!'

'You must of course do whatever seems proper, sir. And now, if you'll excuse me, I have to start organizing our departure.'

Mercedes slowly replaced the receiver. He turned with a pensive expression towards his officers.

'We're still going?' asked one.

'Of course.' Mercedes smiled. 'I think I've said all that's necessary. You'd best be on your way now. The sooner we get out of here the better. And just remember—no one, repeat no one, must be allowed to stop us!'

The barracks looked like an ant hill under threat of attack. Men ran to and fro carrying clothes, arms, files of papers. There was the constant sound of vehicles starting up, other vehicles grinding to a halt. A reconnaissance company were sent out to find the nine tanks. Little John and Porta disappeared in the midst of the hubbub and paid an unexpected and thoroughly unwelcome visit on the Sergeant-Major.

'What the blazes do you two want?' he roared as soon as he caught sight of them.

'Sir,' said Porta, in his best military manner. 'Obergefreiter Porta and Obergefreiter Creutzfeld of the 5th Company, sir——'

'I know who you are, for Christ's sake! What have you come to bother me for? Can't you see I'm up to my neck in work?'

'We've come to offer our services, sir.'

'And what the hell good would you be to anyone?' sneered the Sergeant-Major.

'We're willing to help the revictualling party, sir.'

'Christ almighty!'

The Sergeant-Major's oaths rose to the ceiling, bounced off the walls, filled the entire room with sound. The cigar that he had been smoking was chewed to shreds.

'God help me, I wouldn't let you two clowns anywhere near a bloody revictualling party!'

'If that's the way you feel about it——' began Porta, very much offended.

'It is the way I feel about it! It's the way anybody but a complete moron would feel about it! If I had my way you'd be left behind in Paris and handed over to the French! A more incompetent, useless——'

Porta and Little John, with a great show of dignity, removed themselves from the Sergeant-Major's presence. They took their wounded pride to seek shelter with a friend of Porta's, the medical orderly Obergefreiter Ludwig, who was installed in splendid solitude in the isolation wing of the infirmary. They stood with longing eyes at the window, watching other, more fortunate, men loading food supplies on to the back of a lorry.

'Look at that lot!' Little John lowered his voice to an awed whisper.

Crates of tinned meat, of bacon, of chocolate——

'Coffee!' said Ludwig, gloatingly.

'Cognac!' yelped Little John.

'Take a look at that fat idiot down there.' Ludwig pointed towards a perspiring soldier bent sideways beneath the weight of a heavy packing case. 'What do you suppose he's got in there?'

'Don't know, but I've a bleeding good mind to find out!' Porta scratched thoughtfully between the cheeks of his bottom. 'Whatever it is, you can bet your sweet life it's eatable! And anything that's eatable is worth nicking . . .'

'They catch you knocking off any of that lot, it'll cost you your head,' said Ludwig, gravely. 'Only last week they shot a couple of artillery chaps for pinching a case of tobacco.'

'The way I do it,' said Porta, 'they never even know the stuff's gone. That's the trouble with some soldiers today: they don't know how to do a job and get away with it. When I first joined the Army, a soldier wasn't a soldier if he didn't do a bit of nicking now and then. You picked up the technique quick enough. Nowadays they're so lily-livered, some of 'em, they could spend a whole day locked up alone in the food stores and not even lift a couple of packets of fags.'

'There's a difference,' objected Ludwig, 'between a couple of packets of fags and a bloody great crate full of God knows what.'

'You want to watch how I do it?' challenged Porta. 'Want me to teach you a trick or two?'

From his pocket he took a hand-grenade. Slowly he made his way out into the courtyard, stood idly for a moment or two, awaited his opportunity and slipped unnoticed behind a large pile of crates. On the far side of the courtyard were drums of petrol, waiting to be loaded on to one of the lorries. They made an excellent target for

Porta's hand-grenade. The whole lot roared upwards in a solid wall of flame and the men of the loading party scattered for their lives in all directions. Next second, Porta had swung himself on to the tail board of a lorry and was hefting crates towards Little John and Ludwig, who, with their qualms overcome by cupidity, had rushed out to lend a helping hand. Five cases they managed to secrete in the infirmary before the courtyard became, quite literally, too hot to hold them. They shut themselves up with their booty and watched out of the window the leaping flames and thick black smoke.

Meanwhile, the entire barracks was in an uproar of terror and speculation. Groups of men turned and fought each other through sheer panic. A nervous sentry fired on one of his own side and killed him. Everywhere men believed that the F.F.I. were attacking in force. The final death roll amounted to four, with seventeen men wounded, some badly.

In the midst of the upheaval, Porta and Little John had carried away four of the crates to 5th Company quarters.

'For God's sake!' exclaimed the Old Man, at once putting two and two together. 'You're nothing but common criminals, the pair of you! It's all very well nicking a few extra rations now and then, but chucking hand-grenades about the place and then looting all this amount of stuff is carrying things altogether too far. I'm sick to death of both of you.'

The Old Man turned away in disgust.

'The trouble with you,' said Porta, amiably, 'you're too damned honest. The way I see it, the State stole the best years of our youth from us and we're entitled to steal it back in kind. Stealing from friends is different. Stealing from the State's what anybody's got a right to do. Leastways,' he added, 'that's how it seems to me.'

'There's no call to go chucking bloody hand-grenades about,' grumbled the Old Man.

'Couldn't have got the grub otherwise,' said Porta, cheerfully.

Little John had already opened a tin of sardines. He

speared one of them with a penknife and took it across to the Old Man.

'Here,' he said, 'have a sardine. Fit for heroes, these are, and I reckon you're a hero all right.'

We moved across Paris in a tight-knit column, from the barracks to the Porte d'Orléans. The city was in a state of ferment. Now that we were retreating, everyone wanted to have a go at us and the snipers were out in force. A shot fired from an attic window seriously wounded one of our N.C.O.s. A small party at once detached itself and invaded the house in question. It was empty, apart from two very small boys caught hiding in the attic with an old German rifle. Shaking with terror, they were pulled up into our lorry to await the decision of General Mercedes. He took only a few minutes to make up his mind: in spite of their extreme youth, the boys were to be shot. They were reprieved only to the extent that the execution was not to take place until we were well out of Paris. To shoot them in full view of the enraged crowds of people would be to ask for trouble. And besides, it would be unwise to stop the entire column in the centre of the town.

Half an hour later, under the horrified gaze of the two boys, the wounded man died.

'You see?' Porta forced them to take note of the fact. 'Perhaps that'll teach you to play around with guns. Eh?'

He slapped them both very soundly across the cheeks and made them sit looking at the dead man for the rest of the journey.

By the time we had put a reasonable amount of distance between ourselves and Paris it was growing dusk and we camped down for the night. The execution was postponed until morning. There was great fury on the part of Major Hinka when it was subsequently discovered that the two boys had vanished from the scene. Porta, as usual, was at once cast as the guilty party. Heide claimed that he had woken in the night to see Porta returning alone to the wood that we were camped in. It was almost certain that he had led the boys off into the darkness and told them to run for their lives. Both Gregor and Gunther, on the other hand, swore that the boys had still been there at least a couple of hours after this incident. The matter was dropped for lack of time and lack of evidence, but I think none of us had any doubt that Heide's story was the true version.

Barcelona had somewhere dug up a radio set. He had at last managed to pick up an English-speaking voice, and we eagerly made a note of the wavelength. Thanks to some indefatigable knob-twiddling, he had come upon the command post of the U.S. 3rd Armoured Division. We at once put ourselves in communication with them.

'Hallo Yankees!' yelled Barcelona excitedly. 'Can you hear me? How are things at your end? You getting on O.K.?'

'Hallo Fritz! We're fine, how's yourselves?' rejoined a voice in fairly good German.

'Not so bad,' said Barcelona. 'Hey, tell me, Yank, you got anyone at your end who could answer a rather burning question for us?'

'What's that, Fritz?'

'We've been trying ever since the bloody war began to find out the name of Odin's pig.'

'Odin's *pig*?'

'That's right.'

There was a pause.

'You did say, Odin's pig?'

'That's it,' confirmed Barcelona.

Another pause.

'Hell, is this some kind of a trick question?' asked the American-German voice, suspiciously.

'Not at all!' retorted Barcelona. 'It's a genuine thirst for knowledge!'

'Well, hang on, I'll ask the other guys.'

We hung on, and it was not many minutes before the Yank was back again.

'Hi, you still there, Fritz? As it happens, you're in luck. One of our boys is a Norwegian.'

'You mean you've got the answer?'

'I surely have, but I got one condition to make——'

'What's that, Yank?'

'Just simply this: I give you the name of your pig, you

284

surrender straight away and put an end to this damn war. O.K.?'

'O.K. by me,' agreed Barcelona. 'Matter of fact, we're on our way to Adolf right now, trying to talk a bit of sense into him ... What's the name of this pig, then?'

'"Golden Brush", he was called, and he belonged to Freya, not Odin. Least, that's what our expert tells me.'

A great cheer went up at this. We at once began contacting the other units to tell them the glad news.

'Hallo, Dietrich! We've got the name of Odin's pig!'

'Hallo, Heinz? You know that pig we were on about——'

'Hallo, Wolf! We've found out the name of Odin's pig. Only it's not Odin's, it belongs to Freya, and it's called "Golden Brush".'

'Like hell!' said Wolf. 'I've remembered it myself, and it's nothing like "Golden Brush". Matter of fact it's called Saerimner. And it belongs to Odin all right.'

There followed a passionate disputation. The U.S. 3rd Armoured Division clung stubbornly to the name Golden Brush. They didn't care for Saerimner and claimed that it had Nazi overtones. Wolf, on the other hand, accused them of making up Golden Brush and trying to con us into believing them. The matter never was resolved.

The column moved on. We crossed the Rhine in a sudden cloudburst, with grey skies and heavily falling rain. All along the route were ruined buildings, heaps of rubble, charred remains; entire townships razed to the ground, the inhabitants living in holes like rats. Sometimes we were accompanied by throngs of starving children, stretching out matchstick arms and calling up to us for bread. Everywhere there was the stench of war.

On 25th August we tuned in to an enemy station and heard the following news:

The 28th Armoured Division under General Leclerc had entered Paris that morning. The bells were ringing out all over the city and the population was generally going mad with excitement. Any Germans foolish enough to show themselves in the street went at their own peril and in danger of their lives. The guards at Fresnes had been slaughtered by the prisoners. Any women suspected of having had relations with occupying troops were having their hair shaved off, their clothes stripped from them and their bodies daubed with swastikas. General von Choltitz had been arrested by the Americans. The whole town was to be illuminated throughout the night. Vive la France!

We turned it off and sat looking at each other a while.

'You know what?' said Porta, at last. 'They wouldn't give old Choltitz enough fireworks to blow the place up, so what's the betting he's now busy claiming that he actually saved it from destruction?'

'They'd never believe him,' said Barcelona.

'Besides,' objected Little John, 'it'd all be there, written down in orders and such like.'

Porta shrugged.

'Them at the top always manage to wriggle out of everything.'

'Not this time,' said Barcelona.

'You want to take a bet?' said Porta.

THE END

General

☐ 552 08944 3   BILLY CASPER'S 'MY MILLION-DOLLAR SHOTS'
Billy Casper 40p

☐ 552 08768 8   SEX MANNERS FOR OLDER TEENAGERS (illustrated)
Robert Chartham 30p

☐ 552 08926 5   S IS FOR SEX   *Robert Chartham* 50p
☐ 552 98958 4   THE ISLAND RACE Vol. 1   *Winston S. Churchill* 125p
☐ 552 98959 2   THE ISLAND RACE Vol. 2   *Winston S. Churchill* 125p
☐ 552 98572 4   NEE DE LA VAGUE (illustrated)   *Lucien Clergue* 105p
☐ 552 08800 5   CHARIOTS OF THE GODS? (illustrated)   *Erich von Daniken* 35p
☐ 552 08861 7   THE AUTOBIOGRAPHY OF A SUPER TRAMP
W. H. Davies 40p

☐ 552 07400 4   MY LIFE AND LOVES   *Frank Harris* 65p
☐ 552 98748 4   MAKING LOVE (Photographs)   *Walter Hartford* 85p
☐ 552 08362 3   A DOCTOR SPEAKS ON SEXUAL EXPRESSION
IN MARRIAGE (illustrated)   *Donald W. Hastings, M.D.* 50p

☐ 552 98862 6   INVESTING IN GEORGIAN GLASS (illustrated)
Ward Lloyd 125p

☐ 552 08069 1   THE OTHER VICTORIANS   *Steven Marcus* 50p
☐ 552 08664 9   THE HUMAN ZOO   *Desmond Morris* 35p
☐ 552 08162 0   THE NAKED APE   *Desmond Morris* 30p
☐ 552 08927 3   IS DEATH THE END   *P. & S. Phillips* 35p
☐ 552 08880 3   THE THIRTEENTH CANDLE   *T. Lobsang Rampa* 35p
☐ 552 08975 3   THE YOUNG BRITISH POETS   ed. *Jeremy Robson* 30p
☐ 552 08974 5   BRUCE TEGNER METHOD OF SELF DEFENCE
Bruce Tegner 40p

☐ 552 98479 5   MADEMOISELLE 1 + 1 (illustrated)
Marcel Veronese and Jean-Claude Peretz 105p

☐ 552 08943 5   MEMOIRS OF THE CHEVALIER D'EON
trans. *Antonia White* 50p

☐ 552 08928 1   TELL ME, DOCTOR   *Dr. Michael Winstanley* 35p

Western

☐ 552 08907 9   SUDDEN: TROUBLESHOOTER   *Frederick H. Christian* 25p
☐ 552 08971 0   TO ARMS! TO ARMS IN DIXIE No. 68   *J. T. Edson* 25p
☐ 552 08972 9   THE SOUTH WILL RISE AGAIN No. 69   *J. T. Edson* 25p
☐ 552 08131 0   THE BLOODY BORDER No. 35   *J. T. Edson* 25p
☐ 552 08896 X   HOW THE WEST WAS WON   *Louis L'Amour* 30p
☐ 552 08939 7   TUCKER   *Louis L'Amour* 25p
☐ 552 08922 2   LAW OF THE JUNGLE No. 13   *Louis Masterson* 25p
☐ 552 08923 0   NO TEARS FOR MORGAN KANE No. 14   *Louis Masterson* 25p
☐ 552 08940 0   THE PIONEERS   *Jack Schaefer* 25p
☐ 552 08906 0   SUDDEN: MARSHAL OF LAWLESS   *Oliver Strange* 25p

Crime

☐ 552 08970 2   KILL THE TOFF   *John Creasey* 25p
☐ 552 08968 0   ACCUSE THE TOFF   *John Creasey* 25p
☐ 552 08977 X   UNDERSTRIKE   *John Gardner* 25p
☐ 552 08640 1   RED FILE FOR CALLAN   *James Mitchell* 25p
☐ 552 08839 0   TOUCHFEATHER TOO   *Jimmy Sangster* 25p
☐ 552 08894 3   DUCA AND THE MILAN MURDERS   *Giorgio Scerbanenco* 30p
☐ 552 08884 6   MY GUN IS QUICK   *Mickey Spillane* 25p
☐ 552 08938 9   SHEM'S DEMISE   *Michael Underwood* 25p

All these books are available at your bookshop or newsagent: or can be ordered direct from the publisher. Just tick the titles you want and fill in the form below.

CORGI BOOKS, Cash Sales Department. P.O. Box 11, Falmouth, Cornwall.
Please send cheque or postal order. No currency, and allow 6p per book to cover the cost of postage and packing in the U.K., and overseas.

NAME...

ADDRESS ....

(MAY 72) ....

A SELECTION OF FINE READING AVAILABLE IN CORGI BOOKS

Novels

☐	552 08651 7	THE HAND-REARED BOY	Brian W. Aldiss 25p
☐	552 07938 3	THE NAKED LUNCH	William Burroughs 37½p
☐	552 08849 8	THE GLASS VIRGIN	Catherine Cookson 40p
☐	552 08440 9	THE ANDROMEDA STRAIN	Michael Crichton 35p
☐	552 08963 X	CAPE OF STORMS	John Gordon Davies 40p
☐	552 08868 4	I KNEW DAISY SMUTEN	ed. Hunter Davies 40p
☐	552 08851 X	CHEAP DAY RETURN	R. F. Delderfield 35p
☐	552 08965 6	MY FRIEND THE SWALLOW	Jane Duncan 30p
☐	552 08934 6	THE INTERNS	Richard Frede 35p
☐	552 08912 5	SUCH GOOD FRIENDS	Lois Gould 40p
☐	552 08125 6	CATCH-22	Joseph Heller 35p
☐	552 08652 5	THY DAUGHTER'S NAKEDNESS	Myron S. Kauffmann 62½p
☐	552 08932 X	ALSO THE HILLS	Frances Parkinson Keyes 45p
☐	552 08888 9	REQUIEM FOR IDOLS	Norah Lofts 25p
☐	552 08632 0	MICHAEL AND ALL ANGELS	Norah Lofts 30p
☐	552 08949 4	THE MAN FROM O.R.G.Y.	Ted Mark 30p
☐	552 08950 8	THE 9-MONTH CAPER	Ted Mark 30p
☐	552 08933 8	THE TERRACOTTA PALACE	Anne Maybury 35p
☐	552 08791 2	HAWAII	James A. Michener 75p
☐	552 08124 8	LOLITA	Vladimir Nabokov 35p
☐	552 07954 5	RUN FOR THE TREES	James S. Rand 35p
☐	552 08887 0	VIVA RAMIREZ!	James S. Rand 40p
☐	552 08930 3	STORY OF O	Pauline Reage 50p
☐	552 08597 9	PORTNOY'S COMPLAINT	Philip Roth 40p
☐	552 08976 1	OUR GANG	Philip Roth 35p
☐	552 08945 1	THE HONEY BADGER	Robert Ruark 55p
☐	552 08852 8	SCANDAL'S CHILD	Edmund Schiddel 40p
☐	552 08372 0	LAST EXIT TO BROOKLYN	Hubert Selby Jr. 50p
☐	552 08931 1	ZARA	Joyce Stranger 30p
☐	552 07807 7	VALLEY OF THE DOLLS	Jacqueline Susann 40p
☐	552 08523 5	THE LOVE MACHINE	Jacqueline Susann 40p
☐	552 08091 8	TOPAZ	Leon Uris 40p
☐	552 08384 4	EXODUS	Leon Uris 40p
☐	552 08964 8	AN AFFAIR OF HONOUR	Robert Wilder 40p
☐	552 08962 1	THE HELPERS	Stanley Winchester 40p
☐	552 08481 6	FOREVER AMBER Vol. 1	Kathleen Winsor 35p
☐	552 08482 4	FOREVER AMBER Vol. 2	Kathleen Winsor 35p

War

☐	552 08953 2	TATTERED BATTALION	Laurie Andrews 30p
☐	552 08935 4	ACCIDENTAL AGENT (illustrated)	John Goldsmith 35p
☐	552 08874 9	SS GENERAL	Sven Hassel 35p
☐	552 08779 3	ASSIGNMENT: GESTAPO	Sven Hassel 35p
☐	552 08855 2	THE WILLING FLESH	Willi Heinrich 35p
☐	552 08873 0	THE DOOMSDAY SQUAD	Clark Howard 25p
☐	552 08920 6	SECURITY RISK	Gilbert Hackforth-Jones 25p
☐	552 08892 7	THE FORTRESS	Raleigh Trevelyan 30p
☐	552 08936 2	JOHNNY GOT HIS GUN	Dalton Trumbo 30p
☐	552 08798 X	VIMY! (illustrated)	Herbert Fairlie Wood 30p
☐	552 08919 2	JOHNNY PURPLE	John Wyllie 25p

Romance

☐	552 08941 9	THE BEDSIDE MANNER	Kate Norway 25p
☐	552 08973 7	MY SISTERS AND ME	Barbara Perkins 25p
☐	552 08956 7	MAIDEN VOYAGE	Alex Stuart 25p
☐	552 08955 9	THE SUMMER'S FLOWER	Alex Stuart 25p

Science Fiction

☐	552 08925 7	THE BEST FROM NEW WRITINGS IN S.F.	ed. John Carnell 25p
☐	552 08942 7	A WILDERNESS OF STARS	ed. William Nolan 30p
☐	552 08804 8	THE AGE OF THE PUSSYFOOT	Frederik Pohl 25p
☐	552 08860 9	VENUS PLUS X	Theodore Sturgeon 25p